HOTELLES

HOTELLES

EMMA MARS

Translated by Alexis Pernsteiner

HARPER PERENNIAL

NEW YORK • LONDON • TORONTO • SYDNEY • NEW DELHI • AUCKLAND

HARPER  PERENNIAL

HarperCollins books may be purchased for educational, business, or sales promotional use. For information please e-mail the Special Markets Department at SPsales@harpercollins.com.

FIRST EDITION

Designed by Michael P. Correy

Library of Congress Cataloging-in-Publication Data has been applied for.

ISBN 978-0-06-227417-5

14 15 16 17 18 OV/RRD 10 9 8 7 6 5 4 3 2 1

HOTELLES

ROOM ONE

Love is a great master; it teaches us to be what we never were.

MOLIÈRE,
THE SCHOOL FOR WIVES, ACT III, SCENE V

Paris, the early days of June 2010, in a hotel room in the middle of the afternoon . . .

I have never belonged to that category of women who see all hotel rooms as identical, all one and the same, each an anonymous space without any character or personality. A kind of cold tunnel with a uniform interior, offering standardized comfort for the night. Those women have probably only slept in them on exhausting layovers between trains or planes. To get a taste of a hotel room's unique character, you have to experience it during the day, when the rest of the building is empty, or almost empty. You have to take the time to feel it, to let your senses come alive, one by one, if you want to uncover the stories of its former guests, their laughter and tears, love and ecstasy. These past months, I've learned that there is a direct link between what we give a hotel and what we get from it. If you let yourself sink into sleep, boredom, or melancholy, you will only receive a reflection of your own sadness and futility. And you will leave as you came, regrettably unchanged.

But if you take the time to listen to what a hotel room has to say, you will hear thousands of stories, anecdotes, and sighs.

You will burn to add your own. The most curious among us sometimes find themselves possessed by previous guests and their motivations. A scent of perfume hanging to the curtains or above the bed. A small stain that has survived the cleaning crew. A residue on the mirror tracing a shadow or a silhouette. These details affect you, infuse you, invite you to live your own story.

That is exactly what I am trying to do now as I lie naked with my wrists tied to the headboard of this bed. To write new pages for a story that began long ago, well before my time. Like most rooms in the Hôtel des Charmes, the Josephine contains a gigantic ceiling mirror. So, while I wait for things to heat up, I have all the time in the world to look at myself, Annabelle Barlet, née Lorand, twenty-three years old, just married this year, and ready to give myself without restraint to the man I can hear getting ready in the adjoining bathroom. Who is he? I don't know yet. The only thing that's certain is that he's not my husband. If it were him, would we even be here? Honestly, would this be happening?

They call me Elle. Since forever and in all circumstances. Probably because "Belle" would have been too much. But don't be fooled, "Elle" is even worse. "Elle," like the cover of a magazine, like I'm supposed to be a picture-perfect embodiment of woman in all her grace. A crystallization of desire. A melting pot for fantasies, the raw metal of which men are made.

WHEN AT LAST I HEAR the bathroom door creak open, I yelp in surprise. Perhaps too sharply. Part of me must have thought he was only a dream. The stranger freezes, hesitating as to whether or not to come to my side. I imagine his hand tense on the door handle, his breath suspended.

"Madame? Madame Barlet, is everything as you wish?"

The voice I hear is not his. It comes from the hall. They worry for me behind the scenes. They want me to be satisfied. Madame is a regular. Madame is important here. My man gave them his instructions. He is the kind of person people listen to around here, the kind of person whom others obey.

"Yes, Monsieur Jacques . . . Don't worry, everything is fine."

The first time I stayed in this room, last year, they were not nearly so attentive. Nor was I so sure of myself back then. The large mirrors reflected a very different image. My shape was already a burden, my curves already a promise. But I was not yet aware of their power, and still less of their function. I did not know the joys of another, and even less so of being myself.

What makes you come, Elle? Yeah, what does make me come? Do I really know? What exactly is it that makes me melt, deep down inside? That makes me wet without being touched, just at the thought of it? A man's naked body? His smell? The sight of an anonymous cock erect for me? Against me? In me . . .

Handwritten note by me, 6/5/2010

NO, A YEAR AGO I did not know that every room is a breeding ground for love, where every woman incubates and eventually learns to become herself. I was not tied up like I am right now, and yet I was more imprisoned than I shall ever be again. Don't be fooled, today *I* am the mistress, and not just to the man trembling behind the door. I have abandoned myself entirely, but I have never had this much control.

A YEAR AGO I WAS just me, Elle. Every woman minus herself. A whole woman was waiting to be born . . .

1

June 3, 2009: One year earlier
in the same hotel room

I was curled up in the sheets of the Josephine's unmade bed. On that day, my limbs were free. Free and yet so ill at ease. I had only met the men who was about to share my bed three hours before, four at most. Suffice it to say, I didn't know a lot about him, besides his marital status and the size of his wallet—and soon of something else. Over the course of the long evening that had preceded this exact moment, I had not listened to a single word of his conversation with our dinner companions. My only contributions had been a few brief smiles and docile nods of my head. A wallflower, which is what was expected of me. What exactly did he do in life? Banking? Imports-exports? Or maybe he presided over something, was an honorary president somewhere? In any case, he was important enough to command the respect—and sometimes even silence—of the other guests.

"Which position would you prefer, Elle?" he asked as he helped me unzip my delicate white dress.

Funny: a few minutes ago we were eating poached foie gras with blueberries and addressing each other as "Monsieur" and "Mademoiselle." As soon as we crossed the threshold to our room, we started using our first names. When bodies undress too quickly, a deceptive form of intimacy emerges.

"Excuse me?" I choked between sips of sparkling water.

If a man sincerely desired you, a man you also desperately hoped would worship you, he would never bother asking such a technical question. In its own way, your body would tell him what he needed to know before he even got the chance. Words would not be necessary. Everything would be music, and your bodies would fall effortlessly into harmony.

"I mean . . . Do you object to any positions? Have any limits?"

I turned around and looked at him more attentively. He was fairly handsome. In his forties with graying hair. The athletic type. Probably really sporty, which would no doubt explain my presence in this room. If he weren't, there was no way I would have agreed to spend more time with him after such a boring dinner. I would have stuck to the basic itinerary. This was only the third time I had "followed" a client, to use the accepted jargon. It wasn't much, considering I had been working for eight months.

After his faux pas and the mood-killing way in which he'd asked about my preferences, I figured he couldn't be more experienced than I. Maybe I was his first escort. Not wanting to ruin what was left of the mystery, I didn't ask.

"No . . . No, not really," I lied with what I hoped was an engaging smile.

"Okay . . ." He nodded, visibly reassured. "It's just better if I know in advance."

My mind was miles away . . .

*Doggy-style bothers me because it's animalistic. I only like
to do it with men I know.*

*Doggy-style makes me come more than any other
position . . . precisely because it's animalistic!*

*I fantasize about doing it with someone I don't know,
preferably with a mask on.*

Anonymous handwritten note, 6/3/2009, slipped into
my mailbox without my knowledge

I WAS THINKING ABOUT ALL the notes I'd received over the
past few weeks, ever since I had found a small, blank, silver-
covered notebook in my bag. An anonymous hand had taken
advantage of the crowd on the metro to put it there. A mysterious message was stuck inside, and I did not recognize the
handwriting:

*Studies show that men think about sex approximately
nineteen times a day. Women, no more than ten. How
about you? How many times a day do you let yourself be
invaded by that kind of thought?*

Several days had gone by before I found an unstamped
sheet of perforated paper in my mailbox. It had holes that
matched the metallic rings in my notebook. The author of the
missives obviously took pleasure in imagining my fantasies. He
wrote in the first person as though he were me.

I had almost thrown the handwritten page into the trash
unread. I had even considered filing a harassment report with

the police. But I'm a journalism major and my curiosity got the better of me. Like a good student, I put the piece of paper in my miniature binder; I had already guessed that this would be the first in a long series. The faceless hand wouldn't stop there . . . Oh, no, it would not.

"I DON'T HAVE ANY LIMITS," I told my client.

To be fair, he was not any worse than the small handful of men I had let have me after a few too many drinks or a couple of mediocre dinners. And if I'm honest about my first time with Fred, my only serious boyfriend to date, I have to admit that it wasn't exactly glamorous. The night we'd ended up making love, I had given into it because the occasion had presented itself and the natural course of the evening had led to it . . . not because of any real desire. Where was the harm in dressing it all up as a transaction? Wasn't I worth more than a slice of pizza and two glasses of red wine?

At least this one was rich, clean, good-looking, and, to top it off, well dressed. He was wearing a bespoke, two-button suit with refined details, fuchsia silk lining, and topstitching that matched the buttonholes. Thanks to him, I was going to make more in a night than I had ever pocketed in a week working minimum wage at fast-food chains and other places.

Honestly, I was trying to motivate myself as best I could. The evening's champagne was already wearing off. I needed a pick-me-up, something effervescent like the bubbles that had vanished from my champagne flute.

I HAD JUST GIVEN MONSIEUR Bespoke a blank check. But in spite of this, he unceremoniously, and without saying a word, sheathed himself in latex and pushed me into a tortured and grunting missionary position. The lack of sexual savoir faire in supposedly intelligent people will never cease to amaze me. It is probably the only form of knowledge that can't be self-taught and isn't the subject of private classes or coaches.

"You okay? I'm not hurting you, am I?"

No, no pain or anything else. A strange lack of sensation. The lower part of my body seemed completely anesthetized. I knew I was there, having sex, being penetrated in a very real sexual game, but I did not feel the least bit affected. Still, I put my hands on his butt and gently matched his movements in and out of me.

"I'm fine," I said, trying to sound encouraging.

My own inexperience made it impossible for me to take the kind of initiative he must have expected from me. Was I supposed to sigh, scream, whisper obscenities into his ear? Just how much was I supposed to fake it? Was that part of the job, too?

"Is it good for you?"

That was the best I could manage. I know, it was pathetic. Still, he panted a yes before coming. Being the shrewd business-man that he undoubtedly is, he made the most of the precious postcoital moment, keeping completely still for about fifteen seconds. Then he started up again like a Swiss metronome.

I wasn't really there. I didn't feel embarrassed, disgusted, or even mad. My hand slowly stroked the length of his back, from his ribs to his pelvis. I honestly wanted to give him pleasure. I took the increasing intensity of his groans as a sign of satisfac-tion. Frankly, the encounter wasn't any worse than most of my past experiences in horizontal gymnastics. Besides, boring sex gives you plenty of time to look at the decor. The rooms in the Hôtel des Charmes were worth admiring. With the exception of the ceiling mirror, one of the hotel's rare concessions to our time, my surroundings faithfully replicated the room occupied by Napoleon's wife, Madame de Beauharnais, in Château de Malmaison. On the whole, the circular space resembled the most luxurious countryside tents, held upright by a series of thin gold columns. Between these columns were laced large red wall hangings, which lent an ancient and gracious air to the surroundings. An eagle with wings outstretched, as though taking flight, overlooked the massive four-poster bed. The headboard was decked with a couple of golden swans, and the footboard with two horns of plenty. The rest of the furniture, including the armchairs and chaise longue on the other side of the room, reflected the dominant theme of gold and red as well as the floral motifs on the bedspread and bed skirt.

The ambiance was flawless. It wasn't hard to imagine oneself in the nineteenth century. Did Napoleon treat his Josephine to this same monotonous precision, or did he vary it up? There I was, with my aesthetical and sexual-historical musings, when Monsieur Bespoke gratified me with one last pelvic thrust and a final gasp. He hadn't lasted more than three or four minutes. Perhaps he'd been distracted by the majesty of the place, or maybe he'd simply felt bloated from the meal and weak from the alcohol.

After pulling out, he rolled to one side. His stomach was almost touching mine. Feeling grateful after his orgasm, he paid a banal compliment:

"You're really pretty, you know."

"Thanks."

How else do you respond when you know it's not true? I did not like the person I saw in the mirror above. She had never suited me. And I knew that this kind of activity was not helping things. Too round, too this, too that. What could I say, I was me. More like a young, poorly polished girl than a femme fatale. In a word, I was hopelessly imperfect.

"I don't like thin girls," he confided. "I'm always afraid I'm going to break them . . . and hurt myself on their bones."

That was his way of saying that he liked my curves. At least one of us was happy with what I had on offer. All-around abundant. No sharp angles. Satisfying, it seemed.

I took the small stack of bills he had left on the mahogany side table, glancing quickly to check the amount. He disappeared into the bathroom, and I took advantage of his absence to leave the room as quietly as the ghosts who inhabit it. What could I have said that would not have sounded like a lie or a false promise: *It was really great? Thanks again? See you soon, I hope?*

I PUT MY SHOES ON in the hall. The thick carpet felt good under my feet. I headed straight for the lobby. From his polished reception desk, Monsieur Jacques gestured discreetly for me to come talk to him.

"Did everything go well, Mademoiselle?"

"Yes, yes," I said in a low voice. "Very well."

The concierge at the Hôtel des Charmes was impressive, with his Louis XIV livery trimmed in gold and silver lace. But beyond the uniform, I was fascinated by his physical appearance: the old man did not have a single hair on his entire head, not a tendril—no mustache, no beard, no eyebrows, not even any lashes to frame his large, slightly bulging blue eyes. No one could be more smooth-faced than this man. Nor any paler.

Surprisingly, when Mom had chemo, she didn't lose any of her gray hair. The last six months of her treatment took a toll on her muscles and their strength but not on her head, which remained covered in hair. Maude Lorand was a trouper. She hung on as she always had, with courage and humility. She didn't even complain. Her lungs had gone to hell, but she hadn't lost one inch of dignity. She was a bronze statue rising from the ashes.

"Do you think you'll need another room in the coming days? Perhaps tomorrow?"

"I don't know yet. And even if I do . . . it will definitely be the last time."

He did not seem surprised by my off-the-cuff statement. He almost looked happy about it, flashing me a knowing smile. Monsieur Jacques wanted what was best for me. Or, rather, he saw the best in me. At least that's the feeling I got whenever we met. In spite of appearances and the obvious reason for my presence in his hotel, he thought I could be good, or better. It only took a few seconds for his kind gaze to boost my morale.

But that night I didn't have time for his tonic look. He was still smiling as the doors sucked me out of the hotel and into the gentle night. It was still early.

2

THE SAME DAY, A LITTLE LATER

S o, basic . . . or *base* itinerary?"

The voice behind this terrible play on words came from a girl who loves to flirt with all things vulgar, knowing full well that it adds to her coarse charm. Sophia. My best friend. Kind of my only friend, to be honest. Sophia Petrilli, two years my senior and at least five years ahead of me in the world of men and sex. Chocolate curls that catch everybody's attention. Perfectly sculpted breasts that call out for hands to touch them. Eyes in which all men long to get lost. One of her first lovers nicknamed her Esmeralda because, being the young dancer that she is, she's wildly independent and makes men burn for her. In her everyday life, she is just Sophia, a little lost and without a serious boyfriend or stable job. But she is the most lively and independent person I know, and she has been a solid friend in the face of hardship. Boyfriends have come and gone; *Sophia* is forever.

"Mmm . . . ," I replied, dodging her question with a shrug. "Second itinerary."

"Makes sense, given the hour. I kind of figured."

On nights when we were both working, we typically met at Café des Antiquaires on Rue de la Grange Batelière, which is just a few paces away from the Drouot auction house in Paris's 9th Arrondissement. The rule was simple: the first one to finish up with her client would wait for the other. Option number one rarely kept us out past eleven p.m. Number two could easily go into the wee hours of the morning.

"And you? Did you have a good night?"

"One might say," she said, smirking.

"Rich client?"

"Disgustingly rich, you mean. I've never seen such a flashy Rolex. And he really pulled out all the stops: the Pompadour suite and all the trimmings."

That was another thing about the Hôtel des Charmes: each room, which could be rented by the hour, was dedicated to one of French history's great seductresses and courtesans. The king's favorites, mistresses, queens, and simple ladies of the night whom posterity had not forgotten. A surprising collection of dancers, spies, artists, and half-socialites. All were remembered for their extraordinary powers over men and the ways in which they used them over the course of their tumultuous lives. No reference was made to these men in the hotel; none of them were associated with a room. Meanwhile, as I had noticed earlier, each room was decorated in perfect harmony with the time and period of the heroines I've just mentioned. Each room was a unique setting that embodied one woman and gave life to a whole fantasy.

"Not bad," I said with forced enthusiasm. "I was in the Josephine."

"Nice! Have you ever been there before?"

"No, first time."

Sophia was more of a regular at the Hôtel des Charmes than I. Sometimes she'd go as many as two or three times in a month. On principle, never more than once a week, though depending on what else was going on in her life, these rendez-vous were her primary source of revenue.

"And," she asked, smiling coyly, "how was it? Good?"

"Sophia!" I cried. "You know . . . I can't."

She knew the rules as well as I: the agency that put us in contact with our rich clients strictly prohibited us from talking about them. Nothing was to leave the walls of those quaint and charming bedrooms. Some of the men we met were important and very powerful. Any information related to what they did in their private lives, especially when it came to sexual prefer-ences, could be used against them by their enemies. Their con-fidentiality was paramount, and secrecy became our dogma.

To be completely honest, I liked it that way. The agency's rule put a healthy barrier between me and Sophia's obsession. For Sophia, talking about sex was as much fun as having sex. It was a natural extension, as though language were an organ like the clitoris that could be stimulated. She considered sex a universal subject and would find any excuse to bring it up in conversation, in any context, with friends *and* total strang-ers. "Seriously," she would say, trying to provoke me, "can you think of anything more interesting than sex? I mean, come on. We're not going to talk about the stock market or kids, right? We're both broke. And stop me if I'm wrong, but neither of us is going to have kids any time soon. Thirty-one, that's the average age of a first-time mom in Paris. Thirty-one!"

She could go on forever about her favorite topic of conver-sation, delighting in all the gory details, feeding off anything she could force out of those around her.

"Because my client tonight, you should have seen the size of his equipment! Monstrous! I mean, crazy! Even bigger than his bank account, which says something."

"Soph!" I started, trying to keep myself from laughing.

"Seriously, the guy should join a circus."

"Stop!"

"What? I didn't give you his name! I'm just telling you about his penis."

"Awesome," I said ironically. "You should make a reality show."

"No, but seriously, he was so big I thought I'd choke when I ble—"

"Yeah, you're right." I cut her off so I wouldn't have to hear any more. "It's better not to take forever when you're giving fellatio. Otherwise, they get addicted to it and that's all they want."

My classic response to Sophia's tsunami of inconvenient truths: modestly limiting myself to tired clichés and ready-made phrases, most of which I got from sex columns in women's magazines.

"That said," she went on, "it's hard to beat that guy who wouldn't touch me and who made me masturbate for two hours while he watched . . . He wore me out."

"Yeah, but at least if he watches while you masturbate, he'll learn what makes you come. It's not a total waste of time."

I think I got that from *Cosmo*, July/August 2007. It had to have come from there.

But what did I, Annabelle Lorand, actually know about sex? Not a lot.

Truth is, the agency's rule was a good excuse not to get into too much detail with Sophia. Most of the time it quelled her curiosity or at least put a damper on her shameless logorrhea. I would have been happy keeping my secrets to my little notebook. But there, somebody else's hand was recording them for me, in the intimacy of those white pages:

> *I know it sounds stupid, but I think genitals have soul mates. Every vagina only has one penis in the whole world that's made exactly to its dimensions. And vice versa. So long as it hasn't found its mate, it won't fully bloom. I know that's how it is for me: my vagina has not yet found its penis soul mate.*

Anonymous handwritten note, 6/2/2009, slipped into my mailbox—He isn't wrong.

THE FACT THAT ANOTHER HAND was writing these letters both excited and disgusted me; I couldn't separate the two feelings. In the end, I must have been pretty excited. After all, I did play along. I had kept the notebook, where I religiously filed my harasser's unavowable fantasies. I was receiving several a day. Once or twice, I staked out the mailbox for a few hours, but I never caught him.

Initially, I was able to keep the notebook secret from Sophia, who usually has a sixth sense for these kinds of things. That is, until a few days later, when I dropped my bag in a café, right next to her chair. She reflexively leaned over to help me pick up my stuff.

"What is this?"

"Nothing . . . Give it to me!"

"Fancy notebook! Is it your booty-call list?" she clucked.

"No . . . Stop . . ."

"Yes, it is . . . You're blushing!"

Without asking my permission, she opened it and read the first few pages under her breath . . .

"I am not blushing! Give it back now!"

. . . then louder.

" ' . . . I also wonder how it smells and tastes to a guy who is licking me down there . . .' Wow! Mademoiselle Lorand! Look at you!"

"Fuck, Sophia, give it to me!"

She ended up giving in, but it was too late.

"So, what, you're writing *The Sexual Life of Annabelle L.*?"

"I'm not the one who wrote it . . ."

"Well, well!"

"I promise you. This guy leaves notes in my mailbox every day. I don't know who it is or what he wants from me."

"Really? And you just file them away in that binder?"

"Honestly, it's the truth."

Trapped, I told her about the mysterious circumstances under which the notebook got into my hands. Then about how every day I received these journal entries that could be mine, but that somebody else—a guy? a girl?—was writing.

She was more amused than shocked. It had crossed my mind that Rebecca, the agency's owner, could be behind the poisoned present. But if that were the case, then why was I the only one getting messages? Out of all the other girls at Belles de Nuit? Otherwise, I know Sophia would not have waited one second to brag about them.

"It makes me crazy: out of all the girls in Paris, the nut who thought this up is stuck on *you*!"

"Why do you say that?"

"Er, Elle . . . Let's just say that it's more my thing than

yours. I would have *loved* it if a guy had given me that present. And I'll tell you one thing, I would not have waited for him to write all the entries for me."

I handed her the silver notebook, as if to unburden myself.

"If that's all it takes to make you happy . . . then here, take it."

"Stop, no! It's yours," she said, suddenly serious.

"Yeah, right . . . He could have put it in any girl's bag on that metro car."

"No," she corrected me. "Actually, when I think about it, I wouldn't say it's random. He knew you needed it. You, more than any of the other girls."

To make you less square, she probably wanted to add. I pouted in protest.

EVER SINCE THAT INCIDENT, AND especially since I'd met David, it had gotten increasingly difficult to contain the Sophia inquisition. My boyfriend of three months was not a client. Never had been. So the rules concerning clients did not apply.

"And you never told me about David . . ."

"Never told you what?"

"Well, how's he hung? Normal? King-size? Mini, but knows how to use it?"

"Right, do you really think I'm going to answer that kind of question?"

Doesn't hurt to ask, her smirk implied.

"Aren't you meeting him, like, now?" She tacked to a more chaste line of conversation.

"Yeah. Actually, no. He's getting home late. I'll see him tomorrow morning. If I see him . . ."

David's exceptional personality and stature brought out conflicting impulses in Sophia: the bimbo and the nymph, the dreamer and the man-eater. The fact that I had caught such a specimen baffled her. And in the name of our friendship and all the years we'd shared of emotional struggle, she thought I owed it to her to divulge everything exotic or alluring about him.

"You don't think it's weird to see him after you've been with a client?"

"I just told you, I probably won't see him before tomorrow night."

"Still . . . ," she insisted. "You're not scared he'll find out?"

"And what about you, you don't think it's weird never to sleep with the same guy twice?" I replied, tit for tat.

"Touché. Maybe even a little harsh." Her face suddenly darkened.

Sophia had effortless sex appeal. But that, coupled with her rapacious appetite for sex, made it impossible for her to spend more than a few nights with a man. When she wasn't cheating on her man of the moment with the next lover, she was rekindling an affair with an old and dear acquaintance. There were incidents from time to time, and she paid the price. Whenever she got caught, or whenever she got tired of someone, she would go back to her sex toys. Her collection had seriously expanded over the years.

"Sorry . . ."

"Don't worry about it. You're not wrong . . . Want to get some air?"

WE LOVED WALKING THROUGH PARIS after dark. Taxi lights sweeping through deserted streets. Nothing to do but stroll.

One of our supreme pleasures was to go window-shopping at the antique stores and jewelry shops that filled the streets around Drouot. We couldn't afford any treasures—not even the humblest ones. But that meant we could dream. We imagined the day when we would suddenly fall into wealth, a meteorite of material happiness dropping from the sky.

"Holy cow, look at that watch!" I exclaimed, pointing to the one in front, my face practically glued to the shop window.

"The men's chronometer?"

The shop, Antiquités Nativelle, had placed a small explanatory note beside each object, like some bookstores do to recommend titles.

"Yeah, look . . . It's one hundred percent mechanical, made in 1969!"

"So, what? You looking for an erotic watch?" she joked.

"'69, année érotique," Jane Birkin had whispered over Serge Gainsbourg's oh-so-languorous instrumentals.

"'69 was practically the year David was born. His birthday is January 5, 1970."

"It was the year he was conceived." She snickered. "But don't tell me you're going to get him such an extravagant gift?"

"It's not that I don't want to. It's beautiful, isn't it?"

The watch was fine and understated. It eyed me from its little velour case, its night-blue dial sparkling at me in the half-light. I couldn't help but notice the subtle curve of its protective glass, which certified the age and authenticity of the piece.

"A toy compared to the one my client had . . ." Sophia pretended to be unimpressed. "But I wouldn't turn my nose up at it if someone gave it to me, that's for sure."

"Ha! . . . Did you see the price?"

"Yeah, three thousand two hundred euros. You're going to have to put in overtime, hon, if you want to spoil your nabob!"

That one bauble alone would cost more than my living expenses for two whole months. Without counting . . .

"I could never." I sighed. "Not with Mom's medical expenses."

Her down-market health insurance policy did not come close to covering all her medical expenses. I did my best to make up the difference. I wanted to give her a minimum level of comfort, both at home and during her frequent trips to the hospital. One week of chemo, one week of recovery, one week of something that resembled normalcy, followed by another seven days of intense treatment. That was her infernal schedule. She had sacrificed so much for me throughout my whole childhood that it only felt right giving her part of what I made, even if it wasn't much.

Another object drew my attention from behind the watch. A silver comb "that once belonged to the actress Mademoiselle Mars," the accompanying note pointed out. A glittering remnant from the first half of the nineteenth century, for the bagatelle of one thousand seven hundred euros. Yet another wonderful thing I couldn't afford.

Without warning, Sophia took me by the arm and dragged me away from the tempting shop window.

"Come on, beautiful! It won't kill your Prince Charming if you can't give him baubles costing three months of minimum wage every time you see him!"

"I know . . ."

"And if I may, considering his income, he should be the one giving you nice presents."

"That's the problem," I said, nodding. "It's *his* income, not mine . . ."

My friend wasn't wrong. In the game of courting and gift exchange, I'd never stood a chance when faced with a competitor like David. How many times more than minimum wage did he earn a month? Was his income within the cap that a number of politicians had once suggested imposing on French executives; namely, fifteen to twenty times the basic living wage? In some ways, I preferred not knowing. I came from simple origins. My upbringing had been frugal, and I had strong opinions about what was appropriate and what was not when it came to money. Under normal circumstances, I would never buy such a watch. But I couldn't help dreaming.

"And does the monsieur even deserve it?" Sophia asked in a lighter tone. "I know you'd bend over backward for him, but where would you put him on your 'best of' list? Top five? Top three?"

Now she was back to her favorite topic. She was acting like my little notebook, ever ready to record my deepest secrets. Soon she'd start calling it my "Ten-Times-a-Day," in reference to the number of erotic thoughts I apparently had about it each day.

"David's different . . ."

"Different how? He isn't like other guys? He has you do weird things?"

"I love him."

I had tried to say it without whimpering. I didn't want to seem sillier or more tenderhearted than I actually felt. But judging from the pout on Sophia's face, I could tell she was disgusted. She looked like she'd just eaten some bad whipped cream.

"Oh, sorry, I forgot . . . You loooooove him! So it doesn't matter how he makes love to you. He could be a board for all you care. How silly of me."

"Enough . . . You know that's not what I mean."

"Has your millionaire blown your mind at least once?"

She'd played her joker. I didn't want to respond. No, not just that. I didn't want to ask myself the question. Probably because I already knew the answer.

I shrugged and tried to smile mysteriously. She wasn't fooled. She knew me too well.

I quickly changed the subject, pointing at some posters for cabaret shows.

"So, about dancing . . . Do you have any upcoming shows?"

"Meh. 'The economic crisis,' as everyone's been saying. I swear, it feels like I'm dealing with bankers as opposed to choreographers and producers."

"What about your dance troupe in Neuilly?"

"It closed. Everybody's so broke these days, even the rich are going out of business."

"Are you getting by okay, though?"

"Yeah, I'm managing . . . ," she reassured me, though without much conviction.

I knew concretely what a lack of work meant for her.

"You mean, you're taking on more clients?"

"Mmm," she murmured, as she let her eyes wander up to the multicolored neon lights.

"A lot?"

"About . . . two a week."

Which meant more than her absolute limit. Would she be able to live with it? How was she going to get out of it? It was only supposed to be an occasional thing, and now it had practically become her regular job.

I wrinkled my brow. I was worried. Sophia wasn't going to quit the agency any time soon. People agree to do things they typically wouldn't with the idea that it will only be temporary. It looked like this one was going to last. It was her life now.

3

PARIS, DECEMBER 2008,
SIX MONTHS EARLIER

I'm not just being my usual discreet self. I really do not remember the exact circumstances under which Sophia first spoke of Belles de Nuit. I think it was before she started working there. She wasn't sure yet. She wondered about the exact nature of the services the agency promised its clients. She was troubled by rumors she had heard and by her own imagination. She remembered scenes from books and movies: Luis Buñuel's *Belle de jour*, Ken Russell's *Crimes of Passion*, and, more recently, the very dark *Mes chères études*, which was based on a true story.

How had she learned about the agency to begin with? Had someone approached her? And if so, who?

It was a mystery.

"BELLES DE NUIT, *BELLE DE jour* . . . Granted, they aren't subtle," Sophia critiqued. "But it's not like we're interested in their creativity."

We were standing in front of a pretty posh building in the Marais, on a street that divides the gay district from the rest of Paris. The plaque above the intercom did not specify the nature of the business. Belles de Nuit easily could have been selling pillows as opposed to ladies of the night. BELLES DE NUIT, SIXTH FLOOR.

"I think it's kind of pretty," I said, trying to remain positive, "poetic."

"Are you sure about this?"

"Soph. It's only a first meeting. I just want to learn about it, that's all."

"Okay, okay . . . but I don't want you accusing me later on of pushing you into something you didn't want to do. Okay?"

I looked at the sky and fell back on my throaty, slightly coarse voice, the one I'd tried to erase in my radio training classes, a requirement for the journalism major. In four or five months, I would have my degree and go knocking on the doors of France's most prestigious media outlets. I would be like Balzac's Rastignac; I would do anything to see my byline on an article.

"I'm twenty-two. I'm a big girl."

The elevator was really cramped, and in spite of our small dimensions, we had to squeeze in and hold our breaths.

"Come in, come in!"

The slender fifty-something blonde who greeted us oozed sophistication. Not at all what I'd expected of a brothel owner.

She extended a hand, which was covered in rings and bracelets to hide her age spots.

"Hello. Rebecca Sibony. I am the director of Belles de Nuit," she introduced herself, in the husky voice of a heavy smoker.

A subtle yet intoxicating perfume followed her as she guided us to a soberly furnished office.

"Annabelle is a little . . . nervous," Sophia said. I could have killed her. "She wants to know what *exactly* you expect of the girls who sign with you."

Sitting up in my chair, I defended myself in a childish voice. "Not at all! I understand everything perfectly!"

I was wearing a pair of old jeans I'd patched myself and worn ballerina flats. I hadn't been to the hairdresser in ages, and I looked awkward and penniless. I didn't need Sophia's help in that department. Rebecca scrutinized every square inch of my body before launching into a monologue she clearly knew by heart.

"Listen, I don't know what you've heard about us, but I am sure much of it is wrong. There are a lot of preconceived notions about what we do. A lot of bad-mouthing. In truth, what we offer here is very simple. And I want to be clear, it is perfectly legal: our clients are rich, single men who cannot, in all decency, show up alone to the various events they are obligated to attend throughout the year. If you join us, your role will be to wear your prettiest dress and smile for a whole night without hurting your jaw. You must also be able to speak competently if someone asks your opinion on the latest Woody Allen. As you can see, it isn't rocket science."

"What did I tell you?" said Sophia, with an eloquent wave of her hand.

This was my same friend who, not so long ago, had told me about a hot rendezvous set up by Belles de Nuit. A mission without the slightest social justification. At the time, the episode had given me good reason to reject Sophia's offer to join Rebecca Sibony's agency.

"A booty call and a blind date all mixed together! It was just crazy!"

"Really? And how did you . . ."

"Well, like in the movies, hon. I had an appointment at the Raphael at three p.m., sharp. Above all, I was to be on time. The room's curtains and blinds were already drawn. I imagine he had given the personnel instructions. Then I was to put my naked self on the bed and turn out the light."

"And then?"

"Then the guy arrived. Maybe about ten minutes later."

"You didn't notice when he got there?"

"No, it was a suite with a separate entrance hall that made the room feel hermetically sealed. I'd only just noticed his shadow when he pushed open the door to the bedroom."

"It wasn't kind of . . . creepy?"

"No! The opposite!" she'd cried. "At first, I was just a little cold, waiting like that, completely naked and not moving. But he got undressed and took me in his arms to warm me up."

"Did you make love right away?"

"Not immediately. We kept still, our bodies touching, for a while before he started to caress me."

"And he didn't say anything?"

"Not a thing. He had really soft hands. I swear, no one has ever touched me like that. I got wet crazy fast."

"You didn't try to see his face? What if the guy looked like the Hunchback of Notre Dame?"

"I don't think so, not from what I could tell by feeling his features. But honestly, seeing how he touched me, he could have been E.T. and I would have said yes."

"Seriously?"

"Seriously. He spent at least fifteen minutes massaging me down there. With his fingers, his nose, his tongue . . . I couldn't take it anymore! I was completely drenched. I think

I came at least two or three times like that, before he even entered me. And that was just an appetizer! We spent three hours in bed."

"Two, three times," I repeated, panting.

"What's more, the jerk smelled good!"

"Really . . . how?"

"Umm, I don't know, something really sweet. And I swear to you, his cock tasted like strawberries or raspberries . . . I could have spent all day eating it!"

"Soph!"

"What? It was amazing . . . like eating caviar blindfolded. When you can't see, all the other senses go into overdrive. Especially taste and smell."

"Okay, okay, I think I get the picture."

REBECCA STARTED TALKING AGAIN IN her raspy voice, interrupting my memory:

"Of course, Belles de Nuit has a reputation to uphold. We only hire girls who are pretty, young, and put-together. They speak perfect French and are, above all, cultivated. I don't have time for ditzes and bimbos. But from what I've seen and heard, I don't think we should have a problem there."

"And really, that's all?" I pressed.

"Yes. That is all you are committing to contractually with us, and that is what we bill our clients for."

"Good," said I, laconically.

"You seem disappointed. What were you expecting?"

Her tone had suddenly grown sharper, and she looked as haughty as Uma Thurman in that Schweppes ad. Rebecca Sibony definitely knew how to command respect.

Then a smile as faint as the Mona Lisa's bloomed over her

face, and as she made a reeling movement with her hand, she quietly added:

"And, well . . . if the monsieur is to your liking, that's another story. *Your* story. You are as much a consenting adult as he. And who am I to stand in the way of your desires, or his?"

"That's what I always say," Sophia agreed gravely.

I tried to block out the image of my friend naked in a dark, luxurious hotel room, waiting for that stranger who tasted like fruit, that skilled vagina masseur.

"It's not like I'm going to restrict myself to hiring perimenopausal women like me in order to avoid that kind of incident!"

Downplaying the subject, she punctuated the phrase with a sigh, and then snorted deeply from her throat. It almost sounded like a cough.

The message was clear: we were free to take clients to the Hôtel des Charmes—or any other hotel—after we had provided the service she'd sold them. But she didn't want to know about it, and even less to have it come to her attention. That part was up to us. The time, the pricing, the revenues. That said, we also assumed any associated risks. She warned:

"I offer no assurances about what might happen in those bedrooms. The moment you decide to walk through their doors is the moment I can't help you."

"And what if he becomes violent?"

"Stop being so dramatic!" interrupted my friend. "We're talking about politicians, corporate lawyers, executives . . . These aren't the kinds of people who would take the risk of harming you, even as a joke."

Did she really say "*as a joke*"?

"That's not the point," Rebecca interrupted. "Let me reiterate: the second you cross the threshold of a bedroom with your client, you are alone. No matter what. Under no circumstances will I ever come to your rescue. Do you understand? Never."

"Yes." I nodded.

"And if you ever make the mistake of calling me for help or mentioning the agency to a third party, like the police, I will categorically deny ever having met you. I will blacklist you immediately."

The iron mask she'd been wearing suddenly fell.

"Great! Congratulations! And welcome to Belles de Nuit!"

The next fifteen minutes were filled with paperwork. I was now officially part of the agency. I was also given some elementary advice, which Sophia had already filled me in on: never talk about your missions to anyone, not even someone close to you, not even a parent or another girl from the agency; never reveal any information or secrets learned about a client during a mission; never mention the identity of your clients; never try to see a client outside the appointments arranged by the agency.

"Sophia told me you were a journalist?" inquired the tall blonde, her tone slightly suspicious.

"Yes . . . well, not yet. I'm finishing up my degree."

"Perfect. So I won't be reading about our meeting or your missions in the press . . . right?"

Her question sounded like a threat.

"No. I need the money. You don't have to worry about me."

"Perfect!" she exclaimed, raising both hands. "The day after tomorrow, late morning, are you available?"

I froze. Was it possible she'd already found me a client? Based on what Sophia had told her about me? I could almost hear my friend vaunting my "aristocratic sensuality," my "well-heeled sexual appeal." Had Rebecca presold my services to one of her regulars?

I furrowed my brow, annoyed by the hasty way in which things were starting here at Belles de Nuit. Rebecca's demeanor immediately softened. She got up and put her long, bejeweled hand on my shoulder. A maternal gesture. Her fingers rubbed the cheap wool of my sweater:

"We're going to fix this. I'm going to help you. We're going shopping together. I adooore shopping!"

"Shopping?" I stammered.

From her chair, an overjoyed Sophia was stamping her feet like a middle schooler.

"Yes, you'll see. Two or three simple purchases, and you'll look magnificent!"

Magnificent.

That adjective seemed like an article of clothing that was three sizes too big. I'd have to get used to it, though. And fast.

4

Leaving Paris for the suburbs was a disenchanting com-
mute, a kind of downgrade. Being a small-town girl from
Nanterre, about ten miles west of Paris, I felt the capital had
a certain cachet or appeal. At night, when I boarded the RER
train going west—at the Halles, Opéra, or Étoile station—it
felt like I was riding a chariot of the condemned. Except that
I got on every day.

My suffering would not end until I could afford my own
apartment. And when I could, I knew I would rather have a
run-down shoebox in the heart of Paris than a fully equipped
one- or two-bedroom on the outskirts. I wanted to be in the
center of the big city, the center of the action. The center of the
world.

I COULD FEEL THE AGENCY contract in my pocket that
night as I boarded the train. The car's interior had recently
been tagged, the benches and jump seats included. As soon as
I sat down, I felt several sets of eyes on me. Male, of course.
It still vexed me, even though I should have gotten used to it
over the years. "I don't get why it bothers you," Sophia would
say. "Just wait till you're fifty and your boobs go down to your
knees. You'll miss all the looks on the metro."

In the meantime, every eye was killing me. I didn't know what to do with male interest. I juggled men's latent desires like a penguin with a frozen sardine. Nobody had taught me the rules of the game. My only choice was to stay on the sidelines and throw myself into the first escape that presented itself. Ignoring them and looking at the view—the train only slowed down enough to enjoy it at Nanterre University, which was the station before mine—did not dissuade them, nor did it lessen my embarrassment.

By accident, my eyes fell on the front page of *Le Monde*, which the man next to me was reading. He was in his thirties. He wore a suit and carried a black leather briefcase. One headline drew my attention.

"David . . . David Barlet," I muttered, reaching for the newspaper.

The man on my left seized the opportunity.

"Umm, no . . . I'm Bertrand Passadier. And you?"

He extended a soft hand, which I did not acknowledge. My fingers were already curled around his newspaper. Ignoring him, I started reading the first lines of the article, which talked about the owner of a private broadcasting company that bore his name, the Barlet Group. Notably, the company owned the most-watched twenty-four-hour news station in France: BTV.

Squirming, the man next to me was desperately looking for a new way to catch my attention.

"You interested in television?"

"Umm . . . ," I growled without raising my eyes.

"If you want, I could give you advice on good places to work. Barlet is okay. It's solid. But in the short term, you could do better."

I wasn't listening to a single word this guy was saying. After skimming the piece on BTV's strategy of teasing its viewers, I contemplated David Barlet's portrait. I had already seen him on television and in the media pages of economic periodicals, but this was the first time I'd noticed his troubling resemblance to the deceased actor Gérard Philipe. It was striking. I could practically hear the handsome, soft, and familiar voice, telling me the story of *The Little Prince* or *Peter and the Wolf* on Mom's old record player when I was a kid.

But the similarity stopped there. The eternally young heartthrob was an expression of human fragility, whereas David Barlet was nothing but force, determination, the savage will to do battle, and the absolute certainty of reaching his ends. His face was more angular, and his build could fit right in on a rugby field. Moreover, his eyes seemed to jump from the page, challenging you.

" . . . hardly more than three or four percent a year, which is nothing . . . ," my harasser went on, talking to himself.

BTV. That's where I should apply once I have my degree. Barlet seemed to be beckoning me from the picture in the newspaper, I thought dreamily.

The jarring squeal of the brakes brought me back to reality, and to the blue-and-white sign on the platform that announced my stop: NANTERRE – VILLE.

My station.

I immediately leaped from my seat, stumbling over Bertrand Passadier's legs as I went, and landed on the platform just as the doors clapped together behind me. Inside the train, today's suitor crumpled. His mouth grew slack, and his forehead pressed against the humid window. Waving the newspaper I'd taken hostage as I'd run off the train, I smiled weakly at him. I didn't feel badly about the theft. Looking at me from his column-framed photo, David Barlet congratulated my conqueror's attitude.

MY MOTHER MAUDE'S HOUSE IS less than a mile from the station. An average brick home. No garden if you don't count the tiny roadside patio. Taller than it is wide, with three cramped floors. For as long as I could remember, I'd lived there, with her, just the two of us, nobody to come and break our happy routine.

Since she had gotten sick, I'd made an effort to be around more often. I tried to help her as much as my classes and work would allow. It was hard for her to do basic things now: cleaning, errands, cooking, bathing, etc.

"How are you, my Elle? Were you in class?"

Though she still had a full head of hair, her skin had grayed. A waxy mask highlighted her wrinkles and froze her facial expressions. It was still her, but sometimes I had trouble recognizing her as my mom, the beautiful woman who had made my fatherless childhood a warm cocoon.

Some days she didn't get out of her old damask robe. An insignificant detail. But it was the kind of thing that made me cry. Never in front of her, though; later, in my room.

"No . . . Sophia just wanted to talk to me about a job one of her girlfriends might have for me."

"Something interesting?"

"Yes . . . No . . . I'm not sure yet."

She was always thanking me and telling everyone how proud she was to have given birth to such a nice daughter. Children were so ungrateful these days. As for me, I would never forget all the mornings she'd gotten up before my alarm to go to work. All the Christmases when she had nothing but still managed to make me feel like a princess. And my college education, for which she had sacrificed everything, and at an age when other people start to take it easy. So even though I wasn't making much, I tried to help. Sometimes I was even able to spoil her a little.

"Here, this is for you."

I handed her a small white cake box tied in a turquoise ribbon.

"What is it?" she inquired, her eyes glazing over like candy.

"An assortment of macaroons: strawberry, raspberry, cherry . . ."

That they came from Paris made them all the more special. But I'll admit it, sometimes I cheated. Sometimes I bought treats at a chain patisserie on my way home and put them in a fancier box I'd brought with me that same morning. The important thing wasn't the brand. What counted was the ritual that united us.

The doorbell rang, interrupting our little moment. Felicity, the old house cat who never went out anymore, glued herself to my legs and meowed lazily.

"Oh, shoot, yeah . . . I forgot to tell you. Fred called to say he was coming by to pick you up. It must be him."

I suppressed my irritation and went to open the gate. Fred was waiting on the other side, helmeted and perched on one thousand cubic centimeters of motorcycle—black and still warm. Fred, my boyfriend of three years. The only guy I had ever introduced to Mom. Fred Morino, unemployed sound mixer, loved martial arts and big cylinders. Lanky, blond, muscular, and covered in leather. In my eyes, his major quality was that he'd put up with me throughout my years in school.

Fred, a lover such as you can find by the dozen in this neighborhood: dark, tough, raging against the world.

"Hi, beautiful! Why aren't you dressed?"

"Dressed for what?"

"Umm . . . the movies! It starts in twenty minutes at La Défense. Your mom didn't tell you?"

"No."

"Okay. Well, do you still want to go? We'll have to hurry."

"Fred . . . I don't feel like it tonight. I'm going to stay with her."

I didn't have to turn around to feel my mom's eyes on us. I knew she was looking through the stained glass on the entry door.

"Did she relapse?" he asked sympathetically.

"No. It's just me. I don't really feel like it."

The motorcyclist considered me for a moment. His legs were still straddling the machine. Then he fixed his gaze on the house.

"You wouldn't have blown me off like this six months ago, would you?"

He wasn't bitter. He just wanted—needed—to know.

"Six months ago, my mom wasn't dying, Fred," I said between clenched teeth, afraid Maude would hear.

"Remember how we were going to get an apartment together?"

He wasn't whining, just listing his complaints. And I cannot deny that as the weeks went by, what with the new direction my life was heading, I was creating more cause for dispute.

An apartment together, yes. A wonderful, fully equipped one-bedroom in Nanterre. We had gone to see several. But it was everything I didn't want.

"You know I don't have the money," I began. "If I'm going to pay for Mom's treatment in the States, I'm going to have to—"

"Twenty-five thousand euros, I know," he interrupted, exasperated. "You've told me a hundred times."

Twenty-five thousand euros: that was the cost of this gene therapy treatment—our last hope—that only one clinic in the world could perform, and it was in Los Angeles. Typically, only movie stars and billionaires could afford it. Life had a price tag. But in my eyes, my mom's didn't. I would have done anything to save her.

Working at Belles de Nuit, for starters.

"Let me repeat myself. So long as I haven't gotten the money together, every cent I make is going to that fund."

He nodded, suddenly wanting to be more agreeable.

And to think that at one point all I wanted was his body. And to think that he was one of the first men to enjoy my intimacy. To thrum mysterious chords of desire deep inside me. I couldn't relate to that initial excitement anymore. These days, I only saw a skinny motorcyclist begging for signs of tenderness. On the verge of tears and begging.

"Okay. But what if I treated you?"

"Not tonight . . . please don't insist."

I reached out to caress his forearm. Firmly, but without violence, he pushed my hand away.

"I know what made you like this, Elle," he said, on the offensive.

"Yeah?"

A discreet scratch alerted me to my mother's presence, a few paces behind me on the front steps.

"It isn't Maude's cancer. It's your fucking journalism."

"Whatever . . ."

"Uh-*huh*, all your little bourgeois boys, them, your daddy's boys who read *Le Monde diplomatique* and go on TV to tell us to get off our asses and find jobs! They've got your head spinning!"

"Shit, Fred . . . my head isn't spinning, I'm exhausted!"

Sophia would have said the same thing. Ever since we had started to go separate ways—after college in Nanterre—class difference had opened up like a gulf between us. A "social fracture," to use an expression dear to Jacques Chirac. For them, I was a traitor to the cause. I was rejecting my roots. And my ambition was putting me on the side of the haves. I wasn't any richer than Fred or Sophia, but in my own way, I had already joined the enemy camp.

"And?!"

My mom's voice hit me in the back. Her hand shook against the banister, she swayed on the steps, but she was ready to swoop down on my boyfriend.

"Is wanting to succeed a sin? Is it? What do you want? For my daughter to hang out on the back of your motorcycle for the rest of her life? Is that what you want for her?"

"Maude, I—"

"And then what? You have two kids, and then you dump her because you hate what you've done with your existence?"

"Mom . . ."

I grasped her shoulders and tried to guide her back inside. I was touched by her intervention. As sick as she was, she still only cared about one thing: protecting me. But I didn't want her to wear herself out. *I* needed to deal with Fred Morino. By myself.

From behind the half-open door, I heard the mechanical

backfire of an engine igniting. He had left without further ado, in a deafening roar. That was his way of yelling.

THE NEXT DAY, I WAS much happier taking the morning RER into the city toward Auber station. Rebecca Sibony had kept her promise. She had sent me a text message the night before. Late. She wanted to take me on a shopping trip, or what she soberly called a "makeover."

When I arrived at Boulevard Haussmann, I immediately recognized her long, birdlike frame. She had a cigarette in her beak and was pacing in front of the Printemps entrance, a cell phone glued to her ear. She greeted me with a wink and a carnivorous smile that said, *Today, we are going to make you into a real woman, my dear.*

Rebecca told me that today was about getting the basics I'd need for my missions. That included three complete outfits: one for daytime meetings and official events, where my presence was decorative or lent distinction (pantsuit from Zadig et Voltaire in charcoal gray, black lingerie from Aubade that peeked out from under the jacket, synthetic pearls from Agatha); a second for cocktail parties and small dinner gatherings (black sheath dress with a plunging back from Armani, purple lingerie from Lejaby, and earrings by Fred, studded with a fan of semiprecious gems); and one for galas and balls (a full-skirted dress made of pearls by Jean Paul Gaultier, pearl-gray lingerie by La Perla, and a diadem bracelet by Bulgari). We added three pairs of shoes, the heels of which gained an inch or two with each time of day: three for daytime, four for evening, and six for night.

Before getting to the cashier, our arms filled to the brim, I piped up with concern over how much this was all going to cost:

"Rebecca, all of this is wonderful, but . . ."

The way she lifted her index finger, I could tell she'd been waiting for this moment.

"Don't worry about it. The agency will advance you the money."

So it would be an advance, not a gift.

"But I'll never make enough to pay you back!"

"Rest assured. You won't have any out-of-pocket expenses."

I slowly grasped what she meant. Much like drug dealers and human traffickers, Rebecca provided her new recruits with generous advances on their future salaries.

"What you mean is you'll deduct it from my first missions?"

"That's right."

"And so long as I haven't reimbursed you, I'll be working for you for free?"

She glared at me, then broke into a cavernous laugh:

"And here I thought you were just the pretty one. I'm happy to discover that you're also the smarter of the two."

Intelligent, maybe, but also hers now.

All she had to do was firmly put all the gorgeous clothing in my hands for me to look beyond the poisoned gift and see the promise of a gilded future. A life where I would not need Rebecca Sibony to treat myself to things like these.

Fred was right. I had definitely gone to the other side. And I didn't want to go back.

5

April 2009

"Y̶ou can open your eyes, Elle."

How had he managed to perform such a miracle? In less than twenty seconds, the massive dining hall, its staff and fifty guests included, had been completely emptied. Now we were alone. Just he and I in the middle of all the gilt, drinking magnum bottles of champagne under flickering candlelight. The candles ran the length of the hall, replacing the electric chandeliers that had served as lighting until just a moment before. From an adjacent room, we could hear a harpsichord's crystalline notes singing what sounded like a piece by Rameau.

"How . . . How did you do that?"

He and his honeyed voice, the clarity of which reminded me of the actor who'd recorded a reading of Corneille's *Le Cid* and starred in *Fanfan la Tulipe*. I had my own theory: up to a certain point, individuals of the same physical type are equipped with more or less the same quality of voice. But David Barlet's voice was not content to imitate Gérard Philipe. He had deeper, graver inflections that continued to ring in the air long after he'd finished speaking. His voice, like his person, was surprisingly young, but he was as capable as any bass or baritone of giving you shivers. He was a perfect combination of lightness and gravitas.

> *I know now: a man's voice, and just his voice, can fill me with maddening desire. His voice is like a sex toy that titillates my clitoris with every sentence.* ~~Hmm, I wonder if there's a Rabbit . . .~~

Anonymous handwritten note, 4/15/2009—David's, I can't deny it . . .

A MINUTE EARLIER—AT THIS POINT, we had only known each other for a half hour—he had asked me to close my eyes. I'd had just enough time to see him whisper something into the head waiter's ear and hastily pass a scribbled note to our immediate table neighbors. A few instants later, the miracle had been accomplished. David was that powerful. He was a magician. A man with what seemed like limitless powers.

AFTER MY SHOPPING TRIP WITH Rebecca, I had a busy schedule of missions. One or two a week. Everything was as she'd described in our interview. For the most part, all I had to do was wear one of the extravagant ensembles she had purchased for me; parade on the arm of a man who was double or triple my age; teeter, long-legged, on my extremely high heels; keep my torso and neck as straight as a ballerina; and attend a great number of frivolous and garish soirees. At least I had the opportunity to visit some of Paris's most beautiful buildings—private homes, ministries, museums, and other exclusive locales—and overhear secrets from the flow of conversation that the journalist in me quietly tucked away in the back of my mind.

Other guests rarely asked questions. Typically, they would compliment my clothing, elegance, or supposed grace. No one was fooled as to my role as arm candy. It didn't bother me. I knew my own worth. I swallowed my pride and took my check at the end of each evening. That was it. I kept myself from giving this job more thought or emotion than it deserved. "Where are you cast tonight?" Sophia had asked a few hours earlier.

I had finally graduated. I knocked on the door of every television network in the capital, looking for a job as a TV presenter. In school, I had focused on broadcasting. I didn't want to apply for jobs in radio or print until I had run through all the possible options there. I would have worked for any station, any show, even the ones with the lowest ratings. I don't think I was a lesser candidate than my peers, but everywhere I went the answer was the same: not enough experience.

"How am I supposed to get experience . . . if no one gives me a chance! It's ridiculous!" I complained to Sophia.

"I know, it's stupid . . . I have the same problem: they want *both* the fresh face of the young ballerina *and* the résumé of a star with fifteen years of experience."

"'Not enough experience'—I know what they really mean."

"Oh, yeah? What?"

"Not enough connections."

Your network. If you were well connected, if somebody could call in a favor on your behalf, it made all the difference . . . This typically French evil allowed the elite classes to reproduce faster than a family of rats. Always the same people. By and for the rich. And for people like Sophia and me—nobodies, without money or influence—the doors were closed.

I didn't stand a chance. Not without a good recommendation.

"YOU LOOK RAVISHING!"

The man complimenting me was tonight's date. We were standing in front of the Maison des Polytechniciens, a building in the heart of Paris's very chic 7th Arrondissement. It was an evening for the alumni of HEF, an elite business school. He was the latest in my long list of recent missions, which included a dentist in town for a conference, a diplomat, several executives of prestigious companies, and a number of senior executives wishing to impress management at the big annual gatherings by strutting about with a creature such as me.

"Thank you. That's very kind," I replied, adjusting ensemble number two, the dangerously low-cut Armani dress.

"I mean it."

If I were to compare him to my other clients over the past two weeks, François Marchadeau, a well-known economic journalist, was considerably better than average, physically speaking. Less bald, less paunchy. He was in his forties, brown-haired, and well built. His suit showed off his muscles. It was obvious he worked out. I had to admit he looked hot.

"Do you know where we are?" he asked, guiding me to the reception hall.

"The Maison des Polytechniciens."

"Yes, but I meant the occasion. Do you know what we're celebrating here tonight?"

"Not exactly, no . . ."

"HEF is not as well known as, say, Harvard Business School or HEC Paris, but most of the richest tycoons on the Paris Bourse graduated from it. You're going to meet the crème de la crème of the French business world, and all, or almost all, were top of their class at our school."

As he went on, the president of the Association of French Entrepreneurs, whom I had often seen on the news, gave him a friendly wave. She was already holding a glass of champagne.

"And what about you?"

"I'm my year's loser. I think I'm the only one who doesn't have a bank account in the Cayman Islands or a chalet in Gstaad."

"Why do you come to these things, then? Do you like being humiliated?"

He let out a genuine laugh.

"Because I need information for my magazine and after a couple of drinks they're happy to oblige. And they need me to write favorably about their strategies for handling the economic crisis. They want to reassure their stockholders as well as public officials."

"Win-win."

"Exactly."

Over cocktails, I learned about an imminent redundancy scheme at a major automobile manufacturer, the release of a revolutionary new tablet, and some other exclusive tidbits I pretended to ignore. I played my part of the beautiful ingenue flawlessly. But I filed all the information away in my memory. Just in case. My training as a journalism major hadn't worn off.

Still, what was exciting the first hour quickly grew tiresome. And as we sat down to dinner, all I could think about was my freedom after the last bite of rose-infused meringue.

I have a recurring erotic dream that takes place at a formal reception. As a joke, and also as a form of provocation, I'm not wearing any underwear. My formfitting dress reveals the absence. No panties. The breeze whips up the silk fabric, blowing gently over my exposed parts, tickling and teasing my clitoris.

The men look at my body with increasing intensity. They don't have to say anything for me to know they've all noticed my little secret.

As I walk by, even though they're with their wives, they caress my buttocks, my breasts, my thighs . . .

Their collective desire is like the Fountain of Youth. I feel much more beautiful than I really am.

Suddenly, I stop moving, and then I feel an anonymous hand grasp my crotch. Two fingers spread my lips, exposing my dripping vagina. Just as I'm waking up, they sink into me. The interruption is painful. I need to be taken . . . in my dream as in reality.

Anonymous handwritten note, 4/18/2009

"I BET ALL THIS INTERESTS you more than you let on? Am I right?"

I heard his familiar voice before I saw him. He was leaning over my shoulder. I hadn't noticed him before. Next, I felt a tickling sensation in my nose. He wore a smooth and yet powerful cologne. Its bouquet was surprising, with notes of citrus, leather, tuberose, and maybe a hint of iris. I had never smelled anything like it. It must have been a custom blend. Like his voice, his cologne was a perfect mix of youth and power.

He extended a large hand, and only then did I see his face for the first time.

"David Barlet."

"Ann . . . Elle."

"Annelle?" he asked. "Or Anaëlle?"

His tone was candid, perhaps with a hint of irony. But it was hard to reproach him for it; his smile was just so enchanting.

Rebecca had advised using a pseudonym on missions. All the girls did it. Sophia changed her name almost every time, from Brenda to Zoe to Cleopatra. I'd opted for my actual nickname. It was mysterious enough to entice the messieurs, and familiar enough so that I didn't forget or give myself away.

"No, Elle . . . Like the magazine. Anne is my middle name," I lied.

Seeing him like this, in the middle of such a tedious evening, as though he had been torn from that article in *Le Monde* I'd read a few weeks before, it felt like a dream. I wanted to touch him to make sure he was real. I made do with shaking his hand.

"I should read more women's magazines," he teased.

"I was just saying . . . I don't really read them."

"Oh, yeah? What do you read?"

As if by magic, the decrepit old man sitting next to me stood, leaving a vacant chair. David gracefully sat down, without taking his azure eyes from mine. He didn't say anything. He must have known the effect of his words on me.

"I don't know . . . Dailies, news magazines . . ."

Don't be a groupie, Elle. Don't talk to him about Le Monde*!*

"Don't tell me you read our friend François's rag?" he asked in a voice that was loud enough for my date to hear.

Standing to his right, François turned and parried:

"Don't listen to that old fox! He's a frustrated journalist. Back in college, he was the worst writer among us."

"Fair enough," admitted Barlet, triumphantly. "But my little poems weren't my only method of seduction."

"Right. Well, I wasn't born with a silver spoon in my mouth, old friend. I'll concede that I never could fight you at that level."

We all laughed at their little duel.

"Tell me everything, Elle: How did spoon-less Marchadeau and you meet?"

"We . . ."

I hadn't anticipated this line of questioning. I was afraid my client would reveal our secret. But even though I could feel him standing behind me, listening to every syllable, Marchadeau did not say a word. I had to come up with a credible story all by myself. Posthaste. Everybody knows that the best lies, the ones you can actually keep up over the long term, contain a small grain of truth.

"I'm a journalism major."

"At CELSA-Sorbonne?"

"No, at the Center for Journalism Studies. I just graduated. I did an internship at the magazine where François works."

"And you two got along?"

"Yes."

David's soft, charming look suddenly threw daggers at his old friend. He could have shot him on the spot. The blend of sensitivity and violence in this man was off-putting. From one second to the next, he was as soothing as a salve and then as harsh as a third-degree burn.

I was finally able to release myself from David's spell to take in the ballet of people around us: men and women alike were drawn to him like moths to a lamp. Yet there were certainly others in attendance who could easily rival his fame and fortune. But everyone seemed to want to be near him, to get his attention, to have some of his glory rub off on them. Everyone wanted to penetrate the magical circle that surrounded him. Standing in such close proximity, even I was a source of jealousy, especially as the minutes went by. He was granting me a considerable amount of his time.

"Who is that? Do you know who she is?"

"Never seen her. In my opinion, she looks rather ordinary."

I heard people whispering in the background, some perhaps only a few chairs away from ours, gossiping. Who was I to monopolize the star of the evening? How did I dare assert myself like that? Shouldn't I have taken it upon myself to cut my conversation short with the media prince so that other people could get their chance to talk to him?

"And where do you work now?"

David was completely focused on me.

I was so troubled that I couldn't even see the opportunity in front of me. It was so huge I hardly noticed it. The man was so enchanting that I didn't think to grasp it.

"Umm . . . I have leads. I'm taking my time."

"I see. So, to summarize . . . you have nothing."

That was the kind of blunt statement that normally makes you want to slap the person who's just assaulted you with it. So why was I standing there dumbfounded and smiling piously. Where was my pride?

Since I didn't have anything to say, David slowly reached toward my face and whispered an order:

"Close your eyes, please."

"Excuse me?"

"You heard me: close your eyes. Just for a few seconds."

"What are you—"

"Don't be scared," he instructed, with all his natural authority.

Marchadeau ended up popping his head into the dark dining hall to lay claim on what was rightfully his for the night: me. Maybe it was his way of standing up to his old friend. Maybe it was his way of saying that freedom of the press was not completely dead.

David gamely accepted defeat:

"You know, as much as the exploitation of interns disgusts me, I might just change my mind, François. Especially since you choose such nice ones."

"You think so, too, do you?" The other grimaced, annoyed.

I could tell he wanted to reveal the exact nature of my function with him that night. But for the second time that evening, he was kind enough not to say anything.

"See you later, Elle."

As David handed me a business card, his jacket sleeve crept up his elbow, revealing his left forearm. It was girded by what looked like a tightly cinched silk armband the color of pearl. I stared at it for just a second too long, and David suddenly became more forceful:

"If you don't take this right now . . . Lord knows when we'll see each other again."

"Yes, of course," I muttered. "Sorry."

He left in a halo of light, half convincing me that the whole evening had been but a dream.

"ELLE? WOULD YOU MIND GIVING me a little more of your time?"

My client's invitation was perfectly polite. But to me it seemed completely inappropriate. As uncalled for and vulgar as someone who grabs your behind at a garden party. I could only imagine sharing my bed with one man in the whole world. Only one man could make me lose control. And that man had just disappeared into the night.

"Why not . . ." I hesitated.

"Rebecca Sibony said something about the Hôtel des Charmes. It's supposed to be really trendy. Have you been?"

I had gone once or twice over the past few months, lured by my need for extra cash and even slightly aroused after a few too many glasses of champagne. It was no big deal. I hadn't made it a habit.

Maude, Fred, Sophia, Rebecca . . . David. An image of their faces raced across my mind. What would they think? What would they tell me to do? Take the money, no matter its source? Or go home in the taxi that my date would surely hail me?

I couldn't help dreaming of the four hundred euros he'd leave on the nightstand at the end of the evening. Suddenly, my phone started vibrating.

The text message was from an unknown number, and it sealed my decision:

Let's not leave things like this. No, what I mean is:
let's never leave each other.

6

June 4, 2009

How do you measure the inviolability of your darkest secrets? Perhaps by the fact that they become so much a part of you that you actually forget about them. You become so used to keeping them to yourself and pretending that they end up escaping your conscious thoughts.

AFTER OUR MAGICAL AND UNEXPECTED meeting, David and I got really close. As his first text message suggested, we never left each other's side. Occasionally, I would go home to see Mom in Nanterre and spend the night. But not a day went by that David and I didn't see each other. Sometimes just for a quick lunch at a restaurant near Barlet Tower, an ultramodern steel-and-glass structure that David had commissioned ten years earlier. Located in south Paris, it housed all of his company's activities.

"See you tonight?"

"At Le Divellec," he'd said from his car earlier in the day. "Do you know where that is?"

I knew where it was, yes. But I had never had the chance

to dine there. It was considered one of the best seafood restaurants in Paris, and had been a favorite of President Mitterrand, who would eat there with his secret daughter, Mazarine.

"It's on Rue de l'Université, right?"

"That's right. I have a reservation for eight thirty. Does that work for you?"

David knew I had way less to do than he. Still, he was gallant enough to respect my schedule. Meanwhile, every second of his time was worth a few hundredths of a point on the stock exchange. He had been so attentive the past few weeks: so considerate, sensitive, and full of surprises. Everything was so enchanting and refined with David. He also knew how much I loved scallops and lobster cooked in salted butter. His choice of restaurant wasn't random. It was a sign of his budding love.

THE EXTRAORDINARY HAD BECOME MY ordinary, with exquisite meals at Michelin-starred restaurants. But I hadn't become jaded to luxury. I was too familiar with the other side of the coin, I thought, when I spotted the restaurant, whose blue awning was visible from quite a distance.

"Good evening, Mademoiselle. Monsieur Barlet is waiting at his table."

The maître d' carried out David's instructions with zeal, and had not failed to recognize me immediately at the entrance. I followed him through the hushed room, which was occupied by a handful of graying diners and a few celebrities and politicians whose names escaped me at the time. I was distracted by the thought of the man I was about to meet.

David was sitting at the table in front of a bottle of white wine on ice. His contemplative gaze rested on the lobster tank and its unsuspecting inhabitants. My appearance roused him from his rare stupor. His spontaneous smile was genuinely beguiling.

"Darling!"

He wasn't one to use terms of endearment. I took it as a sign that tonight wasn't just another dinner. The scent of his custom-made cologne had grown stronger after a day of activity, and I could smell him as I reached the table. It was like a familiar welcoming committee.

"This place is fantastic."

"Yes, it will do," he said indifferently. His mood brightened as he kissed me.

"Don't play innocent. You know exactly why we're here," I said, my head gesturing toward the lobsters tied up with blue bands.

His Hollywood smile suddenly froze. He looked like he was in pain, as though he were afraid I would find out who he really was. No, Sophia, David Barlet had not yet given me an earth-shattering orgasm, the kind of erotic roller coaster you rode every night of the week—or practically—with a different partner. But his face was always so open and frank, so charmingly young—like the actor whom nature had modeled him after—that any girl in my place would have followed him to the end of the world.

First course: "A whole blue lobster," the waiter announced, carrying two artistically arranged plates.

He fished David's crustacean from its juices. My eyes shone, and I could not suppress my childish excitement. This variation on my favorite dish was so thoughtful of him. David was always finding ways to please me, but this meal went above and beyond all our other forays into Parisian gastronomy.

"Mmm . . . It's gorgeous!"

"Lobster served room temperature, Jerusalem artichoke, and beet fries," described the man in the black vest, an immaculate towel draped over his arm. "Bon appétit, Madame. Bon appétit, Monsieur."

"Thank you."

Don't worry, I'm not that rough around the edges. I know you're not supposed to thank the staff in that kind of restaurant. You're not supposed to let them think you're on the same level. But I didn't care. I felt carefree in my little black dress—Rebecca had suggested it for "a night when you want to end up in his arms." It was probably much too tight and much too short for this kind of establishment. I figured that was why the other guests kept stealing looks at us between bites of sweet potato. Or were they surprised to see Paris's most eligible bachelor with such an ordinary creature as myself? David dismissed this kind of assessment, but it was a critique I had overheard on prior outings with him.

I couldn't care less. I felt happy, and the fine wine my man had chosen was already going to my head.

"It's delicious," I exclaimed after I'd taken my first bite. The flavors and textures were divine.

"Your mother doesn't mind that I've stolen you this evening?"

He put his hand over mine on the table. I liked feeling his weight on me. It foretold another configuration, another weight, the weight of his body crushing mine. I shivered in pleasure at the thought. But I wasn't brave enough to take the initiative and tear him from the dinner we'd just begun.

I wish he would have led me to the restroom and taken me there. My panties on his ankles. His impatient member

*pressing into my behind. No formalities. Just the urgency
of our desire.*

*I've never been taken by a man in a public restroom
before. Usually I inspire in them feelings of love and other
noble sentiments. I want these things, too. But for once I
would like it if one of them took me in haste and ravaged
me. I want to be made an object for his desire. I want to
feed his raging hunger. I would go down on my knees before him, on the defiled tiles. His engorged tip would open
my lips and enter. He would fist my hair and push his
hard member deep into my throat, fucking my mouth like
a whore, faster, faster, hurrying to finish before the next
guest arrived in the bathroom. He would come quickly
in several spurts, and he'd let out a muffled cry. I would
have just enough time to rinse my mouth and wipe off the
traces of semen. But the smell of his cock would still linger
on my lips. I would be able to taste it with every bite of my
dinner.*

Anonymous handwritten note, 6/5/2009—Would I
really find that exciting? I guess so . . .

I HAD NOTICED THE COINCIDENCE early on, and over
time it was becoming increasingly apparent: my harasser's licentious missives reflected events in my life. They tried to in-
tegrate themselves into my thinking, to give a detailed and
realistic account of the kinds of ideas that crossed my mind.
Where was this stranger? Was he in the restaurant now? Was
he watching me?

Just as I could not bring myself to admit to David what I
did at Belles de Nuit, I did not have the courage to tell him

about my guilty relationship with the crazy poet who had plumbed my innermost depths. In a way, the poet had already won; I had let him penetrate my whole being.

"YOUR MOM . . . YOU DIDN'T want to stay with her?" David asked again.

"No . . . No, not at all," I lied, my mouth full.

I was the queen of compartmentalization. With Maude, I had barely mentioned the marvelous irruption of David into my life. I had been especially careful not to mention his last name, for fear she would make the connection with the glittering businessman she sometimes saw on the eight o'clock news. For now, she only knew the bare minimum: some rich and charming guy named David had taken Fred's place. And she'd never really liked Fred much. It was enough to satisfy her maternal instincts, and had kept my two worlds from clashing. I knew they would eventually meet. It was inevitable, considering how things were developing with the man on the other side of that forkful of lobster.

"You're right; it's excellent," he agreed, his eyes half closed in pleasure as he sunk his teeth into a beet fry.

. . . Mmm, how to rehabilitate such a lowly vegetable.

Money wasn't everything. David wasn't just a living bank account with enough to pay for this kind of banquet every night of the week if we wanted. He had something that no winning lottery ticket or profitable financial scheme could offer: he was cultivated. It was the only ingredient that Fred's pizzas would never have, though they represented so much love and sacrifice.

The following courses did not disappoint: lobster cassolette with black seeds; pan-seared lobster cooked in its own juices, served with shellfish in a champagne sauce, the effervescence of which tickled my tongue and made me groan in delight.

"It's to die for!" I whispered as David reached out to intercept a drop of sauce escaping the border of my lips.

It was obvious that my happiness was his. He was more delighted seeing me so undone by these delicacies than he was tasting all the amazing flavors himself. His enjoyment was vicarious. I for one was happy to flatter his imagination. My taste buds were so sensitive, so inexperienced. They felt pleasure in a way his could not, since for him fantastic dinners like this were so commonplace.

"NO, SERIOUSLY . . . I WOULD love to know how to make something like that."

"Really?"

"You wouldn't?"

"Sure, I guess I would," he breathed.

His laughter winged through the air.

Since we'd started seeing each other, I had barely gotten the chance to show off my admittedly meager cooking skills, a pale facsimile of my mom's culinary know-how. Food, like everything else, was part of the whirlwind David seemed so effortlessly to create. I just let myself be carried away. Now that I think of it, "whirlwind" isn't the right word—being able to choose the perfect word or image to fit a given situation is essential for a writer in training like me. "Tornado" is better, considering its dizzying power. I was being sucked up into his magical world.

David called the waiter with an almost imperceptible hand gesture and leaned to whisper something into his ear.

"Don't tell me you're ordering another bottle of wine . . . I'm already feeling blotto."

"'*Blotto*'?!" he repeated, bursting into laughter. "If you keep using your mother's expressions, beware: next time, I might just invite her to dinner instead of you."

The waiter, who had left during our brief exchange, suddenly reappeared holding a folded note. To my surprise, he handed it to me, gesturing with his head that I should indeed take it:

"Mademoiselle . . . Compliments of the chef."

"Thank you . . . ," I stammered.

A murmur swept through the restaurant: famous chefs never revealed their secrets. Especially not in gastronomic sanctuaries like this. But David had only to express a wish, and management would grant it, even if it went against all the rules. All to satisfy my little whim. I blushed, feeling both pleased and confused.

"Now you don't have any excuses: tomorrow I'll have Armand make the kitchen available to you," said my enchanting king.

Armand was his jack of all trades. He was also his personal chef. Thanks to him, Monsieur Barlet's everyday life went off without a hitch. Armand attended to everything, at any time of day. I twisted my mouth into a pout I knew would make him melt.

"I might disappoint you."

"Hardly. Shall we go?"

That was David. He was already standing, the moment he'd just created over. He was the genie in the lamp *and* the gust of wind capable of blowing all the magic away.

Our fellow restaurant patrons were staring more intently than ever when the staff discreetly whisked us out a back door. I imagine my date had left a more-than-generous tip as we were leaving. Outside, the valet was tapping his well-shod foot against the asphalt. He did not rush to greet us, as one might have expected. He held no ticket or key, but instead handed David a light blue-and-white-striped sweater, which he unfolded and firmly placed around my shoulders.

"We're not taking your car?" I asked, surprised.

No sign of his black Jaguar.

"No. Let's walk a little, shall we?"

The sun had set during our lobster orgy, and though there was a slight breeze, the evening was inviting. David put his arm around my waist, his beautiful hand resting just above the curve of my hip. He led me down Rue Fabert toward the docks, the sparkling dome of the Invalides behind us. I, who had made it a rule never to let other people manage my life, was quickly learning to enjoy letting go. It didn't seem like much of a risk, not with David. He had all the self-assurance and easy confidence of his class, a giant air bag of money, loads of connections and self-confidence. He flattened all obstacles and hardly even broke a sweat.

I liked that he took charge. But once again I longed for more . . . at the very least, a kiss.

When we got to the Quai d'Orsay, he wordlessly guided us toward the Pont Alexandre III, one of the most beautiful bridges in the city. I couldn't help but notice the *Ronde des amours*, three happy cherubs dancing at the base of each lamppost. We walked over the elegant steel-and-stone structure, which had been built for the World's Fair in 1900, and reached the Right Bank, where a few stairs led us to a pier.

"You know," I said ironically, "I may be from the suburbs, but I have actually taken one of these tourist boats before."

In reply, he pointed to a vessel tethered farther away. It had a fresh coat of paint, its bottle-green sides shining with lacquer.

From where we stood, I could see a small canopy under which lighted candles danced in the breeze. Our skiff was nothing like the tourist traps. A uniformed man in white gloves was waiting by the boat to greet us:

"Mademoiselle, Monsieur Barlet . . ."

"Good evening," I whispered, more impressed than I wanted to let on.

As soon as we set foot on the varnished deck, a string quartet started playing Vivaldi from behind the canvas tent. I hesitated: Did I want to laugh or give in to this avalanche of clichés? Everyone clearly expected the latter. Even romance novels weren't this cheesy.

David read my thoughts out loud.

"My white horse has a cold and asks you to forgive him. Unfortunately, he won't be able to make it tonight."

"Well . . ." I feigned exasperation. "You tell him I'm sending a doctor to make sure he isn't lying."

"I will." He laughed. "But if you're going to go to all that trouble . . ."

The servant had just unveiled a small round table, the epitome of simplicity: a white tablecloth, two bottle-green garden chairs, two candles, two champagne flutes, and one bottle of champagne. Only then did I notice the starry spring night overhead.

"I warn you, I won't be able to manage anything more than bubbles."

"Perfect. My plan was to get you drunk."

"Really, that's all?" I simpered coarsely.

He seized my hand, caressing it as though polishing a stone. A distracted gesture that was more of a comfort for him than me.

The boat slowly started to pull away from the dock. A light hum. Our glasses clinked, a crystalline note tinkling amid the long vibrato of the string instruments. As he uncorked a vintage Moët, we floated by the obelisk at Place de la Concorde and the National Assembly. They were both lit up for the night and sparkling. We continued on, passing the Musée d'Orsay's glass arches, which were also dressed in light for the night.

To be honest, I could have gotten used to the clichés. I could pretend all I wanted. Play the young intellectual . . . but he wasn't fooled, and neither was I. Who wouldn't enjoy such a beautiful view, and from their own private boat? Who was I to look down on something millions of other women could only dream of?

I signed my surrender with a sigh. Then I smiled. David and his charming attitude deserved it.

"To what shall we drink?" I asked, tipping my glass in his direction.

"Wait . . ."

He who was usually so self-assured seemed taken aback by my invitation to clink crystal. He shot a furtive glance over the panoramic postcard view as though he were looking for something.

"What, is there a special time for toasting, now?" I teased.

"No, of course not . . . Let's just say, I would prefer a more . . ."

He was looking for the right word.

" . . . *appropriate* scene."

The locale seemed more than adequate to me. The boat had taken us to the Pont des Arts, an elegant pedestrian bridge, a favorite romantic rendezvous for Parisians. From the river, I could see thousands of locks that young couples had fastened to the parapet's fence as a symbol of eternal love. The nod toward loyalty and posterity is the sort of thing of which those known as the Immortals over at the French Academy would surely approve.

"Not everyone would agree with you!"

As we floated under the metallic arch, we were greeted by an enthusiastic salvo. Yes, this was real. Some people were lucky enough to live life like you see it in the movies. And tonight, I was one of those people.

> *I wonder if one of the couples on the bridge has already made love here, in haste, hidden behind a tree trunk or lamppost?*
>
> *One of my girlfriends once told me that several years ago she'd participated in a kind of informal lovers' competition on the Internet. Whoever did it in the most conspicuous or interesting place and got it on camera won. That's how my friend managed to have sex with a fellow game player in one of the Centre Pompidou's subterranean parking lots, in a bush at one end of the Champs-Élysées, and—their masterpiece—in the back of a double-decker bus filled with tourists who were so fascinated by the City of Light at dusk that they didn't even notice the commotion behind them.*

Anonymous handwritten note, 6/5/2009—Sophia?

SQUARE DU VERT-GALANT, A LONG green strip at the tip of the Île de la Cité, was already receding on our left. David was still distracted by something.

"Annabelle, I . . . ," he stammered. His face, which was usually so radiant, was suddenly tarnished by an expression I did not recognize.

Jeez, you really have to be completely caught up in something not to see or hear what anyone else would have noticed ages ago.

"Yes?"

"You know, people always say this kind of proposition doesn't just fall from the sky . . ."

"What are you talking about?"

My face probably resembled one of those stone masks that decorate the Pont Neuf, the ones that look like dithering gargoyles who seem to be hesitating between bemusement, pleasure, joy, and fear. I could feel the pressure of the wind on my face as our vessel passed under the bridge. As I was waiting for David's revelation, it felt as though we had suddenly picked up speed.

What was he going to tell me? Worried, I felt a shiver run through my body. It did not go unnoticed. David immediately stood, his hot lips hungrily covering my neck with kisses.

"You'll catch your death . . ."

"Yeah, I'd rather not," I said without thinking, in my typical ironic tone.

Just then, the arm of the Seine on which we'd been floating lost its charm. Here it was just a thin strip of nothing. Not a single tree was planted on its banks. To top it off, the shadow of 36 Quai des Orfèvres, the seat of the judicial police, darkened the suddenly choppy muddy waters. Would my harasser end up behind those walls?

Probably not, if I didn't say anything . . .

THE VIEW IMPROVED AFTER NOTRE Dame's two towers passed by on my left. And the mood seemed to lighten considerably. I heard a large insect buzzing overhead. I thought David would kill it reflexively, but instead he smiled. He looked relieved.

"What the heck . . ."

I looked up to see a round black engine the size of a breakfast platter, its four small blades whirring as it hovered a few feet above the canopy . . . above our heads. A drone!

It sounded like the seagulls that made it here from the ocean, fluttering and flapping. Who was piloting the machine? It was getting really close, but I could tell it was being driven with extreme precision. When it was about three feet from the table, a metallic claw shot out from the rigid plastic structure and opened with a dry snap. A little package tied in a ribbon dropped onto the tablecloth, making a light and hollow sound.

"People always say things like this don't fall from the sky," David repeated. "But I wanted it to for you. Really: from the sky."

Dumbfounded, I stared at the package. Then, obeying a look in his eyes, I got ahold of myself, though I was still mute from disbelief. The boat trip had already exceeded all expectations. David had already more than fulfilled the kinds of princess dreams I had always disdained.

"Go ahead, Elle . . . ," he cooed, his voice sounding like it could have come out of a Christian-Jaque or Marcel Carné film. "Open it."

So this is what he had been hiding from me these past few weeks.

How to measure the ironclad inviolability of our biggest secrets? By the surprised expression on the face of the person to whom we reveal them. Let's not kid ourselves. At that moment, mine was curled into a foolish grin.

I tore off the gold paper and opened the velour jewelry box.

Inside hid a ring. Pink gold and diamonds, I noted instinctually. It was the most splendid piece of jewelry I had ever seen. It was subtle and well balanced: its size and setting were understated, the quality of its precious stones exquisite. What's more, I could tell just by looking into its scintillating angles that this ring had a history. It did not come from a jewelry shop window. It had a memory.

"It belonged to Hortensia, my mother," David remarked gravely. "And to my grandmother before her. And if you want, you'll be the third generation of women in our family to wear this engagement ring. I've already had it resized."

Family. Engagement. Marriage? My mind went blank. I could only think in keywords, and they were doing some kind of bumper car version of ballet in my head. I had a strange pounding sensation in my temples. Irrationally, I thought my blushing cheeks had started flashing an alarm-signal red.

"Engagement?"

I didn't understand.

"An engagement and wedding ring. It's a tradition in my family. On the wedding day, we take it off and put it back on the ring finger."

To better illustrate his point, he took the ring out of the box and made as though to put it on my finger.

"Wait . . . No!"

I hastily withdrew my hand. A hurtful gesture, I quickly realized. Still, he was the one who apologized.

"Forgive me . . . As usual, I'm forcing things."

The onlookers who had gathered near the cathedral didn't understand the importance or uncertainty of this moment for us. Some even started to applaud. For them, our fluvial tryst was an unexpected bonus in their tour of romantic Paris.

I broke out into hysterical laughter.

"Is this a joke to you?"

"No! Not at all!"

I controlled myself with great effort. I didn't want to dampen the mood any further.

"It's just that it's so . . ."

Unexpected. Huge. Surprising. Fantastic. And even a little cheesy. I wasn't sure how to feel, but I knew I was grateful. Gratitude. It grew within me, warm and comforting. Life with him would be as peaceful, calm, and romantic as the river upon which we were currently floating.

Madame Annabelle Barlet. Me, a girl from Nanterre carted into Paris every morning on the RER train.

"Don't give me your answer right away. Take your time."

"Yes . . . I mean, thank you," I said, matching his distant tone.

Suddenly, I don't know what, but something felt wrong. Something seemed out of place in this otherwise perfect scene. The servant, who had been standing in the background, came to refill our champagne flutes. We'd hardly touched them.

The bubbles foaming in my glass reminded me of something. The night before. The man I'd promised myself would be my last client. And another memory floated across my mind: the circumstances under which David and I had met. A secret I had been trying to forget . . .

And what if François Marchadeau, my future husband's old friend, his tennis partner twice a week since forever, the man with whom I'd shared a bed the very night David had entered my life . . . What if François said something? Belles de Nuit, the online catalogue of girls . . . the room at the Hôtel des Charmes.

"I don't want to rush you, but," David began, "if you give me an answer soon . . . I was thinking about setting a date in the near future."

What was his radiant smile telling me? He was so candid, so blissfully unaware of my troubles. What was I missing?

"What do you mean by 'the near future'?" I asked.

"The eighteenth of June."

My birthday. I'd be twenty-three.

Mademoiselle Annabelle Lorand, will you take Monsieur David Barlet to be your lawfully wedded husband, till death do you part, at an age when you should really let yourself be free to sow your wild oats?

"But that's practically tomorrow!" I exaggerated.

"I know, but don't let that worry you: if it's okay with you, we can do it at our place."

"At Duchesnois House?"

"Yes. Armand will take care of everything. All you'd have to do is give him a list of people to invite. And sign a few papers, of course."

I couldn't torture him a second longer. His mention of what was supposed to be the "happiest day of my life" was the coup de grâce, an irresistibly convincing argument in David the expert negotiator's arsenal. What else could I say but:

"Yes."

On the outside I was radiant and smiling. Inside I felt something visceral hollowing out my stomach. Something was gnawing at me and sending waves of pain throughout my body. It radiated into each one of my organs, shooting out through my limbs.

Was this fear? Happiness?

He leaped around the table, leaned over me, and delivered

one of the most tender kisses my lips had ever received. More tender than sexy, as the absence of excitement between my legs indicated. But these things come in time, at least that's what I tried to convince myself.

This man whose picture I'd admired in a newspaper only a few weeks before, this inaccessible man. David, the boss, my seducer, looked at me beseechingly and asked in an excited voice that sounded nothing like him:

"Yes . . . Yes?"

7

June 4, 2009

Y es."
   One little word and a woman gives herself to a man. Sometimes she knows in advance what she's getting into. But more often than not, she isn't sure if these three letters will mean a few moments or the rest of her life. Just a little bit of her time and body or all of her soul. We make decisions based on our present desires. But what do we know about our future wants? Can we know in advance how many "maybes" and "nos" will follow that one simple "yes"?

> *I haven't had that many orgasms over the course of my life. A few dozen, max. But I know one thing: at the fateful moment, I am one of those women who scream* no *instead of* yes. *I know some women yell, "Oh my God!," "More," or simply their lover's name. What does this say about me? Why am I a "doll who says no, no, no, no, no"? I don't know and I'm not even sure I want to.*

Anonymous handwritten note, 6/6/2009—How does he know???

SO I SAID YES THREE times, as though I were trying to write my own destiny. There I was once again in David's bedroom nestled at the heart of his mansion on Rue de la Tour-des-Dames. This was number three.

"Come!"

I followed him into his private sitting room, where the decorator had taken care to respect the romantic interiors with appropriately colored upholstery, but had broken with the style's characteristic clutter, particularly with the clean lines of unadorned, ultramodern furniture.

As soon as we were inside, he pressed himself to my back and buried his nose into my neck. I felt him grow against me as he rubbed my backside. I liked his responsiveness. His majestic rigidity. I liked that he desired me like that. Without preamble or long speeches, and especially without my having to give him permission.

"Take it off."

My panties, of course. The seams showed through the thin black material of my dress. I couldn't get them off fast enough for him. He reached up my dress and slipped a hand over my buttocks. His fingers briskly pulled at the lace covering my crotch, trying to rip them off.

"Ouch!" I cried, my hips smarting, a red welt already apparent.

My panties hadn't budged. Symbolically, I was resisting him. He who got everything—or almost—he ever wanted.

"Sorry, sorry . . ." he breathed into my ear. He sounded more excited and disappointed than sorry.

"It's okay . . ."

With that, I put one hand on a metallic dresser, arched my back, and used the other hand to push the lacy cotton to one side of my impatient and engorged lips. No more obstacles.

A trembling finger brushed my sex. I wasn't as wet as I had thought or as he might have hoped. That's life: I am not one of those girls who turns to liquid at the first kiss. My juices don't start flowing without some sweet preliminaries. My body is like a diesel engine: it takes time to warm up. David knew it.

But that night, I think he'd hoped that the combination of champagne and his proposal would unleash a waterfall. Instead, what he got was light dew pearling timidly where my lips parted.

"Elle . . . ," he growled into my neck.

His index finger wandered into my flesh, opening me up wide. Once inside me, it moved in a sweeping circular motion that was a little too zealous to be pleasurable. And it wasn't deep enough to reach that treasure spot that hides inside some of us.

THAT WASN'T HOW HE WAS going to make me come undone!

NO, DAVID WASN'T GOING TO make me come, and I didn't need that little voice inside me to point it out.

As if he could hear me, David unzipped his pants, revealing his seriously long cock and its soft, velvety skin that made going down on him such a pleasure. Without warning, he introduced his penis into my recalcitrant vagina. It wasn't fireworks, but I did feel a responsive shudder in my loins. I liked being filled with the man I loved. His in-and-out movements were a little awkward, though. Something about the angle was curving his member. But then he bent his knees and aligned our genitals in a more pleasing way. Sophia would have freaked

to hear me talk about such sacred things in these geometri-
cal terms. But to be fair, now that we were better positioned,
his movement inside me was not unpleasant. Even though it
wasn't earth-shattering, I gave in to the sweet sensation, the
warm, diffuse feeling. Suddenly he came to a grinding halt.

"What's wrong?" I sighed.

"Nothing . . . I don't want to come too fast."

I had to swallow an incredulous "already?!" Instead I said,
in a low, comforting tone:

"Okay . . . Okay, darling, you take your time."

*I've heard my friends sometimes complain about their
lovers, saying they have too much endurance. "It's been
two days, and it still chafes." Apparently men like that do
exist in the world. I'm more accustomed to the standard
model—"three little thrusts and then they're done"—or the
guy who dutifully puts in his ten minutes before giving
in. Just one time I would like to know what it feels like
to have a man fill me, fully and completely, until I forget
what it's like without him inside me. Can it really be all
that painful? Wouldn't it feel so sexy and powerful to be
able to inspire such long-lasting desire? I wonder if a man
could ever stay erect inside me for hours without moving?*

Anonymous handwritten note, 6/6/2009—What the
heck have I gotten myself into?

I HAD JUST *DARLING*-ED HIM for the first time. I was a little
tipsy, and his hands were cupping my shapely ass in what could
only be described as a caricatural position of weakness—yet I
held the key to his pleasure. I was barely even aware I'd done

it. And I don't know if he noticed. Some part of him must have been excited by it because his pulsing movements suddenly became more urgent. He'd never been so ardent, nor shown such a desire to plumb the deepest hollows of my sex.

As he slammed into my hot flesh, I started to feel a light fluttering in my loins, a kind of contraction. I wasn't anywhere near orgasm, but my body was beginning to tremble in pleasure.

"Do you like it like that?"

"Yes . . . ," I moaned, deliberately amplifying my feral cry. "Don't stop!"

As all women know, myself included, exaggerating the responsiveness of our erogenous zones to a man's caress is nothing to be ashamed of. I'm not talking about faking orgasm. I simply mean it can be used as a form of encouragement, a way to coax our partner into getting us both where we want to go. It's about kicking our sometimes lazy, stubborn libido into gear.

Though he had just pulled out of me, I guided his abdomen back toward my body into an achingly slow, penetrating motion. As I could have predicted, he misunderstood my intentions, confusing his sensations for mine:

"You, too . . . You're coming?"

No. I wasn't as practiced as Sophia in the erotic, but my favorite part of sex was that moment of uncertainty when the tip of the penis grazed my soaking lips, tickling and trembling against them nervously, before plunging back into the pink folds of flesh, reaching for that irresistible unknown. As if rewarding David for his efforts, my sex released an abundant flux, bathing his excited penis in fluid. His rhythm grew quicker, and I prepared myself for his moan of release.

We had been lovers for almost three months. We'd recently given up condoms, after our STD tests had come out clean. Most couples would take this as good news, an important step in our relationship. But for me . . .

"Oh, no! No!"

. . . it meant sex would be even faster. Sigh.

Everybody knows that direct contact between bodies increases sensations and makes for a shorter time to completion. (Where had I read that? Beats me.)

He had just come. A long, hot, rhythmic set of bursts. One hand gripping my hair like a sailor clutching a rope in a storm. Then he lowered himself onto my curved back and laced his arms around my chest. We stayed still like that for a moment. At last, he straightened and carried me to his improbably large bed, where we collapsed onto his pearly white silk sheets.

I closed my eyes and felt David's breath against my skin. I, too, was drowsy, though not for the same reason. In vain, I tried to feel other bodily sensations. Except for my stomach, which was happily digesting the evening's delicious dinner, the rest of my parts were completely unmoved.

WHEN I OPENED MY EYES, I found my man curled up in the comforter, wearing pajamas that matched our sheets. He was fast asleep. I had trouble believing we had just made love. How long had I been dozing?

I was even more surprised to find myself dressed in a nightgown I didn't recognize and that David had no doubt picked out for me himself. It was hard enough believing someone had changed my clothes while I was half asleep. Never mind trying to imagine David taking care of my intimate places without my permission. I felt between my legs: it was as dry and clean as a freshly powdered baby.

I propped myself up against the white leather headboard and looked at our two piles of neatly folded clothing as well as the piece of furniture against which he'd taken me. Had we really just done it? Nothing about the room suggested it. It didn't even smell like sex.

"Everything okay?"

The irruption of his voice into the silent room startled me. I jumped. Still, I was the one comforting him. I whispered firmly:

"Yeah. Everything's fine. Go back to sleep."

He didn't argue—proof that he must have been in a deep sleep. I knew it would be impossible for me to get any rest. I got up, put on the pair of Turkish slippers that had been left for me by the bed, and went down to the ground floor.

The main hall had incredibly high ceilings and was flanked on either side by two branches of the same majestic staircase. A graying man was bustling about. It had to be Armand, David Barlet's butler since forever. Before David, he'd worked for Andre and Hortensia—David's parents.

"Not able to sleep, Mademoiselle?"

"And neither can you, apparently."

He was dusting a giant mahogany hourglass that was as big as a rugby player. It was one of David's most recent acquisitions. David loved antiques and was a regular at the nearby auction houses.

"Oh, you know, at my age . . . You become a light sleeper. In any case, there's always something to do in this kind of house."

He spoke without bitterness or reproach. Indeed, the old man seemed extremely affable and even kind. Like his employer—or should I say master?—he looked like a famous actor: the distinguished Michael Caine. I had noticed it on my first visit to Duchesnois House. I remember being so taken with the place and its stunning bow windows that when he'd opened the door, my mouth had dropped. He was a perfect blend of distinction and refinement. I was living in a fairy tale, and Armand did not detract from it.

"Maybe it was the construction next door that woke you?"

Armand had informed me a few days earlier that Mademoiselle Mars's house had been undergoing a remodel for the past several months. Its owner had undertaken the ambitious project of restoring it to its original state. It would take forever.

"Not at this hour," he replied.

"I can't remember, Armand . . . Did this house originally belong to David's mother or his father?"

The truth is my fiancé hadn't told me. He had avoided all questions about his parents, who had both died about fifteen years prior.

"To Madame Hortensia," he replied, visibly afraid David would overhear us. "She was a direct descendant of Mademoiselle Duchesnois."

"And who was she? Wasn't it rare at the time for a woman to own her own house?"

"You're right. But Catherine-Josephine Duchesnois was not just anybody. She was one of the greatest tragedians on the French stage during the First Empire. And the great rival of Mademoiselle George over at the Comédie-Française."

He seemed to enjoy telling me about this little chapter in history.

I played along:

"Mademoiselle George?"

"Georgina!" he corrected, as though it should have been obvious. "One of Napoleon's most devoted mistresses."

So then this had been a house of women and passion. And here I was, humble Annabelle from Nanterre, about to join the history of this place. I imagined the sumptuous balls that must have taken place here, on this very floor as well as in the perfectly restored reception hall.

"By the way, Armand, did David warn you . . . about Felicity?"

"Your cat, right?"

He said it without animosity, but I could tell he was skeptical. He'd have to get used to it. Soon she and I would be part of this household, and not just for a few sleepless nights. Other suitcases would arrive, adding to the overnight bag I left from time to time. As for Felicity, Mom had insisted she come with me: "Take her, take her, she's *your* cat . . . And you know I don't have the energy to look after her. I might forget to feed her, poor thing."

"Yes, everything is ready: the food dish and the litter box . . ."

I began to take my leave. "Thanks for everything, Armand."

"You're welcome, Mademoiselle."

I was already halfway up the stairs when I heard his muffled voice:

"Oh, Mademoiselle . . ."

I stopped and turned. "Yes?"

"David didn't tell me . . ."

He called him David, not Monsieur David or Monsieur, but despite the familiar form of address, I could tell he respected my fiancé a great deal.

" . . . will your mother be moving in with us here after the wedding?"

David's offer had been generous, but Mom had not been enthusiastic. She could not imagine ever leaving Nanterre. She would miss Madame Chappuis, her neighbor and only friend, as well as all her little routines. The neighborhood was convenient for her, which was essential given her condition. She could still manage to go by herself to the neighborhood bakery or the nearby pharmacy. And there was bus number 167 to take her to Max Fourestier Hospital.

"No, not for now. But thank you for asking."

He nodded courteously.

I felt guilty leaving her alone, and for taking the cat. But I was also relieved. I could not imagine blending her world with that of my future husband. Her refusal to come live with us seemed natural. That was how big of a difference existed between the two social worlds. In spite of how much he loved me, David would never accept my mother as she was. And despite our mother-daughter bond, she would never agree to live in this moneyed universe of power and artifice.

"Will she be leaving soon?"

David had offered something else that I could not refuse: he was paying for Mom's treatment in Los Angeles. Twenty-five thousand euros in cash. He and Maude hadn't even met yet.

"She's supposed to leave in less than a month. But I'm waiting for the clinic to confirm."

"Good," he said with sympathy in his voice.

"Actually, while I'm thinking of it: I need to give you my guest list."

"Don't stress over it. Nothing is urgent. Besides, David always has me overestimate the number of guests."

"Okay . . ."

"Good night, Mademoiselle."

"Good night, Armand."

My sleep was deep but disturbed by worry. When I awoke, David was gone. He'd left at dawn to attend to the thousands of obligations that filled his days. A surreal calm had settled over the old building, and morning rays bathed its rooms in light. I slipped into a robe and padded barefoot over the cool floor tiles. It was a daily pleasure. In the hall, the hourglass gleamed, thanks to Armand's nocturnal dusting.

I noticed that the butler had turned the timepiece. Probably at David's request. Sand was emptying from the top bulb into the bottom. A small mound had already begun to form. How many minutes or hours did it represent? And how many were left before the last grain fell?

I noticed a series of engraved inscriptions on the surface of the glass: a graduated scale, from one to fifteen. Minutes? Hours? . . . Days? Considering the slow rate at which the sand seemed to be accumulating at the bottom, I decided it must be the last of these three options. Fifteen days. Two weeks, grain by grain, before our wedding day. I had to smile at David's clever thoughtfulness. I wasn't the kind of girl who turned soft at the slightest romantic gesture . . . but, still, it was really sweet of him.

Only then did I notice a small robin's-egg-blue envelope lying on the ebony console table where Armand usually put David's personal mail. It looked like an announcement. Had Armand sent out the invitations without consulting me first? It was not addressed to anyone. I waited a moment before opening it. I thought about how in the past three months of living together, I had never seen David's handwriting. Text messages. E-mails. But I had never laid eyes on his penmanship.

An absence that could have put him on my list of suspects in the notebook affair. But no! It couldn't be him!

I couldn't take it anymore. With racing heart, I caved. I lifted the flap and withdrew a folded piece of paper. A perforated page resembling those I'd been receiving for the past several weeks . . . and yet the first to arrive at my new address. So my nutcase had found me.

The words on the page were familiar. So familiar that I felt the room begin to sway around me:

That's not how he's going to make you come undone, miss.

8

June 5, 2009

. . . you come undone, "miss." Why would David *"miss"* me? That wasn't like him. Still, I had come to the inevitable and horrifying conclusion that David was my harasser. Yet it didn't make a lot of sense for him to talk about himself in the third person. And why would he denigrate himself like that?

Was he that crazy?

Another equally baffling question: How was he reading my thoughts? Had I said them out loud? Maybe in those moments between waking and dreaming? My mom said I used to sleepwalk when I was little and that sometimes I even talked in my slumber. Maybe it was happening again?

I dressed quickly and spent the rest of the morning feverishly rummaging through the house—the term doesn't really do justice to the place, the luxury and size of which made it more of a palace—looking for a note or anything that David could have written by hand. Nothing in the bedroom, soon *our* bedroom, nothing in the living room or in any of the other common rooms in Duchesnois House. Nothing on the famous console table in the entry. As for his office, the obvious place to look for such a thing, it was locked. And I didn't know how to ask Armand to open it without arousing suspicion.

"May I help you with something, Mademoiselle?"

I was on all fours, digging through the kitchen garbage.

"No . . . ," I stammered. "No, I think I accidentally threw out my to-do list."

"Oh, that's annoying . . . Do you want me to look? I think I know what your handwriting looks like."

If the message in the envelope had not been so personal, I could have used Armand as a resource. He knew David so well. But, alas . . . *that's not how he's going to make you come undone, miss.*

"Thanks, Armand . . . I can handle it. We shouldn't both get our hands dirty over this."

I laughed nervously. He nodded and disappeared into his office.

When at last . . .

Tennis with François rescheduled: Friday 9 p.m.

The fluorescent Post-it spotted with milk and tomato sauce was definitely David's work. Compared with the handwriting on the anonymous notes, David's script was much rounder and more elegant. It was less nervous, almost feminine. This was incontrovertible evidence: David was not my harasser. Immensely relieved, I also felt badly. I froze on the floor next to the garbage, my bottom glued to the cold tiles. How could I have doubted him?

After a while, I put the new message in the silver notebook next to the others. I stared for a moment at the strange writing. Who could have written them? What was his or her problem? Why did the jerky, almost haphazard script make me feel so uneasy? Why did I get the feeling that writing these notes caused their author great suffering?

I SPENT THE AFTERNOON ON the phone with Mom and Sophia. I also received calls from some recruiters with whom I'd recently interviewed—all unfruitful. Then I got this text message from David:

> I'm getting home early tonight. Want to go out?

Early for David meant nine o'clock, at best.

> No, sorry. I promised Mom I'd go to her last checkup with her before she leaves for L.A.

> Your appointment is that late?

It isn't easy lying to a man who deals with half-truths all day for a living. I would have to be more convincing.

> No, it's at 6:30, but you know how it is . . . They keep you waiting for at least an hour, then there's the time with the doctor . . . I don't think we'll get out before 8:30, 9 o'clock, and then I have to take her back home.

> Right. No worries. Text me when you're on your way home.

OK, but don't wait to eat. I'll probably have dinner
with Mom. You know how she is: once I'm with her,
she won't let me go.

I understand. Hope all goes well. Love you.

Love you, too. And thanks again for everything you're
doing for her.

David didn't reply. He'd probably been whisked into a
meeting or off to deal with some emergency. My phone buzzed
an hour later. This time it was someone else:

BDN Mission: Meeting at the Alban Sauvage Gallery,
15 Rue de Sévigné in the 3rd Arrondissement, 8:30
p.m. SHARP. The client will recognize you.
Invitation attached to this message.
Have a nice night.

BDN, Belles de Nuit. Rebecca, my boss, always sent this
kind of last-minute mission. And she would keep pestering
me until I had answered and she was sure I would make the
meeting. The agency's reputation depended on it.

The first time she'd sent me a message like that, she'd
also included instructions on what to wear. Now that I had
more experience—and she'd gotten positive feedback from my
clients—she dispensed with such advice.

But I had been firm with her recently: until further notice,
I wasn't taking any more missions. "For personal reasons," I had
said. Her latest message suggested she didn't care. For her, I was
still in the catalogue of girls. So I sent her a curt *Got it, thanks.*

After all, I needed money now more than ever. My motives were pure: after this final mission, I would be able to afford the vintage watch I'd admired at Antiquités Nativelle. It was to be my wedding present to David. My way of surprising him, of taking his breath away.

I wasn't cheating on David since it would be for him. "I am not cheating on David"—I repeated the mantra to myself several times.

Yes, this would be the last time.

"THE LAST TIME, HUH?"

"The last time."

I tried to sound convincing. But it wasn't easy. I had a hard time making myself believe it: the last time, really, and then it would all be behind me? This part of my life could be relegated to my memory, so long as no one went digging?

"Didn't you say that the other day?" Sophia asked over the phone in a moralizing tone. I was choosing my perfume. "And the day before that, too!"

I didn't want to feel guilty, so I tried to concentrate on the present moment. What was I going to wear? A black dress with a flowery tutu by Repetto, ballerina flats, and a black leather bag by Nina Ricci. And maybe this top my personal shopper said was really "in" this season. And which perfume?

Even in the secrecy of these pages, I'm a little embarrassed to admit it: I love how the male sex smells. To be precise, I love the smell of the man I love. My first time was when I was sixteen; even then I grew intoxicated as I inhaled the scent of the man who was about to possess me. If I concentrate, I can still catch a whiff of that heady bouquet, a blend of vanilla, alcohol, and fading flowers.

That's why I always wonder how I smell. Does my scent awaken desire in my partners, as theirs does in me?

They would never suspect it, but whenever I meet a man I find appealing, be it just a tiny bit, one of the first questions that crosses my mind is: And what about his scent? Will it overwhelm my senses and make me burn for the man who produces it?

Anonymous handwritten note, 6/6/2009—Nonsense!

I FEEL NAKED WITHOUT PERFUME. When I turned sixteen, I started working at the mall every weekend as a greeter in a perfume shop called Quatre Temps. The extra money had made a big difference, and the experience left me with dozens of sample perfume bottles, all free, and a chronic inability to remain faithful to any one scent. I choose my perfume based on my mood.

"Are you still there . . . or did you hang up?"

Sophia brought me back to the present tense.

"Yeah, I'm here . . ."

"Don't tell me you're doing it to pay for that watch?"

How did she know?

"No!" I cried.

"Fuck, I can't believe it . . . *That's* why you're doing it! You're such an idiot. You'd marry the first schmuck who came along."

Perfect: Miss Dior Chérie, an updated classic, a little old for me but not too much. I sprayed both sides of my neck.

"That's not very nice to David," I parried.

"About that, so . . . how was last night? What was his big surprise?"

I don't know why, but I decided not to say anything about all that had happened over the past twenty-four hours, the marriage proposal and the latest anonymous letter.

"Oh, nothing. David just knows how much I love lobster. Last night he took me to Le Divellec."

"Ugh. Don't tell me, 'the best seafood restaurant in Paris,' barf."

"Something like that, yeah." I laughed.

"And after . . . how was it?" she asked, reverting back to her favorite topic.

"Umm . . . I'd give it an A-minus."

"I see . . . So you guys aren't comfortable with each other yet, to put it nicely."

I couldn't pull one over on Sophia when it came to sex. But I could cut the discussion short.

"Soph, I have to finish getting ready . . ."

"Go, get ready, girl!"

A half hour later, I took a cab to avoid being late.

THE ALBAN SAUVAGE GALLERY WAS on Rue de Sévigné, not far from the Saint-Paul metro station in the Marais. Its facade was narrow, but inside it felt spacious, thanks to its depth. The gallery was made up of a series of small rooms separated by white movable panels. The window displayed a giant pink resin phallus dressed as a doll in a white dress, black patent leather shoes, and a pearl necklace. There was no mention of the artist.

A quick look around and I saw that the conceptual installation inside did not vary: a scrotum disguised as a Care Bear, a vulva wearing a Bob the Builder costume, and so on. Each sexual body part was somehow dressed up as a children's toy.

"What do you think?"

A bald young man with five o'clock shadow had hurried out of the gallery to greet me. His smile as well as the glassy look in his eyes suggested alcohol. Behind the door, I could make out the sounds of laughter, glasses clinking, and whispered cattiness: a typical Parisian gallery opening. Nobody really cared about the art. The important thing was to see and be seen, enjoy the free food and drink, and, above all, get an invitation to the next gathering.

"I don't know . . . I'm waiting for someone."

"Come in. Maybe he's already here."

The way he said it, I could tell he was gay, but I still wasn't sure I wanted to follow him in.

"Come ooooon," he insisted, grabbing my arm and sighing dramatically. "Don't be such a ninny!"

I had no other choice but to follow him through the packed quarters. It was a mishmash of people, from journalists in black uniform, to disheveled artists with tattoos or piercings, to half-naked creatures in designer dresses.

I was wondering who on earth would need an escort here, where everyone seemed so well connected and too-cool-for-school, when my bald man in horn-rimmed glasses handed me some champagne and stuck out his hand.

"Alban Sauvage."

"Oh . . . !" I exclaimed. "So this is your place?"

"Yeah, mortgaged to the hilt and costing me arm and leg, but yes, it's my place."

Did he need a beard or something? A mom to impress? Investors to persuade? Or worse: Was I a kind of conceptual happening, something dreamed up by one of the sickos in attendance? *The call girl in the land of contemporary art.*

I didn't know what to say.

"You . . . ?"

"No, not me. Follow me, I'll introduce you."

When I saw my client, I thought it must be a joke: he was wearing an elegantly belted suit that showed off his waist, while his open jacket revealed a matching vest. The man was in his forties and carried a silver-knobbed cane in his right hand. His face was fitted with a pair of sunglasses. Alban abandoned me without introducing us, whispering an excuse:

"I must go. I have some Chinese to fleece. Kiss, kiss, darlings!"

I couldn't move. I was like a statue. The man removed his smoked-glass spectacles and looked me up and down without saying anything. But did he need to? Once he'd removed his slightly grotesque glasses, there was something magnetic about the way he gazed at me. And though the color of his eyes was nothing special—hazel that sometimes looked gold, depending on the light—there was a rare intensity in their expression. If looks could kill, I mused, before quickly banishing the thought from my head. It wasn't easy. He was giving me a deadly look. I felt like I was his prisoner. He was searching me. He was trying to get inside me. Before saying one single word, he'd already taken up residence in my being.

"Good evening, Elle."

He was good-looking: his face was long and egg shaped, with high cheekbones and a straight profile. His demeanor was stately, though his neck a little stiff. And his hands were like those of a surgeon or a pianist . . .

Without contest, he was in the top three of my most attractive clients. He wasn't like those living statues that stand at the entry of some clothing stores. Nothing like that kind of vapid girl-magnet. He had the aura of someone who had come out of a novel and onto the silver screen. Like a god who had at last come down to the level of humans.

I did not have to look around to feel the room's attention on him. Women especially were converging around us like flies to honey. He wasn't doing anything special—he wasn't doing anything at all, just standing there, immobile. And yet he crushed the male competition through his regal attitude alone. He was perfectly present while being completely detached. He appeared to be floating above the vile masses.

"Good evening," I stammered.

With some effort, he took a step toward me, adjusting all his weight onto the precious cane. He wasn't faking his infirmity, and instead of breaking the charm, it only added to it. He was a man of more than one posture, apparently. It was obvious he had a story, and a painful one at that. The mystery only made him more appealing.

"For once, Rebecca does not disappoint."

His compliment, his way of making it clear he was a regular, annoyed me. It was vulgar. Usually our clients at Belles de Nuit tried to lighten the situation by pretending everything was normal, as though we hadn't needed an intermediary to set up our meeting. Not he. And his unusual frankness irritated me. It was as if he were trying to tarnish his first impression.

"And yet we manage it every time . . . keeping our promises," I replied brusquely.

"You have all night to convince me . . . Elle."

I hated the way he detached my first name from the rest of the sentence, playing with it like a cat with its prey.

I had been hoping that on my last mission I would get someone gentle and clumsy, someone who would simply be proud to show me off. But an escort doesn't get to decide these things.

"I don't even know your name," I snapped. "You are Monsieur . . . ?"

"Patience . . . You have all night to find out."

With every passing second, the man seemed less and less charming. I, for one, was having a hard time staying composed. I wanted to leave, and had to keep reminding myself of the watch in the window at Antiquités Nativelle to motivate myself to stay. Without this eccentric man and his money—Rebecca had told me he was willing to pay double for *me*—I might as well kiss the watch good-bye. But how long did I have to endure this?

As though sensing my panic, the limping dandy shifted tones, making himself more affable and even a little playful. He asked questions to be polite: Was I a student? Was I from Paris or the provinces? Did I like contemporary art or not really?

He had at last stepped down from his pedestal.

"Admit it, you're not really that into galleries . . . ?" he said, breaking into an open and almost charming smile.

"No . . . Not really."

"In that case, will you allow me to be your guide?"

"My guide?"

"Yes, here, tonight. You know, David Garchey is an up-and-coming artist. He's already very popular in New York and London."

David. So that was the artist's name. I smiled to myself, pleased by the irony and coincidence. David Barlet. David Garchey. The similarity was troubling.

"Okay, that would be nice," I said, relaxing.

He offered me his firm but slim arm, which was tense and gave off a kind of nervous energy. As he guided me to such and such piece, to such and such corner of the gallery, he allowed himself to behave with me as with an intimate. His fingers ran through a stray tendril, brushing over the nape of my neck and sending an electric current through my body.

"You see," he pontificated in a calm, deep voice, "David isn't just another spoiled child from a good family who feels guilty about his background."

"If you say so . . ."

If I was going to cut this tedious night short, then I'd have to let him do the talking. The less you contradict someone like him, the more quickly he'll grow bored of his own opinions. I figured he was like those university professors who go after naive students. I had been approached by some when I was in college—only to disappoint them.

I could smell his cologne, its notes of vanilla and lavender accentuated by a persistent charcoal that seemed to follow him everywhere.

"I'm sure of it. The social meaning of his work goes well beyond his background."

As he said this, he pointed to a giant statue of Sophie the Giraffe with huge breast implants and a silver lamé string bikini riding up her backside.

The sleeves of his jacket and shirt were slightly bunched and revealed a tattoo of a miniature *a* and the tip of a feather pen on his left forearm. The rest of the word was hidden from view.

"Sorry, but I don't follow. I don't see the interest in making fun of children's toys by turning them into grotesque sexual objects . . . How exactly does that diverge from the petulant bourgeois youth biting the hand that feeds it?"

I hadn't been able to hold myself back. He had awakened my critical mind, which had reacted before my better judgment could kick in.

I expected him to dismiss me for the night—and without pay—or at least shoot me a death look. Instead, his eyes shone with renewed interest, searching mine. He was smiling both in surprise and excitement.

"Notice the choice of characters, Elle: David could have chosen to use toys that are already known for their oversexualized attributes, like Barbies. Instead, he transformed objects synonymous with childhood and innocence into symbols of sexual emancipation . . ."

"Okay, if you say so. And so what?"

"What he's trying to express is how fast children today transition from a state of innocence into sexualized beings. And how violent that is. To the point where the child and the sexual predator coexist in the same person, becoming at once the hunted *and* the hunter."

The moral undertones of his speech made me uneasy. Above all, I was surprised to hear this sort of conversation from a man I barely knew. But he did not seem very hampered by strict principles.

"Do you know the average age at which a person sees a pornographic film for the first time?" he asked in a serious tone.

"No . . . I don't know . . . Fourteen?"

"Eleven. By the age of eleven, most preteens, girls included, know all there is to know about fellatio, sodomy, double penetration, and even more extreme practices."

"Right, clearly, it's a prob—"

"No!" he erupted. "They don't really know anything! That's the whole point! The fact that sex has become so banal has created the *illusion* that everyone is properly informed on the subject. All the porno-chic advertisements, all the suggestive clothing, all the sexualized television programs kids binge on these days . . . none of it actually teaches them anything about sexuality. It's just one big, incredibly lucrative marketplace. But you could hardly call it a sexual education. Everything about it is fake, deformed, ridiculous, and even violent . . . It's everything but erotic. Anything but true!"

"So if I understand you correctly, then the problem isn't simply that sexual content exists, but that children are exposed to it before they've reached any kind of *natural* sexual maturity?"

"Yes." He nodded passionately. "*That's* what David's work is expressing: all this ambient sex is nothing but a trompe l'oeil. And a real education in sexuality has simply vanished. None of these children bombarded with sex at a very young age are capable of understanding sexualized images. Any semblance of truth has been occulted. And somebody is making a fortune off this shit. That's the tragedy! That's the scandal!"

"So then according to you," I inquired, "what would be the right age at which to learn about sex? And who would teach it?"

I immediately thought of my notebook and its mysterious notes. Wasn't the person writing to me trying to educate me, albeit in a way that was brutal, intrusive, bordering on rape?

"It's different for everyone. There is not *one* age at which the libido blossoms, contrary to what some lawmakers and statisticians argue. Each person has his or her own schedule. Some are ready much earlier than others. Sexual education should not follow a one-size-fits-all curriculum."

The man was the Rousseau of sex. His philosophy was that each person's natural sexuality should be allowed to express itself, and that people needed to be protected from society's market-driven mentality. He had not answered my second question, though: *Who* could we entrust to teach it? He was right to criticize the current market-driven model of sexual education, but who would he have replace it?

Thinking about it, I didn't disagree with his assertions. But was this artwork really the best way of getting the message across? What about the teenagers from the nearby high school who walked by the gallery several times a day? Was exposing them to Sophie-Gomorrah monsters without any sort of explanation really all that helpful? Was it really any less toxic than the pornography they encountered online? Wasn't the artist (involuntarily?) complicit in the evil he was trying to condemn?

I kept my ethical concerns to myself. My companion was so passionate about what he was saying that I started thinking he *himself* was David Garchey, the artist and author of the abominations in question.

"Speak of the devil . . . and the scent of sulfur fills the air!"

He nodded furtively to someone behind me who noticed and navigated through the crowd of art show moochers to join us.

"Good evening," said the young man timidly. He was practically a teenager. He wore a white shirt, his long brown hair hiding half his face.

"David, allow me to introduce Elle. Elle, this is the young man whose work I so admire, as you've probably guessed."

That was an understatement.

I threw a polite smile in the direction of the artist, who looked about as confident as a coat hanger.

"Good evening . . . and congratulations on the show."

"Thank you," he replied shyly.

"I bet the media has taken interest."

"Actually," my date piped in, "we've had several nice articles. But that's not what counts. The important thing is that some of your fellow newspeople have seen beyond the most shocking features of David's work, which are only there to grab public attention, and grasped the social and educational thrust of his message."

How did he know about my future profession? Wasn't Rebecca supposed to keep our personal information confidential?

I was about to ask him about this when a tall, ethnic-looking woman, in a sequined dress the size of a swimming suit, sauntered over and glued herself to him. She coiled her long body and perfect curves around my interlocutor. Unlike David, *my* David, he did not look like a famous actor. His feverish demeanor put him in a category with the likes of Willem Dafoe, Christian Bale, or Anthony Perkins—the dark and nervous types. He was not a beautiful statue, but still was rather incandescent.

"Shall we go, Loulou?"

"Yes, let's. Elle, I leave you with the future of contemporary art."

The future in question was staring at his shoes.

"Wait . . . you're leaving?"

It was the first time a client had left me like that, and on the arm of a girl who was a hundred times prettier and more sophisticated than I. My tutu flounced in rage and indignation. I was so irritated I forgot that his early departure also meant I would not be getting the promised bonus. I was just so offended. I felt rejected.

"Don't fear. We'll see more of each other," he promised as he put his arm around the tall and tan Vine, whose dark eyes were glaring at me. "Oh, and I forgot . . ."

What had he forgotten? The most basic forms of polite-
ness? Or maybe to pay me? Typically clients paid me directly
and sent the agency its commission separately. Some of the
regulars settled everything with Rebecca, who would then
give us our share. I didn't ask, but assumed that he must be in
the latter, more exclusive category.

His tattooed arm reached toward my low bun, which had
come undone over the course of the evening. I stiffened at his
touch.

"What?"

"You should use hairpins instead of barrettes," he advised,
as though he could read my thoughts. "It would show off your
neck better. It's a shame to hide it."

"Oh, I don't know . . . ," I stammered.

"Good night, Elle."

The duo was just about to disappear into the crowd, the
loud clap of the man's cane on waxed cement echoing behind
them . . . when suddenly he turned and started back. Now
what did he want from me?

"I forgot to introduce myself."

"Right . . ." About time, I thought.

"I'm Louie . . ."

I was still curious. Louie who? I gestured for him to go on.

"Louie . . . ?"

"Barlet. I'm David Garchey's patron . . ."

Louie Barlet, I repeated to myself, trying to grasp the
meaning of the two names. Suddenly I felt sick.

" . . . and David Barlet's brother."

Again he took his leave, but stopped for a brief instant to
smile and throw what felt like a grenade in my face:

"But I suppose you'd already guessed?"

So this was the brother David barely mentioned. I had never seen his picture, and David had clearly been avoiding a proper introduction. Now we had met. And in the worst circumstances imaginable.

He and his creature disappeared into the night, leaving me there, breathless.

"ELLE?"

Alban was like a jack-in-the-box; he popped up in front of me without warning and handed me a thick envelope.

"Here, Louie told me to give this to you."

"Thanks, what is it . . . ?"

"You'd better get going. Your taxi is outside. Open it in the car."

Without saying good-bye, I ran out the door and found a large sedan idling curbside. I hesitated a moment, unsure of how to address the chauffeur, then said:

"3 Rue de la Tour-des-Dames, please. In the 9th Arrondissement."

He put the car in drive without saying a word. I settled comfortably into the back seat and opened the envelope Louie had left for me with his gallerist friend. It contained eight perfectly crisp one-hundred-euro bills that could have come directly from the Banque de France. Eight hundred euros. Or exactly double my usual rate for a date, including a night at the Hôtel des Charmes. It's what he'd promised. Louie Barlet had decided against possessing me while he was anonymous to me . . . but he'd still paid for me like any courtesan.

His generosity made me a vulgar whore. And he knew it. Just like he must have known I would soon be family.

I started texting David a message to tell him I was on my way home when my smartphone suddenly buzzed. There was no indication of the sender, but I knew right away who it was:

See you tomorrow.

I should have thrown my phone out the window. Or at least erased the two last messages from its memory. I was shaking, my head sweating and inflamed, and I didn't do a thing. I fought to contain my tears, which flowed uncontrollably from who knows what old painful memory.

That is how I met Louie Barlet.

9

June 6, 2009

That morning, David did not greet me. Not in person. He had left his credit card and a little handwritten note on the bedside table for me to find, more proof of his innocence in the notebook affair. It made me smile and gave me energy for the day.

> *Don't you have an interview today?*
> *Go make yourself beautiful—which you already are . . .*
> *I love you.*
> *D.*

He was so charming! He'd been doing things like this for the past three months. Unfortunately, I could not fully appreciate it. Something inside me was stuck. My emotion for him did not course through me like it should. Not like it had. I thought love was supposed to last at least three years. Not three months!

WHEN I'D ARRIVED HOME THE night before, David had

already gone to bed and was fast asleep. I tried to make myself as discreet as possible when I joined him under the feather-and-silk covers. But I couldn't help tossing and turning as I replayed the night's catastrophic events.

I couldn't find the right words to describe the situation: my future brother-in-law had hired me to be his luxury doll behind my fiancé's back. He had set a trap for me, and I did not as yet know why. One word from Louie to David and my future would instantly disappear like a speck of dust in the wind. My dream life: over. Maude's miracle treatment: gone. His disgusting and completely inexplicable ruse could destroy everything David and I had planted over the past few months. And the money, which I had counted over and over in the back of the taxi, and which he had deemed too dirty to touch, had already ruined the token I had wanted to give his brother as a symbol of my love: the watch. I could not buy it for David now. It would be a constant reminder of my shame, and of the secret between Louie and me.

I could hardly believe this man's hostility. Prior to that night, I had never met him. What had I done to him? Did he think I was just another trashy, brainless gold digger, after the family money like all the other leeches? The thought crossed my mind that David himself had asked Louie to test me, as I would imagine he tests all his new recruits in the business world. But no. I couldn't believe such a disgusting thought . . . Not after his beautiful marriage proposal on the boat. A man capable of that kind of romanticism could not be manipulative in matters of the heart. That's what set him apart from Louie, who obviously loved to scheme.

"Are you sleeping?" whispered a muffled voice.

It was so unexpected that I almost screamed.

As if he knew I needed comfort, he pressed his athletic torso against my back, folding my body into his and caressing my neck with his breath. "It would show off your neck better," Louie had murmured not an hour earlier. "It's a shame to hide it."

Remembering his words and the feeling of his touch against my skin as he'd reached for my bun's stray tendril, I felt an unexpected surge of heat. A ball of energy formed within me and shot from my neck down to my loins and into my backside and the fleshy folds of my sex, which quickly engorged with uncontrollable desire. Reflexively, I pressed my posterior against David's penis, instantly waking it from sleep.

"That's how the hospital makes you feel?" he asked quietly, his lips on my ear.

I shuddered in reply, showing uncharacteristic wantonness.

"I want you . . . Take me, now."

"You don't want me to—"

"Take me!" I pleaded.

He did not need more coaxing. He freed his erection from its cotton prison and planted it into me. No foreplay, no liminal rubbing. We were spooning, which limited his depth of penetration and range of movement. Its only advantage, aside from the obvious one of comfort, was that it freed up my hands to wander to the base of my pubis. I spread my fingers into a V and rubbed the mound between my legs. My breath was jagged. As my pink button swelled in pleasure, I felt myself cry out softly. It wasn't an earthquake, but a quiet shudder rose through me. I wanted more, harder, longer. I didn't want it to stop. And the good news was that it was all up to me. To my touch. My hand joined David's and coaxed it over my erect nipple. He pinched it harder, sending an electric arc through my body. My back and thighs contracted. It almost hurt. I would have loved for the release to have lasted more than a few seconds. For me, it was too short.

I don't remember how I first learned the technique to make myself come. It must have been as a young girl in my bed, facing a Depeche Mode poster and snuggled between two stuffed animals.

It hasn't varied much since then: I start by touching my breasts. I haven't given it that much thought, but I've noticed that all my erectile parts are connected. When I graze a hand over my nipples, the little pink button below always stirs. But I do not rush to touch it. I continue exploring my upper body: breasts, neck, nape of the neck . . . Sometimes I run a hand through my hair, allowing light strands to tickle my face like tiny, taunting fingers. As my crotch begins to heat up, I let my hand wander over my belly button, the curve of my stomach, and down to my pubis. I play with it for a moment, curling the wild hair around my index or middle fingers. My other hand brushes over my lips. One or two fingers dart into my mouth, where my wet tongue rolls over them.

Downstairs, serious things start to happen: the index and middle fingers form a V, and I lower the natural fork over both sides. With each movement, the base of my make-shift tool hits the excited little mount. I feel it getting bigger. It is growing out of me at an accelerated pace like a magic bean. I don't stop. I keep rubbing. From time to time, I close my two fingers, pinching my clitoris, crushing it. I imagine it to be scarlet. And then again and again. When my pleasure seems imminent, my second hand comes to action.

Sometimes I move my index finger in a circular motion over my flesh, directly on the little knob, which starts to radiate pleasure. Or sometimes I introduce my finger into my vagina, where I let it wander and knead my moist interior. In response to all this, a first wave surges from my clitoris. It's sharp and strong and crashes through my middle. A second, often followed by a number of small aftershocks, rumbles like a tsunami. Its epicenter lies deep in my loins, unfurling in opposite directions: down toward my toes and up over my chest, throwing my head back. "Oh, no, no . . . ," I moan, before collapsing and curling up on my side, exhausted. Satisfied for want of real happiness.

Anonymous handwritten note, 6/6/2009—Except for the Depeche Mode poster, it's pretty accurate . . . How does he know?

ENCOURAGED BY WHAT HE BELIEVED to be the product of his efforts, David quickened his cadence, and soon emptied himself into me, crying out in a way that almost sounded pained. His contractions inside me felt like a kind of reward. An encouragement.

If David had finished, that meant I had full access to my vulva and could introduce one finger then another inside my wet folds. Soon I began to feel it. Then a wave started to surge up from my belly button and crashed into the shore of my lower belly and legs. Just one wave this time.

"Nooooo . . ."

It wasn't the orgasm of the century, but it was an orgasm, the kind I could give myself, often quickly and discreetly. Sex with David was not that different from sex with Fred or sex when I was single. In the end, I always had to count on myself, and only myself.

I had hoped things would change with my true lover, but I could already hear light snoring at my side. David was sleeping. I was tired, too. Exhausted by an avalanche of contradictory emotions. I had a strange dream in which David Garchey, Louie's little prodigy, was wearing the same doll's clothing as his giant penis, and kept whispering with a half-smile: "Why don't you teach him how to make love to you? Hmm? What are you waiting for?"

I WAS AMAZED AT THE powers of the unlimited platinum credit card! After brandishing David's that morning to half a dozen shop clerks, I felt much better. Each time I signed for him—an ultimate mark of his trust—Louie, David Garchey's teratological work, and all the pompous speechifying on sexual education receded bit by bit. I began to forget about the threat posed by my meeting with my brother-in-law. All I could hear was salesgirl babble, like the intoxicating chant of sirens.

"That will be four hundred fifty-eight euros, please, Mademoiselle."

"Jacket, skirt, heels, small handbag . . . Eight hundred twenty-three euros and fifty cents, please."

"Two hundred sixty-seven euros, please. Do you have our store card?"

"Oh my, you have a lot of bags. Would you like me to call a taxi?"

"Five hundred twenty-one euros, including the fifteen percent discount on purchases above five hundred, okay?"

"Have you seen our new collection? I think you'd love it!"

Floating on my magic carpet of easy money, I could barely hear them. In just a few hours, I had scoured the boutiques of

better- and lesser-known designers in a very chic neighborhood in northern Paris, the Abbesses, a triangle of sophistication bordered by working-class streets: Rue Lepic, Rue des
Martyrs, and Rue des Trois-Frères. The sun was radiant, and
a gentle breeze chased away any residual thoughts about the
Barlet brothers.

With David's card, clothing sellers did not see me as a
shopper with money troubles at the end of the month. I was no
longer that chubby girl, the size 10. I was curvaceous, like the
new generation of models who embrace their bodies, and whose
curves advertising now extols after decades of banishment.

All the positive encouragement made me less shy about
formfitting dresses or puffy short skirts, both of which accentuated my voluptuous form. "Like a Boucher or a Poussin," David,
who appreciated classical art, was sometimes known to say.

PLACE PIGALLE IS ONLY A few steps down from the Abbesses. I took Rue Houdon, eating a greasy, dripping falafel
sandwich, just how I like them. I stopped in front of a shop on
Boulevard de Clichy that was much flashier than the designer
boutiques I'd just visited. Blinking pink and red neon lights
formed a naked silhouette that beckoned those feeling lusty.
Some men pretended not to notice; others stopped and entered
into a mirrored lobby.

"Come in, Mademoiselle. Girls like it here, too," heckled
a smooth-headed bouncer in a thick North African accent.
"Come in!"

"No . . . I just wanted to see a friend of mine who dances
here. Soph—"

I stopped myself. Lord knows what name she went by here.
I didn't want to compromise her anonymity.

"What does your friend look like?"

"Brunette, long, curly hair . . . with . . ." I flushed and did an exaggerated mime of her chest.

"Oh!" He guffawed, showing off his broken teeth. "But you know, my gazelle, they're all brunettes with big tatas!"

"How can I find her, then?" I inquired as soberly as possible.

He clapped a friendly but firm hand on my back, pushing me inside.

"Go ahead, go . . . after the mirrors, take the hall on the right. You'll see a door marked 'Private,' and that's where all the girls are. Your friend is probably in one of the booths."

I followed his directions, cursing Sophia for asking me to meet at her work. "You know, the kind of dancing that gets a man all excited before he goes home to screw his little wifey," she had said, downplaying the job and making it sound like a female version of Chippendales.

In these hard times, she'd been forced to recalibrate her dreams. But thinking about what she did and seeing it with my own two eyes were different things. Totally different.

The dark hall was too narrow for me and my giant collection of designer shopping bags. I saw my friend through a tiny window on one of the doors. Her back was to me, and her thong was so minuscule that I didn't even see it until she briefly turned around, just for a second, enough time for me to notice she'd taken out her two belly button rings. Her lusty hip movements looked nothing like choreographed dance, her only goal in the disco party behind the door being to show off body parts: her breasts, mouth, and bottom. From time to time, she'd press one of these attributes against the glass. A man was no doubt masturbating on the other side.

Five minutes! She indicated to me with one hand. She *had*
noticed me.

*In another one of my sex dreams, I am lying on my bed,
naked, touching myself. It must be summer because it feels
hot, and there's a light mist of sweat pearling on my naked
skin. I'm not wearing anything, and the fact that I'm
giving in to my pleasure so freely must mean that I think
the vacation house is empty.*

*My legs are spread, my sex wide open, and I'm
using my unfailing technique: the upside-down V
straddled over my aroused button, the middle finger
of my other hand plunged inside, where it's already
wet. Inside, I'm burning. Despite the distance, my
light perfume floats up to my nose, and I grow more
excited.*

*But when I feel the culminating moment drawing
near, I hear someone's footsteps behind the door. The old
parquet flooring creaks under the weight of someone who
has suddenly stopped moving. I can almost hear the unknown person holding his breath, afraid to make a sound.
Has he come upon me by accident? Has he been spying on
me?*

*In other circumstances, I would have dressed quickly or
hidden myself under the white sheet. But I am not in control. I carry on, deepening the circles with my fingers, looking for my hidden sensitive zones. I bite my lips. I won't
be able to keep myself from screaming for much longer. My
sensations have been heightened by the knowledge that a
man is so near, so petrified by emotion that he shivers in
desire. I am breathing loudly . . . and he, too. He must*

have taken out his sex. He is rubbing it now, at the same rhythm as I. He is being careful not to make a sound.

I wake up just as we are about to come in unison.
In my state of half-sleep, I imagine him leaving without asking questions or revealing his identity.

Anonymous handwritten note, 6/6/2009—I've never had that dream, but my God . . . I've already experienced that scene!

I WAS REFLECTING ON SOPHIA'S dance, when a red light on the booth's ceiling started flashing. I guess it was the final count.

Ten, nine, eight . . .

Sophia turned to face me and pressed her ass up to the glass in front of the anonymous client; she closed her eyes and inserted her middle finger into her vagina as she pushed the invisible string of her underwear to the side. With her finger, she was simulating the penetration of a very different member, first slowly, then with increasing speed.

. . . seven, six, five . . .

Was that in her contract? She had to finger herself vigorously, as though she were trying to make herself come, as opposed to the customer.

. . . four, three, two . . .

She really seemed to be enjoying herself, but I had a hard time seeing her in such a degrading position. What a game of fools: a few euros for an unsatisfying fantasy. She batted her eyelashes in spite of herself. Was she really about to come, right there, a few paces from me, for that loser behind the glass?

. . . one, zero.

The room was suddenly plunged into darkness. Instinctually, I ran toward the exit as I heard her behind the chipped red door collecting the clothing she'd removed during the show.

SHE MET ME OUTSIDE, NEAR the bouncer.

"Don't tell me you liked that or I'll start to worry . . . but then again don't tell me you didn't or I'll strangle you!" she cried, shaking me affectionately.

I had never dared ask, but I was fairly sure that her collection of lovers had included women. Who were they? What did they look like?

"I didn't say anything!" I laughed.

The early afternoon sun was inviting. I wanted to go for a walk, in spite of all the shopping bags weighing me down. I had two full hours before my interview, and it would only take me about thirty minutes by metro to get to the studio in Levallois-Perret. Sophia's heady perfume, a blend of floral notes and patchouli, was in contest with the enormous, steaming kebab sandwich she'd gotten as we were walking. She may have been eating like a trucker wolfing something down on the side of the road, but men still stared. She effortlessly exuded sexual availability and always drew a lot of male attention. She barely even realized it.

When she'd finished her snack, we sat down at a table in the sun in Place des Abbesses and sipped Monacos, her favorite beverage. Perhaps I was feeling a little tipsy: I didn't waste any time in telling her about my unfortunate meeting the night before.

"That's crazy! You *have* to tell David!"

"Tell him what, exactly? That his brother treated me like a princess for about ten minutes and like a tart the rest of the night? And why, you might ask? Oh, wait, I know: because I *am* a tart!"

Two yuppie men drinking beers and scoping their next conquests from a neighboring table looked at us with lewd intent.

"Elle, he set a trap for you behind his brother's back. You can't just let this go!"

"David could learn a lot about me, Soph . . . For now, he accepts me for who I am, even though I'm about ten rungs down the social ladder from him. But he'd never be able to get over that part of my past. Can you imagine what the press would say? 'David Barlet, CEO of the Barlet Group, marries a call girl.'"

"Fucking shit, Elle, you're not a call girl . . . You're an escort, it's totally different."

More staring from our right.

"Oh, yeah. Try and explain that to the paparazzi!"

She glared at the two oglers, then turned back to me with a smile on her face:

"Did I hear you correctly? Did you say '*marry*'?"

"Er, yeah." I sighed. "It happened the night before last."

"Ooh! No feeling sorry for yourself! One of the hottest, richest men in France wants to put a ring on it—on *you*. So be good and don't screw it all up at the last minute."

My phone buzzed from my bag, cutting her off.

BDN, Urgent: Annabelle, are you available for a mission tonight at the Champs-Élysées theater, 8:30? The client will pay triple your usual rate since it's so last minute. Please get back to me ASAP.

Sorry, no, other plans.

I replied without hesitating. Just as I was keeping David in the dark on my employment at Belles de Nuit, so had I hidden from Rebecca my recent engagement to the famous bachelor.

As for the identity of the person who had requested the surprise mission, I was sure it was none other than Louie Barlet. Who else? He had even told me last night: "See you tomorrow."

"There's one thing that bothers me in this story," Sophia went on. "How did his brother know about you?"

"I don't know. I think he's a regular client at the agency. Considering the girl he left with at the gallery, I wouldn't be surprised."

"Rebecca has literally hundreds of girls in her catalogue. It's kind of a big coincidence he happened to see you there."

"David must have shown him a picture of me . . . ," I speculated. "He must have spotted me while browsing the catalogue."

My phone demanded my attention again.

You turned down three missions last month. You know the rule: one more and I'll fire you. Think about it.

I've thought about it.

Okay. Do you need a reminder of the amount of money I fronted you? You still owe me. Lest you've forgotten, YOU asked me to delay the reimbursement plan. And so long as you have not paid back every

penny, you are bound by contract. I may be understanding, but my business is not a charity!

I had not forgotten. One thousand seven hundred fifty-five
euros left to pay. My current savings could cover it, but then I'd
have to forget about my present for David.

"Are you okay?" Sophia asked, worried.

"Yes, yes . . . Rebecca's just harassing me."

"Tell that old harlot to shove it!" snorted my friend. "A
little pocket money from your billionaire and you can tell her
where to stick it. *Servant.*"

Scowling, she threw an invisible leash over an imaginary
minion. My rebellion against Rebecca gave her an opportunity
to free herself of her own enslaved condition, at least a little,
the time to have a laugh.

"Millionaire, not billionaire," I corrected.

"Yeah, but you should be able to more than cover your
debts. Erase that bitch from your phone."

I did as I was told and deleted Rebecca's text message.
But no sooner had I done that than another popped up with a
chime on my list of unread messages.

"God, the old hag is obsessed!" Sophia cried.

"Umm, no, it's not her . . . Shit."

The polite, concise words on my screen were far more
concerning than anything Rebecca Sibony had to say. Money
would no longer be an issue in my life—a victory, considering
the miserable cards I had been dealt at birth.

But you can't buy professional recognition.

"Who is it?"

"My interview . . . It's been cancelled. They hired somebody else. The weather girl."

"That old cow?!"

"I know . . . But everybody already knows who she is."

"Hmm . . . I don't understand why you want to work for those jerks in television anyway. I think you would be amazing at a magazine."

"Let me remind you that my fiancé is practically the 'jerk' in chief," I retorted.

"Listen, I didn't even know you were getting married until about five minutes ago."

Sophia tried to cheer me up. Somehow, though she had spent the better part of the day dancing faceless in front of a window, she still had energy to console me.

"At least you won't have to worry about being a Hotelle anymore."

"A ho-what? Excuse me?"

"Rebecca never told you?"

"No . . ."

"Apparently, another girl named Elle used to work for her. She got pretty well known for ending all of her missions in a hotel room. And, you know, 'hot' plus 'Elle' equals 'Hotelle.' Not bad, right? I guess it stuck."

The other girl may have been named Elle, but she sounded a lot like Sophia. A girl who sparked male desire during the day from her booth and put it out at night in a hotel room for a fee.

"I had no idea Rebecca was so creative," I joked.

"Anyway, for you, that's all finished."

I wish I could have been more sure. I had really wanted the interview to go well so that I could close the door to the Josephine—and all the other rooms in the Hôtel des Charmes—once and for all. To be simply Annabelle. Not a "Hotelle."

"Do you mind if I call David?"

"No, go ahead. Do you want me to go?"

"No, stay."

I patted her tan forearm for emphasis. The summer had given her a really beautiful glow . . .

"Let me guess, your media mogul is really busy, right?" she said as I hung up from our brief exchange.

"During the day, yeah. But that's what is so weird . . . He wants me to meet him at his office."

"Now?"

"Yes, right away. He's waiting for me."

"Maybe he's throwing you a press conference: 'Annabelle Lorand, you plan to marry David Barlet, and you're also a call girl . . . Is it difficult to straddle such vastly different worlds?'"

"Don't be ridiculous!"

I QUICKLY SAID GOOD-BYE AND, being weighed down by my purchases, hopped in a cab for Porte de Sèvres on the city limits. I had never been inside Barlet Tower before. The tall, scintillating structure dominates Paris's southern skyline, and is a stark contrast to David's taste for old buildings in his private life. Up close, it was even more chilling. I entered the main hall with its dizzyingly high ceilings.

"Mademoiselle Lorand?"

A petite, plump blonde, whose braided bun accentuated her kind of equestrian look, approached me as soon as I set foot inside. No doubt she had been waiting for me.

"I'm Chloe. Monsieur Barlet asked me to take you to his office. Would you please follow me?"

"Yes, of course."

"Actually," she corrected herself as though her life depended on it, "he'll meet you in the conference room. He's with someone in his office right now."

"Okay."

I felt as if I had walked into a machine that was much bigger than me, and in which Chloe was probably only a minor cog and, as such, no doubt under a lot of pressure. In the time it took us to get from the elevator to the transparent door where she left me, Chloe looked at her watch at least a dozen times.

"Would you care for some coffee? Tea? Water? A cold beverage?"

"No, I'm fine. Nothing, thank you."

"Okay. Monsieur Barlet will join you in less than"—she checked her watch one last time—"three minutes. Four max."

"Perfect," I said, almost laughing.

But I stopped myself, trying to imagine this poor girl's life, in which every meeting was calibrated to the second. I realized it was like that for the man I was about to marry, too.

I sat down in one of the shiny new leather chairs on wheels and flipped through an economic journal that was sitting on a corner of the table. A shadow appeared behind the frosted window. I smelled his cologne, that unmistakable blend of lavender and vanilla, before I realized it was him. My nose was just beginning to register the scent when a voice at the doorway seized my attention:

"Elle! Here and in person! What an honor!"

Louie Barlet was pressing his hands into the knob of his cane and looking at me intently. His suit was just as close-fitting and elegant as the one he'd worn the night before. My chest seized, and my breath grew short. I must have resembled a dead fish, or some other such unappealing creature, because his smile grew wider and his usual look of disdain disappeared.

Instead, he put on the affable expression he'd had on when we'd first met.

Could I trust his good-natured appearance? Had he tracked me here after I'd refused Rebecca's request to meet him tonight?

I walked over decisively and planted myself so close to him he couldn't escape my questions.

"What are you doing here?"

"What am I doing here?"

Apparently, he was enjoying this uncomfortable and almost laughable situation. His presence, which seemed even less called for here than at the gallery the night before, infuriated me. And yet he acted so intently self-assured, as though each one of his cells knew it had a legitimate reason to be here.

"I think I was clear when I said no," I railed. "I am not available tonight. Nor any night, for that matter."

"But I understood that from the start."

At least he was admitting to being behind my latest invitation. I was steaming, and had to resist the impulse to wring his neck or unbalance his bad knee.

"So . . . So why did you follow me here?"

"I did not follow you, I promise."

"Liar!" I boomed. I was having difficulty controlling my anger.

"Calm down. Chloe just told me you were he—"

"There you are, you two!"

David's cheerful voice sauntered into my bubble of anger, which instantly popped, leaving his arms to wrap me in measured warmth.

"At last you meet. I'm delighted."

Everything was "splendid" or "delightful" for David. If he

wasn't using overly enthusiastic adjectives, it was probably because he found the situation mediocre or, rather, terrible. In this moment, he seemed sincerely happy to see the two of us together.

Louie faked jubilation and shot me a look to do the same.

"One might say, yes."

"That's my horrible older brother!" David joked, nudging shoulders with his sibling. "He's also Barlet Group's director of communication."

"Director of . . . ," I stammered, horrified.

"Our one and only . . . but he's also the very best, and by a long shot."

It was clear David's excessive enthusiasm irritated Louie. And yet, in the presence of his brother, Louie showed a reserve that sharply contrasted with his attitude from the night before. An employee's respect for his boss? Or that of a prodigal son for his successful brother?

The CEO turned to his right and asked in a professional tone:

"Now, if you don't mind . . . I'd like to speak with Annabelle. Privately."

"Of course."

Louie nodded obsequiously, looked at me in a way I couldn't read, and finally disappeared into the hallway, the shadow of his long silhouette flickering through a play of light over the immense glass panels.

I can make out Louie Barlet's protruding, muscled ass through the light fabric of his tight pants. I want to grab it, squeeze it, maybe even bite it, and . . .

Anonymous, handwritten, and unfinished note,
6/6/2009—No comment!

"DARLING?"

"Yes?"

"Sit down, please."

I sat and found myself facing David for the first time in the position of a docile, good wife.

"I've thought a lot about your interview and everything . . ."

"Let's not talk about it."

"Yes, let's do talk about it. I spoke with Luc Doré this afternoon. He's in charge of what goes on air at BTV. He's been wanting to add a culture segment to his evening programming. Our current Thursday night prime-time show isn't working. I've had my foot on the brakes about it, but I just gave him the green light."

Brakes. Green light. The way he talked, you'd think David's job was as simple and carefree as a game of Mille Bornes. A game that he always won, of course.

"And?" I pretended I hadn't seen his cards.

He grabbed my hand.

"And, Mademoiselle Lorand . . . I should say Madame Barlet . . . I am pleased to announce that in a few weeks, you will be hosting the new general culture show on BTV. It will be called *Culture Mix*."

"Are you joking?"

"Not at all. I got your demo tapes from your school and showed them to Luc. He was really excited about them."

"But, David . . . I've never done a show in my life!"

"So you'll do like ninety-nine percent of television hosts: you'll learn on the job."

He took his hand back and stood up. His internal Chloe-clock must have alerted him to another meeting.

"It's a provisional title, of course . . . If you don't like it, you can change it. I'm afraid I have to leave you. I'm already ten minutes late. We'll talk about it tonight at the house."

My husband had just changed my life more than I could have ever dreamed. And my boss had just left without a good-bye, much less a kiss.

Sigh. They were both the same man.

10

June 6, 2009, early evening

The RER train ride to Nanterre had never looked so beautiful, nor had the trip from the center of Paris ever felt so short. I almost forgot about Louie and my equally disturbing harasser. I think I even smiled at my own reflection a few times like an idiot. I wondered if my happy bubble were contagious and if the other passengers could feel it. Maybe that was too much to ask . . .

Outside, the fading light bathed the gray buildings in flattering hues, and for once they looked beautiful to me.

I was in such a good mood I decided not to stop by the police station, as I had been promising myself I'd do for days, and I even forgot to go to the bakery for Mom's treats. David's proposition had erased all my worries and fears.

"It's no big deal," Maude welcomed me in her bathrobe. "I played grandma today and made a blanquette."

Mom wasn't old enough to be a grandmother, but her sickness made her look like one before her time, with her matte-gray complexion, wrinkles that seemed to deepen by the day, and an increasingly heavy step . . .

I felt uncomfortable at first being so happy in front of

her, but then I couldn't contain myself. With one hand, I idly stirred the veal ragout, whose smell of nutmeg and bay leaves tickled my nose. A purring Felicity seemed to share my joy and wove around my legs.

I tried to minimize the exciting opportunity David was offering, but my mom understood it was a big deal:

"How wonderful, darling! That's wonderful!"

She pressed herself to my back and laced her weak arms around me. It almost felt like she was holding on to me for balance. I reached my free hand back and gave her a pat, keeping my eyes glued to the thick stew.

"Yeah, it is . . ."

"But . . . ?

"His help bothers me."

"Why?"

"Well, you know, I'm twenty-three, and I just got out of school . . . and I'm going to have my own show, prime time, on one of the most watched channels in France. Do you realize what people are going to think?"

"Killer luck?" She smirked, convinced that was how young people these days talked.

"No . . . They'll think somebody pulled some massive strings. And if I'm anything but excellent, I'll be massacred."

She pressed her cheek against my back like children do. Her voice was much smaller as she said:

"But you *will* be excellent, Elle. Period."

"Mom." I sighed, smiling. "You're sweet, but believe me, in television, this kind of favor will come back to haunt me. The boss's girlfriend gets the show. Everyone hates that: viewers, commentators . . . not to mention the other hosts who want the job. I know what it's like."

I brushed aside the thought of the text message rejection I'd received just a few hours before.

At that moment, I caught a whiff of my mother's ever so reassuring rose perfume as it blended with the stew's juices.

"Personally, I don't believe in chance or luck," she replied as firmly as she was still able. "If you get the show, let's be clear, it's because you deserve it."

"Hmm . . ."

"Didn't you say that Luc what's-his-name really liked your demos?"

"Yes . . . Well, that's what David says. But I think he was just trying to please his boss. From what I saw today, my fiancé isn't exactly warm at work."

"That's not very nice," she chastised gently.

Surprised at her critique, I turned to face her.

"Not nice? To David?"

"You could have more confidence in his judgment. After all, as you always say: he owns a very big television network. If he thinks you're up to the job, I don't see any reason not to believe him."

Stunned, I stared at her for a moment on the verge of tears. Then I redirected my gaze through the open door to the living room. A collection of photographs of me sat atop the buffet. It was a kind of memorial to all the triumphs of my young existence. The most recent pictures were of my high school graduation and then with Sophia with our college diplomas.

"Honey, it's normal to have doubts," she said, folding her fragile hands around mine. "But given David's level of responsibility, he can't afford to take unnecessary risks. And he chose *you*."

She knew the right words to say, the ones that soothed and made everything a little clearer, like when I was a little girl and would ask about my father, the only trace of whom I had was an old, faded photograph: him and a chubby me, dating back to the year he disappeared, late 1987.

Richard Rodriguez, the Spanish foreman. They'd had a shotgun wedding, and one day he left to do a job in Quebec that was only supposed to take a few weeks. He never came back. Just like that, a ghost.

"Thanks, Mom."

I hugged her closely, trying to give her some of my warmth.

"Oh, I'm so stupid . . . I forgot the most important thing!" I was so excited I was clapping my hands like a kid.

"What is it?"

"Wait a sec . . . "

I went to the entry, rummaged through my bag, which was hanging on a hook, and came back to the kitchen holding a long envelope on which was printed a line-drawn globe.

Maude looked at me questioningly.

"What is it?"

"Ta-da!" I trumpeted. "What do you think? Your annual Disneyland pass?"

"What?"

She wasn't sure whether to laugh or scold me. I pretended to whack her with the envelope.

"No! Our tickets for L.A.! David's assistant gave them to me earlier."

"La?"

"Los Angeles, Mom . . . Get with the program, jeez!"

So long as I didn't push her limits, she loved it when I teased her. It made her feel more like a friend than a mom.

"You should have seen Madame Chappuis's face when I told her I was going to the United States this summer!"

"I bet she couldn't believe it."

"Honestly, she thought I had lost it, yeah! 'Right, America . . .'"

"You should send her a postcard."

"I'm going to, and you'll sign it. The old bag will have a heart attack."

She took the envelope and stared at the boxes printed on the heavy stock paper with all the dates and codes. She read the first one quickly.

"We're leaving June twentieth?"

Two days after the wedding, I thought to myself. I hadn't told her yet. I didn't want to show how happy I was when her life was in the balance.

My wedding . . . Even to me the prospect seemed unreal. Almost none of my friends and family knew. David, in our few moments together, never brought it up, as if now that he had my answer, it was a done deal and the subsequent events a formality. As promised, Armand was working behind the scenes to make it a perfect day. He hadn't been consulting me on the more basic decisions (invitations, flowers, menu, etc.). I'd only ever hear about them once the choices had been made. And Sophia, who normally would obsess over this kind of topic, seemed uneasy about broaching it, even though the wedding was imminent. Was she jealous? Or annoyed that I hadn't told her sooner?

"Yes, we leave on the twentieth. Why? Did you have other plans?" I bantered.

"And when do you start your new job?"

"In theory on the ninth. In three days. Tuesday the ninth."

She closed the envelope, grasped my hands, and looked at me with determination.

"I'll go alone."

"What?" I stammered.

"You can't come with me. You will have just started a new job."

"But, Mom, the plane leaves on a Saturday. It's not a problem."

"Be reasonable: you're not going to go all the way across the world and back in a weekend. And I know this job is really important to you. You can't drop everything and leave right after you've been hired."

"David is the one who bought the tickets. And David is *also* my boss, Mom. If he thought it was a problem, he would have said something. He would not have chosen these dates."

Although she was weakened by illness, Maude was still my mother, which meant she was still capable of making me do what she wanted with just one look. Just one word.

"No, no . . . You're staying here, daughter. I'll go by myself. I'm a big girl." She said it like she was taking a cruise for a few weeks, though it was hard to tell by her voice whether or not she was just pretending to be brave.

"I'm not just worried about the trip . . ."

"Am I misremembering? Weren't you the one who said that this clinic was *amazing*, and that a nurse would be at my side attending to my every need as soon as I got off the plane?"

"Yeah, I said that," I admitted. "And it *is* amazing. It's truly world-class. It has treated the crème de la crème of Hollywood. As well as at least two United States presidents."

"So what do you think is going to happen to me there?"

Nothing, she was right. The only thing that was going to

happen in this whole adventure was that she was going to be cured, something the Max Fourestier Hospital in Nanterre had been unable to achieve, despite laudable efforts.

"Anyway, you know how it is. When you're happy, *I'm* happy. And if I'm happy . . ."

She stopped herself, probably out of superstition. She didn't want to think of her future but of mine, which she saw as bright. I decided not to contradict her. We could talk about it later.

THE BLANQUETTE TASTED AS GOOD as it smelled, and I was relieved to see my mom devouring the mouthwatering pieces of meat. She had more appetite than usual and was clearly enjoying our meal.

"Did you see your mail?"

I had not yet requested a change of address at the post office.

"No. Why? Is there something special?"

"No. The usual papers: bills, ads . . . Oh, wait, here."

She stood suddenly and made her way to the entry with surprising energy.

"You have a strange invitation."

"Why 'strange' . . . ?"

My question, like my fork, froze and hung in the air.

"Because there's no address on the envelope. Just your name."

In other words, someone had brought the letter directly to my mailbox. And that someone had known not only that I got my mail at my mom's house but also that I came by regularly to pick it up. Like the person who wrote the anonymous letters in my notebook, I thought fleetingly.

I wasn't waiting for anything in the mail, and if David had wanted to surprise me with something, he wouldn't have sent it here.

Maude shuffled back to the table and handed me the envelope. I thought I would pass out. My hand froze on the edge of the paper.

"Are you okay?" Mom asked, surprised.

"Yes, yes . . ."

The color choice, a glittery silver, was one used for wedding or birth announcements, and also for society events like gallery openings or movie premieres.

I recognized the familiar hue of my Ten-Times-a-Day. How could it be a coincidence? The color was so rare, so specific.

"Aren't you going to open it?"

The flap wasn't sealed but tucked into the envelope's folds. Anyone could have opened it and read its contents. Without understanding why, this thought sent a nervous shiver up my spine.

The most visible aspect of its contents was a hard plastic magnetic card. Again, I thought I was going to faint when I saw the printed logo:

The Hôtel des Charmes

So he knew . . .

Since the hotel rooms didn't have numbers, it was impossible to know which door this magnetic key would open. After I got over the initial shock, the first thought in my head was strangely this: without the room number, the keycard was useless.

*I've already made love a few times in this hotel, but I
have yet to orgasm here. I have not added my contribution
to the ghosts of pleasure haunting its rooms. Do I really
mind?*

Anonymous, handwritten, and unfinished note,
6/7/2009—What did he know? He wasn't in my vagina and couldn't possibly speculate about what I felt!

A PINK POST-IT WAS STUCK to the back of the card. I felt a
wave of disappointment when I realized that the handwriting
did not match the one used in the anonymous messages addressed to my body.

> *Dear Zelle,*
> *tonight, ten o'clock.*
> *Be on time.*
> *Do not bring your phone.*

The script was less jerky, more calm and even. It was the
handwriting of a person at peace, as opposed to the worry and
anguish apparent in the other messages.

"Bad news?" Mom asked, noticing my pallor.

After having examined the contents of the envelope, I was
able to say without lying, or barely:

"Yes . . . I mean, you were right, it's an invitation."

A white card with one sentence printed in the center:

1—Thou shalt love thy body.

The reference to the Ten Commandments was unmistakable. In college, I had participated in a daylong seminar on literary forms in the Bible: sermons, parables, psalms, etc. The Decalogue had been an important topic.

"Really? Where?"

Maude, who respected my privacy like it was a sacrament—a character trait that had made it easy for me to dodge her repeated requests to meet David—was suddenly curious.

"To a, umm, a masquerade ball."

"Really? How cool! Is it at your school?"

She was forcing me to improvise.

"Yes. The student council president lives nearby. He probably thought it would be nicer to hand deliver the invitation."

"You don't seem very excited," she said as she poured herself another few drops of wine.

"You know me, big parties have never been my thing."

"You should go! It will be fun."

If my own mother said so . . .

This time, I was almost one hundred percent certain of the sender's identity. Who other than Louie Barlet would summon me to a hotel room to provide a service for which he had already paid? But I was more concerned by another thought that crossed my mind: What if Louie was the person who'd been sending me the indecent messages these past several weeks? What if he was the man behind the notebook? That depraved individual who'd taken it upon himself to perfect my sexual education. The night of the gallery opening I had wondered *who* could be up to such a task. Well, now I had my answer . . .

I flashed back to a few hours prior in the conference room at Barlet Tower with David and Louie. *Their* tower. Being in the presence of the Barlet brothers had left a bad taste in my mouth. There was something unnatural about it. One of the two seemed excessive to me, but I couldn't figure out which. Together, they made an unsettling whole. I remembered their left forearms: David wore a white silk armband; Louie, who was thinner, had a tattoo that I had not yet seen in its entirety.

The doorbell tore me from this unsolvable puzzle. I hadn't noticed her move, but Mom was already perched at the window. She'd probably heard the motorcycle backfiring, a sound she abhorred.

"It's Fred," she said succinctly.

"What does he want?"

"To get his stuff from your room."

"Did he tell you he was coming?"

"Mmm, yes . . . He mentioned he'd be stopping by one of these evenings."

My ex did nothing with his days, and yet he just happened to show up when I was there. The bell rang again; our visitor was impatient.

"Go to the basement," Mom whispered.

"What?"

"Go to the basement. He won't look for you down there."

"I'm not going to hide from him. I don't love him anymore, that's all . . ."

"You don't need this right now," she insisted, her tone exasperated.

But Fred didn't wait for Mom to open the gate. I could already see him through the stained glass on the front door, just three feet from us.

"Annabelle?"

"Go downstairs!" Mom hissed.

"Annabelle? I know you're there. Open up!"

"Don't be ridiculous, Mom!"

He was now banging on the door.

"Christ, open the door! It's me!"

I looked at Mom, who was awash in anger and panic.

"Remember me? The guy you dumped like a little shit?!"

I reached to open the door, but Mom stopped me.

"Annabelle, I forbid you from opening that door. He's completely wasted!"

The motorist's gruff and menacing voice confirmed her suspicions: he was not in a sober state.

"I just want to talk to you . . ." His voice sweetened. "Don't you at least owe me five minutes? Five minutes, then I'll leave you alone for the rest of your life. Elle . . . just five minutes."

"She doesn't want to talk to you, Fred."

My sick mom's voice must have unsettled him because he started acting even more conciliatory.

"I'm sorry, Maude . . . I didn't mean to scare you. I just want Annabelle to tell me to my face."

"Tell you what, for goodness' sake?"

"That it's over . . ."

"Well, I can tell you that: it's over!" she cried, mustering what little energy she had. "Long over at that!"

A few moments of silence went by before he replied, obviously shaken by Mom's bravado:

"What makes you say that?"

"Because it's the truth. She's with someone else now. Someone better."

Don't tell him that, my eyes begged.

"Who?"

And as she crucified him, telling him about David, my new career, my dream house, my guaranteed success, and all my future happiness with somebody else, my thoughts started to wander again.

. . . To the envelope.

With Fred's unfortunate arrival, I hadn't noticed its unusual weight. Deep inside, under the papers, lay a large, jagged key, polished by time and use. There was no indication of what it could open. Nor did I know what would be expected of me that night. And then there was the strange spelling of my name: "Zelle."

Nevertheless, I was sure of one thing, and it was probably as foolish as the drunk man on the other side of the door: I had no other choice but to attend this meeting.

To skip it now seemed impossible.

11

June 6, 2009

In college, my methodology professor for journalism used to say that words carried hidden truths. And that in order to understand what they really meant beyond their banal surface, you had to experience them for yourself, with your own flesh and blood.

"Once you've really lived what you write about, once you start intellectualizing things a little less," he would lecture, rolling his mustache like General Dourakine, "it's crazy how much power words begin to have. They *are* what you experience. They become one with you."

Truth be told, I was at a loss to describe in words how I felt that evening. Butterflies in my stomach? My heart in my throat? Goose bumps? Yes, all of those things—and more. It was disturbing. More powerful.

After Fred finally left, I stuffed the silver envelope in my bag next to its older sibling, the notebook, and hurried to catch the next RER train into Paris. Fred had given in, but only for the time being; he'd promised to return for a final face-to-face.

THE METRO CAR WAS ONLY half full since it was going in the opposite direction of suburban traffic flow at this hour. I braved the terrible cell phone reception and tried to call Rebecca several times—after all, I reasoned, she was the one who had put me in contact with the elder Barlet. Then I dialed Louie directly on his professional line. It was crazy, I know. Felicity meowed her disapproval from her travel crate.

I only got Rebecca's machine. As for Louie, an assistant answered in a surly tone and said her boss had already left for the night.

"Would you mind giving me his cell?"

"No, sorry, I'm not authorized to give out that information," she recited.

"Right, I understand you're not supposed to intrude on his private life. But David Barlet himself has just hired me. You can check with Chloe, if you'd like."

"I don't doubt it. But I am not authorized to give you—"

"Fine," I cried, cutting her off. "But what I'm trying to say is I'm . . ."

What? The boss's girlfriend? Future wife? How could I put it without sounding like I was bragging or snubbing a girl who probably came from the same kind of run-down suburban neighborhood as I?

I ended up going with:

" . . . a new prime-time host on BTV."

I wasn't sure if that version of things would be better or worse.

"There's nothing I can do," she stammered, undoubtedly torn between the fear of losing her job and that of making an enemy of her boss's boss. "I'm really sorry."

The RER train went through the tunnel under La Défense.

We were entering Paris, and the poor cell reception cut our conversation short. It also prevented me from calling Sophia and sharing my dilemma.

With each passing station, I felt my sense of determination waver, until I arrived at my destination and the train rushed off behind me. As I walked toward the Hôtel des Charmes, it occurred to me that I was ceding to the perverse game Louie had set up for me, beginning with our first meeting—and even before that, I realized, red-faced, since his initial correspondence had preceded the evening when David and I had met. If I refused to play along, though, I would run the risk of him telling David everything he knew about me. Moreover, the fact that he was related to my future husband meant I could never report him—as I'd been thinking about doing a few hours earlier. I could not tell the police without inciting legal conflict. And the notebook I carried around with me everywhere was written in the first person, filled with personal details, and in no way proof of anything. I had accepted it into my life, which implicated me in this affair just as much as it did its author.

But aside from these issues and blackmail's persuasive qualities, I was motivated by something I could not have even imagined a few days prior: curiosity. I refused to call the inner turmoil—tinged with anger and bitterness—that Louie caused in me by any other name.

"Good evening, Mademoiselle. David asked me to tell you he would not be joining you for dinner tonight."

Only the ground floor was lit at Duchesnois. The master of the house was absent, and a silence common to old buildings hung in the air. Armand was standing on the front steps holding a lamp and looking like he'd been busy cooking.

"Oh . . . Okay."

I was surprised David hadn't taken the time to tell me personally . . . and then I realized that the cell reception in the RER had probably prevented him. Sure enough, his number showed up three times in my call log.

I let Felicity out of her crate at last. The old servant looked on in silence. She took a few hesitant steps over the checkerboard marble, her nose glued to the floor.

"He has a meeting with the Koreans that will probably go late. He said not to wait."

"Okay, do you want to do a picnic dinner?" I asked, as though Armand were a girlfriend who had dropped by unexpectedly.

"Everything is ready for us in the kitchen, if you're already hungry."

"I'm not hungry. I am *starving*."

That was a lie. I had eaten an early dinner with Mom and was really full. I had no desire to partake in another meal. But playing happy was the only way I could think to suppress the miserable feelings tearing me up inside. Still, I wasn't faking my enthusiasm when I saw our two steaming plates.

"Sautéed gambas on a bed of shellfish cooked in champagne," Armand announced solemnly.

The recipe from the chef at Le Divellec! I was in heaven and beaming like a kid at Christmas. The gesture was so perfect it made me forget my troubles.

"David thought you'd like it."

"It's . . . it's perfect! Thank you."

Carried away with joy, I smacked his paper-soft cheek with a loud and chaste kiss. He replied with a gesture toward the golden shrimp:

"Shall we eat?" he suggested, blushing.

"Let's!"

My taste buds were almost as delighted as they had been the other night. Armand was too modest, I thought; he could have easily been a restaurant chef as opposed to working in anonymity for David. But his smile told me he derived pleasure from my own, and I thought better of saying anything.

"I don't know if you've noticed, but I've been receiving a lot of messages recently. Anonymous messages."

"Anonymous?"

"Small perforated pages with my name on them, folded in four . . . You've been putting them on the console table with the rest of the mail."

"Oh, yes . . ." He winced a little as he said, "I did notice them, but I try not to pry into your—"

"No worries, Armand," I said, reassuringly. "I know you're discreet. I was just wondering if perhaps you'd noticed anything unusual about it . . . or if the mailman had said anything?"

"I did ask him about it. But he doesn't deliver unstamped mail. The person who sends you those letters puts them into the mailbox directly. If you'd like, I could keep an eye out to see who comes up to the house."

"That would be really nice of you, Armand. Thanks."

"Do you think we should alert the police?"

"No . . . Thanks, but I don't think that should be necessary."

Not with Louie being behind them, I thought.

Since it seemed like a good time, I asked, in a confidential tone:

"Armand . . . Do you know Louie very well?"

At the mention of his employer's brother, Armand frowned, his lion's wrinkle deepening, his face sobering.

"About as well as I know Monsieur David. As you know, I worked for their parents when they were still alive. I saw the two boys grow up."

"And, do you . . ." I interrupted my question when I saw the lines of discomfort and worry fold into Armand's face.

"Yes?"

"Do you think Louie might have any reason to be angry with his brother?"

"My mother used to say, 'Show me siblings who don't in some way resent each other, and I'll have them framed and hung on the wall.'"

"I agree," I said. "But in their case, you don't see anything more . . . specific?"

Though he did not seem surprised by my question, it did clearly embarrass him. He took a moment to pour himself another glass of white and drank a few sips before attempting to answer. Armand's penchant for the bottle was no secret to me; I'd noticed his inflamed nose as well as an abnormally elevated number of empty bottles of Pouilly and Montrachet in the recycling. He was maybe even a borderline alcoholic.

"I can't tell you about David and Louie without first talking about Andre Barlet . . ."

"Go ahead." I smiled sweetly to encourage him.

Another swig of wine, and he was ready. If I listened closely, I could hear the tiny grains of silica running through the hourglass, and they would continue to fall until the moment when I gave myself to David, my husband.

"In order to understand the Barlet brothers," he began, "it's important to know that their father started with almost nothing. After the war, he inherited a small, failing business that made wood furnishings near Nantes. It only survived through its production of fir coffins, which weren't even very well made. At that time in their lives, people aren't very picky."

I shivered as I imagined planks of blond wood, barely even registering Armand's uncharacteristic use of morbid humor.

"Coffins?"

"In those days, nobody had any money for furniture. Beer, yes. People needed more of that than ever, believe you me."

How old was Armand during the war? He couldn't remember the Occupation, could he . . . ?

"Don't tell me they got rich off the funeral business?" I gasped, hoping he'd say no.

"No! Pierre, Andre's father, had diversified their business. From wood, he slowly went to paper. And from paper to printing, and eventually to publishing. He invested in several local periodicals. Notably a paper everyone later suspected had collaborated with the Germans: *The Salvation*."

"And what happened when France was liberated?"

"Father and son must have thrown money where it counted because, with the wave of a magic wand, *The Salvation* became *The Liberated Ocean*, one of the leading Resistance papers in western France. And that's also when Pierre put his son, Andre, in charge of the paper."

The portrait of the small-time owner of a provincial newspaper looked nothing like David and his media empire. What had happened to bring the Barlet family from the banks of the Loire to those of the Seine? From a village marketplace to the French stock exchange?

"Andre quickly proved to be more ambitious than his father."

"How?"

"He started by taking advantage of his family's new contacts in the CNR . . ."

I recalled my high school history classes: the CNR, or the Conseil National de la Résistance, was a provisional body that managed the transition after the collapse of the Vichy government.

" . . . and bought all the newspapers, one by one, that had openly collaborated with the Germans. For a song, of course."

"They artificially inflated their readership." I connected the dots.

"That's right, and the business reached proportions Pierre never could have imagined. In the early fifties, *The Liberated Ocean* became *The Ocean* and was the newspaper of record in western France. Remember, this was an era before television really took hold, and there were hardly more than two radio stations in the whole country. With one article, *The Ocean* could make or break anyone; its readership was in the millions. Its coffers filled at epic rates."

The rest of the story was now fairly obvious.

"And from there they expanded their policy of acquisition?"

"Exactly. Pierre died in 1956, and Andre kept buying everything he could: newspapers; magazines; radio stations, what with the FM revolution of the eighties; and then television channels in the nineties . . . In the mid-seventies, the company moved from Nantes to Paris. Before David built the tower, its seat was in an Art Nouveau building on Rue de Miromesnil. The in-house journalists called it the Freighter because its windows were shaped like portholes."

Many other French families who made their money after

the war have similar stories: the Hersants, the Arnaults, the Pinaults, the Lagardères . . . The story of the Barlet dynasty was fascinating. But I was burning to know about the younger generation.

"And the Barlet sons?"

"I was just getting to them. Andre raised them with one thing in mind, Annabelle: who would succeed him at the head of the company. Their whole childhood, he was never a father to them but a referee."

"A referee? What do you mean . . . ?"

"When David was born, he announced that the two were in competition over who would be the best to take over the company. Everything was judged accordingly: grades, athletic ability, friends, popularity with girls. It was as if he were charting their scores. He probably was, actually."

Their youth had thus been a succession of tests and conquests to measure who was most worthy of their father's scepter.

I wonder if in the domain of female conquest the two brothers ever compared each other's prowess in bed. Have they already had a threesome or more?

~~The idea of Louie and David joined by one woman, one plunged in her vagina, the other sucked into her mouth, alternating orifices and combinations, together capable of making the girl come as she has never come before, turns me on as much as it sickens me.~~

Anonymous handwritten note, 6/7/2009

WITH THESE LAST WORDS, ARMAND'S voice quivered. He seemed weighed down by what he was describing.

"That's horrible . . . ," I said with emotion in my voice.

"Hortensia always tried to minimize the impact of the struggle between her sons. Sometimes she would even get violently angry with her husband. But so long as he was in the house, nothing could be done. Andre played them against each other like two crazed puppies."

"At some point they must have calmed down a little, right? I mean, their father eventually made a choice?"

Armand nodded sadly, and I understood that their fratricidal duel had never really been resolved.

"Yes, not long before he died. It may have been an accident, but he must have seen it coming."

Armand's doubts about Andre Barlet's death did not escape me, but I didn't say anything.

"Did they keep fighting?"

"Worse than ever! David taking over the company was a decisive win, but they kept trying to one-up each other: the prettiest girlfriend, the most expensive watch, the best stock purchase, et cetera."

Fated or not, Andre's sudden death had meant no end to the match. The referee had died before he'd gotten the chance to blow the final whistle. Without him, the game went on, year after year, even to this day. The two orphaned players were exhausting themselves in an eternal competition.

"Neither of them will ever feel he's won, will he?"

"That's what I fear," he whispered.

Yet, with his imminent marriage, David was not far from a KO. His final victory would come when we had a child as it would assure the future of the Barlet name. It would seal his ascendancy in the family.

Given the context, I was surprised the loser, Louie, would

so graciously accept his brother's scraps: director of communication. How could he possibly be satisfied with such a consolation prize? Or maybe he wasn't as content as he let on. Perhaps his schemes with me were a plan to exact revenge.

With that thought, I recalled the energy coursing through his lean body that had transferred to me at the slightest, most superficial contact.

"That's the whole story . . ."

His charcoal eyebrows arched expectantly. It seemed Armand had hoped for a different reaction from me. But what was I supposed to say? That I felt like some kind of vulgar trophy? Like the Road Runner caught by one of the competitors? Like the ball in a penalty kick?

I tried to push these degrading thoughts out of my head. Instead, I made a list from my fragile memory of all the romantic things David had done for me, including this amazing dinner he couldn't even attend but had wanted to be perfect for me.

"He really loves me," I said weakly, "and I love him, too."

My voice betrayed a slight tremor.

"I sincerely hope so, for both of you."

Somehow, I was able to profess my love for David to a person I barely knew. Meanwhile, I had yet to find the courage to announce my imminent marriage to my own mother . . . I eased my conscience, telling myself it was because of Fred this afternoon. Today, I had been ready to tell her. But I wasn't really convinced. I had trouble relating to what was supposed to be the "most beautiful day of my life." It was soon, but I hadn't done a thing in preparation.

My phone vibrated, interrupting the emotional moment. I opened the message with a trembling finger. It contained two photos: the first of me entering the Hôtel des Charmes; the second, taken the same night, showed me leaving. Both pictures were taken from the same vantage point. The photographer must have stayed put for several hours, without moving. As for my clothing, I recognized what I had been wearing the night I'd met David; I was sure of it. I remembered spending the after-party in a hotel room with my fiancé's old friend Marchadeau. I shivered.

There was no accompanying message, but I was sure of its meaning. Someone was waiting for me there. And not in two hours.

Now.

12

June 6, 2009, at about eleven p.m.

Discreet, elegant, romantic: that is how I would describe the Hôtel des Charmes that night.

My mustachioed professor used to play another literary game with us in college. He would rub his bald head with one hand and ask us to define a person, place, thing, situation, or sensation in three words: "It's all you need," he would say. "Don't overload your text with images. Three well-chosen adjectives are worth a lot more than long, stilted metaphors."

The Hôtel des Charmes was only about three or four streets from my new house. Despite the sharp incline on Rue de la Rochefoucauld, I was able to make it there in only a few minutes, without getting distracted by the neighborhood's numerous music stores and their flashy window displays.

The junction of this uphill street and Rue Pigalle formed a kind of elongated triangle, which was dominated by a view of the Hôtel des Charmes. Most striking was the narrowness of the building: each of the six floors featured just two slim windows with potted blood-red flowers.

I had dressed in haste, and justified my sudden departure to Armand as a Sophia-related emergency. Breathless, I arrived in front of the building just as a nearby pay phone—a relic—started ringing.

I tore the receiver from its blue base and quickly surveyed the area for a potential observer. I was knee-deep in a bad spy novel, and I felt uneasy.

"Hello?"

But the three scraggly trees—planted by the hotel?—were not hiding any peepers. Nor was the row of scooters parked nearby for the night. I could hear breathing on the other end of the line; then the person—whoever he or she was—hung up.

The hotel entrance on Rue Pigalle was extremely discreet. No obvious signage. No ostentatious awning. The name of the establishment, even, was only indicated by a simple chrome plaque.

THE HÔTEL DES CHARMES
PERSONALIZED ROOMS
RENTED BY THE HOUR

How did I feel: Nervous? Transfixed? Excited?

Though this certainly was not my first time here, as I walked through the hall, I felt like a girl at prom. Or just before her first date. I fought off that ridiculous idea and tried to quell the turmoil stirring at the base of my abdomen. I waved to the tall bald man smiling with complicity.

"Good evening, Monsieur Jacques."

His wide blue eyes recognized me with a kind glint.

"Good evening, Mademoiselle. Would you like a room?"

"Actually . . . I already have a keycard."

I took the hard plastic rectangle from my pocket and

handed it to him. He showed no signs of surprise or approbation, and simply took the key.

"Okay. I suppose someone gave this to you?"

"So you weren't the one who sent it . . ." I said under my breath.

"No, I wasn't. So long as guests return them to me, they are free to do with them as they please."

"I understand. Do you have a way of knowing which room it opens?"

"Yes, of course."

As he said this, he slipped the card into a black magnetic reader and focused his bulging gaze onto the counter-integrated computer screen.

"Hmm. That's strange," he said.

"What is it?"

"Nothing, that's just it . . . The card is blank, and yet . . ."

"And yet?"

"It's still active. It hasn't been reprogrammed."

"What can we do?"

Late? Annoyed? Impatient?

"Unfortunately, there's only one possible solution: we have to test it on all the occupied rooms. Currently, there are . . . eleven spread out over four of the six floors.

Each second separated me from the conclusion of this affair, which had made me feel like a cheater as soon as I'd stepped out of Duchesnois House. I couldn't do this to David . . . and yet I had to do this for him. For us. All legal options were out of the question, so I had to take care of things tonight. And fast. Even if it meant meeting Louie in one of the rooms.

"Wait . . ."

I suddenly remembered the giant key in the silver envelope . . .

"Does this mean anything to you?"

The object made him smile.

"No . . . Sorry. We haven't used that kind of antique for at least twenty years."

"Darn."

. . . Then, as a last-ditch effort, I withdrew the pink Post-it that had accompanied it.

"And what about this?"

Dear Zelle,
     tonight, ten o'clock.
     Be on time.
     Do not bring your phone.

His smile was so wide that he had to know something.

"The person who sent you that note must know the hotel quite well, Elle."

That was the first time, I think, I'd ever heard him use my nickname. One of my clients must have told him what it was.

"What do you mean?"

"'Zelle' is not a mistake on your first name. It's the family name of one of our most famous muses."

Each room bore the last name of a great seductress or courtesan.

"Really? Which one?"

"One of the greatest: Margaretha Geertruida Zelle."

"Excuse me?" I was scanning my memory . . .

"Mata Hari."

Oh.

"Sixth floor." He anticipated my question. "The farthest door to the right of the elevator. But Ysiam will be there to help you."

Ysiam? It was the first time I'd ever heard the exotic-sounding name.

Another peculiarity of the Hôtel des Charmes were the floor boys posted outside the elevators.

WHEN I REACHED THE SIXTH floor, I was greeted by a dark-skinned Pakistani—or maybe a Sri Lankan—with a wide and immaculate smile. His lashes, which were almost artificially long, shaded his eyes and gave him a sweet, trustworthy look.

He asked for my room number in a courteous tone as I got off the elevator, and quickly led me to a deep-red door without any markings.

There, Ysiam made no sign of wanting a tip and simply asked:

"Would there be anything else, Mademoiselle?"

"Umm, no . . . I don't think so."

I didn't need anything, unless he wanted to punch the gentleman waiting for me inside. I would have liked to put distance between myself and the situation, to be able to laugh at it. But I was just a ball of nerves, ready to pop at the slightest noise, at the briefest shadow or burst of light on the crimson door. I was tense as I thought of the room and its contents, childishly imagining all my worst nightmares.

Ysiam left me alone and, after a few seconds of holding my breath, I slid the magnetic card into the slot. The door clicked and let out an electronic beep. All I had to do was turn the doorknob to meet my fate.

STUNNED.

Overwhelmed.

Charmed.

THE ROOM WAS EMPTY BUT gorgeous. It was decorated in Belle Epoque style with a plethora of precious and colorful objects, the kind you can still find in vintage shops or at the Saint-Ouen flea market. It reminded me of one of those early-century photos depicting an Orientalist scene. Murals featured flowers and flitting insects. The armoire, the table, and the dresser were each made from different exotic woods, which I was at a loss to name. But the accent pieces most recalled the era in question: several Gallé lamps in multilayered, ornamented glass, as well as a number of small erotic bronze statues, mostly of satyrs pressed against voluptuous, naked virgins. The focal piece was an enormous moucharaby wood-panel screen.

I contemplated my fascinating surroundings for a long moment. Not seeing anyone, I was about to take off. So Louie Barlet got off on playing with me like a rag doll or a video game avatar? Just as he'd ordered me to come to the Sauvage Gallery only to promptly leave, so he had summoned me here now without even bothering to show up.

Feeling angry and powerless, I started to cry, when suddenly an anonymous shadow slipped a folded sheet of paper under the door.

Take off your clothes.

The command was written in the same handwriting as the note I'd shown Monsieur Jacques a few minutes earlier.

Without stopping to think of the coincidence, I grabbed my bag and turned the ornate door handle . . . only to discover that it was locked. Sweet Ysiam, or maybe someone else, had made it so a person could come in but not out. I did not immediately panic. After all, I was familiar with the place. I didn't spend as much time here as Sophia, but Monsieur Jacques knew my first name and that I was up here. Our earlier exchange guaranteed that my presence had not gone unnoticed.

Still, fear seized me. I began to shiver. My neck grew stiff. I was scared from my head to my toes. Even my cheeks began to burn.

I picked up the antique rotary phone and dialed the number for reception: 00. It rang and rang. No one answered.

Thinking Monsieur Jacques might be wandering the halls, I let out several discreet cries for help. Aware of how ridiculous the situation was, I kept my voice low.

"Monsieur Jacques? Monsieur? Is anybody there?"

The only reply I got was the hushed silence of the deserted hallway, where each step was muffled by extravagantly thick carpeting. Without getting my hopes up, I tried the giant key in the old lock, but it was much too big. The concierge hadn't lied. I was alone in this hermetically sealed room stuffed with furniture and decorations. Even the window looked painted shut. No way of turning its handle. Through its frosted glass, I could make out the elegant, illuminated lines of the Sacré Coeur.

Do not bring your phone. Stupidly, I had obeyed, and now I was cut off from the outside world. Short of breaking the window and throwing myself from the sixth floor onto the square below, forming a sinister red flower on the ground, I would be a prisoner in this room so long as my host desired. How long was this masquerade going to last?

I started banging powerlessly on the door when something surprising occurred behind me: the colorful wood panels lining the walls turned around all at once, clearly being manipulated by some synchronized electronic mechanism. They were re-placed by full-length mirrors.

I was not alone, no. I was now in the company of an end-less series of my own reflection. Every angle, every side, all my grace and disgrace were joined together. I understood that this display was a reminder to do as I had been told: "Take off your clothes."

"Is that how you get off? Watching? That's your thing?" I called out to the invisible voyeur.

Of course, all I got in reply was an echo of my own voice, altered by anger, muffled by thick upholstery.

I took the silver notebook with all the notes out of my bag and shook it like a street prophet brandishes a Bible:

"It excites you, doesn't it, imagining what I'm thinking about? Imagining my ass, too, am I right?"

The silence heightened my anger.

"Do you really think that you can educate people by vio-lating their privacy like this? Do you really think that writing a few dirty thoughts about me somehow makes me your *thing*? Well, I don't belong to you! I will never belong to you! I'm David's! Do you hear? I belong to David!"

A few minutes went by during which nothing happened either in the room or outside. I trembled, and a few tears lit my lashes. After a while, I decided to obey. If I wanted to leave, it was my only option. I was furious. God knows how long Louie would keep me here if I didn't do as I was told. All night? And if that were the case, how would I explain my absence to David? I would have to tell him everything, then . . .

I undid my shoes, a pair of Louboutins from David. Its flower-shaped buttons had attracted the fashionista Rebecca had awakened in me. The rest of my outfit was more subdued:

skinny jeans and a raw silk top whose boatneck showed off my collarbones. I slowly took it all off until I was only wearing my underthings: intricate lace panties and matching bra, through which one could make out my dark areolae and the tuft of hair between my legs.

I knew it was all a big turn-on for the person hiding behind one of the mirrors or watching via hidden camera.

All I saw was the same old Annabelle who looked back at me from the bathroom mirror every morning. The same over-sized hips. The same overly abundant thighs and buttocks. The same rounded abdomen. *Thou shalt love thy body*? And apparently it had to be seductive!

As if in reply, the lights suddenly dimmed without my touching them. The bulbs shifted their intensity, darkening the general atmosphere while spotlighting me in a hitherto unseen light. Every limb, every curve, every bit of me looked different, softer, more harmonious. I was exactly the same, the same height and weight, and yet I was prettier than I'd ever seen myself.

The temperature must have gone up because, though I was nude, I did not feel cold. I was shivering, but not because of the atmosphere; rather, because of internal agitation that registered somewhere between anger and worry.

I could feel at the time
There was no way of knowing.

Familiar guitar chords and a singer's high-pitched and slightly muffled voice played from hidden speakers around the room. I knew the song. But from where? When? I couldn't remember. This kind of smooth soul-rock, with its fairly dated electronic acoustics, wasn't really Fred's thing. When it got to the refrain, I recalled the title and understood the hidden message:

More than this
Tell me one thing . . .
More than this.

More than this. Bryan Ferry's whispered vocals could only mean one thing: he wanted to see more.

Was I still only acting in the interest of getting this meeting over with? Or was there something else? Desire? No. I was caught up in the momentum. Driven by impulse, the fruit of such contrary and confusing emotions.

I unhooked my bra with a surprisingly hurried hand. It fell to the floor, freeing my heavy breasts. They demonstrated their pleasure at being uncorseted by palpitating and then hardening at the nipples. I brushed a flat hand over them to make sure they hadn't just been responding to a change in atmosphere. But they were warm, almost hot. The movement of my palm made them protrude a little more, darkening their pink color.

More than this
You know there's nothing . . .

Yes. There was one more thing.

My cotton panties with lacy details over my pelvis slid effortlessly down my thighs, joining the rest of my clothing on the floor. Now nothing came between his gaze and my private parts. I don't think I'd ever even shown myself to David like this, with such rawness and indecency. I didn't even have the reflex to hide my lower region, where the lips came together and drew a line under my dark curls.

It took me fifteen years to explore that part of myself that can only be seen with a little distance. I think it was also at that age that I actually started to really masturbate. Before that, I had limited myself to rubbing my crotch with either my teddy bear or a pillow.

I borrowed a mirror from my mom and locked myself in the bathroom. I put one foot on the edge of the bathtub and positioned the mirror vertically from my hole. There wasn't enough light to see. I remember I tried the experiment three or four times before finding the right method: I stood a flashlight on its base on the floor so it shined up at my crotch, balanced the mirror on the bathtub, and used my hands to open the two brown folds so I could at last catch a glimpse of the unknown. I was fascinated. I spent several minutes squeezing each part, especially those that were shining and wet. I was a little scared I would hurt myself. When I got to the pink button, I learned that I need not fear pain. I massaged the area, awkwardly at first, but with enough tenacity to make me sigh and then fall over into the enamel tub. I had discovered what I'd set out to know. And for some reason, I never felt the need to explore the area again.

Anonymous handwritten note, 6/7/2009—It happened in my bedroom, not the bathroom. As for the rest . . .

LOOKING AT MY BODY IN the mirror, from all angles and depths, I had the sensation of discovering it for the first time.

So this is what men desired when I undressed in front of them. This woman, as opposed to the one invented by my critical gaze, the one deformed by years of acquired body image issues. My imperfections hadn't disappeared. But seeing my list of faults together in one image, I couldn't deny how attractive they were, though I had trouble really believing it.

My one physical attribute that I didn't hate was my skin. I cared for it with monoi and almond oils as well as shea butter. I favored natural products over the cosmetic industry's expensive synthetics, convinced that my charms were above all located in my silky skin.

Instinctually, I closed my eyes. I swept my fingers over my middle, my neck, my collarbones, and my breasts, confirming that my epidermal care had not been in vain. My hand wandered pleasurably over my body, warming each region as it moved on to the next. At last it skimmed my love handles, buttocks, and the soft interior between my thighs.

The singer was no longer cooing from the speakers. The guitar plucked each elongated note of the melody. The song was coming to an end. Suddenly a screeching sound interjected, startling me.

It came from a two-shelf console, which I hadn't noticed before, behind the screen. A small printer was spitting out sheets of rigid paper. I grabbed the first one and turned it over.

Dazed. Flattered. Grateful?

Color photographs. Each shot showed me from a different angle, framed more or less tightly. The person playing this game of hide-and-seek with me had made a puzzle of my body. Strangely, it didn't bother me. Seeing myself so beautiful in the mirror made me feel calm and happy. Today I wasn't being celebrated for my obvious charms, that part of me that I still hadn't fully owned. This was something more: I felt at peace with myself. My body had been put back together. It was mine.

The automatic lock clicked, putting an end to my captivity. But this new feeling remained. Getting dressed felt like a long, slow caress. I savored every moment, every inch of my skin. I put the pictures in my bag and left the room feeling a little groggy. I wasn't surprised not to run into anyone on my way out. Not even Monsieur Jacques.

Robotically, and yet also with flowing movements, I walked down Rue Pigalle as though in a dream. At that hour, only a few late-night bars were still open. I barely noticed a group of drinkers whistling at me from an outside table.

Sometimes it occurs to me that I've had sex with men for money. Me, Annabelle, Elle. I can try until I'm blue in the face to tell myself that it doesn't make me one of those kept women who spread their legs in order to maintain their lifestyle, but it still disgusts me. Oddly, when I repeat the insulting phrase a few times in a row, "I am a whore," it excites me.

Anonymous handwritten note, 6/8/2009—Once again, no comment.

QUIVERING, HUMID, AVAILABLE.

The stretch of cotton between my legs was moist, tickling my crotch. It pressed against my swollen lips, my excited clitoris, my vagina palpitating with desire. A sense of decency held me back, but I wanted desperately to put my hand in my panties and, right there in the middle of the street, touch myself.

My sex trembled; it was ready for anything, or just about . . . It was ravenous.

13

June 7, 2009

If someone were to ask about my whereabouts that night, what could I say? Alone, I got undressed of my own accord in a hotel room a few blocks from my new house, at a hotel I'd frequented in the past. What could the person who had beckoned me there really be charged with? Who would describe the night as anything but a slightly incongruous whim on my part?

Louie's absence that night at the Hôtel des Charmes may have come as a shock, but it was not a crime. Nor could he be blamed for my crotch's unrelenting dampness. I was still wet when I woke up, even though David had long since left the house. As usual, I spent the morning alone, this time after a night of torment.

One thing that could be held against the elder Barlet was this new note:

You can feel me, can't you, deep inside?

Like the others, it was waiting for me on the console in the entry when I got up. An impressive mound of sand had already formed on the bottom half of the hourglass. Only a few grains left before our wedding day . . .

"Good morning, Elle."

The tone of voice was playful, almost puckish. It interrupted my dark thoughts with disconcerting lightness. It took me a few seconds to recognize who it was:

"Louie!"

. . . the source of my troubles, recognizable by his heady cologne.

"It is I. Your future husband sent me."

He bowed his head in exaggerated deference.

What was he talking about? How dare he show himself here? Wasn't my humiliation the night before enough? Did he have to harass me just as I got out of bed, too?

I held back an expression of exasperation.

"David?"

"Is there another?" he quipped cheerfully.

Was it possible to be such a manipulative monster at night and act so detached the next morning? Apparently. He smiled radiantly, playfully tossing his cane between his hands with the dexterity of an acrobat. Nothing in his comportment betrayed our "meeting" from the night before.

"No, of course not. But what—"

"David has asked me to help make you a 'real Athenian woman.'"

As he spoke, he grabbed my hand and bent down to kiss it. I snatched it back, readying myself to hit him.

"An Athenian woman . . . ," I repeated mechanically, frozen in indignation.

"That's what he said. So here I am!"

Armand appeared without warning and smiled in candid

approval. The interruption stopped me from expressing my feelings physically. With great pain, I contorted my mouth into a convincing smile.

"That's right, Mademoiselle," Armand said. "David wants you to feel at home both here in the house and in the neighborhood generally. As you are now aware, this area is very important to the family."

"Did you see what a beautiful day it is?!" Louie cried enthusiastically, without a hint of the arrogance he'd displayed on our first meeting. "Isn't it a perfect day for a walk?"

Refusing this outing was not going to be easy since the head of the family—and my future husband—had orchestrated it. What's more, there was a witness. I was going to have to find a good excuse, and fast.

Louie threw a sidelong glance at Felicity, who was trotting around a few paces away.

"It is . . . But unfortunately I don't feel very well," I lied.

"A little fresh air will be just the thing to perk you up!" Armand insisted.

"Seriously, Elle, what else do you have to do today? You should take advantage of your freedom before your new job starts. You'll see. Once your schedule adapts to the station, there won't be any time for *recess*."

I pursed my lips to keep from shouting at him in disgust. "*Recess*"? And how exactly would he describe last night? An innocent distraction?

"No, really . . . Thanks, but I just don't feel up to it . . . If I want to be presentable Monday, I'm going to have to get some rest."

Why was David trusting his fiancée with someone who had been manipulating her for days? I clung to this explanation: he didn't know about his brother's schemes. And I had to keep myself from thinking: But what if he was in on it? No. Not David.

"Come on, live a little!"

Louie grabbed my hand again, and this time so strongly that I had to put up a fuss.

"Let go! You're hurting me!"

Armand shot him a reproachful look. Louie bowed his head like a kid being chastised and relaxed his grip.

"As you wish," he stammered. "I just thought . . ."

I cut him off sharply. "What did you think?"

"That this walk would be a good time to tell you more."

"More? About what?"

"About us . . . David and me. I know David. He's so secretive. I'm positive he hasn't told you anything about our childhood. Or this house, for that matter."

Touché.

If he kept his promise, I wasn't opposed to the idea. Moreover, it would be a good time to probe him on some issues. Maybe I could even get him to take off the mask he put on whenever we met. Maybe I could gain the upper hand once and for all.

I also figured he wouldn't dare try anything in the middle of the day in a crowded street. An encouraging look from Armand quelled the anger I'd been feeling all morning.

"Okay . . . fine," I said dryly. "Do I at least have time for a shower?"

"As many showers as you'd like. We have all day."

Coming from him, that sounded less like an innocent promise of fun on a spring day and more like a threat of long hours of torture. I expected nothing less.

I crumpled the handwritten note in my fist—there was one that wouldn't make it in the silver notebook—and with knots in my stomach, I made a beeline for the shower. I reappeared less than fifteen minutes later wearing a simple floral dress that I'd spruced up with hand-sewn felt flourishes, nude flats, and a small bag containing only the essentials. Sufficiently dressed not to draw critique, sober enough not to send any messages. Though it would not be seen, I took the precaution of wearing the thickest and least revealing panties in my collection of lingerie. I tried to erase the image of the sticky pair I had taken off when I had gotten home the night before.

WE STEPPED OFF DUCHESNOIS HOUSE'S antique porch and crossed the crescent-shaped courtyard. Standing curbside in front of 3 Rue de la Tour-des-Dames, we were bathed in the sun's warm light. I couldn't deny Louie's point: it was an ideal day for a stroll.

Louie was in such a good mood that it was difficult not to be infected. Still, every time he looked at me, I remembered the night before, the hotel room, and how I'd undressed for him, showing more of myself to him than I'd ever shown to any man.

"Elle . . . do you have any idea what David meant when he asked me to make you into an Athenian woman?"

The question didn't sound like a trap. It was asked without the slightest hint of acrimony or hidden meaning. It really seemed like he was just assessing his pupil's level. Waiting for a reply, he glued his eyes to mine.

"No," I admitted. "Not really."

"Okay, well, this neighborhood—between Rue des Martyrs to the east, Rue Pigalle to the west, and Rue Saint-Lazare to the south—is called New Athens. Some of the houses here saw the birth of French Romanticism."

In spite of myself, my eyes widened with interest. I had been expecting biting commentary, maybe even a few salacious remarks, but not a history lesson. He was acting as though the scene in the Mata Hari room had never happened.

"How's that?"

"In the mid-1820s, the biggest names in the then-nascent artistic movement came to live here. Poets and writers like George Sand, Eugène Scribe, Marceline Desbordes-Valmore, Alexandre Dumas, and later the great Victor Hugo; there were also musicians like Liszt, Berlioz, Auber, Chopin, Wagner, and painters such as Delacroix, Vernet, Gavarni, and Ary Scheffer. But people tend to forget that the first artists to set up camp here . . ."

He paused his lecture and raised his eyes in childish wonder up toward the building we'd just left. It was unique in that its curved facade opened onto a small three-sided courtyard.

I noticed that since our last meeting, Louie had let his beard grow. The added hair did not fill out his cheeks; rather, it made his face look even more emaciated. On the surface, the beard seemed to express the feverishness inside the man.

"Yes?"

"The first artists were actors, Elle. Simple actors."

"Like Mademoiselle Duchesnois?" I suggested.

"Exactly. But before her other great stars had taken up residence: Mademoiselle Mars next door at 1 Rue de la Tour-des-Dames."

I remembered the hair comb in the window at Antiquités Nativelle, the one that had made my mouth water with desire only a few days earlier. Louie went on, passionate about his subject, clutching my forearm as a way of keeping my attention:

"The great Talma, Bonaparte's favorite actor, in house number nine. And Marie Dorval, Alfred de Vigny's mistress, a little lower, on Rue Saint-Lazare. In the early 1830s, the street where you live was the Champs-Élysées of the new artistic scene."

As I listened to him, I almost forgot his perverted side, that he was the disloyal brother-in-law who asked for strange favors in exchange for silence and the madman who, page after page, detailed aspects of my sexuality in a book from hell.

He was so engrossed in what he had to say that his whole being appeared to be swallowed into the era he was trying to conjure.

"But why 'New Athens'?" I asked, my curiosity piqued. "And why did they all congregate here?"

"According to the official story, the name was coined by Dureau de la Malle, an editorialist at the *Journal des Débats*, in 1823. But I think it's more complicated than that: Greece was really fashionable at the time, what with the Greek rebellion against the Ottomans in 1821. The neoclassical and neo-Raphaelite style of Constantin's buildings also played a role."

"Neo-Raphaelite?" I asked, admitting ignorance.

While speaking, he slipped his arm through mine, in the most natural and chaste way in the world, and guided me toward Rue de la Rochefoucauld. We were retracing our steps from the night before. He was so casual about it that I completely let down my guard, and gave in to the soft and enveloping warmth of his embrace.

"The more you let him touch you, the more you prepare yourself to invite him other places in you."

I think it was my inner arm, yes, that soft, sensitive
skin in the hollow of elbow, that whispered the phrase
in my ear. I wonder if such an innocuous erogenous zone
could make me come?

Anonymous handwritten note, 6/7/2009

A SHIVER RAN UP MY spine as I thought of the indecent, open version of myself he had shown me. Why was I following him so obediently?

"Yes, look at this building: Do you see the rounded niches above the supporting wall between the second and third floors? And on that one, do you see the three Palladian windows, and how the center pane has an exaggerated arch while the other two are narrower, and how they're supported by a simple lintel?"

His erudite observations did not bore me in the least; rather, they opened my eyes to a whole new world. He was uncovering new mysteries in a city I thought I knew by heart. He squeezed my shoulder and I didn't flinch.

"All of it," he went on, "is characteristic of Italian Renaissance Mannerism."

"Raphael?" I suggested.

"Yes, along with Palladio, Serlio, Sangallo . . . Percier and Fontaine, the Empire's official architects, drew inspiration from them. And their style influenced all the major private housing projects into the 1830s. In New Athens especially."

This time, I was gripping his arm, and my left breast accidentally grazed his extremely taut bicep. I quickly unhooked myself from him, pretending nothing had happened. I did not want him to feel my naughty nipple, which had hardened at his touch. I did not want him to see my growing emotion.

"And then the concentration of beauty and intelligence in the neighborhood made it a first-rate cultural center whose reputation quickly spread. People came from all over Europe! Imagine: in 1850, more than a hundred artists lived on these few streets. Posterity hasn't remembered them all, but they did all help to create the neighborhood's spirit."

There was a hint of nostalgia in his voice, as though he missed a time he could not have known but wished he had.

With all the excitement, he'd gotten hot. He took off his jacket and rolled up his shirtsleeves. For the first time, I caught a glimpse of his tattoo in its entirety. No matter how partially, the fact that he was now undressing in front of me was a little troubling. But I tried to focus my attention on the design he'd just unveiled. Why were the two unfurled wings and enlaced scepter so familiar?

He caught my insistent gaze and said with a faint, pinched smile:

"It's Hermes's caduceus."

The caduceus, I remembered, was the symbol I often saw in front of medical offices.

A lowercase letter *a* near the wrist underscored the image. Its font recalled those made by old typewriters.

"And the letter . . . Why just an *a*? *A* like 'artist'? Like 'anarchy'?"

My childish guessing didn't make him laugh. Instead, a shadow crossed his brow, erasing his good mood.

"No, just the first letter of the alphabet," he murmured.

His sudden shift inward should have dissuaded me from digging deeper, and yet:

"That's all?"

"Oh, don't worry, the others will follow."

I grasped his meaning: he would have all the letters of the alphabet carved into his skin. He would become his own alphabet, his own box of tools. It was beautiful and stupid all at once. Touching and laughable. Juvenile, too. The kind of thing you imagine doing when you're a teenager, not an adult.

"And where does the feather fit in all of this?"

When we'd first met at the Sauvage Gallery, I'd noticed that the caduceus was not accompanied by a basic beveled point but a pen's feather.

"Let's just say that the stylus makes them all irrelevant. In the end, it's the power of the stylus that heals, thanks to its ability to assemble the letters into words."

I had read the Bible, so I knew about the creative power of the word. It seemed Louie was borrowing that notion and extending it to health. So for him, in the beginning there was . . . sex, right? How had we been able to accept a genesis stripped of any sort of carnal act, and for millennia?

I had more questions, but I could tell by his reaction that I had touched a sore spot. Suddenly he stopped, somewhere in the middle of Rue Chaptal, and rolled his shirtsleeve back over his forearm, his way of telling me our discussion was over.

We were in front of a building marked 16. A tree shot up between the houses, throwing a leafy shadow over the sidewalk. A narrow, shrub-lined passage stretched at a perpendicular line from where we stood toward a sunny courtyard that looked charming. Farther off, old women sat on a bench, in the shadow of a giant rosebush.

I looked for a moment at the sign on the street:

Museum of Romantic Life

"Speaking of the alphabet . . . ," he said, smiling delicately, "this place will give you the ABCs of Parisian Romanticism. You can't understand anything about this neighborhood and its history without a visit here first."

Did he mean this timeless haven, separated from the brouhaha of modern life by a few feet of paved alleyway? The building at the end of the path was amazing, with its green shutters and balconies that were partially hidden behind tall bouquets of tea roses.

He grabbed my arm when I tripped over the disjointed blocks of granite. Once again, my chest brushed against him; this time it was his dense and muscled flank.

I asked the first question that came to mind, anything to distract him from my state.

"Who owned this house?"

"Ary Scheffer, the painter. He was sort of the official portraitist of the Romantic intelligentsia. Liszt, Sand, Chopin, Renan . . . He painted them all."

He did not lead me directly into the building but instead seized my hand and guided me to the small garden on the right. A bench-lined flower bed of roses gave way to a splendid conservatory, a massive greenhouse at the back of the main building. Outside and in, smiling tourists with cameras hanging from their necks sipped tea at little round bistro tables.

"It's pretty, don't you think?"

I nodded, enchanted. My hand was still imprisoned by his. I couldn't believe a place like this still existed here, in this city, at the margins of all the tumult. It was a miracle. And that he was the one—*he*—who had taken me here was in itself a cruel irony.

Louie offered me a chair, sat down in his own, and looked very much at ease in this calm environment. A few sad notes from the piano flowed from an artificial waterfall. There was probably a speaker hidden somewhere between the rocks. After listening intently to the piece for a few seconds, he announced the title, his gaze distant:

"Nocturne no. 20 by Frédéric Chopin, in C-sharp minor. It's one of his posthumous pieces."

Who else did I know who was capable of recognizing a piece by Chopin after only having heard a couple lines of music? But then I reminded myself that he could have said it was Schubert or Beethoven, and I wouldn't have known the difference.

"Did you know," he went on, "that George Sand and Frédéric Chopin first fell in love here? People tend to talk about their meeting in Liszt's apartment in the Hôtel de France. Or their paradisiacal Square d'Orléans. But in reality, the two overcame their mutual repulsion here in Scheffer's abode. Scheffer had a way of getting his friends to mingle."

As he said this, he slowly gestured toward the building, whose door to the garden was hidden behind a thick gray velour curtain, as though to better protect the secret of the couple's passion.

"Repulsion?" I asked, surprised, "I thought they were crazy for each other?"

"That's right, I said *repulsion*. Do you know what Chopin wrote about Sand after they first met?"

"No . . ."

Our tea and biscuits arrived. Louie kept his magnetic gaze locked on mine as he served me. A delicious scent of jasmine wafted from my teacup. He began citing from memory:

"'What a disagreeable woman that Sand is! Is she really a woman? I have my doubts.'"

"How charming! What a gentleman!"

"Yes, well, it's a good lesson in amorous humility, don't you think? One never knows where a first impression, no matter how terrible, might lead . . ."

I avoided the thorny topic lurking behind his words. I understood that the place, like the conversation, was not innocent. It would invariably lead to a discussion of our story. Or, rather, his unhealthy obsession with me.

I won't transcribe the entirety of George Sand's libertine poem to Alfred de Musset, her lover at the time, but I do remember the first lines:

I want to tell you that I
understood last night that you
still have a mad desire to
dance, so at the next party you should
come and I hope it is
on time, so I can be
in your arms.

Which really meant, once it was decoded by skipping each line:

I want to tell you that I
still have a mad desire to
come and I hope it is
in your arms.

Anonymous handwritten note, 6/7/2009—If he'd
hoped to teach me something new, he failed. Sophia
had told me about the letter when we were still in
college.

I DECIDED TO COUNTERATTACK: IT was my turn to direct
the flow of conversation.

"Is it also a tattoo?"

For once, my question seemed to catch him off guard.

"Excuse me?"

"David's silk armband: Is it hiding a tattoo like yours?"

He paled and searched for words, he who was usually so
verbose.

At least he wasn't angry. I had tried to ask David about it
a few nights before as we were getting into bed, and he'd been
irate:

"It was an accident, and it isn't anybody's business but my
own."

"What about your wife?"

"It's . . . Well, in any case, it's in the past."

End of story.

Louie tugged his sleeve over the caduceus, as though trying
to protect his brother's secret.

"No . . . David doesn't like that kind of thing."

"So what is it?"

He had never known me to be so determined, only having
seen in me what he had wanted to see: easy prey whom he
could manipulate thanks to the information he had on me. A
toy, a simple toy, and a woman whose body he now knew, right
down to the last curve.

Yet I saw a flash of panic darken his eyes.

"David didn't say anything to you?"

"About what?"

"About his arm . . ."

"No. What is there to know?"

He swallowed several mouthfuls of scalding-hot tea and then began, with less confidence than usual.

"It's not just about his arm . . . ," he said gravely and caught his breath.

His introduction indicated this would not be a happy story.

I gave him an encouraging look.

"When I was twenty, and David nineteen, we both met a young woman over summer vacation. And we both fell in love with her. Both of us. At the same time."

I remembered what Armand had said about their rivalry. Power had been promised to the one who could conquer the most beautiful women . . .

"What was her name?"

"Aurora. Aurora Delbard."

The name was bitter on his lips. His cheeks started twitching. What had she meant to him, to the two of him? How was she still able to provoke such emotion?

"How did you meet—"

"It doesn't matter," he cut me off. "In spite of her young age, Aurora chose David. They got engaged and then married over the course of a few weeks."

Married? So I wouldn't be the first Madame David Barlet? I tried to push the thought aside. It cut like a knife. It bothered me, but I decided to concentrate on what Louie was telling me.

So Louie had lost the girl to his brother. I could see traces of this defeat on his unhappy face. Had this been one of David's first decisive triumphs? The kind that would win him the

Barlet family throne? And what about me? Did I mean anything more to him than a consolation prize, a plaything, a toy
to steal and dangle in front of his brother?

For the first time, I was the one to reach for his hand, but
he withdrew it before I had a chance to reassure him.

"They were the perfect couple. People called them the Del-
barlet. Even their last names meshed."

I didn't say the obvious: the play on names would have
worked for him, too. I figured it was better to let him talk. He
had been manipulating me for weeks, and now, for the first
time, I felt like I was gaining the upper hand, like I was in
charge. Nervous, he rolled up his shirtsleeves again, revealing
the lowercase *a* on his left arm. *A* like "Aurora," I realized.

"But neither David nor I realized how troubled Aurora
was."

"Troubled, how?"

He replied with a wild look.

"Destructive. Manipulative. At the time, there wasn't a
name for what she had . . ."

"And today?"

"Borderline personality disorder. It almost exclusively af-
fects women who were abandoned or abused in childhood. I
spent a lot of time researching the issue."

I had to resist the temptation to dig deeper into the horrible past of my future husband's first wife. A wife he had never
even mentioned to me. I tried to reason with myself. I didn't
want to think of David as disloyal or deceitful. I considered
how difficult Aurora's sickness must have been on him. To a
certain extent, his pain justified his silence on the matter.

And, then, who was I to judge? I hadn't even introduced
him to my mother.

"What happened? I mean, after they were married?"

"At first it was okay. David was able to manage Aurora's mood swings, her demands. God, there were so many. It's common of people with that disorder: they're constantly testing their partner in the morbid hope of one day being rejected. For example, Aurora would inhale everything in the refrigerator in one evening, vomit it all up, and then order my brother to restock the fridge immediately, in the middle of the night after all the stores had closed. She could be such a tyrant."

I had trouble imagining David the executive, the charming and slightly authoritative man, letting himself be treated like that. It didn't fit with my image of him. And yet we were talking about the same man.

"Did he eventually just give up?"

"And leave her?" Louie asked, surprised by my question. "No! He hung on till the end. I don't mean he never thought about throwing in the towel. He did, especially after the more violent episodes. But he wouldn't give up . . . I tried to help him as best I could."

"You weren't a little jealous?"

Could a man as proud as Louie really be capable of one day being the jilted suitor and the next his brother's confidant? Again, something seemed off. I didn't trust the noble and chivalrous portrait Louie was painting of himself. It made me empathize even more with the real victim of this tragedy: David.

Had Louie really been as in love with Aurora as he claimed?

"Was I jealous of the hell in which he lived? No, not really . . . In a way, I thanked my lucky stars that Aurora had chosen David instead of me. But in spite of that, I think I still had feelings for her. I couldn't imagine living with her, but I did sincerely hope that she would find some peace with David. I did hope she could find a way to be happy."

The tears welling up in his eyes told me she hadn't. Louie finished his story without any coaxing from me:

"The year after their wedding, we spent the summer at the beach. Our parents were still alive. The weather was beautiful, and we were all more relaxed than usual . . . Even Aurora seemed to be doing better."

"What happened?"

"One night, she wanted to go for a midnight swim. The waters were rough, and David tried to convince her not to go. She didn't have a suit and declared that she wanted to go in the nude."

"So she went?"

His eyes gazed up at the sky as he tried to think of an answer; then they shifted darkly back to me.

"Yes. It was always the same with her: she would challenge David, who would always resist her, and then she would take whatever risk it was she had in mind by herself. And then he had to fly to her rescue. But that night, the waves were really violent . . . There was nothing he could do. Aurora disappeared behind two groups of rocks; she got sucked into a kind of natural siphon . . . She never resurfaced."

"That's how he hurt his arm?"

"No . . . Not like that. That would have been better for everybody."

At least he wasn't making himself out to be a hero, I thought to myself. What a horrible tragedy. And it did not make him look good. Aurora had rejected him, and he hadn't done anything more than his brother to help her. He had stood by and watched the young woman's madness drown the couple, just as she herself had been sucked into the sea's currents.

"Why do you say that?"

Birds chirped overhead, as though they were trying to cheer us up. In vain. His silence dragged on like torture.

A light gust of wind swept through the garden, just as a group of visitors stepped through the gray curtain, revealing a fleeting glimpse into the sumptuous museum interior. From her frame, George Sand, as painted by Ary Scheffer with a red flower in her hair, gave me a severe look.

"It's unfortunate his wound does not date back to that tragic night because it took David many years to recover," he said at last. "Three years after Aurora's death, he tried to take his own life."

"What?"

I swallowed a cry. Louie gestured for me to remain calm.

"Happily, the idiot failed. He went about it the wrong way, and he destroyed the veins in his left forearm. His scars are rather . . . spectacular."

Hence the armband.

Honestly, the mournful and suicidal young man resembled nothing of the implacable captain of industry he had become. The armband was an elementary way of keeping his past under wraps and maintaining his current image in the eyes of the world.

Including me.

I regretted having been so forceful with him about it. I'd been so eager to shed light on his wound, which probably still haunted him, instead of leaving well enough alone and letting his secret remain hidden under white silk. He needed my tenderness, love, and presence at his side. Not an inquisition.

14

JUNE 7, 2009

I wanted to take him in my arms and whisper sweet nothings to comfort him. I wanted to tell him that I wasn't Aurora. That I would never go for a swim in the ocean on a stormy night. That I would not make his life hell or martyr myself. But that I wanted to live a long, happy life at his side. Maybe we weren't passionate about each other, but I would love him as he deserved.

However, the man smiling at me from across the teapot and its wisps of jasmine was not David.

"You believed me?"

He had the triumphant look of someone who had just smashed an insect under his shoe. And the insect was me!

"You believed my little story, didn't you, Elle?"

Filled with rage, I remained mute. I was stupefied, baffled by his extraordinary duplicity. Had he really conjured such a dark tale just so he could watch me believe it, every single detail, like a fly caught in his web?

Louie was beside himself, gloating at how easy it had been to fool me. The spider's silent laugh as it devours its meal.

"It's so easy to get young women like you to believe a soap opera. A garden, a little music, a touch of tragedy . . . and you light up like a match. It's almost too easy. No, but really, I'm touched."

I was shaking but still managed to stand. With what dignity remained, I silently left the premises. I had to push through a group of Asian tourists who were blocking the alleyway.

"Annabelle! Stay!"

In spite of his lame leg, he ran to catch up with me. He reached for my arm, and I shrugged him off, despite the uneven terrain.

"Leave me alone!"

I was done. As far as I was concerned, he could tell his brother anything he liked. I would risk it. Putting David's love to the test. The test of truth. But I was sure of one thing: I would not put up with Louie's guileful behavior anymore. The cruel, wounded, failed man wouldn't get anything more out of me. And he could write as many insane pages as he wanted— they would all end up in the trash unread. My thoughts would once again belong to me.

I broke into a light jog to put some distance between us. With his leg, he couldn't keep up.

"I'm sorry . . . ," he cried to my back. "Annabelle!"

It was unusual for him to call me by my first name. Still, it did nothing to slow me down. Nor did the gaping looks from bystanders. Without further ado, when I got to Rue Chaptal, I turned right and headed toward Rue Blanche.

But I had only gotten a few feet when my phone started to ring:

"David?"

"Hi, beautiful. How are you enjoying the touristy walk with Louie?"

"Er, I . . . It's fine, everything's fine . . . ," I lied in a choked voice.

"Great idea, huh? Isn't it a beautiful day?!"

"Yes . . ."

"I knew you'd love it. Louie is a really good tour guide."

As he spoke, I sensed my pursuer gaining on me.

"Could I speak with him?"

"No . . . no, he's in the restroom," I breathlessly improvised.

"Oh, right. Not surprised. He's kind of a girl in that department."

"Do you want me to have him call you back?"

I prayed for him to accept, he who never had a second to waste.

"No, that's okay . . . I'll wait. It's really nice to hear your voice during the day."

Louie was now only two or three paces behind me. When he reached me, he grabbed my free wrist and his iconic face broke into a menacing smile. Surprised by his strength, I grimaced.

I let out a muted yelp in spite of myself.

"Elle? Elle, are you okay?" David worried on the other end of the line.

Answer him, the lame man exhorted with a look.

"Yes . . . It's nothing, I just ran into a . . ."

"Into a . . . ?"

Louie reached for the phone without relaxing his grip on my arm. I couldn't run or even yell at him. David would have heard.

"Hey, bro!" said the man with the cane, his tone disconcertingly light. "Yes, yes, everything is fine. Annabelle is a . . .

an unfocused but curious student. She'll know *everything she needs to know* about the neighborhood by the end of the day."

He directed his words at me. What kind of message was he trying to convey?

They chatted for a few minutes about the station—some promotional project for the summer—and then at last Louie hung up, though he kept the phone in his hand. Meanwhile, he had not loosened his grip on my imprisoned wrist.

So I exploded:

"'Sorry'? That's the best you could do: 'Sorry'?"

"I don't like your tone," he said sharply. "I just might have to call our dear David. I'm sure he'll pick up since I'll be using your phone."

Today's lies were nothing compared to the sick game he'd played with me the night before. I was ashamed to have participated and wanted to spit in his face.

"Go ahead! Go ahead, call him!" I challenged. "And while you're at it, tell him about the things you do to his future wife in hotel rooms at night!"

"I doubt he car—"

"Oh, yeah, I think he'll be fascinated! And don't forget to tell him about the letters, too. I'm sure he'll be delighted to hear that his own brother gets off on writing about his fiancée's sexual fantasies!"

In spite of myself, I had puffed out my chest. My breasts seemed ready to explode. My nipples pointed through the thin cotton of my dress. They were as cold and hard as porcelain. Breaking the silence should have come as a relief, but instead it felt like I was in quicksand: thinking about the letters bothered me, but forcing them out of my memory would only make me sink further, until the point of no return.

Above all, do <u>not</u> think about his hand feeling them,
pinching them like seeds in pulpy fruit, rolling them
between his fingers until I feel that dual sensation of pain
and pleasure, that intense, localized happiness just before
it radiates throughout my body.

Anonymous handwritten note, 6/7/2009

HE MUST HAVE SENSED MY abrupt shift in attitude because
he softened his voice, acting at once prouder and more determined. He let go of my wrist, now marbled and red-hued.

"I promise you, I did not write those letters."

He spoke with such frankness that I no longer felt angry.

I hesitated before retrieving my silver notebook and opening
it at random to one of the pages with its furious handwriting:

"So this handwriting . . . it isn't yours? Look me in the eye,
Louie, and tell me it isn't."

He let a few seconds pass before saying gravely:

"I'm looking you in the eye, and I promise you it isn't. I'll
even do you one better: I'll prove it to you."

He produced a small black leather notebook and a ball-
point pen of the same color. Hovering the writing instrument
over a blank page, he said:

"Please, dictate something for me to write."

His initiative surprised me.

"I don't know . . ."

"Anything, the first thing that comes to mind."

"'Aurora Delbard drowned at sea,'" I said at last, surprising
even myself.

He stared at me for a moment, in what looked like a mix-
ture of anger and admiration—at least I had guts—then tran-

scribed the sentence without looking up from his notebook. When he'd finished, he handed it to me.

"There. You be the judge."

Aurora Delbard drowned at sea.

I was stunned. To be sure, though blunter and more masculine, his handwriting was just as jerky as the one in my notebook. But the two could never be confused. This script was more rushed, with hardly a space between the words. It trotted breathlessly over the page. Meanwhile, my harasser's writing was rounder, more legible.

I put the two sheets of paper side by side to better compare them. I also reviewed my memory from a few seconds before of Louie tracing the gilded point of his pen over his notebook. It didn't seem like he'd been faking it. There was only one possible conclusion: Louie's handwriting did not match that of my Ten-Times-a-Day.

All the crazy ideas that had been running through my head these past few days, all my anger, everything crumbled like a sand castle under a child's foot after a long day at the beach.

"I'm confused, I . . ."

He looked pleased with himself.

Speechless, I stared into his eyes. I'd never before seen this smile on him before: somewhere between an apology and reconciliation. A Clooney smile, as Sophia, who loved to make celebrity references, would have said.

"Now that we've clarified a few things, I suggest we continue our stroll, this time on better footing. What do you say?"

A fist squeezed my stomach and told me to be careful; I shouldn't take his sudden good mood for money in the bank.

But the excitement in my breasts clamored for the opposite.

"I promise: no more tricks."

What specifically did he mean?

"Not another lie for the rest of the day," he clarified in a serious tone.

"Really?"

To be honest, at that moment, I only wanted one thing: to go home alone and never to see that abject creature for the rest of my life. I didn't care if he was really the man behind my troubles or not.

But I knew that when I started my job at BTV, he would be there, in an office not far from mine. And at our wedding, now only a fortnight away. And then, year after year, unfailingly, at each family event. He was David's brother, and I could not just erase him because I was angry. What would my future husband say if he learned that I had ditched his older brother simply because he'd played a tasteless trick?

"I'll stick to my tour guide duties. There's no way I'll fib about the history of the neighborhood, and I know it better than anyone."

It sounded arrogant, but I knew he wasn't exaggerating.

Wary but calmer, I let him guide me through the streets of New Athens for the rest of our tour. He kept his promise and played his role as a talkative Cicero to perfection.

"Do you see the larger number over the other ones? Above the door?"

We were on Rue Blanche. I had indeed noticed that some of the enamel plaques on the buildings were abnormally large.

"Yes, it's strange . . ."

"Today, it's the only remaining sign that these were once brothels."

"Really?"

He smiled at my naiveté but quickly sobered, as if afraid he might offend me again.

"The 1946 Marthe Richard law put a ban on houses of prostitution, but even before that, brothels had to be discreet. Unlike in Amsterdam, they were not allowed to put up obvious signs, and had to make do with decorations that could be easily recognized only by those in the know."

"Like what?"

"The famous red lanterns, for example, along with more subtle things like frosted glass windows, a peephole in the entry door, or louvered shutters that always remained shut. The 'Big Number'—which is eventually how these establishments came to be known—figured among these discreet signals."

I didn't say anything. The rest of the tour dealt with the same theme of terrestrial love and questionable morals among the neighborhood's past inhabitants: in Square d'Orléans, Louie once again referred to the unbridled passion shared between Sand and Chopin; at 8 Rue la Bruyère, he told the story of the poetess Marceline Desbordes-Valmore and her thirty-year adulterous relationship with Henri de Latouche . . . But the highlight had to be his impassioned description of the ladies of the night who had taken up residence by a neoclassical church while it was under construction:

"Their first clients were the construction workers; then, after the church was finished, they solicited the parishioners. They became known as the 'lorettes,' after the name of the church: Notre-Dame-de-Lorette."

The structure rose before us: four Corinthian columns supporting a classically inspired portico.

"But I thought the area was rather chic?"

"The lorettes were chic!" he cried, defending them. "They were nothing like the cheap whores in the Bastille or Belleville areas who generally worked as linen maids or hat sellers, and hawked their charms to make ends meet."

"And the lorettes were different?"

"Yes! Overall, they were girls of quality. They were educated, knew how to read and write, and were partially supported by their johns. For them, prostitution was more of a way of life than an economic necessity."

"They were more like courtesans than prostitutes, you mean."

I wonder if he spends a lot of time with girls like us, lorettes and Hotelles, like that stunning ethnic woman the other night at the gallery. Maybe he even frequents real prostitutes, the ones you can find in alleys near Bois de Vincennes for a quickie behind a rusty truck. What do men get out of possessing all these nameless, and practically faceless, vaginas? Does it make them feel stronger, more virile, more desirable? Honestly, do they feel transformed after sheathing themselves in latex and penetrating a woman, without emotion or feeling? Just an obedient pussy they'll never fuck again?

Anonymous handwritten note, 6/7/2009—These are the kinds of questions men ask . . . He acts like he's in my head; this time, he has everything all wrong.

MY SUCCINCT WAY OF PUTTING things made him laugh. For once, there was no hint of cynicism or manipulation. Meanwhile, tensions from our most recent spat seemed to have dissipated, at least as far as he was concerned. I wished I could have said as much . . . I was just playing my part as best I could, anxious for it to end.

"One might say, yes."

WE SPENT HOURS OUTSIDE IN the sun. The day was filled with more stories and architectural details than I could possibly remember. It was difficult to admit, but I really did enjoy listening to Louie talk about the Venetian style of some of the buildings surrounding Place Saint-Georges, with all the medallions, friezes, and ornate columns. It was a stark contrast to the clean neoclassicism of Rue de la Tour-des-Dames.

At lunch, we had omelets in a brasserie called Le Central near Drouot. It wasn't far from the antique stores where Sophia and I liked to window-shop. Strange coincidence: Louie stopped directly in front of Antiquités Nativelle. My favorite boutique. After looking for a moment, he made to go inside.

"Will you give me a moment?"

Without waiting for my reply, he stepped into the store. Powerless, my heart stopped when I saw him speak with the clerk, a small man in spectacles, and point to the silver comb I had been ogling for weeks. The one that had belonged to Mademoiselle Mars, my new neighbor, with a couple centuries between us.

It only took a few minutes, and he was back out on the street again, holding a hastily wrapped package.

"Here."

I refused the gift with a decisive gesture.

"Louie . . . I can't accept it. If David found out, he—"

He cut me off softly.

"There's nothing strange or untoward about it, Elle. I am just following my brother's instructions: take you on a stroll . . . and spoil you. He's paying for everything, of course."

It sounded like my fiancé, who must have given this temporary power to his brother unsuspectingly.

"In that case . . . I guess I have to accept."

His eyes gleamed. Right, he was only following David's orders, I thought. But the pleasure he derived was all his. He gave me the present, and in return I offered him my embarrassment and gratitude, two things he seemed to enjoy immensely.

"I have another errand. It's not very pleasant. Would you mind waiting for me in that café? It will only take about a half hour."

I FOUND MY USUAL TABLE at Café des Antiquaires really comforting after the tumult of the past several days. All that was missing was Sophia. Unfortunately, she wasn't picking up her phone. I wanted to tell her about everything that had happened since we'd last talked. Instead, I settled into the familiar café's cozy atmosphere and thought of how Louie's crazy lies had clouded my haloed image of his brother.

Why had he wanted to trick me? What exactly was he getting out of these games? The influence he had on me was not enough to explain his apparent need to test my nerves every time we met.

His sudden entry into the café whipped my face with cool air.

"There! It's done. Are you ready?"

He was holding a red-and-white plastic bag on which was printed a signature uppercase letter *D*: Drouot, the mecca of auction houses. What had he needed to purchase that had been so urgent? The long shape of the package, stuffed with newspaper, did not betray its contents.

I kept my questions to myself and followed him for the last stretch of our walk, through the elegant Jouffroy Passage, another architectural symbol of Romantic Paris. 1846, read the clock overhead, at the junction of the passage's L-shape. Like the clock and the wax statues in the Musée Grévin on our left, Louie seemed frozen in another time. Some of the people around us even stared at him as though he were a touristic curiosity, a vestige of turn-of-the-century dandyism.

"Are you coming back with me? I'm starting to feel a little tired . . ."

We had been walking since morning, and my request must have seemed legitimate to him because he agreed. A few paces farther, as we were stepping out onto Boulevard Montmartre, he hailed a taxi.

Ten minutes later, the car was starting up Rue de la Roche-foucauld, when I spotted a big-cylindered black motorcycle at the next intersection.

"Stop!" I said to the driver.

"It's farther up, on Rue de la Tour-des-Dames, Mademoi-selle."

"Yes, I know . . . but could you leave us here, please?"

"Okay, it's up to you," he conceded, veering his white Mercedes toward the sidewalk.

Torn from his thoughts, Louie looked surprised.

"Is something wrong?"

"No, no, everything is fine," I lied, feeling uneasy.

Then he saw him, too. A motorcyclist stretched across his

mechanical monster, wrapped in a leather jacket, holding his helmet: Fred.

"You've gone pale, Elle. Is it because of that boy?"

"Yes . . . ," I gasped, getting out of the vehicle.

"Who is it?"

"My ex . . . And he has no reason to be here."

"Does he scare you?"

I stiffened. I didn't know what bothered me more: the unexpected appearance of my ex or that Louie was there to see me so shaken up.

"No . . . no. But still, I'd rather go in through the back."

There was a cul-de-sac on the north, at 56 Rue Saint-Lazare, that offered secret access to the gardens of the houses on Rue de la Tour-des-Dames. Only locals knew about it.

But Louie seized my arm, gluing his side to mine, and, with a determined look, dragged me toward the man who was waiting for us.

"You know, I get it. You're not the kind of girl men let go of easily. But come on. Since he's here, we are going to give him something for his money."

Terrible idea!

Fred saw us and started walking in our direction with a quick and precise step. I recognized the look he usually had before a fight: his eyes and shoulders were low, his head tucked, his fists tight.

"So you're the one?" he asked Louie.

"I am."

Holding firm, Louie wasn't the least bit scared. His look was one of aristocratic defiance. Spurred by Louie's attitude, the motorcyclist thrust the palm of his hand into his opponent's chest.

"You son of a bitch! So now you want the proletariat's girls, huh? What, stepping on our backs all year isn't enough? You have to steal our women, too?"

He was oozing hate. Fred thought he was talking to David, and Louie, being a gentleman, played along in order to protect me from my ex-boyfriend's rancor.

Out of desperation, I grabbed Fred's rock-hard arm.

"Fred! Stop!"

"This is your great love? Fuck, he's a cripple!"

"Young man, you've gone too far."

Now Louie approached him, brandishing his cane. Without thinking, I started screaming in the hope that Armand or someone else might hear and call the police.

"Stop it!"

"Oh, I'm sure all their fucking money helps when you close your eyes and open your thighs!" Fred spit, shielding himself with his helmet.

The cane came down hard on the visor, then again on Fred's hand; he shrieked in pain.

"Fuck!"

Drunk with pride and pain, the wounded man charged at his opponent. Just then, Louie rummaged through the Drouot bag. He quickly withdrew a long, flexible object and swooshed a Z in the air. A riding crop!

He punctuated each word with the sharp sound of leather cutting through the air:

"Don't you . . . come near . . . Elle . . . ever again! Do you understand?"

"Freak!" Fred bellowed, his tone markedly less proud.

It terrified me to see them on the verge of fighting. But

I have to admit that it also struck an instinctual chord
inside my animalistic female self: I wondered which of the
two males would win the fight and throw himself on me.
A fleeting desire crossed my mind to see them naked and
tearing each other apart for me.

Anonymous handwritten note, 6/7/2009—"*Animalistic*
female self"? Who did he think he was? A superhero?

AS FRED BACKED AWAY, THE tip of the crop whipped his
face, leaving a red welt—striking but superficial, judging from
the lack of blood. Nevertheless, it convinced him to back off.
Humiliated, he drew his hand to his face and staggered toward
his motorcycle, a wild look in his eyes. Without stopping, he
started the engine and got ready to leave.

But Louie didn't seem satisfied with his victory. He continued to threaten the other with his riding crop, whipping
it all around. It wasn't until the motorcycle roared off in the
other direction that he seemed to remember the person for
whom he'd fought this battle. He collected his cane from
the ground and approached me, acting more sheepish than
boastful.

"I am sorry . . ."

"Don't be."

He took my hand, turned it palm up, and ceremoniously
placed the leather crop in it.

"What are you . . . ?"

"It's your second present. Though I hadn't planned on using
it before giving it to you."

"It's wonderful."

But what am I supposed to do with a riding crop? I wondered.

"It once belonged to an elegant English woman in the 1850s," he added hastily. "At the time, that kind of accessory was very fashionable. Even for women who didn't ride."

"Thanks . . ."

Two presents, one rescue . . . Despite his unpredictable behavior, as well as the odious way in which he was blackmailing me, I could not leave my hero of the day without thanking him. As I kissed him chastely on the cheeks, he put one of his soft, elegant hands on the nape of my neck. For the second time, I could smell his cologne: the fight had dissipated the scent of lavender, accentuating the notes of vanilla. I hated to admit it, but it was delicious. And together with the feeling of his fingers on my skin, it made me shiver, softly at first, then with increasing intensity, in waves that ran from my neck to my pelvis. Was it possible to come by stimulating as unlikely an erogenous zone as the neck?

I didn't wait to find out. I detached myself from him, my forehead burning, my gaze wild.

"Are you okay?" he asked, worried.

"Yes . . . I'm fine. Just a little shaken up."

I pointed to the road where Fred had taken off on his motorcycle.

Armand had heard the racket and come out to meet us.

"I'm leaving you in the best hands in Paris."

"Yes, I know," I agreed. "Armand is—"

"What happened?" interrupted the butler, fraught with worry.

"Good-bye, Elle."

Louie was already leaving. His limp looked worse, and he seemed to need his cane more than ever. Where and how had he hurt his leg? Wasn't he just a faker, an actor seeking to perfect his character? Wasn't the handicap just an eccentric accessory?

Armand helped me up the front steps as though I were wounded. I could have put up a fuss and pretended that I was in full possession of my faculties, but he still would have insisted on supporting me against his surprisingly robust shoulder.

When I saw the missive on the console, I thought I would really faint: a second silver envelope that looked just like the first.

"Who left that here?" I asked weakly.

"I don't know. I found it in the mail this morning. Is there a problem?"

"There's no stamp."

"Oh . . . I hadn't noticed."

"You didn't see who left it?"

Not Louie, I realized, since he hadn't left my side all day.

"No. I'm sorry . . . Is everything okay, Mademoiselle?"

"Yes, yes . . ." I forced a smile. "Thank you, Armand."

I waited for him to turn around before opening the envelope. As before, it contained a key to a room at the Hôtel des Charmes, as well as a handwritten note and a printed card. Clearly this was becoming a ritual.

> *Tonight, ten o'clock,*
> *the usual place.*
> *Bring your equipment.*

My equipment? What did my mysterious correspondent mean?

I was looking at the printed card . . .

2—Thou shalt awaken thine senses.

. . . when Armand came back to the hall.

"With all the commotion, I forgot to tell you . . ."

"Yes?"

I quickly hid the little card behind my back, like a schoolgirl caught doing something wrong.

"David invited some people over for dinner tonight. At nine o'clock."

"Dinner?"

Well, that decided things, much like an alarm clock wakes you from a bad dream.

"He wants you to meet some important people at BTV. Your future coworkers, in a way."

But not Louie, I thought. I agreed hoarsely.

"Okay."

"Nothing formal," he reassured me. "A little dinner between friends. They're all really close to David. It's sort of his intimate circle."

I understood perfectly, and my throat went dry: this dinner would be a kind of test. If I wanted to be accepted by the higher-ups at the station, it would have to be a success. I had to be brilliant, but without overdoing it. Smart, but without overshadowing the other women present. Happy, but not hysterical. And under no circumstances was I to play the role that my imminent marriage entailed, that of the lady of honor. I had to be professional, not silly.

"I'll take care of everything. All you have to do is be beautiful."

Reflexively, I searched through my dress pocket. I had forgotten about it all day, and yet it had never left me. It weighed heavily on the light fabric: the big, jagged key that would unlock a whole new world, about which I still knew nothing.

15

June 8, 2009

No, but seriously . . . he's crazy!"

I had just given Sophia an account of the previous night's events over the phone. At first I wasn't sure if she was talking about Louie or Fred. The Machiavellianism of the one or the hotheadedness of the other. She was not being as frank as usual, but I could tell that she already had a well-developed opinion. My best friend had never really liked my boyfriend. Her favorite thing to say about him: "That guy is a loser *and* a headache." Unfortunately, these past few years, Fred had only proved her right: unemployed, chronically broke, always getting into fights, etc. His violent outbursts at Mom's place and then here the evening before were two more examples of his messy life.

As for Louie, I measured my words, but Sophia wasn't fooled; she could tell that he was a whole other story. And even if there was no formal proof that David's brother was also the twisted man who had slipped the Ten-Times-a-Day notebook into my bag, the very prospect was enough to arouse the attention of Sophia's inner Esmeralda.

"Will you introduce me to him?"

"Who? Louie?"

"Yes! I love that kind of playfulness in a man."

"Soph . . . He's crazy! He took advantage of a historical tour of the neighborhood to spend the whole day talking to me about sex."

"I don't see what's wrong with that." She smirked.

"And he wouldn't stop lying to me. He made me believe that David had hidden his past from me, all in an effort to get me to change my feelings about him. How is that not twisted?"

Was it, though? To be sure, he had recanted and tried to make it all out to be some big joke. But who was to say that Aurora hadn't been real? Or that David's silk armband wasn't really hiding the scars of such an episode?

"Hmm . . . ," she minimized. "In any case, you know for sure that he's not your Ten-Times-a-Day."

"Yeah, but I don't think you get it: in ten days, this guy will be my brother-in-law!"

"All the more reason to dump him on me, girl. It would be so great, right? We could be sisters-in-law!"

"If you don't mind, I'd rather you didn't end up in a psychiatric hospital. Nor do I want to only see you during visiting hours."

She barely reacted when I asked her to be my maid of honor, and continued to daydream out loud:

"A well-connected sex freak like that, and with such a nice pedigree . . . Honestly, I think I could forget about his shortcomings."

Sophia sure knew how to get herself into trouble! She could make fun of Fred, but she wasn't much better. One of her most recent overnight clients, who had taken her to the

Hôtel des Charmes two or three times over the past couple of weeks, had become so infatuated with her that he'd asked her to quit her job to be with him, without any compensation but his eternal love. "Can you believe the rat? If he wants me to be his full-time hen, then he's going to have to give me more than 'my darlings' and 'my loves'!"

As for my own troubling feelings that day in Louie Barlet's presence, I kept them to myself. I remembered the fight and the animal that had taken hold of me, just as my harasser had described. *A real female in heat . . .*

Over our chatter, I was surprised to hear the water running in the bathroom. For once, even though it was a Monday, David hadn't disappeared before my alarm.

"Oh, I haven't told you . . . I spoke with Rebecca over the phone. She's furious about the other night."

"Weren't you the one who suggested I tell her to take a hike?"

"Yeah . . . I just wanted to warn you that it doesn't seem like she's going to forget about the money any time soon."

"I'll handle it," I said elusively.

Soon I would have more than enough to cover it.

The dinner David had put together on my behalf signaled my entry into the enchanting world of the media: the dozen or so guests spent the evening talking about people I had never heard of. I kept myself at a distance from the gossip, and I think it showed my independence and spirit. In other words, I wasn't just the boss's pretty ornament. Alice, a tall, sculpted blonde who had introduced herself by underscoring her title as the "BTV's director of international marketing," spent the evening acting like a potential rival, what with her pointed looks, undercutting remarks, and the insidious way in which she shifted the conversation toward topics she knew were outside my field of knowledge, using cryptic acronyms and name-dropping.

Had she ever slept with David?

Probably . . . Why wouldn't he have been attracted to her perfect lips, her blue azure eyes, her breasts so perky they looked like she'd just had them done, her deliciously sculpted butt and the way it looked in her tight, low-cut sheath dress that tastefully showed off her cleavage? No man could resist such a creature . . .

Alice and David. David and Alice. It sounded so nice. Maybe too nice. And what if one day, to keep him from getting bored, I suggested a threesome? Could there be a better partner for ménage à trois? I could also discover what it felt like to kiss such a beautiful woman. Was her hair down there as shiny as her mane? I don't picture her with a girlish, delicate, and pink vagina, but with a large cleft, fleshy lips, long-winged nymphae spread wide. ~~The pussy of an Amazon woman, of a conqueress with a strong and musky odor.~~ *How would my man like seeing me lick her or put my fingers in her? Would I be able to make her come?*

Anonymous handwritten note, 6/8/2009

THE DINNER LASTED LONG INTO the night, and David, being a responsible host and boss, had to dismiss our guests, whom he expected at work in the morning, though not without reminding them to drive carefully since Armand's beautifully prepared meal had been accompanied by a good amount of wine. We were both so tired he barely asked about my day with Louie, and only half listened to my abridged account.

"Did you like the brooch?" he asked.

"The brooch . . . Oh, the silver comb, you mean?"

"Right, yes, the comb."

"It's wonderful. Thank you."

He smiled absently as I kissed him.

Happily, I had been careful to tuck the English riding crop behind a few piles of clothes before going downstairs to greet our guests. I was aware, however, that it was not a very good hiding place, and that I would have to get rid of the compromising object as soon as possible.

DAVID APPEARED IN THE BEDROOM, a white towel knotted around his hips. Flat stomach, chiseled pecs. He looked really athletic. Aside from his biweekly tennis dates with François Marchadeau—they always made me worry, as I speculated about what the two men might find to discuss—he also spent a half hour every day in the basement workout room. It was brief but intense.

He looked radiant, and his face did not show the slightest signs of the prior evening's excesses. He teased me:

"Get up, lazy bones! We're going to be late."

"Umm . . . I thought I started tomorrow?"

Chloe had left a confirmation message two days before: "Tuesday, June ninth, eight thirty a.m."

"That's right, Mademoiselle . . . But I didn't say anything about taking you to work."

His striking smile was extremely communicative. It had the rare power of calming and reassuring people, of making your soul vibrate to its pitch. Compared to him, Louie was opaque, hard, and unreadable.

"Well, where then?"

"Uh-uh-uuh . . . Get dressed and you shall see the light!"

IT WAS NOT JUST A play on words. The light started shining as we entered a dark tunnel almost two hours later. Okay, fine, I started putting the clues together well before that: the Gare du Nord train station; the escalator that took us up to the mezzanine; the customs official; the hostesses in what looked like airline uniforms; the yellow, white, and blue TGV . . .

My eyes opened wide in childlike delight.

"We're going to London?"

"Yes, Madame. Are you thrilled? Now you can't complain about me not being around during the week."

"You're spending the day with me?"

My feet were practically dancing, I was so delightfully surprised.

"No . . . ," he admitted sheepishly. "I have back-to-back meetings after lunch. But I thought it would be fun for you to come on a trip with me. It's still going to be great . . . You can spend the day shopping."

"No, it's going to be *really* great! When do we come back home? Tonight?"

"*You* are coming back tonight, yes. I have a really boring dinner and then another meeting tomorrow morning. There's no use dragging you to all that. Unless you are as interested in mergers and acquisitions in DTT as I."

"Not really." I fake pouted.

Since my presence wasn't needed at his side, I would be able to spend the evening in Nanterre. I was already thinking about what kind of British goodie I could bring Mom.

I curled into my first-class seat, enjoying the elegant gray leather and its comfy headrest. It wasn't long before I started dozing off. David was attending to some sort of emergency on his laptop, while I cuddled into his firm and warm body, allowing myself to daydream and ignoring the large breakfast we'd been served.

I gazed at the blurry landscape—which was reduced to long gray, green, and blue lines—and collected my thoughts . . . Playing with Hortensia's ring, which pinched my finger (it was still too small for me, even though David had had it resized), I finally settled my eyes on the silk armband peeking out from under David's shirtsleeve.

Who is Aurora Delbard, David? What does she mean to you?

No, I didn't really ask those questions. Yet in the comfort of the high-speed train, I kept thinking about Louie Barlet's cruel story. If the woman had never existed, or if she hadn't occupied the role in David's life that Louie had described, then why exactly had he gone to the trouble of telling me such a tale? And if the story was indeed true, then why had he taken it back? It only made him out to be a fabulist.

Contrary to Sophia's advice, I was not going to bring David in on the secret. Ten days before our wedding, it would be suicide. He would never understand. He would never forgive me. And no watch, no matter how gorgeous, no matter how much humiliation and sacrifice it represented, would be enough to win him back. In his eyes, I was as pure as he had seen me the night we'd met, in the room he had emptied of occupants in order to have a moment alone with me.

But I knew that by going to the Hôtel des Charmes the night before last, I had put my fate in his brother's hands. Now, in addition to the fact that my picture appeared in the Belles de Nuit catalogue, there were the naked and totally indecent photos of me posing for him. One of them was probably still at the bottom of my purse, right there, on the floor.

I shivered when I realized that something that could not be seen or heard, something that was quietly growing deep inside and making my sex palpitate, could hurt me more than any material evidence.

"Elle, is everything okay?"

Unwittingly, I must have stirred in my seat.

"Yes . . . I think I fell asleep."

"Sleep, beautiful . . . Sleep—I want you to."

His order was enchanting. Indeed, the timbre of his voice shifted to resemble that of another sorcerer, who had captivated generations of children through storytelling. Gérard Philipe and his magical tales.

"Stop!" I laughed. "When you do that, it really feels like he's right here."

To kill time as well as get my mind off of all these dark thoughts, I retrieved my tablet and tried to retrace our route from the day before on a map: Rue de la Tour-des-Dames, Rue de la Rochefoucauld, Rue Chaptal on the left, then Rue Blanche up to La Trinité . . .

Hmm, that's funny . . . it makes a lowercase e.

My interest was piqued. I continued mentally tracing our trek: east on Rue Saint-Lazare, then north on Rue Taitbout, then around Square d'Orléans, and back to Rue Saint-Lazare . . .

I can't believe it . . . now an l*!*

Though it was an approximate drawing because of the disposition of the city streets, our stroll spelled out my nickname, letter for letter. Another *l* when we took our detour onto Rue la Bruyère, and then a final *e* when we walked through the elegant Place Saint-Georges, and up to the church Notre-Dame-de-Lorette, where we'd taken the metro to Rue Drouot. Just to be sure, I highlighted the route on my tablet.

"elle" . . . This wasn't just my imagination or a product of my troubled mind. Louie knew exactly what he was doing when he led me, step by step, through New Athens. He hadn't been content to put the city at my feet; he had written me into its history, into the pavement, as though I were one of the heroines he'd described.

An abrupt whistle as we entered the Chunnel and a sudden feeling of compression in the train car interrupted my thoughts. It was too much. I understood his game far too well: taking cues from his beloved Romantic authors, he was planting a "forest of symbols" around me, a vast field of hints and coincidences, in an effort to take me hostage. No matter where I looked, no matter where my attention was drawn, I had to think of him.

List of ambiguous symbols that invariably make me think of sex: tunnels, lollipops, two-scoop ice cream cones, Christmas ornaments, spears of asparagus, triangles pointed downward, flambéed bananas or bananas peeled from the top, cucumbers, acorns, mushrooms, cut apricots, small cartons, the fleshy folds of the elbow, fire hoses, the turgescent stamen of some flowers, etc.

Words have the same effect, even when used in non-sexual contexts: ball, cock, pussy, dick, cleft, hole, bush, fur, poke, fill, ram, suck, lick, wet, finger, discharge . . .

(To be continued . . .)

Anonymous handwritten note, 6/8/2009

EVEN THOUGH I WAS NOW fully awake, I closed my eyes for the rest of the train ride for fear that David would look up from his screen and notice something in my face. I wanted to keep still, as well as weave an invisible thread between David and me, so I repeated a meditation chant that Sophia had taught me when she was going through her Ho'oponopono phase: "I love you. I am sorry. Please, forgive me. Thank you." According to Hawaiian wisdom, when these phrases are repeated over and over, they have the power to purge our bodies of toxins and reconcile us with ourselves.

WHEN WE GOT TO THE British capital, I was almost in a trancelike state. David, who spoke perfect English, was already glued to his phone and hadn't noticed anything. He dropped me off at the Savoy, one of the most prestigious luxury hotels in London. The black-and-white-check marble flooring in the entry recalled Duchesnois House. As he left, David gave me a chaste kiss on the forehead.

"Have fun, darling. If you need anything, ask the concierge, Clive. He's a perfect, pure Oxbridge Englishman. Courteous to a fault."

"Do you know him?"

"Only for the past fifteen years, dear. We used to come here with my parents. He'll bend over backward for you."

"Okay."

"I've got to go. See you tomorrow."

Clive definitely lived up to his reputation. At his suggestion, I enjoyed the spa and its beauty services. Then the man with the mustache and bristly whiskers set me up with a hotel car, and I spent the afternoon going from boutique to boutique.

Spoiled and pampered, I only had one worry for the day,

and that was to spend money that was not yet mine. I had to stock my wardrobe with more than the essentials I had gotten with Rebecca (at an unthinkable cost!). The stunning Alice had given me an idea of the level of dress among women at the station. I didn't want to let my man and boss down. For his part, I don't think this afternoon shopping spree was just an excuse to spoil me: he probably also considered the expense as a kind of investment. It was a fair exchange.

AROUND FOUR P.M., I HAD my chauffeur, Will, drop me off a couple of blocks from the Savoy, and sent him to take my purchases to the room, whence they would be sent to Paris directly—not an unusual perk for regulars of that kind of establishment. I needed some air, and some freedom.

I wandered for a while through the streets of London, which smelled more metallic and masculine than those of Paris. I couldn't help but imagine what sort of licentious anecdotes Louie would tell on such a walk. Was this the hotel where Diana and Dodi met in secret for the first time? Did prostitutes walk these streets once?

Without knowing why, it made me think of Fred. Fred, the loser from the day before. Fred, ridiculous and humiliated. I owed him an explanation and, above all, my apologies. He was right: he did deserve a face-to-face talk. But he didn't pick up his phone. Maybe he was screening his calls, still licking his wounds.

I was mulling things over a few paces from the Savoy when I noticed one of the last remaining red phone booths. Like its French equivalent, in front of the Hôtel des Charmes, it started to ring just as I was approaching it. I turned to look around, searching for a spot from which someone could be spying on me, but I didn't notice anything suspicious. Just the insistent ring. Incredulous, I entered the booth and picked up the black receiver.

"Hello? Hello? . . . Is there anybody here?" I asked in my classroom English.

No, no one was on the other end, it seemed.

However, a local specialty caught my attention: lining the booth was all manner of promotional materials for strip clubs, call girls, and escorts. From an Indian women in traditional dress to a buxom matron of new burlesque, there was something for everyone. The city must not clean the phone booths as regularly as before since the racy flyers had begun to stack up, from the more recent ones to the most yellowed. One of the flyers on top caught my eye:

FRENCH LOVE WITH ELLE

The worst part was not the use of my nickname but the naked photo of me that had been taken at the Hôtel des Charmes in the Mata Hari room, the turn-of-the-century decor of which perfectly suited the choice of font. I tore it from where it had been pinned and was about to crumple it into a ball when I noticed what was written on the back:

2—Thou shalt awaken thine senses.

It was the same message I had received the night before. The one I had decided to ignore.

I leaned my back against the cool window, my head suddenly pounding. The flyer dropped from my hand. I was incapable of any movement. The message couldn't be clearer: no matter where I was—London, Paris, New York—he was never going to leave me alone. Wherever I went, he would find me and remind me of his desires, which I met in exchange for his silence. He didn't just deal in symbols; he was also very real. Invisible but oppressive. He tracked me like an occult power follows the protagonist in a spy novel.

I stumbled out of my vermilion shelter and hailed a cab. There was no point going back to the hotel: everything I needed I had on me, including my return ticket, which I had no problem exchanging for the next train to Paris.

I tossed and turned in my seat for the whole length of the trip, like an insomniac in her bed. I was light-years away from the feeling of excitement I'd had on the way to London, shuddering at the possibility that my picture might be on other flyers, in other phone booths near the Savoy. Who knows? The hand that was working against me on this side of the Channel might have posted some on the public bulletin board in the hotel's reception hall . . . or, even more to the point, directly on David's pillow in suite number twenty-four.

I was having a hard time collecting myself, even with Sophia's mantras, which my anger had transformed: "I don't like you, I hate you . . . I am not remotely sorry. Whether you like it or not, get out of my life! Thank you."

I resisted the temptation to harass Louie's surly secretary—I didn't doubt for a second that she'd filter the call as she had the others—as well as the violent urge to go see him at Barlet Tower in person as soon as I got off the train.

Making a scene at BTV the day before I started my new job would not help my professional future. David could probably forgive me, but what about the others, the Lucs, the Chloes, the Alices? Moreover, I would have to explain to my future husband the reason behind such a show of anger and fear. Why on earth would I have attacked my brother-in-law, the very man who had been such an obliging tour guide the day before?

WHEN I ARRIVED AT GARE du Nord, I took the RER line B and then changed to line A at the Halles. I arrived in Nanterre, my eyes heavy, less than forty minutes later.

"Have you eaten?" Mom immediately asked, worried.

It was after nine o'clock, and I hadn't had a bite of anything since my cucumber sandwich during my afternoon of shopping at Covent Garden.

"No . . ."

"There's still some blanquette, if you want. Or I could make a potato salad."

"Salad."

Once I was seated and poking my fork into small cubes of potato covered in mustard grains and flaky egg yolks, I noticed that her voice sounded weaker than usual and her breathing more haggard. It was clear she was not doing well. Yet she looked happy.

"Look what I got today!"

She disappeared for a moment into the living room and came back with a vase of wildflowers.

"Wait, that's not all . . ."

She gestured toward an enormous pastry box. I immediately recognized Ladurée's celadon-and-gold logo.

"Macaroons?" I guessed.

"*Fifty* rose-flavored macaroons!"

"Your favorite . . ."

"Yes!"

She was like a girl getting a bag of candy after school.

"Do you know who it's from? Was there a card?"

"Nothing. But I have an idea . . ."

The same as mine, if I understood the way she was smiling at me: David. How could he be so perfect? More than perfect, even. I must have mentioned in passing that my mom liked rose macaroons. And now he was spoiling her like he spoiled me.

Of course the fact that he had been in direct contact with her was unsettling. But maybe, with ten days before our wedding, he was just trying to force me into finally introducing them to each other.

I typed a quick thank you text message:

Thank you for the flowers and macaroons. Mom is in heaven. I love you.

Less than a minute later:

I love you, too. But sorry, I didn't send the flowers. Your mom has another admirer!

Louie! Who else? Certainly not Fred. Nor even our neighbor, the resident dirty old man, who had once taken a fetishistic interest in our home.

Louie was trying to insert himself into every facet of my life, every nook and cranny, in his own way. But as fleeting as it was, the joy he had given Maude was priceless. For that, I could not be mad. And he knew it: through her, he was holding my heart, in his elegant hands.

"Anyway, you can't be jealous today," Mom added. "You also got a present."

"A present?"

She pointed to a small box covered in silver paper that was sitting on the buffet in the living room, next to the photos of me. I hadn't noticed it before.

"I think your friend on student council has a thing for you," she joked with a wicked smile. At least she was having fun.

"Oh . . . Yeah, it's not impossible."

I took the precaution of waiting until I was in my room before opening it. Under the disapproving eyes of my old stuffed animals, I withdrew a kind of long metallic egg. Did Sophia have this sort of thing in her collection of erotic gadgets? I preferred not to think of its obvious function and tried to repress images of it in action, in me.

The accompanying envelope contained another keycard for the Hôtel des Charmes, as well as a predictable pink Post-it featuring the same handwriting as the other two messages:

> *Ten o'clock tonight.*
> *Don't forget your present.*
> *I am certain that, this time,*
> *you will honor our engagement.*

16

June 8, 2009

I had been promising myself for months that one day I would verify whether or not the three trees planted in the small square were charms. Charm trees: the kind one plants, vaunts, and sells . . . And I was ready to give my charms away, at a loss, for a little peace and liberty.

I felt light, as though I were about to leave a piece of myself that I didn't want anymore in this room. Shed my dead skin. Yes, that was my plan, to pretend I was giving Louie everything he wanted. But I wouldn't really be there. Not with him. Not for him. All he would get was an obsolete version of the woman he had been circling all this time with his little obscene notes. He thought he'd almost caught her in his net. In reality, he would be devouring a ghost. Biting into a shadow. As for me, I would leave everything that created distance between David and me between these walls. Including the things I'd learned about him and that I never should have known. Then, and only then, I would really belong to him and only him. Annabelle Barlet, David's wife.

I don't know whom I thought I was fooling with such naive ideas. I guess it was what I needed at the time . . .

I was already late. I rushed from the metro station Saint-Georges, where a film crew was getting ready to shoot a scene whose set, a retro booth and an automobile parked nearby, recalled the Occupation. As for me, I was wandering through a scene from the nineteenth century, over the steps where Louie and I had walked the other day.

I recognized the buildings whose history he had described in such detail. I hesitated on Rue la Bruyère in the idiotic hope I'd run into Marceline and her lover, arm in arm. At the intersection of Rue Notre-Dame-de-Lorette and Rue de la Rochefoucauld, a figure of Dionysus stuck its tongue out at me from under a columned balcony. At least someone appreciated the irony of the situation. For a fraction of a second, Louie's face appeared as the impish devil and winked. He was everywhere.

Why had he decided to play the role of the perverted marquis and manipulator? What had David done to him—nothing *he* wouldn't have done in his brother's place, I was sure—to make him harass me? It made me feel like an object in an endless transaction between them. If Louie ever decided to be the man he had been for a few moments during our walk—happy, funny even, delighted to share his knowledge and interest—could we one day become . . . I don't know, friends? Instead of being yet another reason for the brothers not to get along, I could help them bond. I could be their angel of reconciliation.

"Good evening, Elle. I didn't expect to see you again so soon . . . but I am delighted, of course."

Monsieur Jacques, obliging as ever, waved from his counter and folded his long silhouette into one of his little bows, a fleeting bend of the torso reminiscent of Japanese culture. As I approached him, I caught a tart scent of bergamot.

"Thanks," I said. "Tell me . . ."

I withdrew the polished metal egg.

"Oh my!" he exclaimed, his eye gleaming. "A new puzzle?"

I often wondered about Monsieur Jacques's role in Louie's games. After all, this was his hotel. The room keys didn't circulate without his knowledge. Did he simply furnish the elder Barlet with keys and turn a blind eye to what he did with them? Like his bald head, the concierge was as smooth as he was impenetrable.

"It would appear so, yes . . ."

"No clues this time?"

"No. Just this."

I placed the object in his long, arachnidan hands, which were so delicate it was almost worrisome. He closed his fingers around the scintillating metal and inspected it with his bulging eyes.

"Marie . . ." He smiled after some reflection.

"Marie?"

"Marie Bonaparte."

"Napoleon III's . . . daughter?" I guessed.

He corrected me politely, but I noticed his eyes cloud in what looked like worry, which did not fit with his usual erect, unwavering bearing.

"Napoleon Bonaparte's great-grandniece."

"Oh. I believe you. But why an egg?"

He raised his nonexistent eyebrows and fixed his dizzyingly blue eyes on me.

"Hmm . . . No one ever told you about her relationship with the Freud family?"

"No," I admitted.

"Marie Bonaparte was a social fixture in intellectual circles of the late nineteenth century. As a result, she befriended some of the great minds of her time, including the French psychologist Gustave Le Bon."

"I've never heard of him."

"At the time, he was much talked about. His work on crowd psychology was even a kind of bestseller. He's the one who recommended Marie read Freud's *Introduction to Psychoanalysis*."

The rest seemed obvious. At last I understood where his erudition was leading.

"She also managed to meet Freud, is that it?"

"Even better: she became a patient of his, for almost fifteen years."

"That's incredible. But what about the egg?"

"Well, dear Marie Bonaparte had some fetishes. Sexual fetishes."

"Really?"

"She was incapable of knowing real pleasure. And for reasons that are still unclear to this day, she convinced herself that female frigidity originated not from an unconscious trauma . . . but an *anatomical* problem."

He lowered his voice when he said this last word, as though afraid something awful might happen.

"Anatomical? What do you mean?"

"She believed that the clitoris was too far from the vagina to achieve its goal: orgasm. She wrote several articles on the subject."

"And? She thought *this* would solve the problem?"

I pointed at the oblong object he was rolling between his palms like a pebble, having abandoned his gold-accented, black lacquer pen.

"No, not exactly. At first, she thought she could reconstruct the parts where nature had failed. She underwent no less than three operations to bring the ill-placed clitoris closer to the orifice of copulation."

I gasped.

"What? Was she crazy?"

"A little, yes. After that, she put her hopes in the still nascent field of psychoanalysis. But despite all the years she spent on the couch, even Freud himself proved unable to divert her from her obsession. As for this little thing"—he raised the egg, a fragile trophy in his hands, and looked at it admiringly—"it figured among the many intimate toys she used and abused to stimulate herself internally and experience pleasure like she had never known from an external touch. She was so convinced that one day it would 'loosen her up'—excuse my expression—that she became a devoted proponent of a new device: the vibrator. She promoted it and all its forms without any thought of recompense. For her, it was a kind of erotic sacrifice."

"Incredible."

"But don't be fooled. She may have been eccentric, but she was a good woman. During the war—she wasn't so young anymore—she personally intervened to help a number of Jewish intellectuals flee Austria and Germany. Freud included."

He stooped to return my object, his voice vaguely melancholic:

"That's the whole story. The Marie Bonaparte is on the fourth floor, the first door on your left when you step off the elevator. Have a nice evening, Elle."

No hidden meaning in his gravelly voice. Just his usual courteousness.

As I turned around, I was surprised by Ysiam's immaculate smile. Ysiam, who had led me to my first cell. Who hadn't answered my calls for help. The hand that had slipped Louie's orders under the door. Despite his gentle looks, Ysiam was a jailer.

"Please follow me, Mademoiselle."

But was it reasonable to blame the messenger? He waited as I entered the elevator, which jostled us upward. When we arrived on the fourth floor—we didn't say a word to each other during the brief mechanical ride—he moved to the right to let me by and pointed at a night-blue door. The whole floor was that color, just as the sixth was all red and the second, where the Josephine was located, all gold.

Holding my keycard in front of the lock, I was about to question him about his boss when he broke the silence that had been imposed upon him ever since our first meeting:

"This time there won't be any instructions. You'll know what to do. On your own."

"No instructions?" I cried. "And who decided there shouldn't be instructions today?"

"That I cannot tell you."

"That's your instruction, right?"

"Yes." He nodded.

I would have sworn his dark skin blushed.

"I bet you're dying to tell me . . . !" I said defiantly, playing with his show of reserve like a cat and its mouse.

The poor boy lost his perpetual look of quietude. He was so touching, with his scared, wide eyes. He looked lost, as though he were desperately searching for something to hold on to.

"Not at all!"

At last his gaze settled on the keycard in my hand. It was his escape, and he seized it. He slid the card into the reader.

The door opened. My prison was his liberation.

Without saying another word, he disappeared in the flash of an eye to the other end of the hall. Louie could be proud: Ysiam hadn't failed. He must pay him well.

I knew he'd be back to lock the door behind me.

The room did not look like a place for sleeping but more like an office. It had a sober feel, and was decorated according to a turn-of-the-century style: a desk made of polished cherry, covered in green Moroccan tapestry, a metallic ball lamp, a small worn club chair, and, on the other side of the room, under the unique barred window, a velour blood-red sofa on which had been thrown a number of cushions embroidered in gold.

A coherent ambiance, especially considering the person who'd inspired it. What was expected of me seemed pretty obvious, and I lay down on the sofa without further ado.

As before, I waited a long time before anything happened. I heard the faint and rather distant sound of the elevator as it came and went, of doors that opened and closed, and something like the clanking of a room service cart that the attendant on the floor above must have been pushing through the hallway.

There was one modern feature in the room, a flat screen hanging like a painting opposite the sofa. I only noticed it when it flickered on. I checked to make sure I wasn't sitting on a remote. No. The electronic device was responding to an outside command. There was no other possible explanation, thought I. The static quickly gave way to an image of another room.

It looked nothing like the other rooms I'd seen in the hotel. No vintage decor nor gesture toward a historical figure.

Its walls were a bluish black, the furniture consisting of a simple bed with a thick mattress and a comforter, as well as two Louis XV chairs upholstered in dark canvas. The lighting was poor, and I had to wait for two persons, one man and one woman, both naked and wearing masks, to enter, before I understood what was making the atmosphere so bizarre: their bodies glowed in the dark like two fireflies torn from obscurity by a black light, the kind dancers go wild for in nightclubs. Their skin shone brightly from the shadows. It was unreal. Every imperfection erased by the diffuse light and the effect of being filmed.

Did they know they were being observed? And if they did, who were they and why were they so willing to participate? They forwent preliminaries, undoubtedly thinking them superfluous, and got down to business so quickly that I decided they must be simple mercenaries, commissioned and paid for by Louie to put on a private show for me. The girl was smaller and more petite than I. She had two tiny bulges, like little apples, for a chest. She knelt before her partner and began using her mouth to make the flaccid and inert object between the boy's legs grow. She sucked diligently and with delicacy, using her tongue to excite his tip and only swallowing the whole shaft at privileged intervals. He grunted with increasing intensity each time her mouth jetted down his dick, which grew imperiously large, deep inside her throat.

The fact that the show was choreographed exclusively for me, that the two actors probably came from some live show in Pigalle, that it was all so artificial and fabricated, should have put me off. But indifference and disgust soon gave way to curiosity—I wanted to know how she would prolong his pleasure before the final moment. The very thing that I would have found unacceptable in an X-rated movie was now turning me on. The reality effect. I was fascinated by her lips, which were now moving slowly over the throbbing, swollen gland that shone with their desire. I hated to admit it, but yes, yes, yes . . . I found their bit madly exciting.

"More . . . Yes!"

Detecting a strange echo, I stood from the sofa and walked toward the hanging television, where I noticed that in addition to the integrated speakers, there was another source of sound, one that was more direct, more present. Indeed, the troubling fact of the matter was that the couple was making love in an adjoining room, and the wall was so thin that I could hear even the most discreet moan.

Knowing that they were so nearby, so close that I could touch them, unleashed a wild, voracious desire in me to join them. I wanted to participate. Torn between image and sound, I glued my ear to the wall, then took a step back to look at the scene on the television screen. Each peek revealed a different configuration of bodies. Each *Kama Sutra* move elicited a specific form of pleasure. Ysiam had been right, and the man who was orchestrating everything in the shadows, too: I knew what to do. I didn't need orders or instructions.

All I had to do was watch the man's hands, which were now running over the woman's body, pressing into her flesh, dashing into her orifices, a finger pushing into the crease in her ass or brushing across her brown lips engorged with desire. From my side of the electronic mirror, I slowly undressed, piece by piece, each article of clothing igniting a specific area of skin as it brushed across my body: buttocks, belly, thighs, shoulders, nipples . . . I could not take my eyes off the man's hands . . . Standing, my lace panties still in place, I tried to mime each one of his movements. I became my own lover, discovering hitherto unknown sweetness from my own touch.

As I felt my clitoris, which gleamed between my nymphae and pressed proudly into the lace of my panties, I saw the man bury his face between the petite brunette's thighs. With each lick, she shook frenetically and her backside raised over the bed. Her breasts dangled toward him. They were small, but they seemed to become bigger and more extended with each wave of pleasure. Despite the woman's small build, the man's head suddenly disappeared between her legs. He melted into her sex, his nose getting lost in her dark earthiness. He was hungry for her. He sucked, bit, and tasted every fold of her throbbing flesh. Her sighs became more strident, more frequent, and I supposed he must have introduced his tongue—a natural and effective sex toy—into her.

The orgasm took her by surprise. She arched her back in an improbable curve, throwing her head behind her and contracting each one of her muscles. Then she collapsed as though she'd been electrocuted.

When he withdrew his face from her sweet underworld, he contemplated her for a moment, like a painter before a masterpiece. *He* had made her come, and he alone. His tongue was his paintbrush, his dash of genius. But this triumph must not have been enough since he then reopened the woman's thighs and introduced his member, which seemed even bigger than when it had been in the girl's mouth.

The man cried out strongly as he penetrated her. They were facing each other. His legs were planted into the ground. The girl was now lying across a small table in a corner of the room. She sighed in pleasure, and he turned her around and felt her backside with his penis, looking for her soaking vulva. He moved in and out of her as he stimulated her engorged button, his hand resting on the young woman's pubis.

"Yes . . . yes, don't stop," she begged.

Her voice was breathy. Given the camera angle and the mask, I couldn't see all of her face, but I was able to make out her parted mouth—it was probably as wet as her vulva—striped with a few stray hairs. She moaned, in shorter and shorter intervals, at higher and higher decibels.

The synchronous stimulation of her most sensitive areas seemed to have gotten the better of her. Each time the man entered her, she projected her palpitating flesh to meet her assailant. She groaned now, yes, she let out a primitive, husky, animalistic growl. She hiccuped pleasure that seeped through her whole body. I watched as her limbs and nape of the neck shook uncontrollably.

Her second orgasm hit her like an uppercut. Her head tipped to the side, and after a long spasm ran up her spine, she grew still.

I was equally shattered. I felt moisture in the hollow between my legs, which started shaking suddenly, bringing me back to earth. I was no longer floating. I was one year old, I was a thousand years old, I was crippled with unfulfilled desire that had been contained for too long. I rested against the wall, then got on all fours, a rather grotesque position, thanks to which I was able to crawl to the sofa. I buried my nose in the red velour and noticed the metallic egg sitting on the soft fabric. It was looking at me. It was provoking me. It was waiting for me to react.

Behind me on the screen, the action hadn't stopped. Satisfied that he had made his partner come—he patted her backside and improvised a few words, like "nice little ass for my

cock" and other rather degrading phrases—but not yet sati-
ated, he started riding her again, furiously thrusting himself
into her open lips that still shimmered from her first orgasms.
What had preceded seemed more like a warm-up, what with
his show of energy—some might call it roughness or even violence. He crushed his victim with pleasure. The woman was
practically screaming. It was impossible to tell if they were
cries of encouragement or for help. If they were expressing
pleasure or pain.

I pushed aside the small stretch of embroidered cloth that
contained my vulva. A translucent liquid stippled my inner
thighs. I considered the fact that no man had ever put me in
such a situation before: I wanted more, but I also wished it
would end, in happiness, all at once. Contradictory impulses
such as only occur in the unique pleasure that thrills and ex-
hausts us.

Or maybe yes . . . Maybe right now, this egg, this capitulation of my body to the mercy of a triumphant Louie, who was
witnessing every last detail somewhere backstage . . . maybe I
was about to experience my first sublime undoing.

When at last I introduced the oblong object into my dripping vagina, the girl on the screen was orgasming again. I
quickly pushed the thing deeply inside me, as though I were in
a hurry to join her. My sex contracted around the cold object,
surprised by the intruder's unexpected visit, then adopted it.
After I clenched my buttocks and perineum a few times, it
even started playing with it, swallowing it whole, sucking it
into an abyss from which my fingers could not retrieve it. A
new king in my kingdom.

At last I found the strength to sit up on the sofa, which
welcomed my abandon with that smooth softness of old uphol-

stered furniture, worn by other bodies that had lost themselves here. I spread my legs wide, showing my sex to the screen. I felt as though I were being penetrated by the two protagonists. As though their pleasure could be communicated through the screen and touch me, giving me their surplus of delight.

The man's face, which only occasionally emerged from the shadows during their position changes, was softer or more hollow depending on the light. At first he looked like David, smiling, reassuring, his young face between my thighs.

At that precise moment, I felt the egg's first vibrations inside of me. They were so strong that they radiated through-out my vulva, touching my lips as well as the incandescent point of my clitoris, which had grown too sensitive to touch. Pleasure came in waves that were being controlled by an anon-ymous hand.

Then, when I saw him again, as he withdrew his head from between my legs, my virtual lover looked like Louie, with his tense face and sunken, burning eyes. He was a predator, a wolf who would tear me apart with his teeth. The spasms emanating from my vagina felt as though I'd been fanged. As though the most powerful jaw I'd ever encountered had my vagina in its mouth and was ripping me apart, devouring me. Deep down, I felt an explosion inside. A mute and strangely slow-moving explosion, as if I were being reconfigured from the inside out. Each quiet wave chipped away at the terror in which I had been submerged just a moment before. Now *I* was being undone. My head jerked back suddenly. I let out a long, silent cry, my mouth the shape of an O. I savored every second of pleasure, the delicious present tense. I never wanted it to end.

I fell back onto the sofa, my body heavy. It felt dismem-bered. A puzzle of exhausted flesh. I noticed the screen had gone black. The egg had also been turned off, and was now rolling around outside my gaping hole.

He had not touched me at all. He had not even come into the room. And yet, I admitted to myself with a happy sob, an ecstatic and bitter smile on my lips: Louie had made me come. Louie Barlet had possessed me.

And I hadn't held back.

17

JUNE 9, 2009

Nothing on the console in the entry. Nothing in the mail-box at Duchesnois House. The following day was devoid of anonymous missives. I refrained from asking the ever-diligent Armand since I figured he would have made sure I received any new messages.

I could have taken this epistolary silence as good news. I could have interpreted it as a contented withdrawal, an armi-stice. Filled with images from the night before, my predator, whoever he was, was perhaps releasing his prey. Maybe he was loosening his grip for a moment.

But I didn't believe it. The absence seemed even more men-acing than the web he had been weaving before.

I SPENT MORE THAN A half hour getting dressed. I wanted to make a good impression on my first day at BTV. I knew ev-eryone was going to be looking at me, and that all the Alices of the station would start casting perfidious looks in my direction as soon as I arrived. I owed it to myself—and to David—to be without reproach, despite my round curves, which were too voluptuous to be as chic as I would have wished. I finished the outfit with my Louboutins. I remembered trying them on in front of a beaming David, in that boutique in the Galerie Vivienne, and feeling torn between girlish delight and the distinct sensation that such accessories were leading me into a world of artifice. Mom was dying of cancer, and I was slack-jawed at a pair of thousand-euro high heels . . .

"HELLO, ANNABELLE."

"Hello, Chlo—"

"It's eight twenty-eight," interrupted the young blonde in her tight suit. "David will be waiting for you in the main conference room at eight thirty-five with the whole team. If you would like, that leaves you with just enough time for coffee."

She had been looking out for me in the lobby of Barlet Tower, undoubtedly for a while. Her arms were filled to the max with a pile of shirts, a stack of magazines, and a bunch of stamped envelopes. It was all probably meant for her employer: my man.

"That's okay, thanks."

She looked relieved.

"Okay, great. Let's go, then."

Teetering anxiously, she led me to the elevators. Her heels, which were much too high for her, clopped through the lobby. Once we were in the brushed steel box, she reeled off my schedule—as devised by David, I imagined—in a nervous voice:

"After the official introductions, you have a meeting with Albane Leclerc at nine thirty, for at least two hours. Then I will take you to your office. You'll see, it's really nicely situated, with a southern-facing view, and between David and Louie's offices."

Why wasn't I surprised?

I stopped her and asked about something she'd said two sentences before.

"Albane Leclerc?"

"David hasn't talked about her?"

"No . . ."

"She's the editor in chief of your show. She will help you with the content of your first episodes of *Culture Mix*. She'll also help brief your team on how to film the different topics."

Anticipating my questions, she continued:

"Young, but really professional. Her father directed *The Ocean* for the group for twenty years. She works closely with Luc."

LUC DORÉ, THE DIRECTOR OF the station. I'd met him at the dinner David had hosted for me.

"In other words, she followed in her father's footsteps."

"Yes, in a way."

There were limits to David's trust in me. He may have introduced me to his little army as his secret weapon, but I had a chaperone to guide me through this unknown world so that if I made the slightest gaffe, it could be corrected immediately and its impact mitigated.

A discreet beep announced our arrival on the nineteenth floor—the top floor. Chloe rushed out of the elevator, her eyes scanning an illegible scrawl on her notepad.

"This afternoon," she began rattling off again, "at two thirty, you have your first production meeting with Luc Doré; Philippe Di Tomaso, the executive producer; and Christopher Haynes, our artistic director. The order of the day is visual design. Chris has already done some mock-ups. In theory, all you have to do is come to a decision with Luc."

Everything was going so fast! And there was no emergency button on hand to stop it . . . What could I say? That it was all one big misunderstanding? That I didn't belong here? That a crowd of people more competent than I was waiting downstairs?

I recognized the windowed room where I had been introduced to Louie. Instinctively, I looked for his silhouette—the scrawny, birdlike shadow—among the group of people already waiting for us. There were about twenty, all holding cups. To my great surprise, I did not see him. Apparently, the director of communication didn't think it was worth his time.

David appeared at the same time, beaming in a pearl-gray suit I'd never seen before (I had given up on exploring his closet, a veritable Ali Baba's cavern of male elegance).

"Everyone is here. Perfect!"

"Eight thirty." Chloe nodded. "Should we wait another couple of minutes?"

"No, let's get started. I have a conference call with Seoul in fifteen minutes."

During the quarter hour dedicated to my induction, in which David blended light humor with more intense references to "the high stakes of Thursday night prime time, which has to capture our audience's attention so they'll stay with us over the weekend," I kept expecting to see his brother appear. But no one else came to join us. The windows on the corridor were only darkened by journalists in white shirts and Chloe clones.

Sitting at a corner of the table, half hidden by a row of politely scrutinizing heads, Alice, the tall blonde, was silently screaming with boredom over the speech, its orator, and especially its subject. She was playing with her smartphone and resolutely ignoring everything being said, so much so that I was surprised to see a disdainful smile cross her face when my man expressed his faith in me to revamp the time slot.

When David finally announced the end of recess, initiating a small round of flaccid applause, Chloe crept toward my rival and whispered I don't know what kind of reprimand into her ear. The beautiful creature, with her fake breasts and formfitting dress, quickly straightened and exclaimed, visibly irritated:

"Now? What does he want?"

It sounded like she was in trouble. But I couldn't help thinking that a boss trying to seduce one of his employees would behave exactly the same way, if he wanted to lay her in his office without awakening suspicion.

The assistant took her by the arm, signaling that she should be discreet, and led her to the hall. She was like a little tugboat towing a majestic liner, whose swaying hips captivated all the men's gazes. I noticed more than one head turn, even though her colleagues had known her for years.

"HI, I'M ALBANE. YOU'RE ELLE, right?"

In the office's stuffy atmosphere, which was tightly controlled by the all-powerful, debonair David, I immediately took a liking to this young and pretty brunette, this tomboy with a charming smile and a direct tone of voice. She was wearing an open shirt, worn canvas pants, and walking shoes that looked more adapted to a hiking trail than thick office carpeting. Her only accessory was a simple silver chain around her neck . . . She was nothing like all the fashionistas at BTV.

She emerged from behind a wall of people and held out a willowy but energetic hand.

"Yes. I mean, it's Annabelle . . . but everyone calls me Elle."

"The powers that be have decided that at the station you shall be Elle . . . So if you don't mind, let's keep it that way."

"Not a problem. It suits me."

Bossy. But open, and much more pedagogical than her frankness would suggest. She spent a good part of the morning explaining the nuts and bolts of the job, and took the time to go over all the jargon she had herself been using for years. She was patient, but she did not hesitate to scold me if I wasn't being reactive enough. The fact that I was soon to be the big boss's wife did not impress her. And she did not mince words. I realized that the professional friendship between her family and the Barlets put her above the fray . . . or maybe it was just that her obvious ability meant she could easily go elsewhere in case of friction.

"I have to go," she said at twelve on the dot. "But we'll see each other really soon. You can't get me off your back that easily!"

It sounded more like a promise than a real threat. Albane was going to be an ally, I could tell already.

TWELVE OH-NINE, AS CHLOE WOULD say. She had just finished setting up my office. She hadn't lied: the space was bright, extravagantly large for someone of my age and experience, and situated on the top floor with all the directors, an indecent privilege. The bay window had a spectacular view of the outskirts of Paris.

Twelve twelve. Before leaving for lunch, she handed me a building and cafeteria badge, with a picture I didn't remember having posed for (where had David gotten it?). A chattering herd, no doubt her colleagues, called her over, and they all made their way to the company cafeteria on the tower's second floor.

Twelve twenty-two. I was playing with the brand-new phone that sat atop my desk, the only visible decoration, in the ridiculous hope of getting an invitation to lunch. I resisted the urge to call David, who was of course unavailable. I didn't want to get my feelings hurt when he said he couldn't. As for Louie, I still hadn't seen him, and that was out of the question.

Twelve forty-five . . . I couldn't take it anymore, so I called Sophia. By chance, she picked up immediately.

TWENTY MINUTES LATER, WE WERE sipping sickeningly sweet Monacos on a terrace of a nearby brasserie called Le Saint-Malo. We picked up our usual conversational thread over salads. It was reassuring after my morning in the unfamiliar and almost hostile environment of my new job.

"Whoa, your ring is really tight!" exclaimed my friend when she saw the redness of my finger. "Do you think you'll be able to take it off and put it back on, come D-day?"

"Yeah, look . . ."

With a great deal of effort, I dislodged the pink-gold ring from my finger. She took it and inspected it more closely.

Her eyes shone with envy.

"Well, hon, don't get fat . . ."

"I'll have it enlarged."

"Be careful, though, it's not the kind of material that can stretch forever. It's pretty but fragile."

Was she still talking about the ring?

She stared at the object for a while, taking in all its contours. She was mute with admiration, daydreaming. Then, as she brought it up to her eye:

"Whom did you say it belonged to before?"

"Hortensia. David's mother. And her mother before her.

But I don't know her name. Anyway, I'm glad I got it off. Armand is supposed to have our names and the date added tomorrow."

She nodded without taking her eyes off the ring.

"Mmm-hmm . . . What year were David's parents married?"

"I have no idea. Considering David and his brother's age, I would say sometime between the mid- to late sixties. Why?"

"Because then . . . your charming future husband must be the child of a couple of ghosts!"

"What are you talking about?"

Gravely, she pointed to the inside of the ring, which had been filed down to hide the various inscriptions.

"See for yourself."

"I don't see anything . . ."

"Go on. If you turn the ring so the light skims the surface, you can see an old engraving. I can't make out the date, but the year is still visible: 1988."

She was right. Scatterbrained Sophia, the cabaret dancer, the collector of men and sex toys, had deciphered a truth in the very ring I had been sporting for several days.

"You're right . . . ," I breathed. "I can't believe I didn't see it before."

The date had definitely been shaved down, but under the right angle, I could still make out the four numbers. One degree more or less in another direction and it disappeared. If you looked at it straight on, as most people would, and as I myself had admired it on several occasions, the ring kept its secret tightly guarded.

I was overcome.

"How old was your Prince Charming in '88?"

"Nineteen," I said limply.

"They got engaged and then married over the course of a few weeks," Louie had said: 1988, the year of David's first marriage. It was a slap in the face.

Why had Louie felt the need to pretend this truth, perhaps the only truth in all his stories, was a lie? Why take it back like that? Out of fear? But fear of what, of whom?

"Okay. You should tell your honey that it's not very classy to buy a ring at a flea market and pretend it's a family heirloom."

"I'll tell him . . ."

Quick: I had to change the subject. I didn't want to break down in front of her. I forced a smile and asked a non sequitur:

"And Rebecca? Any news?"

"No, nothing. It's getting annoying. I'm broke and two months late on rent. If she doesn't call about another job, I don't know where I'll be next month."

"Worst-case scenario, you can always stay in my old room at Mom's house," I offered.

"Thanks, kiddo . . . But it's not exactly fun at your mom's place right now."

She smiled apologetically.

"Have you stopped by the agency?" I asked.

"Even there she's completely AWOL. I don't know how she manages her business, but that's not how you get rich. Anyway, it doesn't concern you anymore . . ."

She wasn't criticizing me, just a little nostalgic for the days when we both engaged in the same illicit activity and belonged to the same strange and fated community. No doubt she thought the time had been too short, too fleeting. Sophia had always seen us as sisters. David's appearance in my life had changed things.

I knew Sophia would always be in my life. But our good-bye hug in front of Barlet Tower, just before the hordes of lunchers engulfed us, felt final.

I recognized a few faces from my induction in the elevator on my way back to the office. They gave me the silent treatment. No one dared ask how it was going, or if I had enjoyed my solo lunch. First-day hazing in full gear. But what did I know? Really, this was my *first* first day.

Feeling nervous, no doubt in part due to Sophia's revelation, I absently followed the troop out the elevator. After walking halfway down the hall, I realized I was on the wrong floor. Here were located some of BTV's studios and sound-stages. The partitions were also made of glass, but there was no external light, and the hallways were much darker than on the top floor, where it was always extraordinarily bright. Despite the darkness, I immediately recognized two shadows occupying one of the smaller sets on my right. From where I stood, they could not see me, but I was afraid the slightest movement might alert them to my presence. So I stayed where I was, immobile, watching them. I was terrified they would suddenly come out and run into me.

David seemed calm and in control. His interlocutor, on the other hand, looked exasperated. She ran a nervous hand through her hair, her torso contorting gracelessly. From where I stood, it was impossible to be sure, but I would have sworn her chest was heaving more erratically than usual. Was she crying?

In any case, she was not speaking. Rather, she listened to her boss, who, I imagined, was talking in a measured and con-soling tone, judging by the way he placed his hand on her arm, then shoulder.

Suddenly, Alice lost her composure and collapsed into David's arms. For his part, David held her for a moment—to me, it seemed like an eternity—before slowly pushing her away with characteristic gentility.

Really? You're sure . . . you prefer her over me?

When I was little, I used to hide behind the door to the living room to watch whatever movie was playing. I would try to think of what the characters were saying. I did the same here, imagining the words that might plausibly be coming out of the tearful woman's luscious lips.

Yes, she's the one. I'm sorry, David would say.

Whatever he actually said, his words appeared to have calmed the beautiful blonde, as well as crucified her. She had clearly been taken down several notches. With her tail between her legs, she slunk out the studio through a small door hidden in the set, heading out the building, I supposed.

I was proud of him. He had killed her hopes, but without being brutal or gratuitously mean. He had acted like a good CEO, firm but just, concerned about the interests of the whole but also careful not to hurt any of its parts. Alice had been put in her place. I knew other rivals would present themselves one day or another, here or in one of the many cases when I would not be around to see. But his loyalty that day, which closed the door on an old temptation, opened the door to our mutual commitment.

I saw that my mix-up when I got off the elevator on the wrong floor had not been an accident. I had needed to believe in David, to see his love in the world—not just in the amazing presents. To see his love in action, not just hear it in words. The mute show I had just witnessed was worth more to me than all the gifts. I didn't care if he'd been married to an Aurora or even an Alice before me. I was the one he had chosen here and now, against all odds.

Above all others.

18

Isolation: A state or situation of being isolated (see To Isolate) or that is isolated.

   To Isolate: To set or place someone apart from others.

I looked up the dictionary definition, but it didn't make me feel better. Cooped up in my office, I went from contemplating the sky and its infinite meteorological variations to consulting a dictionary that some anonymous hand had left here for me during the lunch hour. I also reread my notes from my meeting with Albane. They made me feel even more inadequate and maladapted. David had given me the nicest present in the world, but it was also a harsh mirror, in which everything I was not—not *yet*, my mother would be quick to correct—became painfully apparent.

I MUST HAVE DOZED OFF because when Chloe burst in, wide-eyed and indignant, I started and felt dazed for several seconds.

"Is everything okay?" she asked, worried.

"Yes . . ."

"Because they're waiting for you . . . in conference room number three. Two thirty . . ."

She didn't say anything, but I could tell she was furious

with me for ruining her beautiful scheduling—and on my first day, no less. But she was magnanimous enough not to notify me as to the number of minutes of which I was guilty. She gestured toward the door in a way that seemed to suggest I might miss it, and invited me to follow her, posthaste. As we wove through the maze of hallways, the characteristic click-clack of her high heels told me to hurry up.

I DON'T KNOW WHAT I perceived first. His silhouette? His laugh? Or maybe the lavender notes of his cologne, which floated out of the room, inviting me in?

He was surrounded by three other men, including Luc Doré, whom I recognized by his silver mane and Buddha-like face. He was speaking loudly, copiously, and looked very much at ease. Yet there was something incongruous about his presence here. And not simply because of what I knew about him or the other circumstances in which we had interacted. I could tell from his excessive confidence: he was not in his element. He was playing a part, and even if it didn't show, this was an act. No doubt he detested his interlocutors.

"Elle!" Louie exclaimed when I at last entered his field of vision. "We had given up on you. I see you've already understood the name of the game here: power belongs to the one who makes others wait."

I blushed. The rest of the group turned toward me. They introduced themselves, everyone except for Luc, who gave me a friendly hug.

"Welcome, Elle. I didn't have a chance to tell you again this morning, but we're all very happy you're joining the team. Truly!"

He placed both hands on my shoulders as he said this.

The gesture was purely friendly—Luc was a hands-on kind of guy—but I could have sworn I saw the elder Barlet brother wince. Though it only lasted a moment, he was annoyed to see me in the hands, however chaste, of another man.

"Louie, are you staying with us?" asked Luc.

"Hmm . . . Why not? After all, the visual design of a new prime-time show *does* affect the station's image. Doesn't it?"

The others murmured agreement.

I hadn't seen Louie since his altercation with Fred two days before. He looked tired, his features more hollow than I remembered. A supreme and sublime injustice: the change highlighted everything about him that was most pure and sensual, his animal side. Despite his infirmity, he reminded me of a wild beast whose every movement expressed all the force and energy of life on the verge of bursting forth. Barlet Tower was his glass cage. He accepted his fate, but like any wild animal, he could not help looking for a way out, a road to the jungle where he could run free. He would devour his keepers and trainers if the moment ever presented itself.

"Chris, will you show us your work?"

Chris, a lanky blonde with a beard, was like so many other young graphic designers in that he looked like a teenager. He opened a laptop he'd been carrying under his arm, and after a few taps on the keyboard, his ideas appeared on the screen.

"Right, so this is more of an urban look." He played up his British accent. "Concrete, all gray, post-hip-hop . . ."

Decoded: giant letters made to look like graffiti on a brick wall.

" . . . and at the same time really laid-back," he finished pompously. "More Berlin hippie-cool than New York speed. See what I mean?"

I didn't like it at all, even if I did get his pretentious vagaries. I didn't say anything, of course, but it must have shown because Luc gave me a look and asked:

"Elle? What do you think?"

"Umm . . . I'm having trouble forming an opinion based on one idea. Can we see the others?"

The artistic director didn't say a word. I had just entered his enemy camp, along with all the other uncultivated jerks without any visual sense who weighed in on his creations like they were choosing wallpaper. He hated me already. It was obvious.

"Yes," he said, his voice pinched. "There are always other options . . ."

Meaning: bad options.

As he went through other designs featuring logos, credits, and some aspects of the set where I would soon be parading around, I felt Louie's presence behind me. From the smell of his cologne—the vanilla was beginning to dominate the floral notes—as well as his feverish natural odor, I could tell he was only a step away. When he leaned over my shoulder, no doubt under the pretext of getting a better view of the screen, I could feel his breath on the back of my neck—I had put my hair up, using the famous comb—where one rebellious strand of hair was idly floating.

Every time he exhaled, I grew weaker. The skin on my neck shivered at each breath of sweet, hot air. In spite of myself, a tremor ran up my spine like a confession.

"I like the more bucolic theme," I said abruptly, my voice haggard.

A naive ambiance that recalled Henri Rousseau's exotic paintings. It was more of a tropical forest scene than one of the countryside in Vendée.

As I said this, I turned toward Luc, forcing the man behind me to step back. Social reflexes, the ones we learn when we are young and which the body performs instinctually, can be really useful sometimes.

He shot me an angry look. And I knew that, here or elsewhere, I could not escape him so easily. The palpitations in my stomach, as well as the iron fist gripping Mount Venus below, were flagrant proof.

"Okay," said the grizzled director, "but why nature?"

"Well," I improvised, "firstly, because it seems less obvious than an urban design for talking about culture and society."

And *bam!* in Chris the aesthete's face. And a point for me, judging from the way Philippe Di Tomaso was nodding his head. He was a short man whose coloring and general physique resembled a crumpled prune. He had yet to say one word.

"Also, it seems like a good way to signal to our audience that we won't just be dealing with what's going on in Paris. And that decentralization is a key feature of our project, and that we're not bohos without any connection to real life."

"Not bad," Luc Doré said approvingly, a smile growing across his face.

I had gone with the first thing that came to mind, the kind of marketing mumbo jumbo my professors in school had always warned against. But it seemed to have pleased the people in my meeting. I was beginning to discover that, in the working world, a little bit of well-crafted bullshit could achieve more than thoughtful considerations. *Sigh.* It was better to impress than convince.

"Louie? Your opinion?"

"On Chris's designs . . . or Mademoiselle Lorand's lovely speech?"

His eyes bored into mine. I was petrified, and absolutely incapable of reacting. Nevertheless, deep inside my stone body,

I could feel some of my organs beating like crazy: my heart, of course, and also my sex, that traitor, which was stirring.

Could he tell? When his eyes finally drew themselves away from my face, they traveled over my black dress, lecherously wandering through every fold, as though it were a thin veil of mist.

Which moment had he preferred the night before? Which moment had titillated him the most? I remembered the egg as it was leaving me, sticky with pleasure, lingering like a misshapen member, laboring to get out . . . as though it were his penis.

"I think that what Elle has just said is actually very sensible."

The producer was coming to my rescue.

"Really?"

Louie straightened as much as his cane and handicap would allow. He looked like a peacock on its territory, his posture expressing exactly how he saw us: vulgar farm animals.

"Yes," Luc affirmed. "If we want to get viewers excited about a prime-time show on culture, we cannot limit our target audience to a small elite that spends its evenings at the Châtelet theater and its weekends in Bayreuth. We have to breathe more life into it!"

Based on the embarrassed silence that followed, I understood that Louie could put the station director in his place without so much as sneezing—and maybe even have him fired right there and then. But he contained himself and even abandoned my trembling body, which was overcome with waves of pleasure and pain, to focus on the man who had contradicted him.

"We want to produce an ambitious cultural program . . . not another *Farmer Wants a Wife*!"

"What are you proposing?" Philippe asked, fearlessly looking him up and down. "Special episodes on your little boyfriends in the Marais?"

To my great surprise, Louie did not grab Monsieur Prune by the collar—which he could have easily done—but remained as cool as a cucumber.

"No. I actually know how to differentiate between my personal tastes and our mission with respect to our audience. And, excuse me, but your example is stereotypical and offensive."

"All right, well, what would you have?" Luc challenged.

"I'm not saying we should do a show for the privileged few. Au contraire. I think having access to pleasure is a fundamental right. In my opinion, exciting the brain is just as vital as bodily delights."

A sultry look in my direction. I recalled his progressive, almost libertine speech from the Sauvage Gallery.

But was he still speaking of art and culture? No, cried my vagina, which was so wet it had spontaneously started to adhere to the strip of cotton in my panties. I discreetly shifted my pelvis, trying to unstick myself. It only made things worse. The fabric worked its way into my fleshy fold, grazing the pink button that was so hungry for contact.

"What do you want to talk about, then? The Eskimo art of smoking fish?"

"Not specifically," he replied, his serious tone a striking contrast to Luc's sarcasm. "Unless it becomes fashionable here. When that happens, why not?"

"So you want to do a trend magazine, a society show?" said Luc.

"Yes . . . and no. I think our audience would get excited about the idea of knowing today what their neighbors won't be able to get enough of tomorrow. You can call them trends if you'd like; I call them nuggets. Things that are still uncommon today, but that everyone is soon going to want in their homes, in their wardrobes, in and of themselves."

He paused to let the turn of phrase sink in.

"It could be a book, an album, an accessory, a recipe, or a new way of behaving in society. That's culture today. It consists of powerful and ephemeral phenomena that dictate what we do more than politics or religion. What moves crowds today? The pope? Protests against legislation? No . . . People get excited about the latest tablet, artistic flash mobs, sneak previews of steamy films. That's what titillates. That's what excites people."

As though addressing this speech to me, and me alone, he stood and walked behind me. Then he took advantage of his newfound proximity to lean over me and rest his free hand on my chair, right next to the elastic of my sticky panties. I would have given anything at that moment to put my hand there . . . and push his hand away from me without making a scene, too.

He went on, pretending not to have noticed his effect on me, like a butterfly who has no notion of its devastating effects.

"It's a world of ideas where everyone can and must look for a way to make everyday meaning. Don't you see how our lives sorely lack sublimity?"

The others were silent. They no doubt had the intelligence to understand what Louie was saying, but were also smart enough to see how his idea, once it was fleshed out in images and shown on television, could be dangerous, subversive even. In other words, it was controversial, and it would be difficult to attract advertisers, who were typically drawn to simple topics that had already been proved to please.

Luc looked to his colleagues for support—Philippe had thrown in the towel, and Chris was quietly despairing over the fact that the conversation had veered so far from his ideas—then, receiving none, said:

"Okay, I am not saying it's not a good idea. But do you have an example of a specific topic so that we can get a better idea of what you mean? Something you could see being on the first show . . ."

"Don't you think we should invite Albane if we're going to discuss this kind of issue?"

I do not know what inspired me to brave the source of my torment, the man whose power over me—my sex could attest to it—grew with every passing day, every passing hour. Perhaps I was trying to break the spell while there was still time, while we were still surrounded by others, he and I.

He straightened brusquely, facing me again.

"I've already spoken with her."

"What? When?" Luc protested.

"More than a month ago. She gave me fifteen minutes for a spot I've been developing."

That was not a simple favor. Even a newbie like me could see that within the station's hierarchy this was a capital offense. The director of communication never should have arrogated to himself such power. He had overstepped the station's director and the producer.

But both men grinned and bore it.

"And what's it about?"

"Considering your delay, don't tell me it bothers you that I found some material?"

For my part, I wondered what he had on my new friend that could have led her to commit such a faux pas. She seemed so fiercely independent. Had he slept with her? Did her self-confidence come from these kinds of secret dealings?

Louie's cane banged against the floor as he walked toward the translucent door.

"No, obviously it's a big help," Luc grumbled. "But allow me at least to ask about this . . . unexpected editorial line?"

"Knowing you, I think you'll like it. It's a completely contemporary topic . . ."

His sardonic smile hinted at something venomous. The two other men pretended not to notice, but Luc Doré challenged him, his tone bitter.

"What's that supposed to mean?"

"Did you know that in Japan more than a third of high school girls and college students are forced to sell their charms in order to pay for their frivolous desires: clothing, outings, mobile phones, et cetera?"

"That's your topic?" Philippe choked.

"No, I'm interested in France. There are less of them here, but there does exist a small community of pretty young women who make ends meet . . . horizontally."

Me, lying on the sofa in the Marie Napoleon room. He wouldn't dare!

Like the night before, I thought I might collapse into one exhausted heap, powerless, completely dominated by his virility, by his sex.

"That's not very novel . . . ," Luc gnashed. "There's already a book on it, and even a made-for-TV movie, if I'm not mistaken."

"You're right. But these days we're not just talking about desperate young girls getting screwed in dingy attic rooms out in the projects. Today the offerings also include high-end women. They're educated, and they circulate in posh environments . . . Some even have careers, high-powered positions."

"Escorts, you mean!" exclaimed the producer.

"Better. They don't just accompany men, but neither are they simply luxury whores. They're like geishas, to get back to Japan. Women who are capable of titillating their clients' bodies and minds."

"And what are these dream creatures called?"

Philippe's lusty laugh betrayed a personal interest in the topic, suggesting he had probably already rented girls by the hour or the night.

"Hotelles."

"Hotels?"

The mention of the neologism made me dizzy: Rebecca and Louie were surely in collusion.

He spelled the word. And with each letter, his lashes blinked at me. The gesture was less emphatic than a wink, more subtle, more intimate. I could feel him touching me from a distance. In my head, my chest, my middle, my sex.

Had I been capable of making the slightest movement, I would have strangled him. But there I was, panting, torn between shame, anger, and an invisible force compressing my vagina, just before pleasure, just after pain, somewhere deep inside me, where my most visceral fears reside. I felt like coming and fighting at the same time, and was incapable of wresting the hate from my being without also losing every shred of fascination and brute desire. It was becoming impossible to sustain, and if Luc hadn't taken it upon himself to put an end to the meeting, saving me from this strange volcanic torpor, I think I would have broken down in tears in front of them all.

Robotically, I left the room, several long seconds after Louie had disappeared into the hall. I made my way blindly back to my office like a zombie, guided by a sense of direction that surprised even me. I collapsed into my leather office chair like a rag doll, with my back to the city and its madness. I gazed unseeing at the empty surface of my desk. "Your computer will be installed tomorrow," Chloe had promised.

"Chloe?"

One major quality of David's assistant was that she always answered on the first ring, or, at worst, the second, but never more.

"Yes, Elle . . . what can I do for you?"

"You didn't tell me if I had any other meetings after the visual design meeting . . ."

The "strip Elle naked" meeting would have been more apt.

"You don't have anything else scheduled. That was already a lot for a first day, though, wasn't it?"

Her tone was smiling, conspiratorial. She sounded more relaxed than the other times we had spoken. Since I hadn't shown myself to be hostile, she had no doubt decided it was time to cozy up to the boss's future wife.

"I guess . . . ," I murmured absently.

"By the way, David asked me to tell you to go home after Luc let you out."

"Oh, okay."

Attentive. Considerate. Giving me special treatment. In a word: David. But he probably did not know about his brother's presence at my meeting, and how much his excusing me from work for the rest of the day was a big relief.

How was I going to be able to manage more than a day in the same office as Louie?

"Also, did you find your package?"

Package, package . . . I scanned the room, looking for a . . .

"Yes . . . ," I stuttered.

She had not left it on my desk but on a chair, which was hidden from anyone entering the room.

Silver paper. A new cousin in my Ten-Times-a-Day's family.

"Perfect. I'll leave you, then. See you tomorrow, Elle."

I hung up without responding. I was already on my feet.

The package was bigger and heavier than the others. In addition to an envelope, whose contents I already knew—the room key; a card (with a commandment); an invitation—it contained a large night-blue jewelry box. It was considerably more sizable than the one David had given me with Hortensia's ring.

I waited to open it and instead began with the card. Magnetic key, nameless and without number, from the Hôtel des Charmes. I knew it. A note in that same round and soft, beguiling script.

Ten o'clock,
in your finest.

He had never been so enigmatic. As for the new commandment, its message was clear, and it was easy for me to guess what would be expected of me in a couple hours.

3—Thou shalt abandon thyself to their unflinching gaze.

The only thing that was really surprising was the jewelry box. I choked when I finally saw what it contained. Atop a silk cushion sat the most extraordinary necklace I had ever seen. Even the rarest of pieces displayed at Antiquités Nativelle did not compare. Three rows of extravagant emeralds—more than three dozen, of varying sizes—linked together with pink gold and accentuated with an infinite number of diamonds that hung in chains or small clusters around the necklace's perimeter. You did not have to be an expert to guess that such a piece contained a fabulous legacy and was of inestimable worth. One would have to be mad to offer such a gift and, what's more, to send it in a simple box, entrusting it to the careless hands of postal workers and secretaries.

Speechless, I gazed at every aspect of the piece, a patrimonial gem that by some miracle had arrived in my hands. Suddenly my phone rang: cruel, banal, modern.

"Hey, kiddo, it's me."

Sophia, obviously.

"Hey. How are you today?"

"Umm . . . Didn't we just have lunch together three hours ago?"

"Right, yes . . . Sorry. I'm kind of out of it."

"I can tell. And you're not the only one."

"What's up?"

"With me? Nothing . . . nothing directly. But I ended up walking by Rue du Roi-de-Sicile again after lunch."

The street where Belles de Nuit was located.

"And?"

"So you know how the last time I went, she didn't answer? Well, this time, I ran into the concierge. I sweet-talked her and told her I'd left some things upstairs . . ."

"And she let you in?"

"Yep . . . And in retrospect I wish she hadn't."

"Why do you say that?"

"Because something is really fishy, chica: the place was totally empty. No Rebecca, no filing cabinets. Not even a trash can with old papers. A total desert. The Gobi Desert in Paris."

As I listened, I typed BDN's URL into the address bar on my smartphone and got "404 Server not found."

When I told her the news, she moaned, sounding more distressed than I'd ever heard her.

"We don't exist anymore. Do you realize? Hotelles don't exist anymore."

Louie certainly would not share her opinion.

19

It may have been a disaster for Sophia, but it was the best news I'd heard in days. Belles de Nuit was out of business. The website and all its files, gone. All that was left of my illicit activities were some stolen pictures, which could easily be explained as the photoshopped products of some mudslinger. These days everyone was capable of pasting a face on a body, in a photograph or movie. Secondarily, the sudden disappearance of BDN also erased my debt to Rebecca.

In short, nothing, or almost nothing from my past, could lead to problems with David anymore. At least that's what I kept telling myself as I left Barlet Tower. Feeling like fate was finally on my side, I clung to the good news like a buoy.

THE JEWELRY BOX ZIPPED IN my bag, I decided to take a detour before going home. I thought of the riding crop Louie had given me—it was still buried in the pile of clothing where I had hidden it—and the flattering things he had said about the appraisers at Drouot. Churlish, but according to him the best in the capital. My intuition had not led me astray, I realized as I entered their office, an austere boutique across from the modern building where the auction house is located.

My treasure worked its spell on the appraisers, making

them forget my gender, age, and naive appearance. One of them was particularly attentive . . . and forthcoming:

"Hmm, I recognize it. It is one of the most famous necklaces belonging to the Empress Eugenie, Napoleon III's wife."

I had been right about its ancient provenance and worth. But the old, bald man dampened my enthusiasm as he readjusted his spectacles over his ruddy nose:

"Actually, the one you have here is a replica from the period. A very nice piece, don't mistake me . . . Jewelers often made less valuable duplicates for their clients to wear. The more precious version would remain in a safe."

"How can you distinguish it from the real necklace?"

"Oh, that's easy, look: the stones are cut less finely, they are slightly smaller, and sometimes the setting is of a less precious metal, which makes them more prone to coming undone . . . There are a number of tells, believe me."

"And the original?"

"It hasn't been in France for a long time, little lady. It belonged for a while to the royal family in Iran, before falling into the hands, thirty years ago, of an Asian collector I know quite well in Seoul."

As interesting as this was, it didn't tell me much about what I wanted to know.

"Are you absolutely sure it belonged to the Empress Eugenie?"

To my knowledge, no room at the Hôtel des Charmes went by that name. And with good reason: Eugenie de Montijo, Marquise of Ardales, Marquise of Moya, Countess of Teba, Empress of the French, and wife of Napoleon III had never been a courtesan.

Was it a mistake? A red herring?

"I am certain. Our organization has identified and catalogued every detail of Eugenie's jewelry collection, one of the richest of her time. In terms of this particular necklace, though, she was not the only famous woman to wear it."

Now we were getting somewhere. I expected he would name some Hollywood star.

"La Païva was without contest the most famous."

"La Païva . . . ," I repeated, racking my brains.

"Her real name was Esther Lachmann. She was a society lady who hosted one of the most popular salons of the Second Empire. She purchased the original of your necklace directly from Eugenie. Six hundred thousand francs: at the time, it was a colossal sum!"

"And where did this Païva live?" I asked out of curiosity.

"Today, a lot of people visit her home on the Champs-Élysées, a present from one of her lovers, Guido von Donnersmarck, Bismarck's cousin. But she spent more time in her house on Place Saint-Georges."

The same square through which Louie and I had strolled.

BACK AT DUCHESNOIS HOUSE, I spent the rest of the afternoon mulling everything over. At Armand's request, I gave him my engagement ring so he could get it engraved: *Annabelle and David, 18 June 2009.*

In exchange, he handed me a checkered sheet of perforated paper, which I recognized immediately. I almost dropped the ring I was handing to him.

"When did you find it?" I asked, my voice shaking.

"After lunch. I'd say between two and three o'clock."

Or when we'd just started our meeting, the one Louie had attended. He hadn't been the one to put the note in the mailbox, then. Did he send a factotum for such minor tasks? Ysiam, perhaps, whose work at the Hôtel des Charmes put him in proximity to the Rue de la Tour-des-Dames. A quick jaunt during one of his breaks and the job was done. Who would notice a humble Indo-Pakistani making a delivery in a neighborhood where so many members of his community lived?

I carefully unfolded the paper like a bomb expert with my own emotions. After two days without, two days of epistolary silence, I had no idea what the note would contain, much less how I would react. Would I be indifferent? Or, on the contrary, would I get all hot and bothered, as I had a few hours earlier with Louie? Would he speak of the way in which I had given myself to him the night before, on the sofa?

A ball of fur threw itself across the room, distracting me from the page between my hands: Felicity. Since she had moved here, she alternated between depressive periods spent inside a cupboard, curled up on my sweaters, or taking refuge in sleep, and rare bouts of euphoria. Now, she had chosen our bedroom as her playing field. The cat suddenly jumped through the half-open window. I went to close it behind her when I noticed the feline climbing the wall that separated our garden from that of Mademoiselle Mars. Felicity's piercing meows told me that she had taken an unfamiliar path and didn't know how to get back.

A minute later, I rang the modern interphone at 1 Rue de la Tour-des-Dames. Above the blue door was an old enamel plaque in the shape of an oval:

Youth Travel Office

After I had pressed the bell several times, a man wearing work clothes opened the door. He made no effort to be polite.

I was clearly bothering him. Robust, shaved head, jaw as big as his forehead, he reminded me of a wrestler from the sixties. He looked me up and down, without lingering on my chest, which was heaving with distress.

"Yes?"

"Hello," I whispered. "I live next door, number three. I think my cat ran into your garden."

"Hmm . . . And so?"

"I think she's trapped on the other side of the wall. She can't make it back."

I don't know why, but I couldn't get the word "pussy" out of my head. I can never bring myself to say the word out loud in public, even in completely asexual situations like this one. *My pussycat is trapped.* I blushed, and I was fairly certain he noticed.

"Are you sure?"

"Yes, I saw her jump."

"Okay," he grumbled. "I'll have a look."

I started to follow him, but he quickly shut the door.

I could hear the sounds of construction from behind the wall. I waited there, listening, for what seemed like a long time. At last he reappeared, holding the guilty animal by the scruff of the neck, just like mama cats do with their babies.

"Is this the one?" he asked curtly.

"Yes . . . thank you."

As soon as Felicity was in my arms, he slammed the blue door without so much as a good-bye. Curiouser and curiouser, as Sophia would have said.

THE PERFORATED PAGE WAS EXACTLY where my three hellions had thrown it. At last I could have a look at what it said.

A bad joke? Or maybe an oversight? How was I supposed to understand this blank page?

I sat down on the edge of the bed, looking out at the garden. It didn't take me long to understand what the blank note meant. It was my turn to write something. All the messages, all the forceful intrusions into the meanders of my libido, had been leading to this precise moment, to when I would hold the pen, when I could no longer contain the need to write my desires.

My phone beeped, interrupting my thoughts. While I had been next door, Mom had left a message. A long message:

"Hi, honey, it's Mom. I hope your first day of work went well, my Elle. No, I don't hope it did: I know it did."

My mother and her unwavering confidence in me.

"I'm not doing so well. I'm beginning to wonder if this trip to the States is such a good idea. And, you know, Madame Chappuis says the Max Fourestier Hospital is one of the top five of the Hauts-de-Seine. She read that in her magazine . . . The top five. Not bad, right? What would they do that's really so much better over there?"

My mother, her insufferable neighbor, and her propensity not to see the forest for the trees. She wasn't ignorant or hardheaded, just humble. She didn't think she deserved better.

"Oh, there was one nice thing that happened today: your David spoiled me again. Calissons from Aix-en-Provence and gorgeous peonies. It's sweet, but you have to tell him to stop, honey! I don't know what to do with all these things . . ."

Maude, my mother, always ready to believe a fairy tale, so long as I was its heroine.

"Okay, I love you. Don't call back. I'm sure you have more important things to do tonight."

I hardly felt up to it, but I forced myself anyway. Her line was busy, and I had to try several times before she picked up. Not a day went by that I didn't call her. It had been part of our routine since before she got sick. Now it seemed even more vital. I always called around the same time, toward the end of the afternoon. I listened to her complain about Laure Chappuis; I even laughed at her expense. We usually talked about simple, shallow things, but it felt good.

AN HOUR LATER, AS THE light streaming through the windows grew orange, I heard a noise in the entry that could not have come from a four-legged creature. Armand usually did his chores with the utmost discretion, to the point of absolute silence; others would have found it suspicious. So the source of the racket could be none other than . . .

"Elle, darling! It's me!"

David arrived back at our home at six o'clock—one word didn't belong. And it wasn't the possessive pronoun. With every passing day, I felt more and more at home in this haven of calm and sophistication.

"Will you join me downstairs?"

"Armand?" he called in a singsong voice. "Would you, sir, please meet us in the living room?"

I was the first to arrive in the neo-Pompeian main hall. Unlike our bedroom or the kitchen and bathrooms, the living room had been restored to its original specifications. Everything fit with that earlier era, from the Empire furnishings, to the floral friezes depicting fluttering clouds of birds of paradise, to the baby grand piano in a corner facing the garden.

The kiss David planted on my forehead also seemed to come from another era. Yet it was not lacking in tenderness.

"You know, everyone was really impressed by you!"

"Really?" I asked, honestly surprised.

He smiled knowingly, as though it were a given, as though the day had simply confirmed his predictions about me.

"Yes! Luc and Albane loved you. And even Louie, who, to be frank, had some reservations about you, was impressed by your poise in the meeting with Chris and Philippe. I don't think you could have had a better first day!"

A day in which Louie had made me his thing. A day in which he'd once again demonstrated that I was at his mercy. If there hadn't been the news about Belles de Nuit, I think it would have been one of the worst days of my young life.

"Armand! Come in, sir!"

Armand hurried from the vast entryway. His round face, the red nose and cheeks of which formed a stark contrast to his white hair and eyebrows, appeared at once. Summer or winter, he invariably wore brown corduroy pants, a white shirt, a buttoned waistcoat, and leather moccasins.

"I wanted us both to get home early because," David said to me, "Armand is going to brief us on the wedding preparations."

"Thank heavens, everything is shaping up nicely," said the domestic in his deep, warm voice. "What should I start with?"

I was surprised to note his casual tone with David, who, for his part, tended to be very formal with him. It reminded me of fathers and sons in old aristocratic families. In fact, Armand had probably played a paternal role to the Barlet brothers after Andre and Hortensia had died.

"You, sir, know best."

Armand withdrew a pair of tortoiseshell spectacles from his cardigan and affixed them to his red nose. He gazed at a set of notes between his hands, holding the paper close to his chest, as though he were afraid we'd sneak a peek.

"So . . . please thank your friend Mademoiselle Petrilli for me. I have received a copy of her identity papers as well as her signed form."

"Perfect!"

For once, Sophia had taken care of something serious . . .

"Your papers, Mademoiselle, are at city hall. It took some doing, but I convinced them to add your wedding to the docket on the requested day. In the middle of June and with only ten days' notice, it wasn't easy. But, luckily, this year June eighteenth falls on a Thursday and not a Saturday. Otherwise, we would have been in a real bind!"

"What time is the ceremony?"

"One p.m. I know it's not ideal, but let me suggest we offer your guests a glass of champagne here, before going to city hall. An amuse-bouche can tide them over until lunch."

"Very good," David approved, delighted.

As for me, I took the ease with which Armand handled each obstacle as a good sign. Thanks to him, the sky above seemed to grow clearer and the ground below flatter. With the exception of my mother's worsening condition, our union was unfolding under auspicious conditions. Or better even . . .

"Do you think I can tell Annabelle our little secrets?"

The white-haired man shot a conspiratorial look at my future husband.

"Please do, sir! There will be plenty of others on D-day."

Secrets? What were they talking about?

I shivered at the idea of what these two might be hiding, but I pretended to be excited as a little girl.

"Tell me!" I said.

"Okay, well, first of all, you should know that everyone on your list is coming."

Even Fred? I wondered to myself.

"And you have to help me with the seating chart. You cannot let two hundred fifty people seat themselves at random."

I had heard correctly: he had said two hundred fifty guests . . . more than my address book had ever contained.

"But how will we fit everyone!" I exclaimed, my eyes scanning the insufficiently large room.

"Barely. That's why we're going to set up two platforms in the garden. It's going to be tight, what with the stage, the bar, the safety perimeter for the firework display . . . But I've done a few simulations; we should be able to do it, and without feeling like we're taking the metro at rush hour."

"And if it rains?" David inquired.

"I called your contact at the Weather Channel. He has promised me that not one drop of rain is to fall on Paris between the fifteenth and twentieth of June. That's a guarantee from the biggest weather service, the one NASA uses, I think."

Armand was like a magician from an enchanted world that David was contriving to build around me. He had thought of everything.

"And about you know who?"

"She'll be here. Don't worry. She even promised to appear live on your show, Elle, at a date of your choosing."

"Awesome!" David said with childlike enthusiasm.

"Depending on her availability and travels to France, of course," Armand was quick to add.

I played dumb; it's what was expected.

"*You know who?*"

In reply, Armand rummaged through his pile of loose papers and withdrew the latest CD by an artist who would perform at our wedding, just a few feet from where I was standing: the biggest star of the last thirty years in person.

Not that I was a big fan, but who in the world wouldn't want such a celebrity at their wedding?

"However, her agent was very clear: a one-hour set, not a minute more."

"What does that mean?" David asked. "About fifteen songs?"

"That's right. A dozen, plus about three encores. The time for a glass of champagne and a slice of cake would be a bonus, if she agrees to stay fifteen minutes after her performance."

I couldn't get over it. Madonna wasn't just going to come to our wedding. She was going to sing for a whole hour!

David was also beside himself.

"Thank you for everything, sir."

"You're welcome, David."

"Now, if you don't mind, I would like a moment alone with Elle."

"Of course."

He quietly retreated, leaving a light trace of cologne in his wake.

While Louie could make my body tremble without touching me, David had the miraculous ability to erase all my childish worries with a few words: I did not doubt for a moment that all of Armand's miracles had been at his behest. With him, I was no longer a modest little girl who had been abandoned by her father and raised by a struggling single mother. I was becoming what he had seen before anyone else: competent, self-assured . . . winning. And it felt crazy good.

He spoiled me with attention and surprises. Still, I felt more like a spectator than an actor in the coming event, as though I were a guest at my own wedding. It was nice not having to handle the logistics, but it disassociated me so much from the process that I would not have been surprised if someone told me that the bride was some other woman. From my golden cage, I would have at least liked to choose the color of my perch or the contents of my feeder. This perfectly scripted event seemed like the exact opposite of David and Aurora's wedding, which had been so spontaneous, so passionate!

"I have one last surprise for you . . ."

A parachute jump from Duchesnois House in my wedding dress, like Johnny Hallyday at the Stade de France?

"Yes?" I simpered.

Our wedding was going to be broadcast live and all over the world on BTV?

"I haven't had the chance to discuss it with you . . . but I didn't want to do our honeymoon in just any postcard destination."

Images of endless beaches and an azure sea faded out, but I didn't really regret it. I knew we had a lifetime, and all the means in the world, for that kind of caprice.

Exaggerating my enthusiasm, I coaxed him to tell me.

"So . . . where are we going?"

"To the sea . . . but not on the other side of the world. Here. I mean, in France."

"You want me to guess, is that it?"

My playful suggestion threw him off.

"No . . . No. I just wanted you to know that this place means more to me than any other. Even more than here. And I wanted to share it with you."

"Okay." I nodded, smiling submissively. "But you don't want to tell me until we're there, am I right?"

"That's right!"

Suddenly he was beaming.

But my next question would squelch that.

The sea . . . A place so important to him that he couldn't imagine spending our wedding night anywhere else . . . A pilgrimage that, by the grace of our love, he considered therapeutic, I supposed. What other place could it be, besides the one where Aurora had died?

My thoughts and my tongue became one:

"The ring you gave me . . ."

"I know, it's too small. Armand told me you gave it to him to adjust."

"That's not it . . . The ring, it was worn by someone besides your mother, wasn't it?"

He froze, suddenly stone-faced.

"You've given it to someone before."

"Who told you this rubbish?"

The man before me was no longer the seductive, honey-voiced David, but the captain of industry, a cold-blooded animal who led his life like a series of hostile IPOs.

"The ring, David . . . It speaks for itself. You and Aurora, you married in 1988?"

His features contracted. Suddenly, there was no difference between his face and that of his brother. His sweet expression had disappeared, and I felt like I was seeing a monstrous hybrid of the Barlet brothers emerging before my very eyes.

"1988," I insisted. "It's the most recent engraving on the ring."

"I don't know what you're talking about!"

He closed the small distance separating us with alarming rapidity. There he was standing before me, menacing.

"Aurora Delbard," I bluffed. "She was your first wife . . . yes or no?"

"Is Louie the one who has been telling you this garbage?"

My silence was like a confession. I saw that David was fighting to control himself. With every breath, he seemed calmer, his discourse more ordered.

"I don't know what that bonehead told you . . . Yes, we did both meet an Aurora Delbard when we were in our twenties. What he clearly left out of his story is that he was the one who fell madly in love with that girl. He even wanted to marry her. Unfortunately for both of them, she fell in love with me."

"What about you?"

"No, I did not."

Without thinking, I suddenly grabbed his left forearm. He didn't have time to stop me before I'd seized his silk armband. He grimaced in anger. Or was it pain?

"So this thing you wear on your arm, it's not for Aurora? Are you sure?"

He tried to free himself from my grasp, but I held on tightly, like a mariner gripping a bulwark in the midst of strong winds and swells the size of buildings. Each of his efforts to liberate himself crashed into me like another wave.

"Let go of me! You're hurting me!"

"Answer me, David . . ."

He struck without warning. The immediate effect: I let go. Then a switch went on, which all women have, and I started crying.

"Elle, I'm sorry . . . I . . ."

I straightened, humiliated and racked with sobs, which my

last shreds of pride and dignity tried to quell. I whispered in a gruff voice that was not my own:

"Fuck off! Fuck off!"

He must have understood that any effort to calm me would be in vain because he didn't try to stop or cajole me as I crossed the room. I grabbed my bag from the console in the entry as well as a cardigan I had left there.

On the other side of the monumental entryway, I noticed, without really thinking about it, that almost half of the sand in the hourglass had already dropped to the bottom. Felicity had her paws glued to the glass and was trying to catch the falling grains of sand. One foot out the door, enraged, I realized that the thing being consumed evaded me just as it did the animal's claws. Everything was going as fast as that sand, including my life.

20

When you reach adulthood, you know how to listen to your body's signals without feeling like it's betraying you. You become determined. You forget your doubts. You take action. Your breath quickens, or perhaps it grows calmer. Your muscles contract or relax. I mean to say that you do not have to be an extraordinary woman to notice the physical signs that come from a desire to fight. Tension before the battle. The élan vital of defense or protection.

IT WAS NOT YET EIGHT o'clock when I left Duchesnois House. I spent two hours meandering, and never even got the urge to sit or have a Monaco. Instead, I needed to maintain my martial resolve, my warrior force.

> Please come home. We need to talk. Calmly. I
> love you.

As I walked, I erased each one of David's messages without so much as a reply. Every time I pressed the delete button, I felt my anger mount. He could send as many messages as he liked; my mind was made up: I was going to spend the evening at the Hôtel des Charmes. To punish him, no doubt, but also to find some of that strange form of comfort that comes from being submissive, as well as that light debasement.

With every step, I grew calmer. I imagined Louie's dark eyes and the way his lashes had fluttered at me when he'd uttered that word during our meeting at work: "Hotelles."

I was going to the damned rendezvous to give myself to him but also to tear what shreds of truth I could from him. I wasn't playing them against each other. I was playing for myself, first and foremost. When I confronted him with David's version, how would he reply? Was the story with Aurora Delbard just an adolescent fling, one more episode in their endless rivalry? If that were the case, then why had David reacted so violently when I'd asked about his armband?

When at last I stepped inside the Hôtel des Charmes, after wandering the neighborhood with no other aim but to air out my fury, I was really wound up, ready to strangle anyone who got in my way . . .

Monsieur Jacques, for instance, and his conspicuous gallantry.

"Hello, Elle . . ."

"I don't know what you and Louie Barlet are up to . . . ," I snarled before he could offer his salutations, "but let me tell you, I won't be locked in one of these rooms. Shut me in again . . . and I'll report you! Do you hear me?"

He was dazed for a moment; then he straightened, regaining his natural elegance and self-assurance. He smiled affably and slowly replied, articulating each syllable:

"But what exactly would you have to report, Elle? Solicitation? Prostitution? Two or three of the hotel's regulars could testify to the fact that you offered them favors in exchange for cash. Is that really what you want, Mademoiselle?"

Though he was at last revealing his true face, he managed to remain as courteous as ever. He was threatening me while maintaining all the tact and grace that the clientele—especially the foreigners—so appreciated in him.

"Not to mention, I could easily deny you access to the rooms at this instant," he added, certain of his power over me. "And I do not believe that would suit you. Otherwise, you would not be here tonight, and right on time, I might add."

So he was in on Louie's schemes. And he understood how badly I wanted to see him, though he was mistaken about my intentions.

I was going to counterattack. I, too, had a story for the police—and the punctilious justice system—about how his famous "rooms by the hour" were camouflaging a vulgar brothel. But a cheerful voice addressed me from behind:

"Elle? Elle, is that you?"

I QUICKLY TURNED AROUND, MY nerves frayed, ready to smack the first person who crossed me, when I recognized my client from the week before, the forty-something sporty but awkward guy, the one who asked all those questions: "Which position do you prefer?" The one I had naively supposed would be my last.

"Hello . . . ," I stammered, surprised and irritable.

But the worst part was not his unexpected appearance. He was with that perfect-bodied ethnic girl Louie had been parading the night we met, the Vine. Her ideal body was once again glued to her date. She gave me a haughty look.

Had she worked for Belles de Nuit? Now that the website and catalogue were gone, I had no way of checking. Regardless, I figured that with her thoroughbred body she could offer her services directly, without having to bother with an inter-mediary.

His look was more one of surprise than desire. The man exclaimed, too loudly for my taste:

"My word! You're everywhere!"

"Excuse me?"

"Wait . . . Didn't I see you five minutes ago in Place Saint-Georges?"

To be sure, I had been wandering the neighborhood, blinded by distress and haunted by ghosts, but I was almost certain I had not been there.

"Yes . . . Yes, that was me . . . ," I confirmed so as not to trouble him.

I TOOK LEAVE OF THEM as politely as I could, considering the circumstances, and hurried toward the elevators, where a bellboy was waiting for me. I was almost disappointed it was not Ysiam, my sweet and timid Indian, but a tall redhead with a stubby nose and cheeks more stippled than my own.

"La Païva, please."

"La Païva," the elevator operator repeated. "Fifth floor."

The doors were silver: the same opalescent, iridescent color Louie used for his messages. Somehow, I understood that this floor belonged to him, perhaps exclusively, and that I was about to set foot in his kingdom.

Without saying a word, the redhead led me to one of the doors and inserted the keycard into the reader. The hinges creaked lightly as the door opened onto the most baroque room I had ever seen in this hotel.

Like the original—which is still open to visitors on the Champs-Élysées—this identical replica of the marquise's apartments was an extravagant profusion of precious materials and ornaments. The most striking element of the room, decorated in the style of the Second Empire, was without contest the wooden coffered ceiling, with its fine chiseling, inlaid work, and gilded ridges. Beyond the traditional square, the ceiling treatment was fashioned into ovals and diamonds that tapered in points toward the floor, like stalactites, and capped with a kind of knob.

Giant mirrors framed by antique columns flanked the room, and elegant bronze caryatids formed the base of a fireplace, which was oddly situated under the window. Was it purely decorative?

Floral tapestries picked up every nuance of the thick purple carpeting, which covered the floor and muffled the clicking of my heels. In the stupid hope of dominating my subject, I had worn my evening shoes, as defined by Rebecca, from my outfit number three. Six inches of lofty femininity and discomfort. That day of shopping with Rebecca seemed so far away . . .

I did not wait to be told to take them off and enjoy the direct contact of my feet against the generous and supple wool. In my own way, wearing my finest—read, Eugenie's necklace—I was in perfect harmony with my surroundings. I was not simply a guest; I *was* the Païva.

I had just observed that this room, as opposed to the previous one, contained no apparent modern technological device, when a few notes of music filled the air around me, betraying the presence of an amplification device somewhere in the paneling. I recognized the piece . . . but I could not put a finger on its title or the artist.

"It's 'Tunnels' by Arcade Fire."

My heart thumped in fright. Then I recognized the voice

that had spoken, that underlined the beating drums and wound through the piano's volutes. It had surprised me, but it was familiar. It was Louie's voice, of course. I felt a sense of relief; undeniable, irrepressible pleasure, even.

On the other side of the room, I heard the lock click. I was his captive again.

I was dazed for a moment, and then set myself to regaining the upper hand. I addressed him loudly and naturally, as though he were by my side. A rush of blood surged through my temples, the base of my neck, my lower abdomen.

"Could you stop the theatrics for a moment?"

"Theatrics? Erotic theater, then . . . and in which you have fully assumed your role, Elle. Do I need to play your performance from last night to convince you?"

That he had filmed everything was no surprise. Just another chink in my armor.

I don't know why, but it occurred to me that my solitary exploration from the other night had not been accompanied by music. Except for the two actors on screen and their yelling and moaning, perhaps the best soundtrack imaginable . . .

"Finding the perfect music for making love is a long-term project," he said from behind the scenes. "For some, it takes a lifetime. I've spent years, and I'm still not sure if I've found the ideal score."

I understood: if I wanted to make him talk, to bring him bit by bit onto *my* turf, I would first have to accept his rules. Only then would I gain enough leverage to convince him to give me a few crumbs of truth and a tiny glimpse into his past with Aurora.

"And what do you think sex music should sound like? I'm curious . . ."

My sudden interest must have startled him, as it took him a moment to reply. Then at last:

"A slow rhythm. Almost mechanical. For most of us, pleasure only comes with repetitive movement and stimulation . . . The accompanying music should mimic this regularity, this stubbornness to make the other come."

"Okay. I'd like to believe you, but give me a few examples. I'm sure your mind is crawling with them."

"Oh, you don't have to be a music buff. Some of the most well-known pieces are poorly disguised odes to sexuality—and its particular tempo. Ravel's *Boléro*, for instance, with its mounting crescendo and final explosion."

The sonorous metaphor was indeed rather explicit.

"And what else?" I insisted. "Something you could play for us right now . . ."

"I don't know . . ."

"Something that would reflect who I am . . . ," I urged. "Me."

Challenging him like that was not going to give me the upper hand, but I thought it might balance our powers. I wasn't one of his bimbos to be sacrificed to his erotic whims. I was becoming his partner, a thought I found extremely comforting.

I had not paid particular attention to the bed until then. It was difficult not to notice it, however, as it was massive. The head- and footboards were wooden jigsaws, on which I made out cherub figures holding lyres and harps.

Sitting atop the bed, I found a mask. It wasn't like the white ones worn by the two anonymous lovers from the night before. It was more of a Venetian carnival mask. I was instantly reminded of one of the few erotic films I'd seen in my life, under the pretext of cultural edification: Stanley Kubrick's

Eyes Wide Shut. It was also one of the few films in my pantheon of cinematographic memories that was capable of arousing me. In a flash, I recalled that magnificent woman, naked, perched atop heels as high as mine today, who ends up stretched out in the morgue, under Tom Cruise's bewildered gaze. He's ready to kiss her blue lips, an eternal kiss.

"This, for example . . . ," Louie said after a while—the time it had taken, I figured, for him to find the right piece.

A pulsating rhythm filled the room, and I shivered as I associated a name with the deafening beat resonating through-out my body: I had always loved . . .

"'Karmacoma,'" I said. "Massive Attack."

"I see you know your classics. It's almost surprising, for someone your age. After all, you were only nine or ten when this album came out."

"Isn't that the definition of a classic? Something that out-lives the generation that saw its birth?"

The music was only one part of his choice. The lyrics were just as important. They expressed a message that Louie was not able to formulate by himself. The voice of the singer 3D in the mythical group from Bristol introduced itself into a silent dialogue between Louie and me:

> *You sure you want to be with me*
> *I've nothing to give*

Between stanzas, the persistent tempo and swaying flute urged my hips into movement. Without quite realizing it, I had started to dance. Slowly, almost imperceptibly. A trance: that was the effect of such music. And of all sexual encounters?

Don't want to be on top of your list
Phenomenally and properly kissed

But I could not let myself get carried away. I did not want to fall into his deceitful and perverse web, not again, though he had known how to affect me, plucking I don't know what invisible chord. I had to stay focused and steer us back to the issue that had brought me here:

"How old would Aurora be today?"

"I don't know what she has to do with this!" he said coldly.

"David says you're the one Aurora drove mad."

"That's ridiculous! He's the one who married her! He's the one who—"

He interrupted himself, as though another part of him were muzzling the one talking.

"Who endured so much for her," he finished.

At least he was now confirming that his initial story, the one in which David sacrificed everything for Aurora to an irreparable point, was probably close to the truth. His subsequent denials were simply part of the game he was playing with me.

"But you . . . You also loved her, didn't you?"

He met my question with prolonged silence, then turned up the sound. The music now hung on the walls like it was part of the decor, lending volume and presence. The room vibrated, was almost alive.

"You would have to ask the Louie of fifteen, twenty years ago," he said. "I can only speak to what he feels today."

I could not hear anything outside the suffocating, almost deafening pressure of the music, but I could have sworn something was moving through the room, around me. A stealthy movement. I stood still for a few instants, then walked toward the wall facing the bed. Something about it had changed, but I couldn't tell what. It was not until other, identical openings appeared around the room that at last I realized what it was: at least two dozen peepholes. Behind each one, an eye was watching me.

"Take your clothes off, Elle."

"You can't possibly think I am going to—"

"They're waiting," he interrupted.

All around me, eyes blinked, as though confirming his statement. *Thou shalt abandon thyself to their unflinching gaze*—I was reminded of his commandment. So this was how he got off? From a distance? Without ever touching the woman he desired?

Perhaps it was all part of an agreement more or less secret, more or less tacit between the two brothers: one consummated what the other could not even touch. David was the imperfect and awkward actor, and Louie the eternal and pure spectator. He had his desires and ideals, a sublimated sexuality, in which flesh was more the stuff of dreams than carnal feasts. Had Aurora been a victim of such an arrangement? And as for me, could it be that David knew all about the game his brother was playing at my expense? Was David aware that he'd been torturing me with meetings and ultimatums?

True story: Weather permitting, Mom used to hang our clothes to dry on a line outside, on the terrace in front of the house. When I was about fifteen or sixteen, at that age when the female figure has first bloomed, my underthings, panties and bras, suddenly started to disappear from the line. At first, we blamed the "mischievous wind," like the

*Georges Brassens song, for stealing the undies of a young
girl and leaving behind the old intimates of a more mature
woman. We chalked it up to chance. But after the fourth
time, we kept a look out from the living room window. After a month, I was the one to solve the mystery:
I saw our neighbor on the left, a retired, single man in
his sixties, casting his fishing rod out the skylight in his
bathroom and hooking my white cotton underclothes. They
were so light he had no problem wresting them from their
clothespins and reeling them in. I even saw him bury his
nose, delighted, in the clean crotch. That day, I felt as dirty
and ashamed as if the gross old man had put his face in
my virgin ~~beaver~~ pussy. Yet in the months that followed,
it was that same odious image that came to mind when I
touched myself most feverishly. Afterward, I was always
careful to ~~wipe~~ dab my moist sex with the small triangle of
cotton, leaving a trace for him to notice of what he would
never be able to smell again in the flesh. So young and yet
already perverted . . .*

Handwritten note by me, 6/10/2009

THE ROOM UNDERWENT ANOTHER CHANGE, coax-
ing me: under each spy hole, a door as narrow as it was high
opened, with just enough room for a hand to pass through. All
at once, several hands rushed in, reaching into the room, eager
to grab hold of what they could not, for the moment, grasp:
me.

"See how they want you! No man on earth could resist
you."

I think the song had started from the beginning again. It

was playing in a throbbing loop, hammering home my distress. My body and mind were under siege. Louie was using any tool he could think of to weaken my defenses, to make me more pliable, to open me like ripe fruit and force me to admit my desires.

"You are so beautiful . . . Show us."

I looked at their hungry fingers with horror and excitement, reeling from one end of the room to the other, eager to let them touch me. That's when Louie urged, with a conviction that smashed my inhibitions:

"Prove it to yourself!"

Like a marionette hanging from its threads, I slowly undressed. Each gesture weighed a ton. Each article of clothing was a lost struggle, falling to the ground, joining the others. When I had gotten rid of my panties and all I was wearing was the emerald-and-diamond necklace, his voice grew deeper, more enticing:

"Put the mask on."

It was like a rerun of my first surrender, here, a few floors down, the time he'd wanted me naked for the camera.

"Don't be scared . . . They aren't dirty; they'll reveal you to yourself."

I approached the anonymous hands. Every inch they touched felt different, taking on a completely new volume or texture. I had never known my backside to be so soft, my middle so round, my waist so narrow. Never had a palm thrilled the heavy contours of my breasts the way this nameless, story-less palm did now.

"If you could see how much they desire you!"

And you? What about you? my vagina silently cried. But I was no longer in a state to reply. I closed my eyes, letting my body—a little ball of palpitating flesh—travel from one end of the room to another. I turned and turned, again and again, an unrelenting merry-go-round, piquing their desire only to frustrate them as I moved on.

After a few times around, some of the fingers grew more daring, darting between my buttocks, gripping the curls of my bush, or even quickly slipping into the folds of my vagina, which was so wet that fluid had begun to run down my thighs in thin lines.

"Continue . . . Continue like that . . ."

The more I ran through their fingers, under their eyes, the more it seemed my whole body was changing consistency. No longer was I simply Annabelle, the sum of my organs and members, the fruit of my lone consciousness. Now, their collective desire was weaving a new me, my new skin. I *was* because they wanted me. Louie could not have said it better himself . . .

Karmacoma, Jamaica' aroma

Yes, the scent of ecstasy, that smooth and familiar perfume of pleasure: that is the aroma that floated through the room. I could smell it through the thin walls.

Karmacoma . . .

Through the walls or rather . . .

What was happening? I was standing motionless in the center of the room. I opened my eyes and noticed that the holes in the walls were at waist-level. One by one, they filled with another organ. Each specimen was varied and unique. Some were flaccid, others fully erect. Some long, others short. Thin and thick, circumcised and not. Two dozen penises were pointing at me, thrusting into the unknown, in the hope that I would touch them as I had been touched.

I staggered toward one, then another, making my way around the room again. I ran the tips of my fingers over the erect members like stalks in a wheat field, for the sheer joy of feeling them bow and quiver with impatience, before resuming their proud position as soon as the gentle pressure of my touch let up. I wiped off drops of seminal liquid that had already begun to pearl on one or two of the members. They smelled so strong, so good . . .

But what was I to do with all their desire? Who was I to think I could satisfy them all? I was just me. All I wanted was to please one man. Louie? David? Which?

The answer should have been obvious, what with my feelings and the coming marriage. And yet the more I perused the army of phalluses, the less I felt capable of giving one up for the other. Louie had succeeded in this: he had made me doubt, and without laying a finger on me.

Louie had not organized a clash of cocks but an immense field of erotic possibility, which I was about to forgo when I sealed my union with David. I would put it away like a good girl, as I had done with the riding crop, between two piles of clothing.

THE MUSIC STOPPED. THE MAN in charge of this strange ceremony must have guessed my consternation, as he gently announced the end of our session:

"You can get dressed now, Elle."

Like the times before, I heard the lock on the door click open. The anonymous penises must have also received an order: they disappeared from the peepholes, and one by one, the tiny doors closed. An envelope pushed through the last one just before it shut, floating to the floral carpet.

I was still half naked, my panties not quite covering my ass and cunt. I leaned to pick up the object, a white envelope containing a stack of hundred-euro bills. I almost screamed in shame . . . Then, when I saw the rest of its contents, I understood what they were for and calmed down: a card with a "List of Mandatory Reading" that featured several dozen, maybe thirty, books. A business card was paper-clipped to it:

> La Musardine
> Paris's Erotic Bookstore
> 122 Rue du Chemin Vert, Paris, 11th Arrondissement

So he was giving me homework.

21

June 10, 2009

This time, I can't refuse . . . My old set only got two channels, and even they were fuzzy."

Mom had just received her surprise delivery of the day: a state-of-the-art flat-screen, 3D television. It was so big it barely fit in her small living room.

"But tell him it's too much. We've never even met . . . and he's already given me *years'* worth of Christmas presents."

"Well, Mom, that's David," I said, feigning exasperation.

"I know I won't be around for very long . . ."

"Tsk, don't say that!" I chided softly.

" . . . but that's no reason to try to make up for future lost time! Even if this boy has the means."

Two delivery men had come by an hour earlier and fought hard to fit the technological beast into her pocket-size house. After plugging everything in, they had only just left, and she was still reeling: a bit incredulous, a bit happy, and wild with excitement over all our recent good fortune.

"Have you at least turned it on?"

"Yes, yes . . . I'm watching my soap. Before, I would have

thought they were broadcasting it from Brazil. Now it feels like the actors are here in the house. It's really nice!"

After so many years of being frugal, years in which every extra cent went to me, she deserved such pleasures. And, to an extent, I was really happy about it. To an extent. Because I knew the source of all the extravagance.

But that day, something else caught my attention.

"Mom . . . did you say you received your new television this morning?"

"Yes, I told you: I just got it. Why do you ask?"

It was probably nothing. And yet . . .

"And what was the present before this one?"

"Let me see . . . peonies and calissons. They were so good, by the way. I finished them all yesterday with that cow Laure Chappuis. You would never guess what she's complaining about now . . ."

She and the hilarious shenanigans of Madame Chappuis. I'd stopped listening. I needed to think. Peonies and calissons: the day after my night in the Marie Bonaparte room, the one with the vibrating egg.

I needed to be sure, so I asked:

"And do you remember when you got the rose-flavored macaroons?"

"I don't know. Two days ago. Maybe three."

Two, I remembered, suddenly certain.

The macaroons had arrived the day after my first mysterious rendezvous at the Hôtel des Charmes.

"What's the matter, Elle? What's bothering you?"

"Nothing, Mom, it's nothing . . ."

Just another knot in the noose around my neck. Another thread he had woven to tie my life to his. There was no other possible explanation: after each of his invitations, and if I duly fulfilled my mission, he rewarded me the following day with a gift to Maude. I obeyed, and he had a sweet treat delivered, right where I was most vulnerable: 29 Rue Rigault, in Nanterre.

I felt the hundred-euro bills from the night before burning through the leather of my wallet. He wasn't remunerating my charms. It was much worse. Since he had the means, he was trying to buy my whole life. My past and cancerous mother included. What were we in his eyes but a struggling small business he could take over on a whim? His brother was perhaps the king of IPOs, but Louie was only interested in making a merger-and-acquisition of me.

I snapped out of it, pressing the phone into my ear to better quell the vertigo.

"By the way . . . I have an announcement."

It was time. At last I would tell her the big news. The family ring that was being enlarged for me. And even the grand ceremony David and Armand had been secretly planning. My mother gasped in delight. I had to delve deep into my memory and recall my old dreams from when I was a little girl. It was the only way I could find the enthusiasm I did not presently feel. I spun a fairy tale for her, blending truth and fiction into a fairly convincing narrative: the proposal on the boat, the presents he'd been piling on me . . . I even pretended that I hadn't been informed of the perfectly chosen date, which was also very soon, until the night before. One final and divine surprise.

Once I had finished, she didn't say a word, but I could tell, even from the other end of the line, that tears were streaming down her face.

"Don't cry, Mom . . ."

"I know, I know . . . ," she howled, sniffling. "You're right. It's completely stupid. But I'm so happy . . . so happy for you, my girl."

"I know . . . So now do you understand why he's been spoiling you with presents?"

Okay. It's not nice to lie to your dying mother. But was I supposed to ruin her happiness, and tell her a strange, troubling story? A story where I gave myself to faceless desires? A tale in which I no longer knew what to believe, what to think, whom to love . . . nor whom to offer my body for the purposes of pleasure. What would she think of the dangerous game Louie Barlet was subjecting me to? Would she be able to accept it? It was a pretty far cry from fairies and magic wands. A pretty far cry from a mother's dream for her darling child.

The dream begins like this: I am the betrothed on the day of her wedding. I am in tears, locked in my nuptial suite. My bridesmaids try in vain to talk sense into me, but I won't let them in my room. The reason for all the drama? I am naked. My dress is ruined. ~~Anonymous hands tore it from me, and I can't remember why.~~ Everything is wrecked. I don't want to go out there in a backup gown. One of my future husband's friends, however, finds the words to convince me. I open the door. He takes me in his arms and consoles me. Then he kisses me and lays me on the ground. I feel so hopeless that I could give myself to him. But he's hovering over me, masturbating. Soon, no doubt too soon for his taste, a flow of semen spurts from his penis, covering my whole body. I am cloaked in fluid. And when it dries against my skin, it forms a white dress. I am dressed in his seed. I am saved.

Handwritten note by me, 6/10/2009

DAVID AND I HAD NOT spoken since his slap and bitter words from the night before. All of his usual habits—his early-morning departure for work, his chronic unavailability over the phone—lent themselves to shared sulking.

"Hello, David Barlet's office, how may I help you?"

"Hello? Chloe?"

She did not recognize my voice, which was perhaps less assured over the telephone than in person:

"Yes? May I ask who is speaking?"

"Chloe, it's Elle."

"Elle . . ."

The zealous secretary was searching her memory. She had clearly forgotten my nickname.

"Annabelle. Elle Lorand, if you prefer."

"Elle! Yes, sorry! I wasn't expecting you. Is there a problem?"

Nine twenty-three, the clock on her phone undoubtedly told her, or almost one hour after the time I was supposed to be in the office.

"No . . . I mean, I don't feel well."

"Nothing serious, I hope?"

"I don't think so. Just a bad cold," I fibbed. "Could you tell David, and Albane, that I won't be coming in today?"

My second day of work and already sick. If there was anyone left at the company who was still on my side, despite my nepotistic advantage, they would no doubt use this occasion to abandon my cause. My pathetic excuse wasn't going to fool anyone, not my future husband, not my new colleagues. Would Louie interpret my absence as a way of escaping him? The only way I'd found to extract myself from his net? I didn't care. I urgently needed to take some distance. To press pause on my chaotic and capricious relationship with the Barlet brothers. I needed to think outside their incomplete, elusive, and contradictory stories. I was beginning to wonder if their flagrant incoherence wasn't a strategy to confuse me, to lose me in a labyrinth of doubt and fear.

I STAYED HOME ALONE. ARMAND was so busy with wedding preparations that I hardly saw him. I had plenty of time to rummage through the parts of the house that I had hitherto neglected. Since I had moved in, I had been lazy, confining myself to our bedroom, its adjoining bathroom, the living room, and, on rare occasions, the kitchen. As I strolled through my new home, I took stock of the size and grandeur of the place. It had originally been designed by the architect Constantin, the very same man who drew up the plans for New Athens.

The room that had once, I presumed, served as a boudoir, and was attached to Mademoiselle Duchesnois's bedroom—our bedroom—was now David's office. An office, as I had already discovered, that always remained locked.

A key . . . The word ricocheted through my head until it came across a recent memory. The large, antiquated, jagged key that Louie had included in his first package. What if it gave me access to his brother's secrets?

As I inserted the key into the lock, I paused. Was I sure I wanted to know about a past from which I would always necessarily be excluded? What would it bring me, in the end? Like everyone, like me with my absent father, didn't David have the right to forget? Didn't he deserve my unconditional love and faith in him? Didn't I owe it to him after all the amazing things he had done for me?

But the temptation was too strong. Coldly and without regret (or so I told myself), I thrust the rounded point into the dark cavity.

"I'm an idiot," I whispered to myself.

. . . And, above all, naive to imagine that it would be so easy. The lock and key were as mismatched as they could be. Try as I might, the object would not go in, much less turn. There was nothing to be done.

I didn't come across any clues in the rest of the house either. In the few furnishings I could access—mostly magnificent Restoration pieces that fit perfectly with the rest of our decor—notably, in the living and dining rooms, all I found were stacks of paper and newspaper clippings of no real importance; they were mostly related to the Barlet Group's activities. Some were jumbled, others organized in random piles, others stuck between economic magazines, the vast majority of which featured David on the cover . . . They told the story of his ascension, year by year, decade by decade. It was like watching the opening credits of *The Persuaders!*, a television staple of my childhood.

Still, I took the time to flip through several large binders containing the most important articles. Feeling nostalgic, I reread the page in *Le Monde* that I had skimmed in the RER just three months before. I couldn't believe I was sharing my life with the man in the photograph . . .

I STRETCHED OUT ON THE sofa in the living room, abandoning myself to my muddled and contradictory thoughts. Felicity crawled onto my stomach and I ran my hand over her tabby fur. It was soft and reassuring. I tried not to give in to black-and-white thinking, remembering another lesson from my mustachioed professor in the journalism department: even in times of war, never consider a subject in terms of sharply divided sides: "Only in the Bible and Hollywood movies will you ever find a pure, immaculate, untainted Good side on the one hand and a truly evil Bad side on the other. Real life is not made up of Cains and Abels, Luke Skywalkers and Darth Vaders. It's always infinitely more complicated than that. And your job is to untangle this impossible web. You have to tug on threads and show your findings to the public, but without blaming anyone for original sin. There is no such thing as a first cause. Only visible points in a long, long chain of causality. It's up to you to choose a point and explain why you've chosen it. And that's the angle of your paper, your subject." To my great disappointment, Mr. Mustache was one hundred percent right.

Everything would have been so much simpler for me if Louie had been content to lie and play with me like a toy, and if he hadn't made me feel anything—neither desire nor pleasure. Everything would have been so much clearer if David had controlled his hand rather than his secrets.

I was trying to curb my emotions, but I was livid. My time off was misleading. I owed this moment of respite to my temporary withdrawal, and it couldn't last long.

I rummaged through my bag for the papers I'd received the night before in the Païva room. I took a moment to scan the list Louie had written. While some of the titles were vaguely familiar—my knowledge of erotica was extremely limited—I had to admit that I hadn't read any of these books. The ones that were most familiar to me had been adapted to the silver screen:

1. *Secret Women*, Ania Oz
2. *Lady Chatterley's Lover*, D. H. Lawrence
3. *The Eleven Thousand Rods*, Guillaume Apollinaire
4. *Sexus*, Henry Miller
5. *Story of O*, Pauline Réage
6. *Philosophy in the Bedroom*, Marquis de Sade
7. *Emmanuelle*, Emmanuelle Arsan
8. *Delta of Venus*, Anaïs Nin
9. *Fanny Hill*, John Cleland
10. *Portnoy's Complaint*, Philip Roth
11. *Irene's Cunt*, Louis Aragon
12. *Story of the Eye*, Georges Bataille
13. *The Butcher: And Other Erotica*, Alina Reyes
14. *The Lover*, Marguerite Duras
15. *The Mechanics of Women*, Louis Calaferte
16. *The Black Notebook*, Joë Bousquet
17. *The Ages of Lulu*, Almudena Grandes
18. *The Sexual Life of Catherine M.*, Catherine Millet
19. *Tales of Ordinary Madness*, Charles Bukowski
20. *My Secret Life*, Anonymous
21. *The Surrender: An Erotic Memoir*, Toni Bentley

Whether it was *The Eleven Thousand Rods* or *Irene's Cunt*, I could not imagine reading any of these books in front of David, much less in a public place like the metro.

I did not feel ready—would I ever be? did I ever need to be?—to show that part of myself to the world. But the desire was there. Undeniable. Pointing its finger at me.

As far as I could tell, neophyte that I was, there did not seem to be any kind of logic behind the list: it was not in chronological order—it went from Sade to Philip Roth without skipping a beat; there was no linguistic or even erotic consistency since light and crude readings were all mixed up. Was I simply to trust him and begin reading from the top of the list to the bottom? I didn't doubt that he'd spent a lot of time thinking about these books and compiling them for me.

> *Crude thought:* ~~*Sex*~~ *Physical love, the kind that tears us from earthly concerns, the kind that makes us forget everything, is never just a question of anatomy, of two bodies in fleeting union. The only kind of sex that really thrills us is the fruit of our imagination, of our doubts, our questions and hopes about an unknown world. To fantasize is to believe you are the first to plant your flag on a new planet. You know it's not true, but if the dream is big enough, you can take flight—and come back! One small step for my pussy, one giant step for my dream life.*
>
> *Sex blooms in the hollow of our thoughts and wet dreams. There, it is even better than in the flesh of our bellies and buttocks. By letting our spirits wander and our bodies be caressed, we become capable of deep pleasure, here and now.*

Handwritten note by me, 6/10/2009

LIKE THE DAY BEFORE, I heard the door open at an unusually early hour. I was immediately pulled out of my torpor, away from the moist and craggy, oh-so-exciting lands toward which Louie beckoned me.

"Elle, are you there?"

David's voice chimed like a bell. His spontaneous cheer

seemed to ignore our row from the day before, treating it as a minor obstacle to be fixed with a simple change of mood.

"In the living room," I said lifelessly.

He appeared at once, beaming, more solar than ever, his arms loaded with a gigantic garment bag, his body half hidden. Only his gaping smile managed to peek over the mass of pink plastic. My instincts told me that this puffy, impossibly large thing did not contain men's suiting.

"Ta-da!" he trumpeted childishly.

If any one of his hundreds of employees, those gentlemen of the economic press, or his close financial partners saw him like this, the Barlet Group's stock would plummet!

"What is it?"

I had decided to play it cool. I had not gotten a half-confession from Louie without a little sacrifice. Nor would I be able to get David to talk unless I played my part.

"Your dress!"

"My dress?"

I greeted his surprise with a conciliatory smile.

"I mean . . . It was Mother's. It dawned on me the other day: she had the same curvy figure as you. More or less, of course, I've had it altered. And here it is!"

Do not strangle him. Do not ask if the dress is like the ring he gave me: something that once belonged to his mother, and also someone else. His first wife. The dead one.

"But darling," I purred, "aren't you forgetting that you aren't supposed to see it before D-day?"

"Who says I've seen it?"

He gloated triumphantly, an expression I imagine he developed as a teenager after beating an opponent on the tennis court.

"Well now . . . I'm guessing you have."

"You guess wrong, Madame Barlet. It has not left its opaque garment bag since it's been in my possession. Except when it was with the seamstress, of course, but I didn't cheat!"

"What about your parents' wedding? The photos, I mean."

"They're yellowed. You can barely make anything out . . ."

His pout was touching. How could I refuse such a frank—and generous—offer of reconciliation? And when I took the dress out of the bag, all my anger vanished. Taking him at his word, I slipped into the dining room to look at it in private. I had never seen, much less worn, something so extraordinary.

"It's . . . It's fabulous!"

"It's a Schiaparelli," he hollered from the next room. "Elsa Schiaparelli was already very old at the time, but she designed it specially for my mother. It's one of a kind!"

One of a kind, yes. It was splendid. Nothing about it, no detail or finish, not even the state of conservation, betrayed its age. Unlike most wedding dresses, it was not a sickening, misty soufflé of tulle or gauze, iced in embroidery. My first impression of the dress came out in a hushed cry:

"It's a real dress . . . quite simply, a real dress."

"What's that?"

"Nothing, I was just saying: I'm going to try it on."

"Go ahead, beautiful! That's why I brought it. If there are any adjustments to be made, we need to know ASAP."

There wouldn't be. I could barely feel the silk, the color of mother-of-pearl, against my skin. My hips, my waist, my breasts, and even my overly generous backside, everything that I normally had so much trouble jamming into ready-to-wear clothing . . . My whole body fit, naturally, fully, as though molded by a sculptor. The top hugged my torso perfectly. The

V-shaped bust, with its scientifically measured flounce, flared
out into a draped corolla at the waist. The three superimposed
movements of the skirt swished back and forth like a waltz.
Every layer was linked to the next by large flowers of the same
material. And dotted inside each flower was a cluster of diamonds that made the whole dress shimmer.

"So?"

"So . . . it's perfect!"

Led by some invisible dance partner, I spun around to face
myself in front of the large mirror in the dining room. I recognized the woman whose reflection was smiling at me, and
yet she seemed different. Nothing had changed on the outside: I had not lost or gained one ounce over the past several
weeks, but something had changed in her, in me, Elle. I found
myself more radiant, more generous. Even my complexion
seemed clearer. The freckles sprinkled over my face, which I
had always hated, suddenly looked like the most sublime and
natural of jewels. Two or three had recently budded on my lips,
like blossoms over a fresh and moist field.

So what they said was true: a gaze of desire can make you
see the most beautiful, lovable parts of yourself. And the eyes
from the night before had definitely pulled me out of my adolescent shell where, until today, I had been trapped. I'd left
my old skin in the Hôtel des Charmes and walked out of the
building a new person dressed in a new me. I could now see
myself as beautiful, desirable. It no longer seemed absurd to
me that someone might want to possess my body.

BEHIND THE DOOR, WHICH I had been sure to lock, David
was growing impatient. I figured now was a good time to drop
my act of gratitude and submission.

"If you don't mind my asking, *she* never wore it, did she?"

"Wore what? Who are you talking about?" He feigned ignorance.

I persisted in my sweetest, most loving tone:

"Aurora . . . Did she ever wear this dress?"

"No! Why would she . . ."

He was lying. I could tell from his shrill, wavering tone. He never sounded this unsure. And at once, he started casting around for ways to change the subject.

"May I come in?"

"No . . . Not until you answer my question."

"Elle," he begged. "I told you everything there is to know: a prosaic love triangle. Louie loved Aurora, who loved David . . . who didn't love her. Period. There is nothing else to add."

I pretended to buy his overly tidy story, then tried another line:

"And was that the reason for her depression?"

"Not at all. She had been sick long before Louie and I ever met her."

"So then why did she decide to go swimming on a stormy night . . . if not for her broken heart?"

"I don't know. No one knows what really happened. Not even Louie. And yet he was the first one to arrive at the scene."

"Did he try to save her?"

Louie's story had been quite different. He had cast his brother in the role of the hero. But why?

"Yes. But there was nothing he could do . . . except shatter his knee on the rocks. In the weeks that followed the incident, we thought he might never walk again."

"Is that the whole story?"

"Yes," he said, with renewed confidence. "Except the police did a small and theoretically routine investigation."

"Why 'theoretically'"? I asked.

"Because Louie kept contradicting himself."

"But nothing came of it, did it?"

"No . . . the cops concluded it was an accident."

His voice had gotten closer. I guessed he had glued himself to the door, ready to burst in at any moment.

"And you . . . what do you think?"

A few seconds went by before he said gravely:

"Knowing Louie's dark character, I admit that some unsavory thoughts have crossed my mind."

"Like what?"

"Stupid things . . ."

"You do know that I'm not letting you in until you've answered?"

"I've considered that he might have pushed her off the rocks, there!" he barked. "He and Aurora knew that part of the beach by heart. What I mean is, I was surprised a wave caught her off guard there . . . even on a stormy night."

"Do you really think he'd be capable of such a thing?"

"No . . . I don't know . . . I think it is impossible to know in advance what a bitter person is capable of doing."

He was right about that. But I wasn't going to let him off the hook so easily. There were holes in his story: What about his arm? What happened to it?

But I was wise enough not to provoke the same outcome as in our last exchange. He had just confided more about the topic to me than he probably had to anyone.

I took off the dress and carefully put it back in its bag, adding simply:

"You were mad at yourself . . . Weren't you?"

"Yes . . . I suppose I was. But it's all ancient history . . ."

Was he trying to convince himself? To bury guilt and ghost under the heavy weight of forgetting?

He tapped lightly at the door, and I unlocked it. It wouldn't be the first time he'd seen me in my underthings . . .

. . . But it would be the first time he took me in this room, where the old-fashioned decor was more reminiscent of quiet evenings by the fire than gasping and excitement.

He glued himself to me before I was able to decide if he was looking for pleasure or consolation. He remained still for several seconds, his nose buried in my neck, jerking slightly as his body adjusted to mine. Like a wounded child taking refuge in his mother's bosom.

I ran my hand over the nape of his neck, a long, gentle movement that I thought more comforting than erotic, and that he took as an invitation. His palm caressed my back, wandering down the valley to my rounded buttocks. Reflexively, my pelvis responded to his touch. Again, he took this as a sign to continue. He and I had not made love since the two times I had given in to Louie at the Hôtel des Charmes.

Which part of the new Annabelle, the woman I had just discovered in the mirror, still belonged to him?

"We haven't christened this room yet, have we?" he whispered in my ear.

He had never said that kind of thing before. Our lovemaking was usually so ordinary, so devoid of challenge. It lacked any sense of play. What was going on with him?

I contemplated the two of us in the giant mirror, and how the raw lighting of the summer afternoon sculpted us; we were as beautiful as we could be. Any third-party witness would have said we were well matched. I was not the only one who had changed. The difference was more subtle in him than me, but for a second I could have sworn I saw that same rough and carnivorous, cannibalistic smile that Louie reserved for his prey.

"Come!"

Without further ado, he carried me to the bronze-footed marble table and laid me across the cold stone. I barely had the time to shiver before he pulled me toward him, my legs spread wide, my feet hanging in midair. He pushed my thighs up toward my hips and leaned down until he was facing my panties. I could feel his hot breath through the satiny cotton, titillating my hitherto bone-dry vagina.

He pushed the material aside with one finger and began licking my vulva from bottom to top, as though painting me with his tongue. Whenever he reached my erectile mound, which was still hiding under its protective skin, he started from the beginning again. His diligence was textbook worthy.

Happily, he made up for such studious awkwardness: his tongue moved at an excruciatingly slow pace, driving me wild:

"Faster . . ."

"Otherwise, is everything okay for you?"

"Yes," I fibbed. "But faster."

He obeyed, and not without success. With each lick of the tongue, I could feel my lips opening wider, readying themselves for entry. Of course, with his metronomic movements and concentrated efforts to moisten the entire area, he never lingered long enough for my taste on my sensitive button. It wanted more, much more. His hands wandered to my breasts, kneading them in a not at all displeasing way. I placed my index finger on my lonely clitoris and began rolling it under its jacket, such as I had learned to do long ago.

Disconcerted by my initiative, David froze:

"You are so beautiful like that . . ."

But I heard more than his smooth, enchanting voice in those sweet words. It was joined by ten voices, one hundred or even one thousand voices, as many as the Hôtel des Charmes could fit men at my mercy.

I continued rubbing myself under his submissive gaze, his subservient fascination. For the first time, it did not feel wrong to give him such a show.

A foreboding shiver ran up my spine, as a question shot through me: Among the penises pointed at me in the Païva room . . . had one belonged to Louie? Had I touched it without knowing? If I hadn't been so drunk with desire, maybe I would have noticed. Maybe I would have felt a telling tremor, a special vein. Would I have squeezed it more ardently?

David's penis suddenly penetrated me. Decisively and without warning. I hadn't seen it coming, and the irruption petrified me. I didn't want this. Not yet, at least, not now.

"Touch yourself again," he ordered.

I didn't have a problem with him dominating me. But, true to his male instincts, he was in a hurry to finish. He was about to blow everything into a million pieces, right when I was just getting started.

"No, you . . . Get out!" I said now.

I had to use a decisive tone so he would obey me without question. Thank God, it wasn't all lost. David, hungry to satisfy me, glued his avid lips to my sex, sucking on the sweet juice of my deliverance:

"Put it in me!" I ordered.

The poor man was seized with panic: Why did I forbid him something only to demand it again a moment later? I clarified the misunderstanding, in an unrecognizable voice that swelled from the depths of my belly:

"Your tongue . . . I want you to put it in me . . . Go ahead!"

He prostrated himself. His pink, fleshy tip darted in me, stretching its full length, diving deep inside. I felt penetrated but not dominated. Attended to but not conquered. His mouth stuck to me like a leech as he firmly rotated his tongue at my vagina's point of entry.

His lips disappeared into mine, which were now bathed in a thick fluid. A white froth lined the contours of his mouth, like a sticky mustache of love.

I read in one of my women's magazines that a French gynecologist had solved the mystery of the G-spot. Apparently, it is not an autonomous erogenous zone that some women are lucky enough to have and others not. In truth, according to this gynecologist and her supporting medical imagery, it is an internal extension of the clitoris. Contrary to what is commonly thought, the clitoris is made up of far more than the few millimeters we can see.

Inside each woman, the clitoris extends over a territory of ten or so centimeters. And, in function of one's anatomy and size, it innervates the surrounding organs. Apparently, the sensations that some women feel in their rectum during sodomy come from that hidden and mysterious presence.

Handwritten note by me, 6/10/2009

"FASTER . . . YES!"

With each rotation, his tongue pressed my sensitive bulge,

that tiny mound of pleasure that had all but given up on such forms of attention.

"That's it, don't move! There!"

He got the message, focusing his efforts on that one essential point. But suddenly and without warning, he withdrew. It was, to say the least, disagreeable. Then, he rapidly replaced his tongue with his member. He, too, had grown impatient—I could tell by the size of his erection and its pearling tip. He couldn't take it anymore. He could only be at my service for a few more seconds. In the end, he needed to dominate, to conquer, to invade me. As luck had it, his preliminaries had prepared my sex so well that his mechanical thrusting ended up prolonging the sensations. I opened myself wider, inviting him to my innermost depths, not far from the uterus. That is where, I knew, a tiny tongue of mucus, which is softer and more sensitive than the rest, is capable of making me come instantly. It is almost impossible to reach it with my fingers. But he was there. His manhood rhythmically rammed into it, there where my body suddenly seemed to concentrate, drawn by an improbable force, like a black hole, which fragmented me, limb by limb, right down to my cells, and then threw them all around me, into every corner of the room, flying on shafts of light from the outdoors, straddling an abyss in which I at last fell, heavily.

For the very first time, he had made me come. He alone, with no help from me. He and his mouth and his cock, all of which were now covered in my humors.

But was he really the only one behind this miracle? In his sigh, I thought I heard the voice of another.

22

June 11, 2009

My notebook! My notebook, my notebook, my notebook ...

I was still naked and panting in the dining room. My crotch and thighs were sticky with pleasure. But I couldn't get those two words out of my head. Over and over I repeated them to myself, like the miser who has lost his coffer. My silver notebook was still sitting on our bed. My Ten-Times-a-Day, which now included my own notes. I would never be able to live with the shame if David saw those pages. As for the entries that were not written by me, I didn't want to think of all the untruths I would need to invent to justify them to him. And I would have to lie if I wanted to preserve even a shred of his trust and esteem.

I climbed the stairs on all fours, my rump in the air, my clothes hastily drawn to my chest and middle. I prayed I would not run into Armand on one of his hurried rounds through the house. Upstairs, I could hear my man walking through our room. Then he stopped short. When at last I made it to the room, his back was turned to the door and he was contemplating the garden. I could not see the contents of his hands, which were clasped in front of him. My heart stopped when I noticed that the notebook had disappeared from the bedspread.

At last he put me out of my misery and turned around:

"Tell me . . ."

His hands were empty. I breathed deeply. The end of a nightmare? Or had there been enough time for him to hide the object among his things?

My heart seized, pounding into my naked chest.

"Yes?"

Against the light, his face looked dark and expressionless. Even his voice seemed less warm and welcoming than usual.

"You're going to have to go back . . ."

Where? To my mom's house? In Nanterre? Near Fred? To my old mediocre life from before?

"Don't get me wrong, my choice has nothing to do with my feelings for you."

What was he talking about exactly . . . ? If I was there, wasn't it because he loved me?

"But I did have to fight to get everyone on board about you."

I shivered apprehensively, finally seeing what he meant. Still, to be sure, I asked:

"On board?"

"At BTV. What did you think I meant? The unions really don't like favoritism, you know. For them, so long as you haven't paid your dues, you're no better than girls who sleep their way up the ladder."

Did he know a lot of girls like that? I pushed the thought aside and commiserated:

"Yes, of course . . . I understand."

"They keep harassing me about it," he added, his expression darkening.

A rush of air into my lungs. So that was what was bothering him. I wouldn't lose everything. Not right away. Not yet.

But . . . where on earth had my notebook gone?

"If you want them to take you seriously," he stressed, "you're going to have to work at their level. You're going to have to be better than them. With these people, it's make or break. They don't do things halfway."

Christopher and Louie had already given me a taste of how intransigent business culture could be. I was going to have to earn my stripes with them, on their turf, that was clear. There was no way I was going to gain their respect and support if I stayed locked up here or in the glass prison that was my office. I still had everything to prove.

"You are one hundred percent right . . . ," I admitted.

The silence following this statement came with a big "but." *But I can't stand your brother? But Louie is working on a report for my program that could reveal all my secrets?*

"So . . . chin up!"

He took me in his arms. He was a comforting bubble, generously sharing his inner calm every time we touched.

"Do you think it would be okay if I stayed home again tomorrow? After that, I promise, I'll be a good little soldier."

I rarely used the kinds of vapid girls' tricks that tend to be so effective with the male sex: wide eyes, puckered lips, batting lashes, cocked head . . . but now seemed like a good time. And even though my position in his arms made it so he couldn't see me, he must have felt it because he caved.

"Okay, but just tomorrow. After that . . . work, young lady! No discussion!"

He breathed a conciliatory smile into my neck, giving me the opening I'd been looking for:

"I was wondering, you didn't see a notebook on the bed earlier, did you?"

"A notebook?"

He detached himself and looked me in the eye. I didn't detect any sign of duplicity in his face.

"Yes, a silver notebook . . ."

"No. Have you looked under the bed?"

It was in fact lying under the bed. We spent the rest of the evening on the bed, with one interruption from Armand, who left us something to eat outside the door—perk of the privileged few, who get to live at home as though in a hotel—and a few urgent calls that David had to take.

Alas, in all those idle hours, I did not have another orgasm like the one in the dining room. A return to our usual, mundane sex.

THE NEXT MORNING, IT WAS not my notebook waiting for me on the breakfast table—this time I had carefully zipped it in an internal pocket of my purse—but a stack of typed papers held together by a silver paper clip that looked like an eagle's talon. I should have seen that as a sign . . .

"Good morning, Elle!" Armand surprised me.

He was already familiar with my morning routine, and didn't have to ask before serving me a large cup of green tea, steeped to perfection.

"Good morning, Armand."

"David left this for you to read."

"I see that . . . But what is it?"

Master Christian Olivo, Notary in Paris, I read the austere header on the first page. A stylized Marianne, a French national emblem, was half hidden under the raptor's claw.

"A draft of your marriage contract. I also have a red pen and a block of Post-its for you, in case you want to make any changes."

A prenup? David had never been so formal about our union in my presence.

With one hand, I stirred a spoon in my steaming mug, while the other leafed through the thick document. My gaze paused randomly on a line or paragraph, whenever a word or phrase caught my attention. Despite my limited experience with contracts, I had no problem understanding that the purpose of this document was essentially to protect the Barlet family's assets and estate. The paragraph on Marital Property didn't mince words: "Separation of individual assets," it stipulated.

It was understandable. The independent woman in me, the one who loved her autonomy and believed women should be self-sufficient, tried to downplay what I was reading. But the cold way in which I was being subjected to the terms, the absence of dialogue, felt like a slap in the face.

"When am I supposed to have this read?" I asked icily.

"If possible, by the end of the day."

I gazed for a moment at the neat stack of papers, then raised my eyes toward Armand, who was wearing his usual woolen waistcoat.

"It's fine. You can take it back now."

He was momentarily taken aback, then asked:

"Are you sure you don't want to read it more closely? Or maybe show some passages to a third party? A lawyer?"

"No, no . . . it's fine as is."

"The contract is binding, Elle. I wouldn't take it lightly."

His advice reminded me of the fine print on ads for credit cards in France with exorbitant rates: "Credit is a binding commitment and must be repaid." I tried not to hear his words in such bleak terms.

"I know. But I trust David."

"Yes, of course," he agreed meekly. "But still . . ."

"I'm right, am I not?" I interrupted, searching his eyes. "To trust him . . . ?"

He had trouble suppressing a little smile from his lips. Had he been drinking? So early?

"Yes . . . Yes, clearly."

I dipped a piece of toast in my tea, which clouded with melted butter, and concluded with false optimism:

"All is well then."

He took the stack of papers, Post-its, and pen, and added, as though he were also David's clerk:

"Well then, I'll have a final version ready for your signature this evening on the console."

"Perfect." I dismissed him with a look. "Thank you, Armand."

NO SOONER HAD I FINISHED breakfast than I received a call from Sophia, whose infectious happiness was like a breath of fresh air. I threw on some sweats and took the metro to meet her. She lived in a small, cheap apartment in Nogent-sur-Marne, at the other end of the RER line A from Nanterre. It only took thirty-five minutes from Mom's house, and without having to change trains. Her studio was on the top floor of a charmless block building from the seventies, but it was ideally located, just a few steps away from the Bois de Vincennes. The unobstructed view of the bus terminal and train tracks was depressing—probably why her rent was so low—but at least she didn't have any neighbors across the way peeping in on her Homeric, legs-in-the-air sessions.

She was wearing a light-pink tracksuit and standing in front of Le Relais, a big café with a veranda where the avenues Clemenceau and Marronniers intersect.

"Hey, ritzy!"

"Hey, fanatic . . ."

The kind of friendly jibes that showed our mutual affection, while also gently expressing whatever we found annoying in the other.

We started at a light trot down Avenue de Nogent. The bridle way was already scattered with turds from the early-morning cavalcade. On a Thursday midmorning in June, there wasn't a legion of runners, no more than there were cyclists and horseback riders. It felt like the park belonged to us, and I was glad, though I was also out of breath. I hadn't been running with Sophia since we used to go regularly in college. She had kept it up, but not me: every stride awoke a group of dormant muscles. I'd soon start to feel the pain.

"Come on, old lady!" she prompted. "Don't forget: in a week you're going to have to squeeze a dress over all that flab you call your body!"

The sky was clear, the air cool, and a breeze that smelled of flowers gently brushed past us, adding to the already enjoyable atmosphere. The road was almost entirely empty of vehicles, save a few rusted trucks whose purpose in these parts was unclear. The prostitutes, illegals from western Africa who had paid a fortune to get here, gave themselves up nearby for a few tenners. But they didn't leave their shabby stalls.

"If this keeps up," Sophia wailed, "that's where I'll end up!"

"Don't be ridiculous! What are you talking about?"

"I'm broke, Elle! I received my first eviction notice. I haven't paid rent in months. I wish it were winter. At least then they wouldn't legally be allowed to evict me. But it's not. It's June!"

"Have you tried Rebecca again on her phone?"

"That bitch has totally disappeared. Her professional line has been cut. And I never had the other one."

"Okay, it's not so bad. You still have your 'shows' . . ."

The air quotes I drew around this word, so as not to say "peep show" in public, only added to her frustration. She stopped suddenly. Her face was flushed with effort and nascent anger, her hands on her hips.

"I would like to see you on stage, Madame-Barlet-and-her-golden-spoon!"

"Ha! Well then it would have to be the tiniest spoon," I said, trying to lighten the mood. I remembered the prenup Armand had handed me that morning.

But my friend didn't give me time to explain.

"Shit, Elle . . . I'm almost twenty-six, I've got no boyfriend, no stable job, my parents are broke and, in any case, they don't care."

"Soph—"

"Don't you get it? I'm out of options. Nothing! And I'm not going to shove my finger up my pussy for some nasty old men twelve hours a day in order to pay my rent!"

"I already told you. I can lend you some money."

Suddenly, as we started down a narrow alley, we heard the sound of a motor from the road behind us. We turned around.

A dark limousine with tinted windows—a rare German model, I thought—hugged the raised sidewalk at a crawling pace. It would soon reach us.

A passenger window opened on our side. As in a spy movie, we could barely make out the face hiding in the shadows of his luxury vehicle, a study in shades of gray.

"Hello! You're Sophia, right?"

We could hear Ravel's *Boléro* playing in the background. The voice did not address me.

"Yes . . ."

"I am Louie Barlet. Annabelle's future brother-in-law. And also the director of communication at BTV."

Sophia, whom I had always known to be self-confident and even cheeky, was now tongue-tied and speechless.

"May I borrow her?" he asked, pointing his chin in my direction. "You won't be mad, I hope?"

Only then did Louie's emaciated face appear, smiling, just as affable in that moment as he could be ferocious in others. The notes of vanilla and lavender wafting out his window mixed with the woodsy perfume of our environs. That was Louie Barlet's power: leaving his mark, shaping a place or situation to his exact image, reconfiguring the world through his sheer presence, as he had wanted to do for me when he'd inscribed my name in the city.

"Elle and I have a little emergency having to do with her show."

How can a person be so careless about lying? It was obvious he had followed us here, and that his sudden appearance had nothing to do with our professional world.

His shoulder rested idly in the open window, his eyes transfixed by Sophia's figure, which was perfectly sculpted by her leggings and formfitting top.

"So . . . ?" he insisted in a playful tone. "You're not going to charge me rent, are you?"

He did not seem to be implying anything, but I could have sworn my friend blushed.

"No!" she cried at last. "Have her. In any case, she dawdles like a cow!"

I interjected.

"Thanks! Maybe you could let the 'cow' speak for herself!"

"Go on, don't make him beg. Your *colleague* insists."

"Are you sure? You don't mind being alone?"

"Don't worry, I can run faster than the perverts!"

She bored her jet-black eyes into those of our surprise visitor. Then she slapped me on the back, and I couldn't tell if she was encouraging or getting rid of me.

Louie opened the door, making room on the bench for me to enter. Then he knocked on the opaque partition between the chauffeur and us, signaling our departure. I barely had time to close the door behind me before the limousine took off, its cylinders growling.

I have never ~~fucked~~ made love in a car. And yet it's so commonplace! Sometimes I get the impression I'm the only one or, to be exact, the last one, having these ~~sexual~~ erotic experiences that everyone else has already had. ~~Starting with Sophia, who has told me some pretty good stories about what's possible in such a confined space.~~

In this instance, if something had happened in that limousine, we would have had all the necessary comforts. There was plenty of space at the foot of his seat to crawl on my knees between his legs and pull out his cock. The car's supple suspension would have rocked me back and forth, and my mouth would have sucked up and down his shaft, effortlessly. From time to time, I would have nipped the base of his gland to anchor myself and keep potholes from throwing him too far down my throat. In the end, when he came, I would have pulled a cotton square from the nearby tissue box and wiped my mouth of semen with one movement, like a windshield wiper.

Handwritten note by me, 6/11/2009

"WHERE ARE YOU TAKING ME?" I screamed in a tone that annoyed even me. "The Hôtel des Charmes? My nights aren't enough for you now?"

"I would love to, believe me . . . But I don't do anything without your consent."

He seemed sincere, and almost shocked that I would question his manners and good faith.

"I would not say you've been holding back!"

"Now, you listen," he seized my hand. "If ever I had felt that you had doubts about doing something, I would have stopped everything at once. I mean, you saw, the other night . . . I put an end to our session. I'm not forcing you into anything, Elle. I am simply accompanying you on a journey that you began at your own will."

His nerve was baffling. Me, of my own volition, in those rooms? Me, whom he had held hostage in his bacchanalia? The victim of his odious blackmailing?

His hand squeezed mine, imprisoning it momentarily, confirming my captivity. Then, as though remembering himself, he suddenly released his grip. Though he struggled to hide it, I could see an internal battle play out across his features. He felt me looking at him and turned his head to avoid my scrutinizing gaze.

I noted, however, that for the first time, we were speaking openly about our secret meetings in the hotel managed by Monsieur Jacques. In a sense, his frank intimations were a kind of confession. At last, he was showing me his true face. At last, I saw the social Louie and the secretive and manipulative Louie at the same time, as each one tried to conquer the other.

I wished I had something to keep a trace of this: the Dictaphone on my smartphone, for instance, which I could use to trap him. But the pockets of my gray sweats barely had room for my keys and a tissue pack.

"And what's keeping us from going further, huh? Who said I didn't want more that night?"

The field of erect penises pointing at me, trembling under my fingertips, rippled through my memory. I could almost hear their gasps and sighs echoing from the not-so-distant past.

"You weren't ready, Annabelle . . . Not yet. You have much to learn before we can go further."

He was no longer wearing the expression of disdain that he tended to project in public. No hidden irony, no arrogant swagger. This had to be the real Louie. His cologne tickled my nose, but I resisted. I kept control over my attitude and voice. I didn't want to let myself get distracted again.

"Like your reading list? Is that what you mean?"

What was the first one on the list, again? Oh, right: *Secret Women*. Was that a hint? The first part of some kind of training? Is that what he wanted from me, in the end? That I, too, become a secret woman? His thing, his toy? For as long as he wanted and unbeknownst to his brother?

"Yes, that's part of it. But there's more . . ."

He let his sentence hang enigmatically.

Instead of answering me, he leaned toward the microphone that communicated with the chauffeur:

"The Tuileries, please."

The motor purred. The car shifted gears, gluing us to the soft leather bench. I liked the sensation of power and gave in to it for a moment. I peered at Louie from the corner of my eye. He was as nervous and reserved as ever. Why didn't he trust me? He was the one uprooting me from my friend and my life. He was the one playing with my life as though it were just a game.

Outside, buildings had replaced trees. Our pace slowed, and the cacophony of impatient horns told me we were in Paris.

"You see, Elle, one cannot get to know oneself and one's sensations without becoming fully aware of the environment in which the body resides."

I recognized the pontificating register from the visual design meeting. To be honest, I found it hollow: "Don't you see how our lives sorely lack sublimity?"

And yet the way he said each word resonated in me, thrumming an invisible chord whose delightful wave spread bit by bit to each of my organs. I could reject him, but he had this power over me: he thrilled me, no matter what he said, no matter the topic.

"And so?"

I pretended he could not win me over with ready-made phrases.

"Look outside! There is not one street, not one porte cochere, not one bench or even one simple cobblestone that is not filled with sensual history. Everywhere you go, no matter how small the nook or cranny, you can be sure that dozens, or even hundreds of kisses, sighs . . . and perhaps even orgasms have taken place there!"

I didn't back down.

"Yes, but the same goes for murders, calls for help, tears . . ."

"That's where you're wrong, Elle. To be sure, pleasure needs a certain dose of the morbid to blossom, but it always wins out over death. Do you hear me, always!"

Eros, Thanatos, a drive for life, a drive for death, and their eternal struggle to dominate the human psyche: his theoretical underpinnings, which he'd borrowed from Freud, were fairly apt. But where the Austrian psychoanalyst had imagined a tension that sought to bring balance between these two forces, Louie seemed to believe in the victory of pleasure over nothingness. What was troubling in his thesis, and also fairly seductive, was the way in which he integrated a spatial and historic dimension:

"And do you know why, Elle?"

His eyes were shining with newfound intensity. He gradually leaned in, and I could feel the fire in him at that moment.

"No," I admitted.

"Because, quite simply, for every *one* death, *one* destruction, and before that the birth that led to it, hundreds of bodies have come together, somewhere in this gigantic erotic landscape you are contemplating. They have come, hundreds of times, there, all around us. For those who know how to look, traces of pleasure will always be easier to find than remnants of the kinds of tragic events you've just evoked."

"Okay, why not? . . . But what does that have to do with us?"

"Patience. In a moment, I will give you a very pertinent example. You'll see."

He murmured to the driver again, his mouth almost touching the partition:

"Richard, would you please accelerate a little? Thank you."

Instantly, the car merged into the bus lane, extracting itself from the magma of vehicles crowding Rue Saint-Antoine. It then hurtled full speed down Rue de Rivoli, with no regard for the police, who were teeming.

Him, his look, his voice, his scent, his proximity in the other passenger seat, his hands grazing over the soft leather. They could have just as easily been running over another kind of skin . . . I was suffocating and took the liberty of opening the power window beside me. A little air for my overexcited senses.

I needed to get ahold of myself. Regain control. I couldn't let his sweet torpor get the better of me.

"Okay," I finally agreed. "But on one condition: stop using Aurora's story to toy with me. I want to know how she died. I want the truth, Louie. The whole truth."

He looked at me in surprise—was this the first time I had called him by his first name?—and a kind of respect. Or something more, maybe, deeper and filled with esteem.

Another wave rushed through me before I had the chance to fight it. I realized that in this confined space he'd had a thousand opportunities to slip a hand under the distended elastic of my sweats, and then into my panties. This thought made my labia contract as well as my perineum, which I struggled to control. And what if I got really wet down there, what then . . .

It's not really a dream, but a thought, one of those wet daydreams I have sometimes, while idling at a red light or when the metro stops in a station; they vanish as soon as I feel movement under me again.

In that brief space of time, I give all the men around me the same face. I choose the most handsome among them,

*of course, and copy-paste it on all the others in his vicinity.
That way, everyone is equal in front of my desire. No one
looks repellent to me. Everyone is worthy of my attention.
I can sense their diversity, their differences in odor, for
instance, and yet I see them as one. In this way, though
they are numerous, I have no scruples about abandoning
myself to their hands, which graze and pinch me, or to
their penises, which penetrate me one by one.*

*~~With each new partner, the penis seems bigger and
harder in me.~~ When I come back to myself, it is always
with the realization that I am not big enough, nor do I
have enough holes, to satisfy them all. I chastise myself for
this shortcoming. And as the train or car starts moving, I
feel heat in my cheeks and moisture in my panties. And I
promise them I'll do better next time.*

Handwritten note by me, 6/11/2009

AND YET, ASIDE FROM WHEN he'd held my hand for a few
seconds, Louie had refrained from all contact. Yes, to be fair,
in his own contradictory way, this man did respect me. Or
was his reserve just a more subtle way of using me, however
and whenever he pleased, and not simply a question of circumstance?

"We are almost there . . . ," he whispered, impatiently
scanning the urban landscape. "And you'll see: what I have in
mind will satisfy your curiosity."

I did not really see the relationship between the Tuileries
and Aurora's death, but I could not think of anything to contradict him either. So much the better, since anything that
came out of my mouth at that moment would have sounded

like a plea for him to throw himself at me. To take me. To spare me the pedantic explanations and give me what he kept deferring, at each one of our encounters.

At last, the Louvre's long body appeared on our left. And with a couple powerful pumps of the accelerator, we raced past the palace and arrived at the Tuileries, a patch of greenery in the dense city. It had not always been like this, I knew. Where today there were trees, there had once stood another building, the Palais des Tuileries, which the Communard insurgents had burned in 1871.

"For fun," Louie went on, "we could each take the identity of a historical character. It's a fairly amusing game."

What road was he leading me down now? I decided not to put up a fight, and even fed into his present whim by choosing a character to suit his ribald tastes:

"I have always seen myself as a Ninon de Lenclos . . . But I am probably overestimating my talents."

His hands were now crossed in an apparent attempt to maintain control. Each one appeared to be fighting the other, restraining the other from jumping at me.

"David, for instance," he went on, ignoring my reference, "has all the qualities of a little Bonaparte. Charismatic, determined, a conqueror . . . A man who takes everything by force, and who almost always succeeds."

His panegyric smacked of criticism or, rather, incomprehension with respect to a nature that was so different from his own. But I had to admit that the comparison was not unfounded, even if, physically speaking, it did not hold. David was pleasant and attractive, and the emperor of the French sharp and disturbing.

The car stopped at the point where Rue de Rivoli and the

Avenue Lemonnier intersect. The Tuileries Garden spreads over half the length of this latter. Louie maintained his stance as he refreshed my patchy notions of history:

"The palace that stood here one hundred and fifty years ago was the Louvre's centerpiece. Napoleon I figured among its list of prestigious occupants. For him it was a point of pride to live where Louis XVI had fallen during the Revolution. But that is not why we're here . . ."

"Why, then?"

"Almost the entirety of Napoleon Bonaparte's romantic life took place here. His first time was in the Palais-Royal when he was just a penniless young officer. A few streets down is where he first saw Josephine. And it was in this now long-gone palace that he received the vast majority of his countless mistresses."

I wanted to shake him: Once again, what did this have to do with David, with Aurora? And above all: What did this have to do with us? With our obvious desire for each other? Every molecule of rarefied air in this vehicle was vibrating with it . . .

But I didn't have to say anything to encourage his erudition, which eventually told me what I wanted to know:

"Like Napoleon when he met Josephine, David fell under Aurora's spell. She did whatever she wanted with him. You know, her borderline episodes . . . She even cheated on him without the slightest remorse."

I had trouble imagining David as a mistreated and betrayed suitor.

"Then, after they got married, he started taking on more responsibility at the company, just like Bonaparte, who began his career as a cadet and quickly moved up the ranks, from officer to general to supreme magistrate. And as he grew more powerful, the relationship of power became inverted. Now he was the star, the man all the women wanted . . ."

"And Aurora?"

"She wilted. She stewed impatiently at the house and eventually gave in to her depression."

"David started cheating on her, too, is that it?"

Just as I was now cheating on David, in my own way . . .

"Almost compulsively, and he didn't bother hiding it," said Louie, without judgment. "There was a service stairway in the Tuileries that linked the ground floor to a second, smaller bedroom above the emperor's office. Napoleon's valet, Constant, led young women from court up to this room for his emperor's pleasure."

"Why are you telling me this?"

At last, he turned and faced me. His look was severe and intense, like a predator who was so certain of his power that he could afford to let his prey wander. But there was no doubt he would be eating it in the end. In fact, his gaze was already devouring me.

"Because at the time, David did not yet reside at Duchesnois House. He lived in what is today my apartment, on Avenue Georges Mandel, in the 16th Arrondissement. An apartment that is entirely reminiscent of the Tuileries: there is a small one-bedroom flat, which we also own, over the apartment. It can, of course, be accessed by the main staircase, but there are also stairs in my apartment that link the two. I sealed the access a long time ago. But, back then, David often made use of it . . ."

I wondered what kind of women David used to choose for one-night stands.

*How many women has David known before me? We
have never discussed it. Have there been dozens, hundreds
. . . more? Is there a way not to be jealous of past affairs?
When once you possess a body, is it possible to erase the
memory and forget the men or women you once knew?*

Handwritten note by me, 6/11/2009

WAS THAT DAVID'S TRUE NATURE? A tireless hunter, always searching for fresh prey, while Louie tended to be mono-focused—on me?

I wondered if there were any hidden staircases in Duchesnois House.

"Did he talk to you about them?"

"Yes. With me, David would brag. It was another competition for him." A tiny smile passed over his otherwise blank expression.

"Were you surprised by his behavior?"

"No . . . I was revolted! I hated that he was treating Aurora like a broken toy, just because she was more fragile than he. Just because she . . ." He flattened his hand against his window, as though trying to erase the view.

"Because . . . ?"

"David justified himself by saying that Aurora had very limited *talents*. He said he'd really tried to resist temptation, but that she could not satisfy him."

He did not have to specify what he meant by talents.

"And you saw things differently . . . ," I ventured.

Saying this, I placed a hand on his knee. He stared at it with desire and pain, and I quickly took it back. I did not want to ruin the moment, as chaste as the gesture may have been. Nor did I want to frighten him out of telling me his secrets.

Louie the libertine, Louie the pervert, had been transformed. I saw him now as Louie the bashful lover, a man torn between desire and the crushing weight of his memories. I could tell he was trying to spare me his pain, and this concern for me was confusing.

"Yes. I think David was the one who suffocated her. When they first met, he saw her as a perfect object, a kind of untouchable being. He idealized her too much. And when he learned of Aurora's troubles, he did everything in his power to cut her off from the world."

"He made her pay for them."

"I would say, rather, that he wanted to regain control in their relationship. Don't forget: David is Napoleon. He will let you take everything, except power. Locking up Aurora in the house was the easiest way for him to assert dominance. He blamed her health and paid doctors to prescribe constant rest."

"So she never left the house?"

"Toward the end, almost never . . . On Avenue Mandel or in Dinard, she lived under a bell jar. The worst is that she never complained. She had become completely dependent on him."

Napoleon and Josephine, the sovereign and his old, abandoned mistress. But the passion between David and Aurora had not died because of a difference in age. What, then? Was this bitter conjecture the answer: their divergent sexual needs had driven them apart?

"And then?"

He knocked on the partition, signaling to Richard the chauffeur that it was time to go.

"The day of Aurora's death, we were all in Dinard, at

Brown Rocks, Dad's immense villa on the cliff tops of Saint-Malo in Brittany. He had bought it for himself some twenty years earlier on a whim, after having sold some of his shares in *The Ocean*."

Dinard.

"To the sea . . . but not on the other side of the world," David had proposed for our honeymoon. Is that where he wanted to take me? Where his memories were etched into the tormented landscape . . .

"Do you still go there?"

"No . . . ," he replied quietly. "I have never returned. The villa is as it was, or almost. I believe Armand goes once a year to clean house."

"So what happened that day?" I urged.

"As usual, David had run off somewhere, supposedly on business. Aurora locked herself in her room. She cried and cried. She had found a message from one of his lovers."

"You were there, too?"

"Yes, with my girlfriend at the time."

So Louie Barlet had had "girlfriends." He, the wild animal, had let himself be locked in the prison of coupledom. Would he ever choose to do it again?

"My girlfriend was the one who managed to get Aurora to talk, through the door, and learn what had happened. A banal episode . . . and, unfortunately, nothing new as far as she and David were concerned."

I did not interrupt. Judging from the serious look on his face, I understood that he needed to get it all off his chest.

"Then she and I went out for dinner in Saint-Malo. My parents were there. Armand as well. There was no reason to worry."

And yet . . .

"She snuck away in the night. You'll see when you go . . ."

Had David told him about our honeymoon destination?

"The house is built on a cliff. The only way to access the beach is via a very steep set of stairs that leads to a coastal path that gets submerged during high tide."

I could not ignore the dark image that suddenly came to mind:

"That's where she drowned?"

"Yes . . . I mean, it's not very clear. But there are big, angular rocks just under that path. When they are covered by the sea, it looks as though you could walk on them. But in reality, they are full of holes and crevices. All it takes is for a foot to step into one of them, and you're trapped."

"Why?"

"The water acts like a vacuum. It sucks you in. And it does not take long for the sea to rise and submerge you. If no one comes to your rescue in the minutes after you get caught . . ."

The story echoed the one he had told me the other day while we were having tea.

I didn't say anything, but I noticed that our car was now going west, past Place de la Concorde and then the Arc de Triomphe.

"Do you think it could have been an accident?"

"Honestly, no. I don't think so."

He spoke without emotion.

Throughout our conversation, he had been gazing out the window. Now, he turned toward me, visibly relieved. Could it be that I was the first person in whom he had been able to confide like this?

"In any case, we'll never know . . . When I got there, it was too late, of course. A swath of white nightgown floated on the water's surface. Like an idiot, I dived . . . All I managed to achieve was get sucked in, too. I was luckier. All I lost was this . . ."

He tapped his bad knee.

"How did you survive?"

"A fisherman on his way back to the port. He was not supposed to bring his boat in so close to shore, but he took the risk, to save me."

"You owe him your life!"

"Yes. And I don't even know who it was. He refused to give his name to the staff at the Saint-Malo hospital. He took off as soon as we arrived."

"And Aurora?"

"When I awoke, my girlfriend told me that they could not find her body. Her remains are no doubt still there, somewhere on the seafloor . . . Maybe they've already mixed in with the shells."

"And David . . . What was his reaction?"

"Exactly what I've already told you, Elle. He who had been so bad at loving her could not handle her death. Several years later, he cut himself on the arm. And for a while, he even blamed me: he went around telling everyone that I was the one who had pushed her onto the rocks."

Another point for his version of the story. It included what David had recently told me.

"It's absurd, of course. My girlfriend could testify to the fact that I was with her in the car when everything happened."

And the authorities concluded that it was an accident. End of story. End of Aurora. "Pleasure always wins out over death,"

Louie had claimed earlier in the day. Personally, I was having trouble figuring out how. How had Eros won out over Thanatos in this tragedy?

I sat up in my seat, the leather squeaked under my weight, and Louie abandoned himself once more to quietly contemplating the landscape. The story had dissipated the sensual fog that had been floating between us since our departure from the park.

Near La Défense, we drove through a long succession of tunnels, which spat us out onto a peripheric avenue I knew well, the N13, where it crosses lower Suresnes and Mont Valérien, then Nanterre. I was terrified that he might be taking me to my mom's house, but the car kept going west, without any sign of stopping.

At last, after going through Rueil's city center, we turned left onto an alley lined with chestnut trees. The car parked in front of an elegant castle, which I had no trouble recognizing: Malmaison, a haven of peace and greenery, known today for its roses. It was a gift from Bonaparte to his Josephine, once his fortune had been assured.

What did Louie expect? That we would visit the original version of the room whose replica I had experienced at the Hôtel des Charmes? I doubted it, given his mood.

Yet after telling me his weighty secrets, he was suddenly himself again: light, unpredictable. He was an ungraspable piece on a strange chessboard, whose spaces were always shifting color and place.

For the first time on our journey, I turned and faced him head-on, ready to confront him. I was tired of putting up with his mood swings:

"What exactly do you want with me? What game are you playing?"

"I am not playing, Annabelle," he replied in all seriousness. "I never play. All I do is . . . reveal."

His eyes were sincere, innocent. They were also piercing through me from head to toe.

"Reveal?"

"Yes, that's right. Consider me . . . like a solution in photography. The agent that makes the invisible image contained in your silver crystals appear. No doubt you do not notice it . . . but I do. I see it beginning to work on you . . ."

The color of my Ten-Times-a-Day and the wrapping of my other presents was not random? Silver. The color that reveals.

"Photographic solutions don't exist anymore" was my retort. "Nobody uses them. They're finished. Everything is digital now."

"Not for me."

A SMILE BLOOMED OVER HIS face like a new flower in his garden. Discreetly, modestly, he pointed toward the neoclassical building with its white stone and slate roof:

"You already knew I was from another age!"

He jumped brusquely from the limousine—with all the vivacity that his injured limb would allow. His pant leg briefly rode up his ankle, revealing another tattoo, of which I only caught a glimpse: another letter that vaguely recalled the 'a' on his wrist. This time, it was an uppercase *D* in an ornate font.

A and *D*. In other words: *AD*.

"Aurora Delbard," I couldn't help murmuring.

23

The rest of the day unfolded into a succession of light and playful moments, in the sweet presence of rosebushes and under the shade of linden trees. The floral scents reminded me of my mother, and a wave of guilt passed through me as I considered how little time I had been spending with her recently.

Happily, the modest park at Malmaison was delightful: it was a no-frill affair, without elaborate water displays or other such things, but it offered an immense space for strolling that was cut off from both the city and time. As in Paris, Louie labored to be the perfect guide, providing spicy and even sulfurous anecdotes that transformed history into a veritable encyclopedia of dissolute mores. And he went into more detail than was necessary on the annex that Napoleon had built to receive his mistresses without having to disturb the woman of the house.

We ate a late lunch in a nearby brasserie, and the afternoon was already at its end by the time the limousine dropped me off outside Duchesnois House.

"See you soon?" Louie asked, with a hopeful and humble smile.

I had not noticed it until then: a little dimple at the bottom of his right cheek that only seemed to appear when he was being sincere. I instantly dubbed it his dimple of truth, and remembered that I'd seen it on the few occasions when he'd been open with me. In the garden at the Museum of Romantic Life. And also, earlier that same day, in the car, when he had told me the complete story of Aurora's death.

"Perhaps," I replied. "In any case, we will definitely have a chance to see each other at one of BTV's exciting meetings!"

He appreciated the irony and rubbed my hand with his fingertips.

The door on my side suddenly opened, before I even had the chance to grasp the handle. Richard the Chauffeur, who had spent the entire day behind the wheel without showing himself, appeared on the other side.

"Mademoiselle," mumbled the giant as he moved aside to let me out.

Surprisingly thoughtful, after so much discretion.

But once I had stepped outside into the light, I instantly recognized the bald head, the jaw, and, above all, the surly expression . . . "curiouser and curiouser." The rude neighbor who had found Felicity and handed her to me like a turd. It was him!

I gaped. He got back into the driver's seat and slammed the door. The motor purred. I was wondering about this strange mystery when the car ambled to the other side of the street. A modern pumpkin, loud and fast.

AS WAS OFTEN THE CASE at that time of day, and even more now that Armand had so much to do for the wedding, the house was empty. As for the three hairy rascals, they were probably in the garden, enjoying the sun on the south side of Duchesnois House.

Beside the silver envelope—could I really call it a surprise anymore?—I noticed a handwritten message from David, proof he had stopped by at some point during the day.

> *Another work dinner with the Koreans.*
> *Considering how they do things, well lubricated,*
> *I probably won't be home until late. Don't wait up.*
> *I love you.*
> *D.*

I took my time opening the silver message, which seemed slimmer than the others. Sure enough, its sole contents were the usual magnetic key from the Hôtel des Charmes and two cards.

The absence of a note was a kind of test: by now, I was supposed to know the place and hour of our rendezvous. The Hôtel des Charmes, at ten p.m.

I turned over the two rectangles of rigid paper and was surprised to discover that each one contained a different commandment. Louie didn't need the first one to convince me to go. He knew I would show up, and that now he could pull out the stops. Step it up a notch:

4—Thou shalt submit to thy master.

Then, perhaps more menacing, though in all appearances indulgent, this second order:

5—Thou shalt listen to thy desires.

What did I really know about my desires? Louie's strategy had awoken in me wants that time and botched experiences had erased—he called himself a revealer—but was I so sure I wanted to abandon myself to him? What were these moments of pleasure, their sharp and inherently ephemeral delight, really worth? Especially compared to the immense landscape of peaceful happiness with David Barlet.

For the time being, I decided to respect David's deceitful silence. If his older brother's story was true, then David was not really a despicable liar. He was at once the first victim of Aurora's madness as well as her torturer. And I could only imagine the shame and infamy he had borne over the years. Time could not erase the sharp pain of these events. It was powerless to lighten the burden of his errors. For him, I was virgin territory, an enterprise at which he could succeed this time, and such an aim justified a few secrets, as weighty and disloyal as they may seem at first.

I locked myself in the bedroom and dug out the treasures Louie had given me over the past few days: mysterious key; riding crop; egg, which made part of me contract when I saw it; Païva necklace; and precious comb, which David may have paid for but which Louie had chosen. I turned the objects over in my hands, noting the softness of one or the rich ornamentation of another. Hard and refined, smooth and rigid, penetrating and impenetrable, they made for a strange mosaic, a collection of odds and ends that reflected their sender's contradictions. Subtle and equivocal. However, all these erotic objects would mean nothing if I decided not to give them power. Louie's lessons only had one aim: to make me an agent of my own pleasure, and the inanimate objects my living partners.

Why, then, had I not received an object for today's meeting? Would another surprise be waiting for me there? Or was I to expect something more *incarnate*?

YES, I HAD CHANGED, I could see it in the bedroom mirror. No doubt definitively. I wasn't a Hotelle anymore. Nor was I a malleable thing that David could fashion as he pleased. And what if I continued acquiescing to the luxuries he offered—this house, that dress, the first-class wedding—and had carefully adjusted to me, what part of me would remain? Was it still me in this gilded life? Had the little girl from Nanterre survived in me? As for the new Elle, the one who was blossoming with each secret rendezvous, what did she want? Did she even know? In which room would she soon find herself?

I HAD NO MATERIAL CLUES this time when I arrived in front of the Hôtel des Charmes a few minutes before the usual hour. Ten o'clock minus a few ticks.

I entered the lobby with neither a glance nor a word in Monsieur Jacques's direction. He was busy writing something. After our recent dispute, I did not want to ask for his help and instead made a beeline for the elevators.

"Good evening, Mademoiselle!"

I was happy to see Ysiam's smile. His long lashes blinked a little faster, a sign that he, too, was glad to see me. He may have been Louie's submissive servant, but I still saw an innocence in him that made me like him, in spite of everything.

"Good evening, Ysiam. Will you please take me to the right room?"

"Of course. Which one?"

His lips spread wide. He was playing.

"Well . . . You know, don't you?"

"Me, yes. But you have to tell me!"

Well, if that was how it was going to be . . .

"Okay. Let's see, what do I still have: a key, an old key that might open any door . . ."

"Any door," he confirmed, thrilled to continue the game. "So no door."

"Hmm, I've used the necklace and the egg . . . I have a silver comb."

"Are you sure that's one of your tools?"

"No . . . You're right. In that case, the only thing I still have left is . . . a riding crop!"

He winked, delighted.

"Yes! That's a tool!"

"A riding crop . . . ," I repeated, thinking.

Which legendary courtesan could have used such a toy? I tried to remember all the room names I knew, but nothing came to mind. When suddenly, a few paces behind Ysiam, I noticed a retro poster . . .

Ysiam caught the direction of my gaze. He turned around. The framed poster was a recent replica of a period advertisement featuring a Spanish dancer holding a fan in one hand and, as if to highlight her martial attitude, a switch in the other. Now all I had to do was read the name of this dark beauty: Lola Montez.

"Lola Montez?" I asked, accentuating the final z. "It isn't spelled 'Montès'?"

"*Lola Montès* is the movie that Max Ophuls made of her life. But her real name was Montez."

After this little lesson—the source of which I didn't doubt

for a second—he led me to the elevator and pushed the button for the third floor.

The decor was striking. Where the other hallways in the hotel were known for their bright colors, the third floor was dressed in black—walls, doors, and carpet included. The lamps let off an intense light that barely pierced through the obscurity. And afraid we might fall, we had to proceed carefully, almost on tiptoes, to the room.

THE ROOM, WHICH WAS PLUNGED in thick darkness, was hardly any gayer. The gilded baseboards and ceiling glowed under the iridescent light of one or two small lamps. This sepulcher to the memory of the most mythical darling of the Romantic era inspired more reverence than excitement. But the click of the lock on the door suddenly reminded me why I was here, like a first lash of the switch at my senses.

"Come nearer . . ."

Like the last time, the irruption of these faceless words in the closed space drew me out of my stupor. The sudden sound almost made me scream in fright. But this time, it did not come from a set of speakers. The metallic timbre, which was distorted by some electronic artifice, did not come from above but from the other side of the room, whose tenebrosity made it impossible to see anything, bodies and decorative features alike.

Nevertheless, I did perceive a hurried movement within the opacity. I could have sworn: someone was approaching me. And I took a step back. My movements grew slower, from a mix of fear and desire—old friends in our most odious nightmares. I was frozen, half expecting to wake up.

"Do not be afraid. If you are here, it is because you are no longer afraid."

The sound was terrifying, but something about the inflection told me he was trying to be reassuring. At last, with these words, he half appeared. He was still anonymous, though. He wore black latex over his head and slight body, right down to his toenails. This surprising costume resuscitated random images from my childhood—a wrestler and a circus Hercules—as well as more adult fantasies—Catwoman, the submissive in an S-M role-playing game, and I don't know what else.

A bulge in the elastic material, a shard protruding under his lower abdomen, told me that he was already erect.

"Right?" he insisted.

Out of prudence, I agreed:

"No, I am not scared . . ."

From behind his back, he withdrew a long, thin object that I could not immediately identify.

"Come here. There's nothing to be afraid of."

A riding crop! Like the one Louie had sent me, and which I had remembered a few minutes earlier with Ysiam.

Suddenly I noticed something: despite the darkness, it was clear that the man in front of me was not holding anything that resembled a cane, nor did he seem to need any support.

"You aren't going to . . . ," I choked.

"Whip you? No. Not unless I have to. Not if you're good."

I tried to control my voice and slow my racing thoughts.

"Okay, okay . . . This is going a little too far for me."

"Tsss . . . ," he whistled as he came toward me. "We haven't done anything yet and you're already retreating!"

"I do not want to be beaten."

"Who said that you would? You know, there are a thousand other things we can do with *this*."

To illustrate his point, he started caressing my body with the soft tip of leather, through the minimal shielding of my clothes. It was electrifying, as if it were his tongue.

In other circumstances, as a simple spectator, I probably would have found the gesture grotesque. But now, it released a sweet and venomous elixir in me. Being the center of his attention toppled my reason, a fragile screen between my desires and myself. My defenses fell one by one, and I felt the pressing need to let myself give in to his injunctions.

"Close your eyes . . . Concentrate on what you're feeling."

I did not need to open them to know that he had drawn nearer—almost in direct contact, judging from the breath that swept across my face and neck at regular intervals. What confused me, however, was the flagrant absence of body odor. Nothing emanated from him, not even a hint of cologne. Nothing but the overwhelming, artificial, and acrid scent of latex.

He took my hand and, with the utmost delicacy, led me to a bed dressed in black sheets. Then he slowly bent me back onto the silken bier.

Odd occurrence: When I fell onto the bed, it set off a musical piece, which swelled throughout the room and fell upon us like drizzle that grew stronger and stronger.

I did not recognize the piece, but I had to admit that it fit the situation perfectly. A bewitching chant with just one musical layer, in a language I was incapable of naming. It sounded like a Gregorian chant by a new religious group, in which women were high priestesses. The words mattered little. I let the high-pitched voices carry me away, up to their peak.

One by one, the man took off my clothes—I had dressed soberly and simply that night—and continued to tease my naked body with languid strokes of the leather whip. The precision of his movements hinted at a developed but lithe musculature.

"This piece is called 'Forever Without End' . . . ," he murmured.

That's what I wanted from his riding crop, which seemed to know in painful detail my most sensitive erogenous zones. It only targeted the best, lingering over the ones that sent the sweetest, longest, and most visible shivers through me. The base of my neck trembled approvingly. The tops of my shoulders responded with an irrepressible tremor, a blend of pain and pleasure. Even the nameless triangle between my ear and nape of the neck expressed contented pleasure. And my breasts, my middle, my ecstatic inner thighs, which opened wider with every stroke. They quivered in anticipation of what might come next.

An avid, impatient tension ran through my whole body. It wanted to learn and, more than anything, feel more. Harder?

"I love this . . ." I sighed, without knowing if I meant his touch or the music.

I twittered at the sudden intrusion of the leather rod between my labia. He rubbed my cleft several times, with just enough pressure to torture me. My back arched, projecting my pubis as far as possible in his direction.

"Ow!"

He'd given no warning before the switch smacked my middle. It was light but biting.

"You're not supposed to beat me!"

I sat up, furious. He pushed me back onto the bed with one hand. I could not escape his weight.

"Whipping is not beating."

"Really? Well, you explain the difference to my skin!"

"Don't get caught up on words . . . Feel it."

My anger had actually amplified the sensations in my body. With each lash of the whip, I wanted more, was suspended in anticipation, wondering how hard the next one would be and which part of my body it would touch. He striped my breasts in turn, then my thighs, the sides of my buttocks. He was careful to avoid my face, which twisted in pain and desire.

Still, I felt a wave of panic when he straddled me and pinned his knees to my arms. Crushed under his weight, they could not make the slightest movement. I knew what he would do next: the icy feel of metal on my wrist, the pinch of the cuff as it closed, then the same thing on the other side.

Handcuffed.

I opened my eyes to see what he had in store for me, his willing martyr, and discovered that everything had disappeared: the night-lights had been dimmed, and the room was pitch-black. Now, the only way I could situate him in the room was by listening to his breath or feeling the subtle heat of his latex-sheathed body.

He must have read this last thought because I heard the squeak of latex and understood that he was at last undressing. This freed not only his body but also his oh-so-familiar fragrance, which the latex suit had been holding prisoner.

Vanilla. Lavender. In a word: Louie. Or a man wearing his cologne?

My doubts evaporated when I heard his voice, now in its natural state:

"No darkness could hide you."

Was he talking about . . . my beauty?

The riding crop was not the only replica he had with him that night.

"Oh, no!"

The metallic egg he had just plunged into my sex with authority was identical to the one he had already used to transport me.

"Oh, yes," he confirmed.

I did not know what to expect next. I heard his feet rubbing across the carpet, then the door click twice as it opened and closed.

Had he really left?

I did not have time to think of another hypothesis. The little seed of pleasure he'd planted in me was sprouting. The egg had spontaneously come to life, moved by what I imagined was a distant order. My hands were bound. I had no control over its strength, its movement inside me, the duration of its vibrations. Nothing.

The first orgasm hit my innermost depths like an implosion. It wasn't like being broken into a million pieces; rather, it was as though I had been collected into a ball of fire and pleasure. I was as compact as a modern sculpture, from which only the sex and a stunned vulva emerged.

"Not that . . . You . . . ," I wept, ecstatic and frustrated.

I wanted it to be over. Or, rather, I wanted to begin. I was done with these games and this mechanized pleasure. I wanted him. In me. Posthaste. Only the time it took for us to make each other come.

And just as he was crossing the threshold, I added, desperately and plaintively, with gratitude and abandon:

"Come . . ."

Without saying a word, he melted over me and withdrew the egg from my vagina. Fluid trickled between my legs, sending a wave of relief through me, even up into my chest.

I felt submerged. Sucked into the whirlwind of my orgasm. Drowned, and happy to be.

"Take me . . . Take me," I begged.

He ignored my request. Instead, he kneeled between my legs, brusquely pulling my backside to the edge of the bed. He started licking my soaking sex like a man who has just left the desert.

The contrast with David's method was striking. Where my future husband excelled at metronomic regularity, Louie licked haphazardly, with plenty of interruptions and changes in rhythm. He did not have to introduce himself inside me to mine my depths. And what should have delayed my pleasure—don't they say that cunnilingus only works if it is long-lasting and ardent?—aroused my desire, engorged my nymphae and lips, made my clitoris stand more erect than ever before.

I don't remember what Sophia and I could have said that would have made one of our professors in college think it was appropriate to provide an example of an erotic book of photography: Born from the Wave, *by Lucien Clergue. After our conversation, I was curious to see the photographs and did an Internet search. I found the pictures of nude beauties both fascinating and unsettling. Most of them were headless, surrounded by waves and foam.*

Seeing them reminded me of an aspect of my vagina that I had always found off-putting, though it was the very same thing that drove me wild in men: the scent of ~~my pussy~~ *my sex. It would have been easy to tuck my obsession away in a secret corner and chalk it up to one of my complexes, except that, in spite of my perfume, I smelled it delicately emanating from me several times a day. At my desk in high school, then in college, at the movies or on the metro. Anytime life put me in contact with strangers, I was convinced they could catch a whiff of the odorous, musky fragrance of ~~my pussy~~ my crotch. Like my vagina, the pages of Lucien Clergue's book also seemed to smell of the sea.*

Handwritten note by me, 6/11/2009

HE SLIPPED HIS TONGUE UNDER the folds of my vagina and played for a long moment with my button, erasing this final barrier and my remaining scruples. For a second it was almost painful, but then lightning shot through the room and struck the tiny organ of happiness, ripping open my middle, burning my innards with a shower of flames. I was blinded, deprived of my senses.

"Oh, yessssss!"

I was devastated. Scorched. I was no longer a woman who screamed *no*, but *yes*.

This time, I did not hear him leave. I moved my arms and realized he had unbound my hands.

But even without the cuffs, even though I had been freed, I knew one thing for certain: I belonged to him now. I could marry whomever I pleased. Including his brother. I could make a comfortable life for myself.

From here on out, I only had one master. And that was Louie.

He was the one.

24

June 12, 2009

Whenever I had a personal issue or, worse, a dilemma, I always handled it in the same way, which is to say, by following the least journalistic and professional method possible: rather than ask my friends for edifying examples or points of comparison, I watched movies that dealt with more or less the same problem. In many ways, when it came to personal questions, I trusted filmmakers more than other newspeople or experts, psychologists, or sociologists. For instance, when I first learned Mom had cancer, I rewatched Nanni Moretti's *Dear Diary* several times. Of all the movies on the subject, his is the most apt to cheer you up.

On sibling love, you can't do better than Woody Allen's *Hannah and Her Sisters* or this other Italian film, *The Best of Youth*, with the sublime Jasmine Trinca, whose pout and wide eyes I was always trying to imitate as a teenager.

Unlike Hannah's Elliot, who has a passionate affair with the fiery Lee only to return to conjugal life, I rejected bourgeois fatality, its morality and conformism. Not making a choice is already a kind of choice. I tried to convince myself of this maxim the following night as I tossed and turned beside an inert David.

After all, couldn't I live somewhere between the two, divided among brothers? Wasn't I myself split between desire and reason, body and heart; between the one who had conquered me through ruses and force, and the other side of myself, where the days went by without passion or pain, lulled by the soothing music of comfort, tenderness, and ease?

"Hello, Elle. I have finished the final version of the contract. It's on the console, as promised. If you could please give it one last glance and sign . . ."

Armand had appeared in the kitchen at breakfast as discreetly as a ghost. The closer we got to the wedding date, the worse he looked. Was it stress? Too much drink?

"Yes, thank you, Armand. I am sure it will be perfect."

Where Louie's commandments were deviant, searing, exciting, the imperatives laid out in David's prenup were a list of rules meant to make our common life a drive on cruise control. No conflict, no accidents. A calm stupor in which the good days would not vary much from the bad ones. Life cushioned by the air bag of his money and my concessions. I could even close my eyes. Everything would remain under control.

"Oh, I almost forgot," he exclaimed before returning to the day's urgent tasks. "I picked up the ring from the jeweler. It's on your bedside table."

Next to the contract, I found another, slimmer pile, which was surer to have an effect on me: tucked inside a plastic folder, a stack of blank perforated papers, identical to the one I had received before. Apparently, my purveyor of stationery did not doubt for a second that I would need more space in my Ten-Times-a-Day. Better still, he'd made a comeback. On the very last page, I found his unmistakable handwriting and the following words:

When I lay at your feet an eternal homage,
Shall you ever wish me to change my visage?
I am a man with captured heart,
Make sure to read the first word of each verse from the start.
Love is the thing for which you were created,
With you, my dear, my pen is never sated.
You inspire me, love, to write these words I dare not speak,
Darling, only you are the remedy that I seek.

I was stunned by the chosen form—since when did he write in verse?—and even more so by his meaning. To declare himself so openly and, despite the rhymes, without varnish, did not seem like him at all.

I grabbed the tablet that never leaves the living room coffee table and typed the first words of his poem into a search engine. The reference was at once clear: "Alfred de Musset's reply to George Sand." But though I was familiar with Sand's coded poem, this was the first I'd heard of her lover's response. The key turned out to be simpler, especially since it was explicitly stated in the middle of the poem, in the fourth verse: "Make sure to read the first word of each verse from the start." Following his instructions, I pieced together the following question: "When shall I make love with you, darling?"

I clicked on a link to learn George Sand's answer in the literary game that she herself had initiated: "This favor that your heart so desires I fight / For it may plunge my reputation into the darkness of Night." The message was clear: "This Night."

A smile blossomed inside me: Was that his plan? For us to

write each other letters like the ones exchanged between those great writers?

I dug my Ten-Times-a-Day out of my bag and penned George Sand's two last verses. Even if Louie never read them, at least our dialogue would not be broken.

> *I wonder if I have ever taken the initiative, even fleet-*
> *ingly, since I've been sexually active. I don't think so, and*
> *I'm not particularly proud of it. I'm not ashamed, but I*
> *regret it, since today I think that the person to express his*
> *or her desires first in a couple gets a kind of bonus. Would*
> *I have known more pleasure or been a better mistress of*
> *their fantasies if I had thrown myself occasionally on my*
> *previous lovers? I'll never know. My sex, my entire body,*
> *will forever be the orphan of such missed opportunities.*

Handwritten note by me, 6/12/2009

GOADED BY THIS NEW GAME, I dressed in haste, cheerful and light. The time was passing like lightning, and after two consecutive absences, I could not be late. I did not want to be the object of more gossip. I figured people were already talking about me and that the whole of Barlet Tower was abuzz with how ridiculous I was.

"PHEW! I WAS SCARED YOU wouldn't be coming back!"

As usual, Chloe threw herself on me as soon as I stepped through the sliding doors. She seemed more stressed now than two days before. Had my absence caused that much trouble with the personnel? I remembered what David had said about the unions.

"Why wouldn't I?" I defended myself.

She looked at me like I was a crazy person or a hermit who had just come out of hiding after ten years of isolation.

"David didn't mention anything to you?"

Mention what? Had he buckled under all the various pressures and sacrificed me on the altar of social peace?

"Should he have mentioned something in particular?" I asked, unsettled.

"Alice!"

I recalled an image of David consoling the tall blonde.

"Alice and Chris!"

Alice-and-Chris... It sounded like the beginning of a playground song. But I didn't think now was the time for childhood jokes.

"I'm sorry, Chloe, but I have no clue what—"

"Chris Haynes, the artistic director, and Alice Simoncini . . . Somebody walked in on them in a special meeting, if you know what I mean. In her office!"

Had the ravishing director of marketing given herself to that pretentious oaf out of spite?

"I'm sorry," I said, pretending to be above office gossip, "but I don't see what that has to do with me."

"Well, they were both fired! On your first day. No severance package, no unemployment, not even a farewell party . . . Nothing."

I could not believe my ears.

"It's all anyone is talking about. I guess Yves, in IT, used the network to activate her laptop and film the whole thing. But there's no way I'll watch it. It's disgusting!"

The lascivious way in which she adjusted the bun on her head said otherwise.

I kept playing the scene I'd witnessed between my man and the woman who had been fired. So it hadn't been the end of a liaison, as I had initially imagined. She had been sacked. Though his gestures had been empathetic and almost tender, his decision had been one of an unwavering boss. One evening, he had invited her to dine at his home. The next day, or almost, he threw her out like a pariah.

This thought made me freeze with doubt and fear. And what if he found out about his brother and my strange relationship with him? Would I face the same fate? Thrown out, repudiated . . . cast off!

Our arrival on the nineteenth floor proved that the turmoil had not died down. People scrutinized me from behind the bay windows as I made my way down the hall. But it was not because I was marching to the scaffold. They simply wanted to read how I was reacting to the news. Whether I liked it or not, I was now one of the people at the station whose opinion ricocheted from ear to ear. It mattered.

"Don't pay attention to them," David's assistant whispered. "They're wondering who will be next. They're worried . . ."

Me, too!

" . . . but deep down they're not mean."

When we arrived in front of my office—at first glance, I did not notice any silver envelopes—Chloe ran off to attend to her regimented schedule:

"Eight forty-eight . . . I'm already six minutes late in my day. I'll leave you. But don't hesitate to call if you need something. Anything at all."

That, I supposed, like her meeting me in the lobby, was part of her duties, as prescribed by the boss. One of the little privileges that my peculiar status afforded me. I found a note from Albane on my otherwise empty desk. I was expected downstairs at nine for my first camera test. That meant I only had time for a foul cup of coffee from the asthmatic machine. Then it was time to get back in the arena.

THE JOURNALIST WAS WEARING HER combat clothes: a shapeless sweatshirt and khakis. She welcomed me with a smile and two loud kisses on my cheeks before I even had time to extend my hand.

"Hey! Feeling better?"

"Yeah . . . I'm okay." I faked the voice of someone who had been suffering.

"Okay. Great. Because the fun and games are over. Today, we have serious work to do. Today, you're going to step into the light!"

"I saw that . . ."

"Follow me. I'm going to introduce you to the technical crew."

This is how you have the spotlight thrown on you in the darkness of a soundstage, in front of a dozen pairs of scrutinizing eyes, a judgmental bubble of condescension that no amount of smiling can pop.

"Hello . . ."

But it was not their number nor the fact that they looked like old, tattooed truckers that left me speechless after my timid greeting. I was stunned to see . . .

"Fred!"

He detached himself from the group and took a few steps in my direction, as cool as though we were meeting for brunch.

"Hello, my Elle."

"*My* Elle," he had stressed, so that everyone could hear the possessive pronoun.

I caught his sleeve and led him away from the group, toward the dark and empty stage.

"What are you doing here? Wasn't it enough to create a scandal in front of my house?"

"First, you should say hello, then calm down. I'm on a six-month contract. And, FYI, everyone is looking at us."

Sometimes I think it's stupid and even a bit unfair that the things we learn about our own sexuality, or what our former lovers were able to discover about us, cannot be transmitted to our current partner. We have medical files—why can't we have sexuality files, to be filled out not by our doctors but by anyone with whom we've ever shared our bed? That way, whenever we find ourselves between the sheets for the first time with a new conquest, that new person can review it and immediately proceed with the things that please us, as opposed to spending days, months, the entirety of a relationship, trying to figure it out.

What would Fred have written on the Elle he used to know? Maybe that he hadn't been able to find a way to make me come with his tongue? ~~Or maybe that I gave a mediocre and timid blow job? That I was incapable of swallowing him as deeply as he would have liked? That the idea of having his semen in my mouth disgusted me and I continually refused to do it?~~

Handwritten note by me, 6/12/2009

A SIDELONG GLANCE THROUGH THE thick, windowed partition confirmed that the gang of technicians was enjoying our heated reunion. The boss's girl comes face-to-face with her ex. Now that broke the routine.

"You were hired on *my* show?"

"Yeah. They were looking for a competent and available sound guy. And here I am!"

"Surprise, surprise!" I railed quietly. "Are you fucking with me?"

"Does it look like it?"

HE TOLD ME ABOUT HOW, after he'd left Duchesnois House, Louie had found his number and contacted him. The two men went out for beers one night, after which a slightly tipsy Louie offered him a job at his brother's broadcasting company "to make up for things."

"He said what?" I shrieked, furious. "'*To make up for things*'?"

"Yeah, that's what he said. It seemed like a fair deal to both of us: his bro steals my girl, he finds me a job."

The worst part of this story was not that Louie had taken advantage of Fred's distress and desperate need for a job. No, what was even more humiliating than everything else he had put me through so far was how he had relegated me to the debased status of an object to be traded on the job market.

"I'm guessing that David knows nothing of your little arrangement."

"Oh, no . . . I don't see why. It's between Louie and me."

The longer our discussion went on, the more the crew laughed at us. Some of them must have worked with Fred before. I noticed two or three scowling at him or making inappropriate gestures.

In the end, what could I say? And what could I tell David without sounding like I still had feelings for my ex-boyfriend or suspicious friction with his brother?

I decided on another option, seizing an opportunity to gain control:

"Okay. Fred, there's something you should know about Louie."

"He has a thing for you, right?"

It was amazing how, in the space of a few days and through the magic of his miraculous new job, Fred seemed at last to have cut affective ties with me. Louie had made a good calculation: by giving him back his pride, Louie had quelled my ex's anger as well as his feelings for me.

"Not exactly. Let's just say that he acts strangely."

I was careful to omit the parts about invitations, commandments, and our rendezvous at the Hôtel des Charmes, and insisted on the way he tried to get at me through extravagant gestures, like with my mom.

"Oh, yeah, you're right . . . That's shady."

"I hate to have to tell you this . . ." I pouted.

"What?"

" . . . And of course it doesn't mean anything about your abilities. But I think that if he chose you it wasn't a coincidence. He's been using you and Mom to get under my skin."

He considered me for a moment, circumspect. Suddenly, he sobered and I saw a familiar violence growing inside him.

"Okay . . . So according to you, if somebody offers me a job, it's not because of me but because of something to do with *mademoiselle!*"

I reached for his arm, but he withdrew it brusquely.

"Don't be like that, Fred, shit . . ."

He was already halfway back to join his peers, when my question stopped him in his tracks:

"He didn't tell you, did he? Did he?"

"Tell me what?"

"That you would be working for me? I'll bet he was careful not to fill you in."

"Hmm . . . That's true. He didn't tell me. Human Resources did. But what does that prove?"

"Just that he's manipulating you. The list of technicians was decided over a week ago," I bluffed. "If you landed here, and David doesn't know about it, it has to be because Louie intervened."

"It's possible," he admitted, guarded.

"You can't see that he's playing with you, with all of us? We're nothing to someone like him. Insects under his shoe!"

The image must have hit home, considering the look of intensity in his eyes.

"What are you suggesting?"

"If David learns how you were hired, he'll void your contract. I guarantee it."

"What makes you so sure?"

"When did you start work?"

"The day before yesterday."

"Well, then you saw how he fired those other two, the tall blonde and that cretin fucker . . . In less time than it takes to blow his nose."

I snapped my fingers for effect.

"Okay. I'm guessing your silence doesn't come free," he suggested, a sharp look in his eyes.

"Let's call it quid pro quo: you keep your job . . ." I paused, evaluating what exactly Fred had the power to give me. The only way of evening out the playing field with Louie, a new page in the silent dialogue we had begun.

"And me?"

"And you . . . you will record as many conversations as you possibly can between Louie and his entourage."

"Are you crazy? Who do you think I am, James Bond?"

"I don't want to know how you manage it, Fred. But get me tape of his landline, whenever he's near a set . . . Anything, I'll take it."

Albane interrupted our negotiation, but I saw him nod in resignation. Poor Fred: even good news turned on him.

"Elle? Will you get in makeup? If we want to tie this up before lunch, we can't dawdle."

THE MORNING PASSED IN A flash. Albane, whom everyone respected—regardless of title or seniority—stayed by my side. That, together with Luc and Philippe's brief visits on set to ensure that the first stage was going smoothly, helped to create a calmer environment between the crew and me. Even Fred laid low, keeping his wounded male ego in check and even, at times, making special efforts, like telling a joke to lighten the mood.

The girl on screen looked as much like me as an actress looks like her understudy, which is to say, very little. Still, after a few hours, I got used to my strange double, and my expressions and movements became more natural, despite the camera's intractable eye.

"Are you coming to lunch with us?" Stan, the show's director, asked.

I would have infinitely preferred a salad and a Monaco with Sophia, but I wanted to fit in, so I accepted the invitation and nibbled my shepherd's pie, trying to be as agreeable as possible.

Albane, whose nonexistent curves testified to a certain nutritional imbalance, left us when we got to the cafeteria. However, she was also the one who nabbed me as soon as I put my food tray on the dishwashing counter.

"Elle! Can I speak with you for a second?"

"What's up?" I asked, noting her irritable attitude.

"I hope you ate well—you're going to need the extra fuel."

"Why?"

Without a word, in her authoritative and slightly snippy way, she led me to the ladies' room next to the self-service food court. Then, amid the brouhaha of powder room conversations, she stated simply:

"We start tomorrow night."

To keep myself from fainting, I played dumb and asked:

"Start what?"

"The show."

"Is that a joke? Did the others put you in charge of hazing me?"

"I wish, believe me . . ."

"But why? Who decided?"

"Who do you think?"

She suppressed a bitter smile.

David had decided to throw me into the lion's den before I was ready. I didn't understand the meaning behind the sacrifice. What was he hoping to achieve by sending me into a battle I could not win?

"I can't imagine the idea just came to him this morning when he got to work?"

"No, obviously not. We've just learned that our direct competitor pushed up its launch for a new variety show by a week."

"And it starts tomorrow night," I guessed.

"That's right."

"But that's absurd! I thought we were slotted for Thursday because it was an underexploited time."

"I thought so, too."

"You don't send a cockleshell led by a ship's boy to face your biggest enemy!"

She must have liked my naval metaphor because she gave me a friendly pat, a rare thing for her.

"Well, we're going to have to learn to swim. We don't have a choice!"

We exchanged a few pained looks, both haloed in clouds of powder and perfume.

"What does Luc think?"

"Same as you: that we're going to get massacred. But tell that to an admiral who only has eyes for the seaman in question . . ."

I lowered my eyes, then my head. She was right. David's feelings for me were deeply impacting his judgment. He was not acting like a boss but a man in love: impulsive, overly confident, incapable of heeding the alarmed cries or sound advice of his entourage.

WHEN I PEEKED INTO HER office, Chloe's eyes widened, sensing the urgency of the situation.

"Can I see David?"

"Yes . . ." She panicked for a moment before consulting her computer, then her watch. "Ten minutes. Then he's leaving for a meeting. Shall I announce you?"

"Yes, please do."

My future husband received me with open arms, as though I were just dropping by for a visit.

"Elle! Darling! Have they told you the news?"

I had trouble reconciling David's stark office with the fact that he was such an important man. Outside of his desk, three chairs, and a small sofa, the only decoration in the room was a bronze bust of his father, Andre Barlet. It was the first time I had laid eyes on him.

David hugged me for a moment, then pointed to a chair facing his, as he would have done with any other colleague.

"It's wonderful, isn't it?"

"Wonderful, yes," I agreed unenthusiastically. "But also completely impossible."

"Why? Because of that lowlife Chris Haynes?"

"No, I—"

"I really don't give a damn about him. We have at least twenty sets on hand. They simply have to be installed, the lights adjusted . . . and onward!"

It sounded easy—possible, even—when he said it with that kind of enthusiasm.

"David . . . You're forgetting something."

"What?"

"I've never been on television!"

"Don't be silly!" He laughed.

It was like trying to tell Dr. Strangelove *not* to press the button.

"No, really!"

"You're stressing over nothing. You have the best team in French television at your side."

Including Fred, my ex . . . the guy who wanted to whack you a few days ago.

"Super! And what are we going to be talking about?"

"Relax! Albane told me she had enough stuff to cover three shows."

Including a report on Hotelles! I silently cried. I could not hold back my exasperation any longer. If anyone could open his eyes in this madhouse, it was me.

"David . . . are you trying to be obtuse?"

"What do you mean?" A cloud crossed his brow.

"I'm terrible! Terrible, you hear? I failed all my auditions, David. And not just because your competitors are blind idiots."

"No, they really are idiots."

I stood at once.

"You cannot launch a show at the most important time slot of the week with a beginner like me at its helm, especially without any preparation! It's insane! I am not ready, David, period!"

I saw the effects of my verbal explosion on his impassible expression.

"I won't do the show," I concluded calmly.

"You will do it," he replied, tit for tat.

"No."

"You will . . . because it's what I want . . . because you are my wife . . ."

Not yet, I couldn't help but think.

"And because if you leave this office without having changed your mind, don't bother coming back tomorrow. Or ever, for that matter."

He was ready to fire me, his fiancée, the one he'd been praising to heaven only a moment before, as he'd fired Alice and Chris, cutting off their heads on an irrevocable whim.

"Think hard, Elle. If you don't do the show tomorrow, you'll still be my wife, the woman I love . . . But you will never again be employed by this company. That part of your life will be over."

25

Okay, even though we have to make this show happen on a dime, we are not going to half-ass it, right . . ."

The more time I spent with Albane, the more I appreciated this woman's energy. She was less rough around the edges than she seemed. As we worked on the following night's catastrophic deadline, I understood the reason behind her attitude: in a world dominated by men, there are only a limited number of ways to survive. Either you make yourself into a captivating and untouchable creature, a femme fatale like Alice, and then you have to have been blessed with the right attributes and accept life on a six-inch pedestal, your compact in hand—or you're like Albane, challenging men on their own turf, professional and loudmouthed. I had the whole afternoon to appreciate her innate sense of devastating humor and her capacity to make the most prosaic subjects fascinating.

"We can't just string the reports together like a kid making a noodle necklace for his mom. We have to find a common theme. Even if it's random, we have to stuff it all into a more general idea."

"Do you have something in mind?"

"Mmm, yes . . . It's very junk drawer, but considering the

timing, we'll have trouble finding better: something like 'Summer's Top Ten Pleasures.'"

"Not bad," I approved. "We could even refine it: 'Summer's Top Ten Pleasures—Five for Him, Five for Her.'"

"Not idiotic . . ."

"Five pleasures each, including a taboo," I added, ridiculously proud of myself.

"Excellent! That will give me a chance to include the idea Louie had me tinker with the other day. I couldn't think of a way to introduce the idea of occasional prostitution into a segment on summer break. But now it fits perfectly!"

This is how you shoot yourself in the foot while smiling.

"Are you sure? Something about that report bothers me."

"Really?" she asked ironically. "Does it tickle your feminist side?"

"Yes . . . There's that. But I'm particularly worried that it might overshadow the rest. I know Louie considers societal phenomena as cultural. But if we could avoid starting the show off with trash . . ."

"I agree. But it has one major quality."

"It's ready to go?" I sighed.

"Exactly. What's more, it was produced with Louie Barlet's secret funds. It will save us ten percent on the pilot, which is nothing to sneeze at."

"Is that really all that important?"

"If our numbers are low, it will be vital."

"I see. But who is to say that we'll fail?"

"I am. We've never done a show without preparation or even any promotion. With Louie's little caprice we can at least make the argument that your show cost less than any other . . . I say we should take it!"

I could not think of a viable argument against it. I was going to be presenting a segment on Hotelles. All I could do was swallow the bitter pill, and with a tall glass of water. For the moment, I made do with a few sips of the smoked tea Albane had made for us both.

"If you want, we can view it now," she offered. "You'll be less nervous on screen if you have time to prepare something that will help you put distance between yourself and the spot . . . You know, like, 'I'm going to show you a piece that's more about denouncing the jerks who use this kind of service than anything else.'"

I have not seen many X-rated movies in my life. Four, maybe five, all during this period when Fred thought it would be a good idea to watch them together, to stimulate our mutual waning libido. The only thing I remember was this baseless yet irrepressible fear that crept over me during the opening credits. I wasn't scared of my reaction or troubled by the degrading show. No . . . It was an absurd fear that I would see my own face and body on the screen, like I had a twin who might have participated in the filming without my knowledge. I was completely stuck on this idea. And Fred could not understand what was terrifying me. Inside, under my marble skin, I was boiling. My sex was on ~~red alert~~ fire. And the more one of the actresses looked like me, the more my cleft grew wet with a thick and abundant ~~fluid~~ nectar.

Handwritten note by me, 6/12/2009

HER CONCERN FOR ME WAS kind. Clearly, under her crude exterior, she was a much more subtle and empathetic being than she seemed.

"No, no, if you say it's okay, I trust you . . . ," I said reluctantly. "You're the pro."

An expert in capitulation, I spent the rest of the day watching her put together *my* show. What had I hoped, really? Hadn't I told David a few hours before that I didn't know anything about it? And if Albane weren't there to mitigate my incompetence, this show would be about as interesting as a DIY student project. Faced with her seasoned reflexes, my amateurishness was painfully obvious.

I was so busy going with my new friend's terrifying flow that I almost forgot about the Barlets, their tangled lies, and the traps that were becoming more and more complex.

My phone was on silent, and I wasn't checking my messages. Then, during a quick break, I listened to Mom tell me about how three workers had come by the house that morning to fix everything she had been letting deteriorate—for want of energy and funds—and that were such a daily burden: broken electrical switches, disjointed tiles, blocked pipes, chipped paint.

Albane returned to my office with a young brunette in glasses, who was weighed down by several spring outfits.

"Elle, meet Géraldine. She'll be in charge of your wardrobe."

We exchanged respective greetings.

"We'll improve the concept for subsequent episodes," she went on. "But for now, I figured we were going for a pastoral beauty, straw hat theme, so here are some ideas."

Five tiny floral dresses, each one shorter and more transparent than the last. I waited for her to hold them all up to her chest before making my choice: pink and white, decidedly virginal.

"That one is not bad."

"Sold!" Albane approved in a definitive tone. "If that doesn't rake in preadolescent to old men . . . then I know nothing about male fantasy!"

HER LIGHTHEARTED REMARK UNDERLINED SOMETHING I had been trying hard not to think about: soon I was going to appear in front of thousands of anonymous eyes; they would be counting on me, judging me, scrutinizing my oh-so-imperfect person, and there was nothing I could do about it. Worse, I was choosing to put myself out there. Suddenly, in the face of this ordeal, the exhibitionism Louie had put me through at the Hôtel des Charmes didn't seem like a very big deal . . .

THE WARDROBE DECISION MARKED THE end of our day. Géraldine left, holding the chosen dress before her like the blessed sacrament of the coming televisual ceremony.

"What time can you be in tomorrow?"

She was really talking about tomorrow, Saturday, the first day of the weekend. But she did not have to remind me: from now on, I was going to have to make such sacrifices.

"Early. Before eight. David will probably be here, too, so we'll arrive together for a change."

I instantly regretted mentioning my special status. But her giant good-bye smile showed she was not offended.

"A word of advice," she yelled from the corridor. "Don't plan anything for tonight. Above all, get to bed early!"

I WAS ABOUT TO LEAVE Barlet Tower when Fred appeared at my office door, visibly impressed by my sanctuary.

"Come in!" I said encouragingly.

He closed the door behind him, with a conspiratorial look I had never seen on him before.

"I have a little something for you. Two things, actually."

"Already?"

"Yes. Louie is a very busy man. Always glued to his phone. Which makes me wonder what he's up to, besides being on the teleph—"

"Okay, get to the point," I interrupted impatiently.

"He spent a while talking to his brother on your set."

"Really? About the show?"

"No, not really . . . I couldn't record everything from the beginning, but let's just say that Louie seemed to be angry with David over Alice's firing."

That was a surprise. What did her fate have to do with the egotistical dandy that was Louie? "My girlfriend at the time"—he had not mentioned her name when he was telling me about Aurora's death. For how long had Alice Simoncini been working for the Barlets? Could she be . . . ?

"Here, listen . . ."

He pressed play on a digital pocket recorder. The brothers' voices swelled to life:

"SHIT! YOU CAN'T FIRE HER as though she were just a tart! Do I have to remind you of all the little sluts you've had sent to your office these past fifteen years?"

"Shut up! You will be silent now!"

"Oh, it's easy," Louie mocked. "All I have to do is ask Chloe to take an inventory of all the blocks in your schedule marked 'Do not disturb' . . . You're as easy to decrypt as a hotel room door, my poor boy . . ."

"The difference being that this place is *mine*. I can fuck whom I please when I please! Not Alice!"

"Is it because she dared to dream it could be a little bit hers, too? Is that why you threw her out? Was that her big fault? To have been stuck on you for too long?"

"That has nothing to do with it, and you know it."

"Or is it because she's been hooking up with that idiot Chris Haynes? You don't want her anymore, but you hate that someone else is playing with your toy, is that it?"

"You're starting to piss me off, Louie! Keep it up, and they won't be the only departures this week!"

"Go ahead! Do it! If you only knew how long I've been waiting for this!"

SUDDENLY, A MECHANICAL NOISE COVERED their voices, interrupting the conversation. Some technicians had probably shown up on set.

Under Fred's watchful eye, I said nothing of the blow I'd just taken and asked instead:

"And what about the other recording?"

"Telephone call from his landline. I had trouble intercepting it at first, but in the end it's pretty clear."

"Whom was he calling?"

"Apparently someone called Rebecca. He didn't mention her last name."

At last she was resurfacing. Though it didn't come as a surprise, her return made me uneasy.

"Go ahead," I coaxed. "Play it."

"Elle . . . I don't know if you want to hear this." His embarrassment seemed sincere.

"Why?"

"Because they talk about you. And about David."

What could they be saying about me that I didn't know already?

"Go ahead. I can take it."

He pressed the button on his digital device.

" . . . Becca? It's me."

"Hello, my Lou. How are you?"

"I'll be fine. But the situation is getting harder to bear here."

"I'm not surprised."

"David and I almost came to blows earlier. I don't remember when we last had it out . . . but we were only seconds away from fighting again. Like when we tore each other to pieces over Aurora."

"That's old history."

"Yes . . . well, I don't think so. Not really."

"Don't lose your cool," she advised. "Not now. He has to keep believing that you're batting for him."

"I know, I know . . ."

"And the other thing, how's that shaping up?"

"Yes. We're getting there. I think . . ."

"Do you think she'll leave him?"

She. Was Rebecca talking about me?

"I don't know. Armand told me that she agreed to sign the prenup."

"Don't get discouraged: so long as she has not said yes, there's still hope."

"Yes, of course," he agreed, his voice unusually worried.

"Do you want me to speak with her?"

"Hmm . . . Maybe. But I don't see what that will change."

"Do you trust me, yes or no?"

"Yes . . . yes . . ."

"Look, you asked me to dissolve the agency, and I did it!"

"That's true. Thank you."

"I'll call her and let you know."

"Okay, thanks. Good-bye."

"Chin up. You know I'm here for you, my Lou. All of me."

My head was spinning. I would need to listen to the recording several times in a row to fully grasp it. The familiarity between them, the way she called him "my Lou," and especially the second part . . . the one about getting me to leave David. Why? I couldn't figure out the missing link between the secrets I'd just heard and the big erotic game Louie was playing with me. Was the whole point of it all to get me to give up on marrying David? And if so, where did Louie's dark designs come from? He had only known me a few weeks. And why had he made contact with me in the first place, with those perforated notes, even before I'd met the man I was going to marry? It didn't make sense, none of it . . .

I was deep in thought when I heard my phone ring. *Blocked number,* indicated the caller ID. I asked Fred to leave with a tense smile.

"Fine," he grumbled. "I'll go."

He froze at the door when he heard my voice:

"Fred!"

"What?"

"I'm sorry."

"Don't worry about it," he said, misunderstanding.

"I mean, for *everything* . . ."

He shrugged and then dragged his feet to the other end of the hall. In the meantime, my mysterious caller had left a voice mail:

"Elle, it's Rebecca. Rebecca Sibony. I know you and Sophia have tried to get ahold of me . . . I owe you both an explanation. Perhaps to you especially. There's a little Lebanese restaurant at the corner of Rue du Roi-de-Sicile and Rue Ferdinand-Duval. Layover in Lebanon. I'll be there around eight o'clock. Please come. Alone. See you this evening."

I LEFT A MESSAGE FOR David with Chloe and jumped in a cab on the company dime, arriving a few minutes early. I had only really started to discover the neighborhood a few months earlier, when Sophia had first brought me here.

As I waited, I did a little window-shopping. Every boutique seemed to speak to me. Every storefront reflected an aspect of my person or the present situation: the Queen of 2 Hearts was a rather racy lingerie store; One Way sold custom perfume; as for Dollhouse, which was located at the bottom of the building where the agency used to be, its small storefront was divided between erotic underwear and sex toys.

Sophia once told me about how she had started collecting sex toys. One of her girlfriends in college, a particularly liberated Swede, gave her a pink plastic vibrator. Ordinary but effective. Sophia's English was spotty, so she misunderstood what Jenny the Swede had told her. She honestly thought it was a gift so, naturally, a new object . . . when really it was a loan. In other words, Sophia had already experienced the joys of the little toy on several occasions before she found out that her friend had made abundant use of it before her. This discovery might have put her off sex toys, Jenny, and sex in general, but for her it was the height of excitement.

She never gave it back to the Swede, who ended up being gracious enough to let her have it.

Handwritten note by me, 6/12/2009

WHEN I ARRIVED AT THE Lebanese restaurant, Rebecca signaled discreetly from the back. She was the same as ever: excessively groomed, outrageously blond, scary thin, and, to top it off, doused in enough Shalimar by Guerlain for everyone in the neighborhood.

She pretended to be nibbling on Middle Eastern pastries, which she pointed at with her long nails:

"Do you want one? The almond is delicious."

"No, thank you . . . I'm not hungry."

It was a fib. But I wasn't there for a tea party.

She began by telling me a lie that was as impossible to digest as her pastries seemed. She claimed there had been a police raid a few days before, in one of the hotels frequented by her girls. Without a place to land, some of the girls were put in a position where they could not offer their clients the full service. As a result, business at Belles de Nuit suffered almost immediately, which was why she had been forced to temporarily shutter the agency.

To the point of emptying the place? Of suspending her professional line? Of not answering her phone calls? None of it held. But I couldn't tell her what I had heard from her very mouth, thanks to Fred's pirate recording.

"Have you known Louie Barlet for a long time, Rebecca?"

She hid her surprise like an old fox who never bats an eye. Nevertheless, it wasn't hard for me to guess my question's real effect on her.

"Fairly, yes. Why do you ask?"

"Because he and I are going to be crossing paths rather often now."

Her smile was wide as she tried to regain the upper hand in our conversation.

"That's right! I hear you and David are getting married. Congratulations. Yours will be at the top of the list of prestigious unions that the agency has made possible."

"David Barlet was never one of my clients."

"Oh, really?" she asked evasively, her gaze wandering absently.

"Did he ever go out with one of the other girls from the agency?"

She was still avoiding my face, so as I asked the question, I seized her hands firmly in mine. I could not care less if David had slept with all the Hotelles in her catalogue. That wasn't the past, the one over which he and Louie had practically come to blows, that interested me.

Her azure irises glared at me. Then, slowly overcome by my determined grip, she softened. Her eyes settled on me, heavy and tender. They were deeply sad.

"I've known Louie since I was twenty-one. He was barely fifteen. We met at one of the parties his mother used to organize for David and him. With all their money, and that stupid competition, the Barlet brothers didn't make many friends. Hortensia thought that if she invited the right kind of young people, plucked from among the children of their business acquaintances, they would learn how to mix with others. Apart from myself, who didn't have much to do with that milieu, it was a failure."

"Were you lovers?"

"With Louie? Yes, you could say that. He would be angry

if he knew I was telling you this, but for a long time I was his emergency wheel. Every time he got his heart broken, he'd come to me. For as long as it took him to repair his wounded pride . . . Then he'd go after someone else. Someone younger. Fresher."

Rebecca, the old mistress, a haven of indulgence and tenderness in his otherwise tumultuous sentimental life.

So then, that night in Dinard, at the restaurant in Saint-Malo, in the car on the way back from Brown Rocks . . . It hadn't been Alice!

"When Aurora died . . . You guys were back together, right?"

"Yes. I was there. Just like every other time he needed me."

She wasn't bitter. What she had for him was an endless love. An unrequited love.

"But it wasn't enough to keep her from being stupid and throwing herself in the water," she lamented.

"He could have saved her."

"No. She would have done it eventually, on that night or another. And David, too, in the end."

She knew that with a suggestion like that I would have to ask.

"David? Are you insinuating that he wanted her dead?"

"Not exactly. But now that she was sick, Aurora wasn't much use to him. She was a faulty stone in his crown."

That was how Louie had described him when we were at the Tuileries, as a monarch who only saw his relationships in terms of glory and ambition. A man who was sufficiently hardened as to wish for the death of a woman who was tarnishing both his image and potentially brilliant career.

"You think he let her condition worsen without doing anything?"

"Nothing . . . He even had a hand in it."

I remembered the living situation Louie had described: the bachelor pad above the apartment on Avenue Georges Mandel. The endless mistresses. The secret staircase. The perfect Don Juan, consuming women without a second thought.

Tarnish his image—wasn't that exactly what Rebecca was trying to do right now, at Louie's behest? I kept myself from spitting contempt in her face. Sure, David was authoritarian, egotistical. Sure, he used others like pawns. All that was undeniable. His hasty decisions, including his tyrannical fit with me earlier that same day . . . But did that make him a monster, a quasi-murderer, such as these two accomplices were trying to paint him?

I tried to determine what obscure contract bound these two together.

"How did Louie recover from the accident? I mean, outside of his knee?"

"Poorly. He felt guilty he hadn't been able to do anything that day. And even worse for not having intervened sooner with his brother. When there was still time to get him away from Aurora."

"Why didn't he?"

"The game," she said simply.

I was not sure I grasped her meaning, in this context.

"The game?"

"The constant competition between David and him. Louie may be the elder . . . but at the time, it was already clear that David had won. Definitively."

"With what Louie knew about him, he could have challenged everything," I played the devil's advocate. "Blackmailed him!"

"It was too late. Andre, their father, had already chosen his heir. There was nothing Louie could do . . ."

She spent a while telling me about how Louie had taken refuge in an imaginary world of belles lettres, romantic and ephemeral passion, and more or less twisted erotic games. She excused him everything: according to her, Louie was the first and, in some ways, the only victim of Aurora's death. Rebecca painted a picture of a sensitive and fragile man who had been crushed more by his father's madness and the harshness of his brother than by the rocks in Dinard. But I couldn't shake the image of the manipulator who wanted to nip my happiness in the bud. Him, my master?!

The more she spun her tale, the more I felt I would explode.

"You asked how he recovered? The answer is: by giving himself the illusion that he was in control of every aspect of his life. By inventing ever more convoluted scenarios for himself . . . It is no doubt hard for you to believe, but back then, he wasn't the dandy you see today, lecturing everyone on life and elegance."

He was as handsome as a bronze statue. As magnetic as a wild animal. And as . . .

I knew all that. I didn't need his old, jilted mistress to tell me. I was in a pretty good position to know the kind of power Louie had over women.

"He was such a nice boy . . . so generous."

She said this last bit like a close friend whispering a secret over tea. I snapped.

"Enough with the theatrics! If he was as great as you say . . ."

We were there. I had reached a critical moment, one where I had no other choice but to show my cards. Lower the different masks I'd had to wear at the Hôtel des Charmes. Even Sophia didn't know this much about me.

My anger did not unfurl like a wave in the Saint-Malo bay, hitting the shore with big, sonorous crashes. It unfolded like a long current of water, large and powerful. No seawall could stop it.

"If he's so great, why is he playing this game with me? Why does he want to ruin my marriage, Rebecca? What am I to him? A pawn on an old chessboard? His revenge against David? The epilogue to their twenty-year-old war?"

"None of the above."

"He doesn't see that he could shoot twenty girls like me without even scratching his brother? He can massacre me like cannon fodder; he can fuck me or have others fuck me, in all the hotel rooms on earth if he so pleases . . . He will never be better than David. Never!"

She shook her equine head. I may have been sure of myself, but there was something sincere in her quiet denial.

"You don't understand anything. Nothing."

It sounded like she was having a revelation.

"Understand what?"

She continued to shake her head incredulously, tirelessly, as though it could erase everything.

What had initially rattled me was now beginning to get on my nerves.

So, in spite of the waiters, who were serving hors d'oeuvres, and driven by the visceral need to empty myself, tired as I was by the constant pressure of their secrets, I screamed at the top of my lungs:

"*Understand what???*"

Every revelation in their web of interlocking lies trapped me inside a smaller and smaller Russian doll. Their dollhouse was going to suffocate me. Soon I, too, would be a broken toy on their hands. A dead toy. Like Aurora.

"He isn't doing all this to hurt David."

"Why, then?"

A gentle smile suddenly made her lips look beautiful. Before, I had always found them thin and dry.

"He isn't trying to hurt anyone. He's doing it for you."

She smiled like she was passing the baton.

She looked at me candidly and repeated:

"Simply for you."

26

S imply for me.

I spent several minutes trying to grasp the full meaning of this revelation, feeling it diffuse through me, a long perfusion of disbelief and joy. In the face of my silence, Rebecca felt the need to specify that she was willingly ceding Louie to me. She had long since accepted that the happiness of her one beloved depended on other women. She continued the thought—I was only really listening to every other word, if that—by listing everything that she and Louie still shared. Starting with their home. Ever since he had moved into the vast apartment on Avenue Georges Mandel, she'd occupied the one-bedroom upstairs. David's old bachelor pad. As Louie had told me, access between the two apartments had been sealed. So well that neither he nor she could burst in uninvited. So close, and yet so independent. Sometimes they didn't see each other for days on end. But just knowing that the other was only a few steps away was a comfort.

"But soon it will all change . . . ," she lamented with a sigh.

"Why?"

My question appeared to come as a surprise.

"They haven't told you?"

Shocked, my mouth formed an O.

"Told me what?"

"Well . . . The construction!"

The racket of hammers and pickaxes we'd been hearing from our garden. Richard the Chauffeur in construction garb. A few snapshots flashed through my mind.

"When they first moved in on Rue de la Tour-des-Dames, Andre and Hortensia bought the house next door."

"The one that used to be owned by Mademoiselle Mars . . . ," I muttered to myself.

"Yes. They renovated the first, the bigger of the two, and moved in there with the boys. For a long time, Mademoiselle Mars's old house remained untouched, and such as it had been since the forties."

I remembered the enamel plaque outside: YOUTH TRAVEL OFFICE.

"In fact, Mars House was deserted until Andre and Hortensia's death. In their will, they left David Duchesnois House, and Louie the other."

My voice cracked.

"Louie . . . Louie is our neighbor?"

Why had they hidden it from me? David; Armand, who had even commented on the inconvenience of the work next door . . . Why had no one told me?

"Not yet. He started this completely crazy project ten years ago to restore the house to its original state. Every fresco, every door handle, identical. From what I've seen, it's magnificent. But it's also a money pit. All of his inheritance has gone into it."

At least one of the thousands of little mysteries surrounding him had been solved: the day Felicity escaped, Richard's presence behind the blue door at 1 Rue de la Tour-des-Dames hadn't been random. Louie's chauffeur had an active role in his employer's project.

AFTER A LONG AND WARM embrace, which caught me by surprise, Rebecca drove me in her cream Mini Cooper to Duchesnois House. I was no longer indifferent to the building on its left. Knowing that Louie would be living there soon threw everything into question again: my resolutions and my desires. I didn't know what I wanted, in the end.

"Take care," she whispered as I got out of her car.

WHICH IS WHAT I DID with my next hour. David was absent again, and I decided to take a long, hot bath. Try as I might, I could not get Rebecca's words out of my head. They played in a loop, floating all around me like my bath bubbles. Alas, they did not disappear when at last I unstopped the bathtub. They stuck to my skin. They fit me better than any bathrobe or article of clothing: "He's doing it for you. Simply for you."

I went down to the ground floor wearing a simple robe—I could hear Armand in the kitchen. I found the new version of the prenup and a silver package on the console. Was Richard the Chauffeur his messenger?

I tore the paper and opened the box like a kid at Christmas. In addition to the usual magnetic key and note card, it contained a splendid black lace fan with a varnished handle the color of ebony whose tip bulged like a phallus. The accompanying note was like the others:

Ten p.m.
As usual,
it's up to you to find
our room.
Bring everything with you.

The last recommendation left me panting. *All* the objects he had given me? I climbed the stairs to the bedroom and took a rapid inventory, throwing everything into a light handbag.

Would I be playing with toys, as his latest commandment seemed to suggest?

6—Thou shalt master thy pleasure.

Was he planning on deferring our moment of physical contact much longer? It was driving me mad.

As I was leaving the house, I noticed the giant hourglass. Three-quarters of its contents had already changed sides. And what about me? Which side was I on? Did I really have to choose?

With no clear answer, I let my body decide: my feet led the way, my pelvis rushing toward pleasure, my sex throwing itself on whatever might flatter it, suck it, lick it, cleave it apart, everything it liked so much.

I was no longer in charge. I was but the sum of my organs, which were hungry for sensation. An erogenous puzzle that hoped to glue itself back together, and would moan with pleasure every time a new piece found its place.

THE RUE PIGALLE WAS VIBRANT that night. Ambient happiness—groups of young people speaking loudly and drinking much on terraces—perfumed the air with a scent of summer. I should have been like them, with them, sipping a Monaco with Sophia and letting boys my age hit on me, footloose and fancy-free.

But I was the exact opposite, driven toward a single goal, drawn by one force, inconsequential but lucid. I was so focused that I had no trouble cracking the day's enigma. Monsieur Jacques could bugger off. The fan was the biggest clue in my bag. It could have only belonged to one courtesan at the Hôtel des Charmes: Caroline Otero, better known as La Belle Otero. She was a dancer at the Folies Bergère around the turn of the twentieth century. The dark beauty was famous for her loose morals and the dazzling grace of her perfectly sculpted breasts. In addition to her male lovers, she entertained sapphic friendships, notably with the writer Colette.

I could not be wrong. I had visited her room before, when I was still a Hotelle.

Like the last time, I entered without so much as a wave in the direction of the concierge and found Ysiam faithfully on duty in front of the elevators.

"You are very beautiful tonight . . . I mean, even more than the other times," he said, charmingly awkward.

"Thanks, Ysiam. Could you take me to La Belle Otero, please?"

A few moments later, he confidently announced:

"Second floor. Would you please follow me?"

I found it touching how he remained ceremonial, despite the repetitiveness: the hall, the gilded door, which he opened, then locked behind me . . .

The room was as I remembered it, decorated like a brothel from the roaring twenties, with red velour wall hangings and rococo mirrors framed in arabesques. On the wall were hung original posters of the Folies Bergère, a testament to the glorious past of the woman who gave the room her name and soul. From first glance, I could tell that this rendezvous would be markedly different from the others. Starting with the chandeliers, which gave off a bright, almost garish light, a sharp contrast to the darkness to which I had grown accustomed.

Another major change: For the first time, someone else was present in the room before I stepped inside. I excluded the previous encounter from my comparison since Louie—or the man pretending to be him—had been hiding in the shadows when I'd first arrived, and had not made his presence known until later. Finally, and this was hardly a minor change, the person in question was not a man but a woman.

She was wearing a mask that hid her identity, but there was no doubt about her sex, not with that voluptuous body and its telling feminine curves. I eyed her chest, waist, hips, buttocks, and tapered legs supporting the whole. She was quite simply magnificent. Her skin, whose amber shade elegantly accentuated her long and lean limbs, glowed luminously under the array of lights floating above. The girl was immobile, but everything about her, from the nonchalance of her jutting hip to her slender hand resting on her waist, betrayed the flexibility and grace of a dancer, like La Belle Otero. Indeed, like this latter, she had the most beautiful breasts I had ever seen, firm and haughty, perfectly curved.

But it was only when she took a few steps toward me, with all the feline grace of a runway model, that I recognized her, the Vine, the stunning ethnic woman I had seen with Louie the night we'd first met and again another time with that former client, in the lobby of this very hotel. Her flawless physique oozed disdain. She was the kind of woman whose perfection crushes us simple mortals.

"I have no desire to . . ."

She placed a finger as long and light as a reed on my lips, commanding silence. Her mouth formed a mute "shh."

She guided my movements with natural authority, though without being brusque. I was surprised to discover that she possessed a languid, almost kindly, gentleness. There was no doubt her services had been ordered, but like all high-flying call girls, she knew how to give off the illusion of emotion. An actress more than a prostitute.

A piano piece swelled through the room, one I didn't recognize—Chopin again?—and she began undressing me, slowly, carefully as a wardrobe assistant, at pains not to wrinkle anything. Every article of clothing was a new opportunity for her hand to brush against my skin, which shivered with every touch.

When she finished the striptease, she rummaged through my bag of treasures, without asking permission, and withdrew the fan.

She presented it to me like a sacrament, as though my approval mattered to her. Stupefied, I did not move, and she began rubbing the handle against her vulva. She pushed her panties to the side, revealing herself to me. There was one thing she was not faking: when again she brandished the object under my eyes, it glistened with her desire.

"Lick it," she instructed, her voice deep and thick.

I complied, timidly at first, then with more ardor. I swallowed the bulge of the black lacquer handle as though it were the most delicious penis. She encouraged me, stretching her hands onto my shoulders. They were long and fabulously satiny, and as supple and light as leaves on water. Her caress was dizzyingly slow, but it grew faster as her hands moved over my throat, my breasts, and below. Her fingers played with my fuzzy pubis, skimming it with the flat of her hand, a finger or two wandering over the edge of my cleft.

Reassured by my submissiveness, she became more enterprising. She kneeled before me, one hand firmly placed on my waist, gripping my little love handle with all her might, and inserted the varnished handle into my vagina. My legs trembled, and I thought I might stumble. But the combined pressure of her palm on my hip and the handle that was slowly slipping deeper inside me maintained a kind of balance. The fan was like a stick on which I was being delectably skewered, one sigh at a time.

The dimensions of the object did not exceed those of a penis. But its extreme rigidity provided a new sensation, pushing into the walls of my vagina with authority. I did not feel ripped apart or excavated. I felt full, invaded, incredibly dominated. And that such happiness came from that ordinary object, and at the hands of the most exquisite of women, well, I was in a state. I let the stake planted in me sink in, bending my knees, seeing just how deep the intruder could go.

"Come, now."

She did not withdraw the fan as she led me to a bed covered in a single white sheet. She laid me down as cautiously as if I were a flower, making sure not to jostle the handle and wound my interior.

I realized that by accepting this new posture, I was abandoning myself fully to her. I was no longer capable of calculating, reasoning, or arguing with this sweet madness. So sweet . . .

Sophia's fingers coming out of her pussy. The girl in the black light screaming in pleasure. The frightening chest of an unknown woman on the metro a few days before. A carousel of images flashed through my head, with women front and center, affecting me in ways I could not deny. I had never so much as touched any of them, but now their combined forces were offering me ecstasy. I was the one who desired them, but through the proxy of the Vine's delicate hand, they were the ones who possessed me.

"Faster . . . ," I heard myself beg in a voice I didn't recognize. "Go on, faster!"

She plunged and withdrew the fan in and out of my vagina with force and regularity, relentlessly prodding my sex, demonstrating a kind of vigor that was surprising for her willowy frame. From under my half-closed eyelids, I read the excitement in her creased eyes and in the way her teeth sunk into her lower lip. Her whole being was concentrated on my enraptured cleft, which she would not relinquish until I had orgasmed.

It came from my innermost depths, like a ball born under my belly button. Heavy and overinflated, it rolled slowly, crushing each of my organs as it passed them by. When it reached the edge of my uterus, it swelled, stopped for a moment, and then at last unfurled in the wet and distended canal, taking everything, ripping pleasure from every millimeter. Howling, I had the distinct feeling that my cries came from my dilated cunt rather than my mouth. In the moment, I could not distinguish between the two orifices, and the astonishing pleasure being expressed by both.

"Very good . . . ," she said pedantically. "You're coming from your vagina."

True, and it was so pleasurable that when she withdrew the fan, I almost screamed in pain. It felt like she had just torn out my entire pelvic region.

Louie had dubbed himself the revealer. As I discovered hitherto unexplored territories of my sexuality, I found myself panting, my sex unsatiated and hungry for more. I longed for whatever he had planned next, like an expectant child waiting for her dessert. Not doubting for a second that he would give it to me. Confident in both him and my ability to receive whatever he offered. My fears had vanished. My senses were awake. And one by one, each new experience was unveiling new facets of a new woman. Up until now, my education, my principles, and, above all, my ignorance, had kept them locked up. At last they were free. They began to speak, one after another, expressing their unique desires, their particular fantasies. At that exact moment, I was not only La Belle Otero; I was also Marie, Josephine, and Lola.

MY EYES WERE STILL BLISSFULLY closed when I heard the door shut. The Vine had left the room without saying good-bye. I was alone, my body exhausted by pleasure, abandoned on the soft bed, with the keys of a piano—playing the mazurka?—running over me, making me shiver.

I could not believe I was being left to my own devices. Unsatisfied and longing for more. Nothing could sate my need but him. I wanted Louie. I wanted him for me, and only me. Now, even if it meant just this once, one more Hotelle in his cap. If only he could possess me once, just one time, maybe I could get his intoxicating scent out of my system; maybe I could forget his dark looks and that dimple on his lower right cheek; above all, maybe I could rid myself of the no doubt false idea that if I were his, all these disparate women would be united in me and I would become the center of a perfect, unified pleasure. No longer would I live off my fantasies alone. He would be a lover unlike all others.

Yes, if only he could penetrate me one time, with a penis I imagined to be as long and hard as the fan's handle, as adept at satisfying me . . .

When I was a teenager, before I had known any boys, I was so impatient to experience penetration that I improvised my own sex toy. I procured an individually wrapped condom from a dispenser outside our neighborhood pharmacy—I had waited until it was late, so no one would see me; I took it out of its package and awkwardly stretched it over a small green banana I had pinched from the kitchen. Alas, I only managed to introduce the tip of my makeshift dildo between my lips—not far enough to deflower me. The pressure against my taut hymen dissuaded me from going deeper. Short of breath and terrified I would do something stupid and Mom would find out, but also incredibly excited, I gave up on the banana and rubbed my clitoris, which was more engorged and hungry for caresses than ever.

Handwritten note by me, 6/13/2009

BUT THE MORE HE MADE me wait, the more he delayed the moment, drawing out our desire ad infinitum, fraying our nerves with his absences and furtive appearances, the more Louie haunted me. He was my master because he knew how to make me long for him: by circling around me, touching and surrounding me with as much subtlety as the sweet piano piece that was now playing.

I could have called out to him, cried his name, banged the door, and roused the whole hotel. I knew it would be in vain. I knew he would choose the hour. Had he already decided when it would be? Was it already written somewhere, in an agenda or on a notebook's perforated paper?

As the minutes passed, it became clear that no one else

would be joining me. And that I would have to set myself free. For want of inspiration, I let my gaze wander through the room. A lamp on the bedside table with a pyramid-shaped shade; a mahogany writing table with such slender legs it was hard to believe they managed to support it; a frosted molten glass vase with a bouquet of white lilies . . .

My hand wandered over the sheets, where they found the fan. I was momentarily surprised it had not been taken, when suddenly I remembered the day's commandment: *Thou shalt master thy pleasure.*

So that is what was expected of me. And so long as I had not fulfilled the command, I would remain prisoner of this room.

Nevertheless, I did not rush. I took my time considering the object more attentively. On closer inspection, the handle was not a crude sketch of a bulging gland. The black lacquered protrusion contained subtle details of realism: the fold of skin at its base, the thin strip of the frenulum, and even the protruding veins on the shaft, which I remembered had felt very pleasant inside me. I wondered if the fan's handle had been modeled after someone. Could it be . . .

I didn't expect an answer. I only wanted one thing, to thrust the handle between my pink, wet lips. It was my turn to produce the pleasure he refused to give me, through my own talents. I was tentative at first, progressively accelerating my cadence, until the object was deep inside me, violently assailing the whole of my lower body. I fell heavily to the bed's surface, gasping. The orgasm jolted through me in spasms, relentlessly crashing through my groin. I felt tears rolling down my cheeks. I was the land under the hail, a little piece of earth in a storm. Suddenly, my hand froze, the object trapped deep inside me like I was its sheath. It stayed there, stuck, until the muscles surrounding it relaxed, freeing me.

I offered him so much, and Louie gave me so little . . .

Or was it the other way around?

27

June 13, 2009

A few years ago, back when we both had trouble making ends meet, Sophia convinced me to do this thing she'd recently learned about. That is how, in exchange for thirty euros, I gave her a pair of used cotton panties, which she then sold on a specialized website. After I pocketed the money, I tried not to think about whatever became of my underthings. I was kind of grossed out by the whole idea and refused to do it again.

But today, years later, I sometimes wonder what happened to that barely moistened panty. Did it still smell like me? Did the man who bought it still sniff it while ~~jacking off~~ masturbating? Had he tossed it in with all the others, making it anonymous? Or had he thrown it out after one use?

Handwritten note by me, 6/13/2009

"*AURORA DELBARD*"—THE SEARCH ENGINE ONLY came back with two results. Only two, and both wrong. Come to think of it, Aurora had died at a time when our private lives weren't available for all to see on the Web and social networks.

Still, it was surprising not to find her anywhere. No class photo, no scholastic or university affiliation, no genealogical tree, nothing. Had her family or even David himself contacted one of those businesses that can erase your online existence? In any case, the result was the same: Aurora Delbard had left no virtual trace of herself or her time on earth.

This idea crossed my mind in a flash, a brief instant of exhilaration and panic, and then it was gone: What if Aurora wasn't real? What if she was the fruit of a sick imagination? It was unthinkable. What would be their interest in inventing this woman? Why dupe me like that?

That morning, as I slipped the ring back on my finger, I had the sensation of entering into a ghost's life, an ectoplasm with no past or shape. Worse, a purely fictional being.

The surest way of sending the ghost back to the other side, of getting it out of my life, was with my pen. When I signed the contract Armand had left for me, David's prenup, I would be giving our union and our present life much more consistency than any memory—real or invented. But I couldn't. Ten times that morning I had hovered the point of my pen over the places where I was to initial. Ten times I had withdrawn my hand, impeded by an invisible force whose name I knew all too well. Louie had a hold on me.

See you at the station, beautiful.
I believe in you.
I love you.
D.

I found David's note on the breakfast table. It didn't lift my severely low spirits. Today was the big day, however. My first television appearance. Something I had wanted for a long time, and which any girl in my place would have seen as a blessing. Yes, everything should have receded—my evenings at the Hôtel des Charmes should have vanished overnight, Louie's voice and scent evaporated—in the face of this important and imminent event. I should have been quaking in fear, hopping with impatience, squealing with excitement. But instead, I felt switched off, my attention drawn elsewhere, far, far away from these happenings and my ambition, which was beginning to seem pathetic and vain.

I DRAGGED MY FEET, TAKING all the time in the world to meet the team that I knew awaited me on set. Moreover, I allowed myself the luxury of a detour, surprising even myself when I exited the metro at the Père Lachaise station, a business card in hand.

Avenue de la République, a wide and affluent street, stretched out from across the famous Parisian cemetery. A little road to its left, Rue du Chemin Vert, was markedly narrower and more working-class. I followed its gentle decline, the scent of kebab wafting over the sidewalk, even at this early hour, and trash cans overflowing at every step. The smell of grilled meat and garbage was nauseating. Happily, there was a light breeze.

Sandwiched between a Pakistani bazaar and a wholesale craft store, the bookstore's bordeaux-colored facade was visible from a distance. The signage was discreet, however, and made no mention of the kind of books it sold: La Musardine. But a quick glance inside left no doubt.

I PUSHED OPEN THE DOOR and stepped inside the hushed space. It had red carpeting and well-appointed display cases, where a few customers were browsing. I had expected to find perverts in raincoats, sleazy old men, Amazons in skimpy outfits. But despite the fact that they were mostly men, the patrons seemed rather banal. The two or three couples present weren't even acting overtly intimate, or hardly. There was a man whispering into a blushing woman's ear, and another who let his hand wander over his girlfriend's ample posterior. Were they planning on making love after their errand? Would they find what they needed to fulfill their fantasies here?

The thematic organization was clear: erotic literature to the left and by the entry; photography and art books to the right and near the register; in the back right, graphic novels and comics; and in the back left, essays, guides, and a few related gadgets.

My list in hand, I had no difficulty finding the first recommended books and piling them one by one into a teetering heap. Since I was in a hurry—a few lingering glances on my curves were making me uneasy—I started toward the bookseller, a charmless brunette with short hair who was slumping behind the counter. But several covers caught my attention on my way: a series called *Pink Pussy*. Inside, young, smiling women spread their vulvas wide open. They seemed delighted to show themselves. True to the title, their pussies were as bright and pink as possible, somewhere between an exotic flower and a fleshy butterfly.

Was I still under the influence of the night before? Had Louie and the Vine really gotten so far under my skin? I couldn't stop turning the pages, fascinated by such openness. I wondered if I could pose like that, too, and what pleasure

I would derive if ever confronted with one of these perfect, open, and humid clefts. Would I arm myself with a hard and oblong toy to insert inside?

The pyramid of books in my arms tumbled, drawing me out of my daydream. Two dozen eyes stared at me, reproaching, mocking. I mumbled an apology and stooped to pick everything up without letting my skirt ride up my heinie. I hurried to pay for my purchases, red with shame, my cheeks and voice flustered like the little girl I thought I had outgrown.

BACK ON THE METRO, I felt calm again. Still, I did not dare open the dark plastic bag printed with golden drops. One humiliation was enough for the moment, especially since the evening's challenge probably had more in store for me.

"You're late, but it's no big deal . . ."

David had charged into my office without so much as a hello.

"For now, all I care is that you are at your best. Did you have breakfast, at least?"

Hearing him speak and feeling his eyes sizing me up, I felt like a yearling on the morning of its first race. All that was missing was a tap on the muzzle and knead of the rump to evaluate my chances of winning or losing. Is that what he had seen in me when we'd first met, at that formal dinner: his station's next gem, a diamond in the rough that he could fashion as he pleased and whom he would make into his jewel?

"Yes, yes, I'm fine . . . I ate."

"Dried fruit? Did you have some dried fruit?"

He was circling me, sizing me up, clearly concerned about how his filly would perform. He was as nervous as a cyclist's dope-pushing trainer before a race.

"No, but I'll be fine. I promise."

I did not want to imagine what would happen if I disappointed him.

"Right . . . I know you're going to *tear it up!*"

The youngster expression fit him like a kilt on an undertaker. But he didn't care. He was high on his own adrenaline; he was all revved up, before the racing flag was even waved.

And if I proved as lackluster as I suspected I would onscreen, there was no doubt I could expect a fate similar to Aurora's. Would he push me to the same extremes? Would my name also disappear into a digital hell, never to be seen again?

He kissed my neck with tenderness, sweeping away all my dark thoughts. He buried his nose into my hair, his hand stroking my half-bare shoulder. So long as he did not speak of the prenup, so long as he continued to see me as his new goddess, I could abandon myself to his muddled caresses.

"I want you," he whispered into my ear.

I bent my neck to escape his kisses, which were becoming more and more insistent.

"Not here . . ."

"Why? Are you afraid the boss will walk in on us?"

He chuckled at his own joke, self-satisfied, as usual. Everything he touched supposedly turned to gold. And it always had. He won at everything. Except with Aurora . . .

"Oh, sorry . . ."

Fred's blue eyes were at the door, staring at us in surprise. A familiar look of anger crossed his brow. But he contained himself, unlike David:

"What do you want? What are you doing here?"

I realized that the two men had never met. And while Fred had to know what his employer, the big boss at BTV, looked like, the same did not go for David, for whom this unshaven young man in jeans and a T-shirt could only belong to the ranks of the hoi polloi in his company. The expendable masses, for him, and he treated them as such.

"I . . ."

Was I supposed to introduce them? And if so, which parts of our respective histories was I to discuss? I figured Fred was afraid I would tell David about how he had started at the station; that would explain his silence.

"'I' what? Leave us alone!"

"Darling . . . ," I intervened, "this is Fred Morino. He's the sound guy for the show. I suppose everyone is waiting for me on set?"

I shot Fred a meaningful look.

"That's right." He nodded, suppressing his rage.

"Oh . . . Very good."

David never lost face, never, no matter his interlocutor. So he straightened, more annoyed than angry, and scolded Fred in a paternalistic tone:

"But next time knock—I don't care if it's an emergency."

He pointed to the door of my office, which had been wide open when Fred first appeared. His gesture was so obvious that it could not be confused.

And to think I had added my ex to the guest list for our wedding. Would the master of the house kick him out of the reception before he got the chance to show his invitation?

"I have to go," I said lightly, following the technician.

It was now or never to sway my hips, bat my eyelashes, pucker my lips into a heart. In other words, play up my feminine charms as though I were in a Z-list movie. Perhaps it would help mitigate David's reaction after the evening's imminent disaster.

"I'll be thinking about what you *said* earlier," I purred . . .

I FOUND FRED IN THE corridor, and we hurried to slip away. I was as embarrassed as he. The incongruity of the situation had not only been torture; it also had lifted the curtain on a vitiated part of my relationship with David. God knows I had wanted it all, the perfect man, a life of power and comfort, privileges to make daily life invulnerable. But I could not forget who I was. I could not leave the girl from Nanterre or those who had grown up with her outside an open door . . . I could not be inside and out at the same time.

I refrained from sharing my nerves with Fred, the involuntary cause and collateral victim of this maelstrom.

"Nobody told you to come and get me, did they?"

"No," he admitted. "But I found something interesting while messing with Louie's phone line."

"What is it?"

"A list of all of his calls over the past three months."

"And?" I said impatiently. "He orders a call girl every day at six o'clock?"

"Not really, no." He suppressed a smile.

"Who does he call, then?"

"I know you're not going to believe me, but there is no doubt about the number. I recognized it immediately."

"Shit, Fred! Tell me!" I growled, teeth gnashing.

"He calls your mom. Maude. It's your house number."

My gaze wandered over the office landscape, in which an army of journalists was preparing for the news update at noon. Then it rested on him again, stunned.

"My mom? Are you sure?"

HE RATTLED OFF HER HOME phone number without hesitating.

"This week alone, he's called her three times," he read off a sticky note in his hand.

I remembered all the presents he had given her, those outrageous rewards for my horizontal services.

"And do they speak for a long time?"

"Kind of, yeah. Monday, twenty-two minutes. Wednesday, only eleven minutes. And yesterday, eighteen, with a little thirty-second interruption—he must have put her on hold."

That was much longer than a courtesy call or a basic verification—verification of what, by the way? They were real conversations.

"She couldn't have answered and then put the phone down without saying anything?"

It was not necessarily an absurd idea. Not more than my real-fake lover, real-fake brother-in-law, calling my mother to chat like two old friends.

"No, I don't think so. Phones that sophisticated automatically time-out so the line won't be busy for no reason. If no one is talking, it will cut out after one or two minutes. Not twenty."

The one thing Fred's technical expertise could not tell me was the nature of their conversations. And the identity Louie was disguising himself under to get to my mother. Was he pretending to be his brother? Or maybe Armand, under the pretext of needing information for the wedding preparations?

"When did you say he started calling her?"

"I didn't. It's been going on since late April."

Or shortly after I'd first met David, when our relationship was still a secret . . . and well before Louie had sent any presents to my mom—as far as I knew, in any case. What had been the nebulous pretext under which he had first entered into contact with her? And why had she agreed to converse with this faceless interlocutor?

AFTER A BRIEF SNACK WITH the voluble Albane, the afternoon unfolded like a dream, with all manner of activities that I performed like a robot.

Two p.m., Chloe had said: Rehearsal on set with Stan, our director, who would lead me through the blocking for the show. The bucolic set had been put together in haste. The only part of Chris's work that they had managed to salvage was the logo, which was printed on a large cardboard sign in the background and lighted to stand out.

Four p.m.: Practice reading the cue cards Albane's team had made for me. I was glad to learn that she had been sure not to make me into one of those petulant bimbos like the ones so favored by our competitors' shows. My script was sober, concise, succinct but not too much, fairly close to what I would have written myself if David's confidence in me had extended to that task, too.

Five p.m.: Meet my two guests—a star bookseller who was going to give his list of must-reads for the beach and a professional dancer who would give us a demonstration of a "killer move" for summer—and chitchat "informally."

Six p.m.: Tea and biscuits, followed by what seemed to me like an endless session of primping, wardrobe, hair, and makeup. I felt like a cream puff getting bigger and bigger.

This doll caked in foundation, this porcelain being about to go out into the spotlight wearing a floral dress . . . Was this really me?

"Pretend you're twelve years old and playing television

host with your girlfriends," Albane said, dispensing some last-minute advice.

"At twelve I wanted to be Marie Curie or Françoise Giroud, but okay . . ."

"You know what I mean: act the part. All the big people in TV today were once kids making faces in a mirror. The rest will come later, with practice."

It wasn't very reassuring, but maybe it would take the wind out of my detractors' sails. There was no doubt they would lambaste me for my inexperience. So goes the world. Everyone is so quick to forget their own faux pas, and eager to trip up anyone new whose youth might outshine them.

SEVEN-THIRTY P.M.: A WHOLE HOUR to wait. I pretended I needed to be alone so that I could wander the deserted halls of the nineteenth floor in my floral dress, primped and proper, looking for an escape that I would never dare take. Fate led me by an office that had recently been vacated. ALICE SIMONCINI, read the white plastic sign that was still posted to the right of the door. I lowered the handle: it was open. The only thing that struck me in the soulless space was the lingering odor. I detected the beautiful blonde's perfume, floral and sweet, and a hint of other, more acidic notes. Was it the smell of love? The bouquet created by their respective sexes? How many times had she and Chris cavorted in here, just a few paces from David's office? I tried to imagine the two of them, the tall, flaccid body of her lover with his buttocks pressed against the bay window, grasping at her vagina with an excited hand, drooling his desire on her delicate neck, and so proud of his prey.

One should never surprise one's friends when they are in the midst of making love . . .

Before Sophia, my best friend was Sabina. People thought we were twins we looked so alike; it was even troubling for us. We spent hours together looking at ourselves in the mirror, hunting down our differences. The only trait that distinguished us was her pair of bright blue eyes. It was an advantage over me, in terms of seduction, and she used it to the best of her abilities, attracting the hottest boys in high school.

One Wednesday afternoon she invited me over to her house. I got there fifteen minutes early, thinking I'd find her watching TV or reading one of her vampire books—"They're so sexy!"—that she loved so much. The door to the parental home was open. So was the one to her room. For good reason, since at this time of day in the middle of the week, she was supposed to be alone at the house. But that was not the case. From the staircase, I heard moaning—almost meowing— that told me what was going on upstairs. But I couldn't resist the temptation. I tiptoed up the steps and peered into her bedroom, admiring Sabina's prowess for the entire quarter hour before we were supposed to meet. Her way of arching her rump to the point of breaking her back while the boy was going down on her. It seemed totally indecent to me back then. ~~Her shocking use of language, in which he was reduced to his "cock," and she called herself a "bitch," a "whore," and "the biggest slut in school."~~ The voracious way she swallowed her partner's member, all the way down to its hilt. The hyena's cry at the moment of ecstasy . . .

I left without making a sound, no questions asked.
I was still a virgin, and the scene had ultimately been
disturbing. I didn't speak to her for the rest of the year. She
probably guessed the reason behind my sudden coldness
but never dared address the issue head-on. I've thought of
that image of my friend, fucking like an animal, raw, on
numerous occasions while pleasuring myself. It is also the
last memory I have of her.

Handwritten note by me, 6/13/2009

Where are you? Luc, Stan, and I are going over a few
last-minute details. We're waiting for you. Get your
butt down here, you diva!

Albane's text message brought me back into the present.
And as she would have said herself, I got my tush downstairs
in double time. As soon as I arrived, I could feel that particular tension that precedes the launch of a new program. David
himself was present, an extraordinary occurrence judging from
the terrified and excited murmur of the troupe.

Meanwhile, one absence had not gone unnoticed: Louie, I
was told, had not been seen in the building all day.

I pretended to watch the eight o'clock news with my team,
who were acting like a bunch of schoolkids—to lower the
stress, I imagined. As for me, my mind was far away from
Barlet Tower.

Where could he be? At the Hôtel des Charmes? Haunting
Mademoiselle Mars's old house, ambling through the construction site? Or at home in front of his television, waiting
like any other viewer for the fateful hour of my televised doom?

WHAT FOLLOWED WAS A COLORFUL nightmare in pop culture, replete with forced laughter and artificial enthusiasm. As Albane had intimated, I was to be something of a ridiculous mime whom everyone pretended to take seriously, though my delivery was too supercharged to be intelligible . . . Not to mention my one hundred fifty "So, nows."

The script prepared by the editorial team burned in my hands. My eyes glued themselves to it as a kind of crutch for my stress. And I could not listen to a single word of the reports off set. I even missed a few cues, despite Stan's reminders in my earpiece and the red light on the camera.

"Breathe, it's not a race!" the director whispered several times into my hearing device. "At this pace, we'll be done in a half hour. Stay cool!"

Five minutes before the end, during Louie's spot, the last one, I got a touch-up on my makeup and a bathroom break. After that all I had left was a brief conclusion to read off the teleprompter, and this ordeal would finally be over.

"You're doing great!" Albane said encouragingly while I made my way to the restroom. "Slow down a little, though. Let your guests talk. You'll always have time to cut things short at the end if they go on too long."

Alone in the bathroom stall, my bladder was about to explode, but I could not release even a drop. I tried to suppress the strong desire to empty my stomach.

I didn't want to leave. Never. I wanted to stay in my little floral dress, smelling pee in this warm, protected world. Here there was no husband, no lover, no viewers to laugh at me.

" . . . No, I started by accident, I didn't really have a choice . . ."

I caught more or less intelligible scraps of sound from the speakers on set:

"I don't mean to pry, but do you ever feel any pleasure when you're with these men?"

"Yes, of course. Rather often, in fact . . . It's not just a job."

It was true. Being a Hotelle was not just a job. I could attest to that.

Prudence, even fear, should have kept me where I was. And yet I left the bathroom, curious to hear what this girl had to say. Her voice, which had been distorted to protect her identity, had a cadence that was not unfamiliar. When I got back to the set, where two dozen screens featured the same masked face, I thought I might collapse and vomit all over the technicians.

I recognized the mask: it was an exact replica of the one Louie had given me once before.

But there was something even more familiar: the broad gestures, the shoulder-length chocolate curls, and that direct way of speaking . . .

"I mean, it's not just about the sex. Not at all!" the modified voice twanged. "We talk, we discuss our lives. Sometimes there's a connection . . ."

The only words to come out of my mouth, in a thin and desperate voice that only I could hear:

"Fuck, Sophia . . . No. Not you."

Her face white with stupor when Louie had introduced himself to us on our jog in Bois de Vincennes.

Her sincere interest, her bawdy laughter, when I had told her about the trap in which Louie had been ensnaring me day after day: "Will you introduce me to him?! . . . I love that kind of playfulness in a man!" Her obsession with my Ten-Times-a-Day, which she had been sure to mention would have suited her far more than me.

One by one, these memories resurfaced, tearing the mask from the woman everyone saw on the screen.

Why had she put on such an act? And above all, what had been her price for betrayal? Just enough to make ends meet, perhaps. A couple of big bills like the ones he had slipped me at the gallery or for my erotic shopping at the Musardine bookstore. Or maybe—and this thought killed me more than anything—they were lovers? Did they make fun of me, of my gullibility, when they were between the sheets? Did they have a laugh over my virginal awkwardness, my silly trepidation, when they rolled on top of each other in boundless ecstasy, the perfect couple in their unquenchable thirst for passion?

Since when had he possessed her?

"Back on in thirty," Stan cried from somewhere in my vicinity.

"Elle! Elle, you okay?"

Albane's voice did not penetrate the thick cocoon that was weaving itself around me. Was I okay? How could I answer that?

Her hand squeezed the nape of my neck, but it wasn't I who shuddered at her touch.

"Elle! Elle, crap! Are you with me?"

No, sweet Albane, I haven't been with you for several long, long minutes now. I had lost all contact with reality. Mine was a long, cold sob that engulfed me like an icy cloak. A giant Eskimo in the middle of the studio. I saw the world outside through a foggy porthole. Everything was muffled. Nothing could get through to me.

"Back on in twenty! Girls, get your butts on stage . . . Now!"

"Shit, I don't know what's gotten into her . . . ," Albane stammered, panicked. "We've lost her. Call the doc!"

On the monitors, Sophia was answering the interviewer's—Louie's—last question:

"I hear you call yourselves Hotelles, is that right?"

"Yes, exactly."

"Can you explain for our viewers in two words what that means?"

"Well, 'Hotelle' is a portmanteau word. First, there's the adjective 'hot,' I think that's fairly clear . . ."

"It is!"

Another desperate call from Stan:

"Back on in ten! What do we do?"

"Go to credits! Whatever!" Albane bellowed. "I don't care!"

Through my tears, the mask was melting.

" . . . And then there's 'Elle,' which is the name of one of the original girls. Our mascot, if you will . . ."

"That's very pretty. And how about you, do you feel more hot or more like Elle?"

"Oh, I'm definitely hot!" She burst out laughing. "Elle . . . I'm not an Elle. I have a friend who's Elle . . ."

JINGLE. SHOT OF THE SET. Without me.

Credits.

28

June 14, 2009

When I finally came to, everyone pretended nothing had happened. They'd have just as soon forgotten my freak-out. They no doubt thought that for now denial was the most charitable reaction.

Better, everyone was really complimentary about my "amazing performance," even Luc, Philippe, and Stan, who were all excessively enthusiastic, despite the fact that they had the most to lose and would certainly take heat for my professional inexperience. I may not have been their first choice, but it had been up to them to transform my rough self into a little soldier who could go into battle. I wasn't supposed to freak out or act like a diva. And judging from their crestfallen faces, over which they had plastered smiles, I could tell David's wrath would fall on them. My failure was also theirs, and they couldn't hide it.

"Albane! Do you know where David is?"

I grabbed my friend by the arm. Her eyes were a mix of disappointment, pity, and compassion. Albane was not an affectionate person, but she was independent enough of spirit to commiserate. She was pretty, young, competent . . . Would this incident put her out of a job?

"In his office. Why?"

"I want to speak with him." I met her eyes proudly.

"Not possible. He asked not to be disturbed by anyone."

"I have to explain to him what happened . . ."

"I know, I understand . . . but he was clear, 'absolutely no one.' I presume that includes you. Sorry."

A lord in his castle, David was probably letting his anger steep and deciding how to react. On the one hand, he had to handle this at the station, where he could not lose face or show any signs of weakness or favoritism; on the other hand, there was our relationship, and though this incident was not a direct threat, it had put a chip in it. One could have imagined a better wedding present from me . . . A luxury watch, for instance, which seemed to be disappearing bit by bit from the window at Antiquités Nativelle, like a receding memory.

I braced myself for anything: kingly contempt, a sign of his clemency and generosity, or, rather, a proper repudiation and anger unfurling on me like a torrent. How much did he want to preserve our relationship? How much did he want to maintain his image as an inflexible boss? One thing was sure: he could not show himself to be softer on me than on his other employees. The nepotism he had shown in hiring me was already a major source of reproach. If he afforded me any special privileges, he would lose all credibility, and his authority would wither under the sun of his love for me.

I WENT HOME ALONE TO Duchesnois House, jostled in the back of a taxi that seemed to cross the city in the blink of an eye. I found a busy, almost excited Armand, clearly unperturbed by the drama of my day. He was so preoccupied with other things, in fact, that I did not dare ask what he'd thought of my show. He jumped on me with notes and papers in hand.

"I finally have the definitive menu. Do you want to see it, Mademoiselle?"

I acquiesced with an absent smile. My eyes skimmed over the paper more than they read the impressive courses of food. From the depths of my stupor, it seemed that Armand had more than accommodated my tastes. Much of the menu was devoted to seafood, and in the desserts red fruits dominated.

"It seems perfect." I forced delight.

"Are you sure? We can still make changes, you know."

"No, no, don't change a thing. I am sure it will be . . ."

Do not say "sublime" or "splendid" or "magnificent" or any of the superlatives David tends to overuse.

" . . . divine. Yes, it will be divine."

He met my compliment with a gracious smile, which quickly twisted, however, into a scowl.

"I hate to bring it up . . . but the notary keeps asking for your signed copies."

"My copies?" I asked.

"Of the prenup . . ."

"Oh, yes . . . the prenup."

"Everything has to be decided before the civil wedding; otherwise the terms of the agreement will be voided. And we'll have to redo the whole thing."

"Of course, I understand. I'll get it to you tomorrow."

"Signed?" he insisted, raising one of his bushy eyebrows.

I got the feeling he wasn't just expressing his need to get things done properly. Beyond the interests of his master, he seemed personally invested in my accomplishing this task.

"Yes, of course," I answered. "Signed."

I BELIEVE EVERYTHING HAS BEEN said and written on the comforting power of cats. Their contagious sense of calm, their sweetness, their apathy, their rhythmic purring that can put you to sleep . . .

I glued myself to Felicity in the hope that she would bring me a little peace, even fleetingly. I wrapped myself around her as though I were her mother. I used to do the same thing as a kid when I needed consoling. Once or twice, I interrupted this outpouring of warmth to call Sophia, but of course the traitor did not pick up. At last I fell into a disturbed sleep. I dreamed Albane was chosen to replace me on *Culture Mix*, and she decided to do it in the nude, and the technicians and viewers were strangely indifferent.

When I awoke, there was still no sign of David. No balled-up towel on the floor, not a hint of his cologne. Had he even come home? Again, I called and there was no answer. Then, midmorning:

"Elle? Hello, it's Chloe."

"Chloe . . . you work on Sunday?"

"No. I had the line transferred to my house. I always do that when I think the weekend might be hectic at the station."

I presumed it had been an order from my fiancé and not her personal initiative. Even on days of rest, his army needed to be at the ready.

"Okay . . . Why are you calling?"

"David asked me to contact you. He spent the night in his office."

I remembered the sofa facing his work table. It looked uncomfortable but doable for a night. I figured it had never dissuaded him from ending long evenings there. Chloe probably kept one of his drawers stocked with clean shirts and underthings so he could dive into work the next day.

"He would like you to join him," she added, and she wasn't asking.

My heart skipped a beat. This was it. And it occurred to me that my procrastination over the prenup had been a sign of prudence on my part rather than flippancy.

"When?"

"Now."

The noose around my neck got tighter; I had just enough air to murmur:

"Okay. I'm just going to get dressed . . ."

"Super. I'll let him know."

However, David could wait, and Chloe could deal with his ensuing reprimand, because I was in no more of a mood to be scolded like a child than he was to let it go. Oh, I would show up to his Sunday summons, of course. But I would do it on my time, and when I felt ready to deal with him. Not before.

I lazed a while in bed with Felicity, my Ten-Times-a-Day open on my thighs. I tried to write, but my mind was miles away from sweet thoughts of sex. My pen scribbled over the blank page, and I crossed out every word I put down. Like Louie, I would have loved to capture traces of lovers before me, in all places and circumstances. To fill myself with their moods, to sigh as they had once sighed, to shiver with them in unison. But nothing came that day in Duchesnois House, in spite of all the suitors whose shadows still haunted this place—including the emperor himself.

Is sex always ~~better~~ stronger than everything? Can the mind become so tortured by serious and urgent preoccupations that all our risqué thoughts disappear? Or does the libido always end up submerging the rest, like an endless torrent?

Handwritten note by me, 6/14/2009

AS THE MORNING WENT BY, I expected to start receiving angry calls from David. But though this gentle time seemed endless, nothing disturbed the spring day's tranquility, which blew a cool and calming breeze through the half-open window. What I found even more surprising, considering my television appearance the night before, was the silence from all my friends and family. That Mom hadn't hurried to hash out what I knew was a historic event for her, that a few old girlfriends from college hadn't taken advantage of this moment to call . . . that Rebecca hadn't exploded in anger over the fact that I had broken my promise of confidentiality—it was all so strange . . . almost suspicious. Had my absence at the end really been that obvious? Had it really hurt my image that much? Perhaps it had made waves? I preferred not to waste what pride I had left by exposing myself to their fake compliments.

It was Sunday. A day of rest in this country. The one day of the week when there wasn't a recap of all the best moments of television from the day before. No one would publicly notice my disappearance until the next day. Except maybe online, that hive of useless activity?

No, nothing on the station's official Facebook page, nor on my personal page, which had been transformed, at Louie's request, into a professional tool with my public name: Elle

Barlet. The most recent messages dated back two days, and were from Louie's subordinates trying to create buzz. *Culture Mix* did not yet have a cultural presence, and for good reason, considering the haste in which it was born.

With nothing else to distract me from what was awaiting me, I killed time digging through the pile of books I'd bought at La Musardine. Dreamily, I skimmed a line here, a paragraph there, not really focusing on anything. Everything slid under my eyes like a scene after a disaster.

The fact that Louie had not made a peep did not surprise me, though it was disappointing. If he saw me as anything but prey, a new cog in the alarming erotic machine he used to obliterate his melancholy, well then, now was the time to show his support. Or more, who knows . . .

I ended up reading the preface of the Divine Marquis's *Philosophy in the Bedroom*, a book he wrote for his mistress. In it, he addresses "libertines" in these terms:

Libertines of all ages and sexual persuasions: to you alone I dedicate this work! Feast upon its principles: they champion the passions that frigid, insipid moralists would have you despise, passions which are merely Nature's way of guiding man to her ends. Listen only to these delicious longings; for only your passions can lead you to happiness.

Lascivious women: look to the voluptuous Saint-Ange for inspiration; like her, scorn all that contradicts the divine laws of Pleasure, which enchained her all her life.

Young girls too long constrained by the absurd and pernicious bonds of Virtue and disgusting religion: emulate the hot-blooded Eugénie; destroy and trample those ridiculous preconceptions that your imbecilic parents have instilled in you—and do it as fast as she.

I imagine that Louie would not have written otherwise if he had wanted to express his ideas for me—I, who may have been his thing but not yet his mistress. As apt and virtuosic as these words were, they also seemed quite vain. I wanted neither discourse nor speeches. Neither lessons nor remonstrances. I did not want to be treated like a princess, much less a slave, a simple object of pleasure or a decorative piece. What I wished was for one or the other, David or Louie, to take me in his arms and offer me love. I would give him my faith. And the past in which they were holding me captive and which had nothing to do with me would be swept away. I wanted to exist before them, for them, against them. I didn't want to be a series of concepts in a skirt or an abstraction of their family strife.

> *It's a debate I have never been able to resolve for myself:*
> *To what extent is it pleasurable to be a sexual object for*
> *your partner? By that I mean, being a toy for him, an in-*
> *strument that he uses depending on his needs. A whore at*
> *his mercy. The way one of my few clients at the Hôtel des*
> *Charmes once used my mouth was painful; it even kind of*
> *disgusted me. He didn't penetrate it with care, as ordinary*
> *lovers do. No, he fucked it hard, violently plunging his*
> *shaft between my lips, his lower abdomen knocking into*
> *my nose, obviously trying to hit my glottis with his enor-*
> *mous gland, which seemed on the verge of coming with*
> *every thrust. I was suffocating, and there was something*
> *degrading about his brutal invasion of my mouth. I felt*
> *objectified, as though his cock were trying to silence me*

forever, obliterate my words, so that he could use my mouth
as he pleased: just another orifice to ravage.
    Would I have been as disgusted if I had loved him?
Could I handle being my lover's thing?

Handwritten note by me, 6/14/2009

THIS THOUGHT REMINDED ME OF the telephone conversations Fred had discovered between Louie and Mom. Why had he been interested in her all this time? What could have motivated such a surprising and inappropriate course of action, if not his interest in me and the construction of this enormous scheme to undo me—to destroy me?

Can I call you?

Fred was at last resurfacing. But I didn't have the heart to listen to his sarcastic remarks or the ones he might have heard the night before with his new coworkers.

Around noon, another message, this time more glacial, reminded me of my obligations.

I'm waiting for you. D.

I quickly showered and threw on my outfit number one, the pantsuit, pearl necklace, and low heels. Sober and professional.

After a twenty-minute taxi ride, I arrived in front of the glass tower, which shimmered in the sun. Yet from that angle outside, there was nothing in the world so opaque as those immense glass surfaces. Under all the flash, the Barlet mystery was decidedly well preserved.

WITH CHLOE GONE, DAVID'S OFFICE door had been left ajar, a clear invitation to enter. I slipped through the crack, trying to be as slim and discreet as a sheet of paper, when suddenly a cork flew past my face, moments after its telltale pop.

"You're the host of *Culture Mix*, aren't you?" he greeted me in a playful tone, a champagne bottle in hand.

I kept my guard up from my corner of the room, maintaining a respectable distance from his voice and especially his hands.

"Umm . . . It would seem."

He filled two glasses and stepped toward me, the two delicate flutes between his fingertips. He handed me one, smiling.

"In that case, drink with me, Mademoiselle . . . Something tells me you deserve it."

"Some . . . something?" I stammered, speechless.

" . . . And that I was right to push you a little. Listen to this," he trumpeted, grabbing a table of figures behind him. "Five point two percent market share!"

"Is that good?" I played innocent.

"Are you kidding? Do you know what the best score for a DTT channel was last year, news and general channels combined?"

"No."

"Seven point eight. And on a major Hollywood film! Five point two percent on a news magazine program and for a launch . . . It's a miracle!"

"Really?"

"Do you realize we're at the bottom of the top twenty? From the get-go!"

His figures mostly eluded me, but faced with his disarming joy and after a few sips of bubbly, I let myself give in to the feeling of triumph.

My premature and catastrophic debut had been pardoned. My beginner's awkwardness: forgotten. The fear of being unmasked by Louie's report: gone. The bitterness I'd assumed I'd harbor for Sophia for the rest of my life: vanished.

All that remained was an unexpected number that transformed my failure into a breakthrough, my defeat into victory. It was a blessing for my future appearances. I was so relieved that, suddenly, I wanted to laugh and celebrate the event with him. To thank him for this extraordinary opportunity that I, ingrate that I was, had tarnished.

"So . . . next time, we'll be in the middle of the top twenty!" I cried, stupidly overconfident.

"It's such a hit that all of Paris has been calling me since last night. Everybody wants a piece of it, honey."

That justified his night on the sofa, I thought, glancing at the rumpled sheet and blanket. It wasn't anger that had kept him awake but excitement. That also explained his silence and the fact that Chloe, not he himself, had summoned me.

"Even that idiot Haynes came groveling to be put back on the show!" He laughed.

When he hugged me with unusual ardor, I abandoned myself to it entirely. I was enthralled by that energy and fire that had enchanted me since the first time we'd met. Napoleon-David had just conquered new territory—in large part thanks to me—and, being the good Josephine that I was, I thought I should reward him. At least that was how his hand, which had just slipped into my panties, saw things.

The telephone rang, and his hand quickly dislodged.

"We're never alone! Yes?" he barked into the receiver after a couple nervous steps.

"It's Louie," he mouthed, pointing to the phone. Then he wagged his finger in a way that suggested, *Go to your office, I'll join you there.*

Louie? Where was that animal hiding at the moment of my triumph? And what had he ever done for me that could compare with what David had given me in one day of hard work? It was completely childish, but I could not suppress images of me being featured all over television. Stolen moments in the society pages. Evenings when I would rub shoulders with France's high society, and not as arm candy but as an equal. My teenage fantasies flashed across my mind, and I was the heroine.

Louie confined me to the role of a courtesan. A precious butterfly, to be sure, but for his eyes only. Meanwhile, David was putting the world at my feet and fulfilling all my dreams. He shared me with everyone. I wasn't his thing; I was a masterpiece in his museum, and those who wanted to see me would have to pay.

I had barely closed the door to his office when I heard the first boom of his voice:

"You don't speak to me like that! Do you hear? I forbid you to . . . I forbid you! . . ."

I stood for a moment listening, but my own phone rang, betraying my presence. I had no choice but to take a few steps down the hall.

"Shit, Fred, bad timing! What's so urgent?"

"Your show."

"What about my show?"

It was a success. *And that annoys you, doesn't it?* I kept myself from spitting at him.

"Did you see the show from last night? I mean, the one that got broadcast . . ."

"Yes . . ." I hesitated.

"Not on the set monitors. The real show on a real television."

"Right, okay, no . . . What's the difference?"

"There was no show."

"Excuse me?"

"You heard me: the first episode of *Culture Mix* was not broadcast on television last night. They went with the originally scheduled TV movie."

"Are you kidding?"

He didn't reply right away, and I understood he was being serious. Deadly, even.

"Since we were all at the station last night and I couldn't watch it live, I called my friend this morning to ask him how it was on a home screen. You know, from your living room. I wanted to record it, but with the stress and everything, I forgot to program it."

The friend in question had watched a crime movie being shown on BTV for the zillionth time at the stated hour.

"He isn't messing with you?" I choked.

"No. I checked. I called two others who don't know each other. I wanted to make sure they weren't all pulling my leg."

My voice shook like it does in winter, while beads of sweat pearled on my forehead.

As in a dress rehearsal, we had done our show behind closed doors, without any real viewers. For us, and for glory.

"Listen, it has to be a joke . . . I was just with David. He read me the ratings report. We were a su—"

"It's crap, Elle," he interrupted. "I don't know where he got those numbers, but it's a lie. I had trouble believing it at first, too. So I ended up calling the technical manager of broadcasting, Guillaume. He's the one who handles everything being broadcast here. We've known each other for a while, and after chatting him up a bit, he spit it out."

"Spit what out?"

"It wasn't an accident. He got a call from David himself, when you were getting ready."

I refused to see the connection:

"A call for what?"

"Shit, Elle . . . I swear I'm not saying this because of us or to get back together or something . . . But fuck, open your eyes to your man!"

"A call to say what? Shit!"

I kept myself from yelling, afraid it might boom through the deserted corridor.

"To ask him to ignore the signal coming from your set and to broadcast the TV movie instead."

I didn't know what to say. But at last I snapped out of it. My feet carried me to the elevators:

"What came over him? I mean, *why then*?"

"No idea. He has a viewing station in his office on the nineteenth floor where he can see everything on set in real time. He has the power of life or death over what gets broadcast, even the live shows."

"Yeah, okay. But that doesn't explain . . . *this*."

"All I know is that David saw you on his screen . . . and he gave Guillaume the order. That's it. You know the whole story."

The whole story, right, in which I was trying to find a few positive points like a man drowning at sea fights to find a buoy. At least Rebecca wouldn't sue me; at least Sophia hadn't exposed herself as a Hotelle; at least no one here could discover my double life. At least, and this was perhaps the most important point for now, my meltdown at the end of the show would have no real consequences.

But I could not quell the rage growing in me. Should I scream? Charge into David's office? Strangle him? Hit him? Settle all the issues that were straining our relationship?

I didn't even feel like exposing this charade. Or understanding the reason behind David's change of mind. I was done with the Barlet brothers and their deceit. What could I expect from his mouth now but more lies and humiliation? Another chance to betray me . . .

"Elle? Elle, are you okay?" Fred drew me out of my thoughts.

"Yes . . ."

"Are you sure? Do you want me to meet you?"

"No, no, I'm fine . . . ," I said, pressing the button for the elevator. "Can I ask you a favor?"

"Yes, of course."

"As long as the story hasn't leaked, can you not say anything to anyone about this? Can you do that for me?"

The elevator's steel doors opened. As I entered, I had the sensation of willingly stepping into the jaws of a beast: the genie of Barlet Tower, which would soon swallow me. The network cut out as soon as the elevator started to move, and I didn't hear Fred's reply. But I figured I could count on him.

Who else but him?

29

A fireball in a Japanese manga.
An explosion in an American blockbuster.
The frequency of the bass in English techno.

I CONTENTED MYSELF WITH THESE three thoughts. My mustachioed professor would be proud, regardless of his opinion on these metaphors from a younger generation than his. Seriously, I felt devastated. David, Louie, Sophia, Rebecca . . . and even Maude, my own mother—everyone was lying to me. Everyone was faking. Each person was giving me a truncated, amputated, or made-up truth. It was like a virtual reality, the kind you see in video games or science fiction flicks, where the protagonist watches entire swaths of landscape melt before his eyes as he progresses. Like a gigantic, pixilated scene that is no more tangible than a dream. *The Matrix* for dummies, for this one dummy here.

How ironic that the only person I could trust was the man I had abandoned. And in the heat of the midday sun that struck me as I left the tower, I almost started to laugh. From impotence and rage.

WHEN I GOT BACK TO Duchesnois House, I learned that I was not the only one to have been wounded. I found Felicity huddled in a corner, trembling in her new surroundings. I tried not to overthink our shared fate, hers and mine, and not to see her trauma of the day as a sign. But it wasn't easy. Unhappiness feeds on anything that might have meaning, as a source of torment and relief. For the moment, every little thing was painful and seemed to be dragging me into an abyss.

I kept myself from calling all the players in my drama. What would they have to say anyway? What new lies would they concoct? As for me, all I felt right then for them was incomprehension and rage. No tangible thing with which to confront them, except maybe Fred's recent discovery. But that wasn't enough. Some could plead ignorance, and others would feign, *Oh, no one told you? It was just a dress rehearsal. The real debut will be next week.* Come on . . .

Listening to their lies, hearing their voices alter, or seeing their eyes shift to the left, all incontestable signs of their duplicity, it was too much for me. Or, rather, not enough. In the midst of this affair, whose overarching aims escaped me—who was manipulating whom? what was everyone's role? who was aware of the fraud?—David seemed like the darkest mystery, the most difficult player to understand. He of the luminous, sunny, and charismatic disposition was in truth a black star. Only one side, a lying sliver of a crescent, was bright. The rest was in shadows. The more I thought about it, the more I began to wonder how I had fallen in love with him in the first place.

How had he appeared the first time we met? I remembered his voice, so close, so smooth, so beguiling. Why hadn't I seen his other sides? How had he been able to deceive me? I, who have long prided myself on my capacity of discernment, a quality my professors in college thought foretold a brilliant career in journalism?

That was it. My thread. My angle. If I wanted to gain access to the secrets of David—the one who was conspiring against me, the one who was hiding his past from me—I would need to go back to the beginning. To the night when we'd first met. With Felicity purring gratefully at my side, I breathed deeply, containing the fire that had been burning me up ever since Fred's revelations. Soon, I was calm enough to start making my round of calls. Embarrassing but necessary.

"MOM? IT'S ME. HOW ARE you?"

"I'm fine . . . now that I've got you on the phone."

I knew she was being sincere, and in no way wanted to reproach me, but her dull tone of voice constricted my heart.

Some of my personal things were still in the drawers of my miniature desk in Nanterre. They included a disorganized pile of business cards from professional contacts, bars and restaurants where Sophia and I used to hang out, and nightclubs and other dance spots where my friend used to perform. I hated asking Mom to go through the mess, but I didn't see any other way of procuring the contact information for . . .

"Marchadeau . . ." I spelled the name. "*E*, *A*, *U* at the end. Right, like in '*eau* de toilette.'"

Oh, if only things could be as crystal clear as the sweet-smelling liquid in a bottle of perfume.

"I think I've found it, my girl . . . François Marchadeau. Assistant editor in chief at *The Economist*. Is that it?"

"That's him. Could you give me his number?"

"You know some important people!"

I decided against asking her about her mysterious telephone conversations with Louie Barlet. Whatever her role in the brothers' schemes, she could only be an involuntary cog, an unconscious pawn. If anyone loved me unconditionally, it was she. I could call anything into question but that.

Her voice was weak. Every time I called, she seemed further away, like she was disappearing behind a thick curtain that filtered out all happiness. Her voice was becoming increasingly hoarse, thick, and at times so muddled that I barely recognized it. The invisible hand that was strangling her from the inside wasn't letting up for a second. Not anymore. And probably not ever again, until the very end.

I masked my number and dialed the journalist a dozen or so times. At first, it rang and rang before going to voice mail. In the end, after a number of attempts, I was automatically directed to his automated message, a sign that he had turned off his phone. I had forgotten one thing. Would I answer my phone if some anonymous person were calling me on a Sunday afternoon while I was taking time off with my family? Probably not. I hesitated, then left a crafted message:

"Hi, François. Annabelle Lorand here. Elle. I imagine you remember me. And I think I saw your name on the guest list for our wedding next Thursday. Which means we'll be seeing each other again soon . . ."

Only four days, I remembered with surprise, trembling from stress rather than impatience.

"Listen, the reason for my call is a little delicate."

If I wanted to catch his attention and convince him to betray two decades of friendship with David, I would have to bluff. Sadly, I didn't have any tools at my disposal besides those of an imposter. But it was my turn, after all!

"I've recently stumbled across some sensitive information concerning the Barlet Group. And also David . . ."

I paused for effect. The idea of the future Madame Barlet seeking to unearth an unsavory story about her husband would come as a shock to the old tennis partner.

"Could you call me back at the following number? It's fairly urgent. I don't want this kind of rumor to fall into the wrong hands."

As I expected, he took the bait. Ten minutes later, he returned my call:

"You do remember the circumstances under which we first met, don't you?" he asked sharply, without so much as a hello. "And you do remember *who* David is for me?"

"Of course I do, François. And I haven't forgotten with whom I finished that night, at the Hôtel des Charmes."

Reminder for reminder, threat for threat, our positions were divided, and though the discussion unfolded in this despicable manner, we were at least on equal footing. Both forces could consider the other from a solid and visible vantage point. There was nothing to pretend. Our masks had fallen.

"And I suppose he knows nothing of all that?"

"That's right."

"Okay," he said after a silence. "Let's just get something clear between us. David is my friend, a kind of friend like you only get once in your life, and I have no need or desire to spend a Sunday afternoon listening to all the gossip surrounding him. In any case, I already know most of it."

"That's not what this is about . . ."

"That is always what this is about," he interrupted. "You've only known David a short time, Elle. You probably don't yet realize what it's like to be a man in the spotlight, with so much influence and so many admirers. Nor to live in his immediate entourage. For the moment, you've only seen the pleasant aspects, I would even say the recreational parts, of his kind of life: doors that open for you as if by magic, rooms that empty with a snap of the fingers, boats under starry skies . . ."

Direct references to all the little miracles David had performed for me, since the night we'd first met and when he'd asked me to marry him. So the two friends did not simply hit a ball over a net two times a week at that ultraexclusive club west of the capital, La Châtaigneraie. How much did they tell each other over backhands and smashes?

"I am neither stupid nor young enough to believe that my life with him could be reduced to that. Don't take me for a bimbo."

I could tell from the sound of his breath in the receiver that he was smiling. François Marchadeau was the kind of man who liked sassy young women. It probably even excited him to have someone fighting him like that. During our brief encounters, he had already shown himself to be playful. He was certainly subtler and more skilled than his humble position with respect to his former classmates suggested.

"I don't doubt it," he said, more composed. "But you haven't experienced everything yet: the paparazzi, spiteful articles, jealous backstabbing, and sycophantic flattery . . . Not to mention the threats."

But he *was* mentioning them, and he knew what effect they might have:

"Do you want an example? One of our mutual friends from business school found his wife at home, her throat slit by some thugs with a gas conglomerate from the East."

"When?" I asked, trying to mask my emotion.

"Ten years ago. But men like David have to be prepared for that kind of *industrial accident*."

"*Industrial accident.*" His way of describing the death of that innocent woman sacrificed on the altar of financial interest was chilling.

Still, I maintained my resolve and racked my brain for the best argument to convince him to meet me in private.

"That's just it."

"What is?"

"What I have to tell you concerns *me*. Directly."

"In what way?"

"My integrity is also at stake."

My tone and choice of words were dramatic enough to stir his interest. I knew how to titillate his journalistic instincts. I had the same, though they were still in their nascent state, the kind that come to attention at the slightest sign of a scoop.

"Integrity . . . physical?" he asked gravely.

"No, professional."

He let out a nervous little laugh that was interspersed with loud sipping sounds. I guessed the beverage was still hot. He was probably in the middle of his Sunday brunch.

"Okay . . . Let's meet. But we agree that this conversation never happened, nor our rendezvous later today."

"We are in complete agreement," I said seriously.

Not that these conspiratorial commonplaces didn't excite me. They awoke thrilling cinematographic memories that titillated my imagination and called forth the ghosts of real and fictional spies. But these childish thoughts were fleeting. After all, none of this was fun. It was my life. And two brothers were playing with it. I was afraid of being consumed by the murky meanders of their ancient rivalry.

"Do you know Café Marly under the arcades at the Louvre?" he asked me.

"Yes . . . I've never been, but I know where it is."

"I'll be there in an hour. No more."

"Okay."

"I also have a family, you know. And they're not too happy with me at the moment. I would rather not go out on a Sunday evening, and just two weeks before summer vacation."

The childish reference to summer break showed how much he cared about his kids, and I found that touching.

My cell phone screen indicated three missed calls from Sophia as soon as I hung up. I didn't feel capable of talking to her for the moment. I didn't know if I ever would.

I quickly showered and changed into something a little more revealing than my pantsuit. My future interlocutor was not indifferent to my fleshy charms. I might as well take advantage of that fact to try to pry a teeny bit more out of him than he was prepared to give. So I opted for a plunging neckline, together with a push-up bra and a midthigh-length skirt.

I had no desire to seduce him. Moreover, during the interview with Marchadeau, my charms played their role without me, for once. I was a pretty package with no one at the helm controlling my attributes. My breasts heaved if they wanted. My naked thighs peeked out from under my skirt as they pleased. ~~My sex let itself be seen through my panties' thin layer of cotton.~~ I didn't care . . .

And yet, as I was dressing earlier, I couldn't help but think of the time Sophia put herself up to that challenge: finding the perfect outfit, one capable of defrosting the most frigid of men, the ones who were most in control of their impulses. An ensemble that included a dress, underthings, high heels, which together were so short, so formfitting, so

transparent, so sexy, so entirely devoted to playing up her
charms that no one could resist her. Anyone who witnessed
this masterpiece of feminine wiles would have the irre-
pressible desire to throw themselves on her. I wonder if she
ever found the magic formula, although I don't think she
needs an outfit to bed anyone she pleases.

Handwritten note by me, 6/14/2009

ONCE I WAS DRESSED, AND more chic than I'd been in a while, I started down the large circular staircase. Armand caught me on the last step:

"Annabelle . . . Are you going out?"

I could have sworn I heard reproach in his voice. His large stature obstructed my path.

"Yes. Not for long. Why?"

"I have a few details I'd like to go over with you."

"What kind?"

"Well, the canopy supplier is out of ecru. We'll have to choose another color. And soon . . . Otherwise we won't be able to get anything at all."

I felt so removed from ecru canopies, suppliers for the wedding . . . and this union, regardless of the tent . . .

"Later, okay," I said lightly.

I was trying his good nature, when suddenly an idea occurred to me. I quickly rummaged through my bag, looking for that large, lockless key. An intuition.

"Armand . . . You recognize this key, right?"

He looked surprised, narrowed his eyes under his bushy brow, and said at last:

"No, I don't . . ."

"This key wouldn't by any chance open the door to Brown Rocks, would it?"

His embarrassed look quickly turned into a warning. He was forgetting that I was not supposed to know about the Barlet family's coastal retreat.

"No idea. You know, I've only ever been once or twice."

I knew he was lying. I could still hear Louie's words ringing in my ears: "I believe Armand goes once a year to clean house."

"Okay. I see." I was being purposefully enigmatic.

For the time being, I preferred not to say anything. After all, wasn't it where David and I were going for our honeymoon?

I wasn't so sure anymore how much honey there would be. I wasn't so sure of anything anymore.

30

The car sped over the mostly deserted highway. Mile after mile, we passed trucks braving the Sunday ban. The sun was still high in the sky. Every segment of tunnel eclipsed its light, a frequent occurrence on this strip of road approaching the tollbooths. Sophia only ever slowed when there were signs for radars. We hadn't spoken a word since we'd left Rue de la Tour-des-Dames, and even if we'd wanted to, the cabriolet's top was down and the wind would have blown it all away, past my friend's chocolate curls, which whipped gracefully behind her.

"You have a car now?" I'd asked over the phone, my expression icy.

"It's not mine. It's Peggy's. She's always said I could borrow it if I needed . . ."

Peggy. Her *other* best friend. The one Sophia had known since early childhood. The one she had generously introduced to Belles de Nuit before me.

" . . . and, well, I think today is the day."

But, to borrow Rebecca's expression, "Peggy was a pain in the ass, a girl with issues." She ended up quitting the agency under troubling circumstances, pressing charges of rape against one of her clients, who had insisted on finishing the night somewhere other than the Hôtel des Charmes, at a less chic establishment than the one run by Monsieur Jacques.

Apparently, once they were in the hotel room, he had tried to reenact a few particularly raunchy scenes from an erotic bestseller. The more violent episodes offended the tastes of the delicate Peggy, a little woman with a disproportionately large chest, who captivated men with her triumphant bust. Police report, trial, financial settlement . . . Enough to satisfy the young woman, though it had also tarnished the reputation of Madame Sibony's Hotelles.

The convertible Beetle turned onto an access road and was soon heading due west, away from the capital, away from the recent revelations of these past few hours . . . I was leaving Paris so that I could return in a better condition. That was the reason I had so urgently needed to see Sophia, the traitor.

TWO HOURS EARLIER, ON THAT Sunday in June, sitting on the terrace of Café Marly with a gaggle of tourists: I could make out every language in the world around me except French. Discretion assured. And I didn't doubt for a second that that had been the reason behind my interlocutor's choice of locale.

François Marchadeau arrived ten minutes late, without so much as an excuse. Instead, he pointed to the glass pyramid inside the Louvre's courtyard and said:

"Did you know that Andre Barlet was the one who initially gave Mitterrand the idea to build that pyramid?"

"No . . . ," I admitted, skeptical.

Who said so? The Barlet family? I could believe that Andre, like Pierre before him, and David after, had walked the halls of the Republic in search of support. At a certain level, everything is political. Everything happens or comes undone in gilded ministerial offices. But to believe he had whispered into the ear of the president . . . into the ear of the Sphinx . . .

"Mitterrand could not in all decency leave the Élysée and move into the Louvre. But, among intimates, he did say he wanted to send a message of presidential authority."

"What kind of message?"

"Symbolic. To speak plainly, he wanted all the trappings of being king without the title. So Andre had this genius idea, which he got from the nickname that Mitterrand's detractors called him. And what do you find behind the Great Sphinx of Giza . . . but a pyramid?"

I sipped my ideally proportioned Monaco, determined to cut short this erudite chatter. I didn't care about the thousands of anecdotes with which the Barlet family wove its own legend. I wasn't their biographer, much less their hagiographer . . . I was barely even a journalist. I was just a lost girl looking for truth.

"Are you interested in what I have to say . . . or do you want to queue up for the museum?"

I pointed toward the line of tourists stretching from the glass entrance all the way to the Arc de Triomphe du Carrousel. Marchadeau had obviously dressed in haste, and was wearing a pair of linen pants and a crocodile polo shirt; he could have easily blended in with the mini backpacks and cameras slung over shoulders.

"You're as beautiful as I remember you," he flattered me, smiling playfully.

"Apparently not enough for TV . . ."

The difference between the sexes will never cease to amaze me. We women are quick to forget the men who have

possessed us, ~~fucked us, rammed us, depending on how~~
~~much they put into it.~~ In any case, that's what the author
of this one magazine article claims, and I agree. I tend
to remember the feelings they've inspired in me, but their
hands, their cock, all those sensations simply disappear.
And I don't feel that I have a claim on them anymore.

Men, on the other hand, maintain a proprietary attitude
with respect to their conquests, no matter how dated. A body
embraced is theirs forever, even only tenuously, and even if
they no longer desire it. That explains a good deal of male
comportment and their general propensity to want to sleep
with their exes, ~~go back to familiar vaginas.~~ But a woman
would find that anachronistic, incongruous, just wrong.

Handwritten note by me, 6/14/2009

NOW ALL I HAD TO do was unload my angry and bitter little story: the preparation of *Culture Mix* in record time, the way the debut had been pushed up, and the fact that, in the end, the show was never broadcast. Of course, I did not mention the part concerning Louie and his special report.

I extrapolated a little, applying the same sequence of events to other shows and other young female journalists who'd started at the station before me, and arrived at this sentence:

"David messes with shows and fake viewer reports to advance women he wants to bed or is already bedding."

Marchadeau's gaze lingered a second longer on my cleavage, as though proving a point about his friend's motivations. Then he straightened and said in a blasé and unexpressive tone:

"If that's true, and if I'm not mistaken . . . it's benefitted you more than anyone else! David is not really the type to ask the first girl who comes along to marry him."

"The CEO of a telecommunications company is lying to his employees, spending his company's money for personal gain . . . and that doesn't shock you?"

"If I got emotional over all the abuses of company funds by CEOs on the CAC 40, I would spend my life crying into a hankie, Elle."

He wasn't being cynical. For him it was obvious. A reality that nothing and no one could make more moral.

"Believe me," he pressed on, "the dodgy dealings of many business leaders disgust me. David knows it. He and I have gone head-to-head on this issue many times. Either because he was involved in something or because he was covering for his cronies."

"But you don't say a word of it in your column!" I replied haughtily.

"If I went on that crusade, I would be thrown out of the game. I don't need to tell you that, you're not so naive: a counterpower is much more effective if he wears a mask and sucks up to the prince than if he goes tilting at windmills."

The reference to Don Quixote did not make his metaphor more convincing. When had his pen ever served as a weapon? Had he ever confronted the economic powers that be and said out loud what so many journalists were whispering among themselves in the shadows?

"Your loyalty does you honor. David is lucky to have friends like you . . ." I pretended to take his side. "As for me, pardon my sins, which are no doubt the result of my excessive youth, but I still have illusions about the integrity of *our* field."

The thrust of the sentence lay in the possessive pronoun, which I had chosen specifically to associate the two of us, him and me. Two journalists, despite the massive difference in age and experience.

"Don't you tell me about how integrity fades with age, Elle . . . Not *you*."

Now it was his turn to play with subtleties. The "*you*" to which he so forcefully referred was not the wise young girl in front of him but the courtesan to which he had treated himself at the Hôtel des Charmes for a few bills, several months back. Despite the inherent risks, I decided to continue with this train of thought:

"You're the one choosing to take it like that, François. It's your choice," I bluffed. "Just as it will be my choice when I reveal to David how we ended the night together that one time."

"You would never do that." He was trying to convince himself. "You have too much to lose."

"You're wrong. I've already lost what matters."

"Yeah, what's that?"

"My illusions. About him . . . about you."

I got up to leave in anger, pulling at the hem of my skirt as I stood, when his hand reached for my wrist and pressed it into the little round table's wooden surface.

"Wait . . ."

"Let go," I said in a measured tone.

"What you're telling me is nothing compared to what I have on the Barlet Group . . ."

He freed my hand, certain he'd caught my attention. I let myself fall back into my crimson seat.

"Really?" I challenged him to say more.

"Really."

His shoulders slumped, suddenly overwhelmed by an invisible weight. He seemed exhausted by what he was about to tell me. His eyes escaped for a moment out the open arcades. A refreshing zephyr fluttered by us. Rays of sun beamed on our side of the terrace. He was without sunglasses and blinking furiously.

When he brought his gaze back into the shadows, he shot me an ambiguous look that I took to mean this: I was at once the worst and best thing that had happened to him. A curse, but also an opportunity that would not otherwise have presented itself to him so soon to cut the cord that had tied him to David for all these years. The hour of revenge. The hour to bite the hand that had been weighing him down for so long. Too long.

"We are in agreement," he whispered. "This meeting never happened, and I never said what I am about to say."

"Okay."

He swallowed two mouthfuls of beer before he began, a bit of foam sticking to his upper lip. A thin lip that I had pressed against mine one night, I remembered involuntarily.

"The Barlet Group does not just produce television programs for a French audience."

"I know that."

"Of course . . . What you don't know is that in some markets it makes rather unconventional shows."

I understood what he meant, but I wanted to hear him say the rest.

"What kind?"

"X-rated stuff. Pretty hard-core. Through lots of different fronts, of course."

The euphemisms used in X-rated book and movie titles have always made me smile. And blush. Gone With the

Minge, Citizen Cock, *or* Horny Potter. *I often imag-*
ine one of these films while playing with myself: the hero,
a well-equipped and energetic hardeur, comes out of the
screen to satisfy me in my bedroom. ~~He bangs me, sparing~~
~~none of my orifices.~~ *Although he's arrived in my home*
by accident, he ends up preferring me over the siliconed
actresses, who become dispirited on the other side of the
mirror by his absence. All they can do is watch us, the
actor and me, demonstrating our (almost) perfect sexual
harmony. In truth, his sex is much too big for mine, which
forces us to get into positions where only his tip and the
upper third of his shaft are penetrating me. The title of this
masterpiece, which is only showing in one theater, the one
in my fantasies: Cairo's Enormous Snake.

Handwritten note by me, 6/14/2009

I CONSIDERED THIS PIECE OF information for a moment
before replying:

"And why? After all, other media groups don't hide the fact
that they *also* produce adult content. It doesn't bother anyone,
neither the general public nor their stockholders."

"You're right. It's less a question of what's in these pictures
than the conditions in which they're filmed."

"What do you mean?"

He cleared his throat, rinsing it with another glass of
amber.

"Young girls from Eastern Europe are much cheaper and
more open: Hungary, Bulgaria, the Baltic states . . . Some will
even work for free. And that is very interesting for a producer
and distributor like Barlet. Economically speaking. With the

production costs reduced to nothing, or almost nothing, the group maximizes its profits."

"For free?"

I could not suppress my horror.

"Practically. The local producer sets up a give-and-take relationship: the girl plays in three or four films in exchange for a residency card in the country of her choice. France, the United Kingdom, Germany, et cetera. Greasing a government worker's pockets ends up being much cheaper than paying a French porn star."

There was one thing I didn't get.

"What's in it for the producer? If the girls are so cheap, why can't the producer simply pay them directly?"

"He could. But the method I've just described attracts a larger pool of actresses, which keeps the product fresher since there are many more girls interested in immigrating than in double penetration. Porn is a genre in which the star system has little impact. There are only maybe two or three actresses who are famous enough to make money off their names alone."

The way he was talking, you would have thought we were having a conversation about the frozen food section in a supermarket.

"That's disgusting . . ."

"Totally disgusting. But less so when you're a twenty-five-year-old doctor in chemistry making three hundred euros a month, with no prospects of job growth in your home country. They grin and bear it, thinking of the El Dorado they'll find when they get here."

His way of synthesizing the problems these girls faced was raw, but unfortunately it reflected their sad truth.

He was clearly lucid about life's harsh realities. I could hear and read it in his haggard face—it was hard to believe he and David were the same age; he looked at least ten years older. But why did he apply this insight so parsimoniously? Why hadn't I paid the price the night we met?

I could not forget the real object of our rendezvous: a certain gala when David first appeared to me.

"Why haven't you said anything to him?"

"Said what?"

He looked like he was coming out of a bad dream.

"About me. About what I was to you that night . . ."

"To David?"

"Yes. To David. Parties, tennis matches . . . You've had plenty of opportunities to do it. It would have been easy to leave out any *details* that might embarrass you."

The ones we attended to and explored in a beautifully decorated room like the Josephine, the Mata Hari, or another.

Since he didn't say anything, I put the final nail in my own coffin:

"Isn't that what friends do? You tell each other when you learn something compromising about the other's girlfriend. You protect each other from stepping into a bad marriage. You can call me an escort, a Hotelle if you want . . . But that night, I was nothing more than a whore."

His eyes widened with almost childlike candor. I could tell he was not faking his surprise. A little girl running through Café Marly, down the long arcade where the central passage was barely wide enough for two pedestrians, crashed into his chair. He didn't react. He considered me, a rueful smile on his lips.

"Annabelle . . . He knew exactly *who* and especially *what* you were to me that night."

Despite the rush of blood ringing in my ears, I had heard correctly.

The blast ricocheted off the walls of the gallery and fell heavily on me. No one in our vicinity had moved. My world was crumbling, not theirs.

"What makes you so sure?"

"What makes me so sure . . . ," he repeated to himself, his eyes glazed. "So you know nothing about his business outside of broadcasting?"

"What do you mean?"

I gripped my chair as though it were threatening to disappear from under me.

"The agency, Belles de Nuit . . ."

"What about it?"

"He owns it," he concluded sotto voce, as if to soften the blow.

And being a good manager of his estate and careful to make wise investments, he had put some money into what was for him a "small business," according to François Marchadeau.

In other words, he knew all of the girls in Rebecca's catalogue—at least all of their sweet little faces on glossy paper—if only by reputation.

DO NOT SAY ANOTHER WORD.

Not even good-bye.

Leave the café without staggering. Or bumping into one of the children on my way.

Go to the metro.

Lose myself in the train car, and hope never to leave, and pray that the sharp screech of the metro takes me away and dissolves what is left of me.

Get back to Duchesnois House (empty), pack a bag, stuffing it with things at random. Without really thinking about what might be useful or the length of my time away.

Call Sophia, a lead weight in my stomach, another in my throat. Barely able to articulate. Feel her concern on the other end of the line. She is still my friend, unconditionally.

Then wait for her to take me somewhere far away. Collapse in a chair in the living room, Felicity on my knees, tears frozen on my eyelids. Incapable of falling, just as I am incapable of understanding what's happening to me.

I OPENED THE DOOR, DECIDING to wait for Sophia outside. There I saw Ysiam, as gawky as usual, standing at the gate holding a small package inside a plastic bag. I hadn't been wrong. He was a cog in the machine set on my destruction after all. An innocent pawn, but still the person who had been delivering my ruination, day by day.

"Hello, Mademoiselle."

"Hello, Ysiam."

"Are you leaving?"

"Yes . . . ," I stammered, as though he'd caught me. "Not long. What brings you here?"

"I have a package for you."

"From whom?"

"I don't know. Monsieur Jacques told me to deliver it. So I'm delivering it."

Click. The Ysiam gear had fulfilled his function.

"I understand. Give it to me."

I opened the gate for him to hand me the bag, then sent him away with a smile that was infinitely less sweet and disarming than his.

"I hope it's good news," he said as he walked away.

"Yes. I hope so, too."

Standing on the cobblestones of the little circular courtyard, I opened the package in two nervous gestures. I wasn't hoping for anything. I just wanted to leave. Leave and understand. And I knew that, as usual, the box would offer more mysteries than answers.

However, no magnetic keycard for the Hôtel des Charmes. No note giving me a rendezvous. At the bottom of the box, one lone object accompanied by a card. A Venetian mask like the one I had already worn for Louie during one of our encounters. I stuffed it in my bag and seized the white rectangle. I read the commandment. One more. The seventh, and which I had no intention of fulfilling:

    7—Thou shalt explore the unknown.

Yet I realized, just as the screech of rubber tires drew me out of my melancholy, that was exactly what I was about to do. Go spelunking in an abyss where I hoped I would find myself again.

31

The sun, which had been so radiant all day, was starting to set, and the atmosphere grew cooler. We stopped at a rest area to put the roof back on the Bug. I didn't notice which one. Two weeks before summer vacation, and it was still fairly empty. But soon, I knew, screaming children and litter would invade.

I gave Sophia some cash to fill up the gas tank. We still hadn't said a word. Sixty miles later, as we were veering right, toward Rennes, I broke the silence. Why then? I don't know. I guess I was just ready. And anyway, I've never been one to hold a grudge. Since I knew she'd already betrayed me, all that was left to figure out was why.

"How did you meet Louie?" I attacked head-on.

"I swear I didn't know it had anything to do with Louie Barlet."

She seemed sincere.

"Who did you think it was?"

"A client . . . A client like any other."

First painful realization: They had slept together.

Since I was now taking my turn at the wheel, both hands firmly gripping it, I was limited in how I could express my anger. I had only closed my eyes for half a second when I heard Sophia shout:

"Whoa! Be careful!"

I came back to attention.

"He never told you his name?"

"No, he went by a stupid first name, Richard."

Richard, the name of his chauffeur.

"But he wasn't the only one to give a fake name," she went on. "You know that: plenty of men prefer to remain completely anonymous, just in case . . ."

Just in case their wives got too curious. Just in case he ran across one of us in a . . . less private context. And why not, just in case the guy in question turned out to be the brother-in-law (and lover) of your best friend.

"Did you *see* him often?"

"Two, three times, I don't remember exactly."

Yes, she did. But I could tell from the tone of humility in her voice—a rarity, I had to admit—that she was trying to spare me. And despite the rage I couldn't help feeling, I was grateful.

"And . . . how did he end up suggesting that you do an interview?"

"He pretended he was a journalist and a writer."

"Did he say for whom?"

"No. Just that he worked freelance and then sold his work to production companies, news agencies, and sometimes directly to certain channels. He downplayed everything, though, and was always saying things like 'if it ever even makes it on air.'"

I trusted Louie to look sincere while piling on the lies. Sophia probably hadn't had the chance to discover his tell.

"But you knew Rebecca had forbidden us from talking about our missions."

"Yes, of course . . . But he promised that he wouldn't show my face. And that they'd modify my voice. Everything was supposed to be completely anonymous."

Anonymous for everyone but me.

"Did he pay you?"

I checked my side-view mirror before passing the car in front of us, a maneuver that momentarily let Sophia off the hook. But I wasn't fooled. The tick-tock of the turn signal was like a confession.

"So?" I probed. "Did he pay you a lot?"

"Two thousand."

"Euros?" I was practically choking.

"Umm, yeah . . . not rubles."

"In cash, I guess?"

"Yes. Bills of five hundred. I've never had so much in my hands at once . . . It was crazy. You can imagine how powerful that makes you feel!"

Under the circumstances, what had first seemed like a stab in the back finally showed its true face: she had only acted out of necessity, through her survival instinct. Also out of greed. Louie must have known about her situation, and her spend-thrift ways, and also that she would accept his offer without hesitation.

I didn't believe for a second that he had chosen my friend by accident. And it certainly hadn't been innocent. Obviously, he had been targeting me.

So many details and questions remained unanswered. If the purpose of the report had been to unbalance me, what was Louie's endgame? That I get fired? That I quit? Leaving BTV would certainly make me more available to him. But did he need to humiliate me to do it?

Mile after mile, kilometer after kilometer, my thoughts turned from one brother to the other, from Louie to David. Because, and this seemed to be the crux of the mystery, if David had known all along about my actual role the night we'd first met . . . why had Louie blackmailed me?

My thoughts remained muddled as night fell. A pinkish-gray veil settled over the green landscape; then everything darkened.

"Have you seen him since?"

"Not since the interview, no. Rebecca told me once or twice that 'Richard' wanted to see me again, but I said no. I thought it was a little weird, to slee—" She stopped herself, then began again: "To keep seeing the man who had interviewed me. Especially on that subject."

The alarm and panic I'd seen on her face at Bois des Vincennes had been real. And that also explained why she had been keeping her distance from me ever since. She'd been clueless as to what she had gotten herself involved in. And as far as I could tell, from her state of confusion and the way she was curling up into the gray plastic of the car door, she knew even less than I.

After a while, she said in an almost playful tone:

"You know, he's kind of crazy . . ."

"Why do you say that?"

She turned toward me, her impish smile now mouthing surprise:

"Don't tell me you haven't seen his tattoos?"

"Yes. An *A* and a *D* . . . Why?"

I had mentioned the two that were visible to everyone, and that I had seen on my walks with Louie. Her look told me that, unlike me, she had seen them all.

"But that's just the tip of the iceberg. The very tip of Alphabet Man!"

"'Alphabet Man'?" I almost burst out laughing. "What kind of nickname is that?"

"He didn't tell you? He has the entire alphabet tattooed on his body."

"Right, I know," I said.

"That's not crazy? It took him four or five years to have all twenty-six letters etched into his skin. Not all uniform, you know: he varies the size, the font, the decorations, et cetera."

"He's obsessive . . . ," I agreed.

As I said it, I realized the descriptor's ambiguity: Louie was crazy, but at the same time, he was also kind of brilliant. The contrast suited him perfectly; it was perfectly coherent. I didn't need Sophia to tell me the rest: Louie dreamed of living off his pen. He would have given anything to write and only write. Even his own body was like the living matter of his art, to be used like a palette.

I briefly recalled the body of a man in a latex suit, then naked, and how it had escaped into darkness. I tried to imagine each letter of the alphabet on his tight muscles, whose feline movements accentuated every stroke of every symbol.

I knew I should not lose myself in such fantasies. After all, this was the man who had trapped me! Who had been playing with me this whole time.

"Soph . . . I have just one last question . . ."

I gulped. An unexpected pain shot through my throat. I felt as though I were swallowing a bocce ball.

"Yes?"

"You have to tell me the truth."

"Of course!" she cried, clearly wanting to make amends. "Of course I will."

Another giant lump in my throat.

"Has . . . Have you ever had David as a client?"

"What?" She was practically screaming. "No, are you crazy?! Never!"

"You've done it with Louie without knowing who he was."

"Yeah, but that's different. David is a public figure. I've already seen his picture."

I didn't recall ever having shown her his portrait or one of his newspaper articles or one of the images on my phone.

"Admit it," I teased, smiling. "You've Googled him!"

"Well, yeah, obviously. What do you think? My best friend is going out with a billionaire. The least I could do is see what he looks like! Am I right?"

"Right, right . . ."

The headlights swept over a sign that told us we were about to enter Rennes. We would have to exit soon to go west around the city and head north, toward Saint-Malo.

"Why do you ask? Do you think I'm so twisted I'd sleep with your fiancé?"

"Of course not. Don't be stupid . . . ," I replied lightly. "It's not that."

"What is it, then?"

"I don't know, really. A hunch . . ."

A nightmare was more like it. One of those ghosts that come out onto the road from the woods. I suddenly realized that we had just gone through the Mayenne, a region known for its dark legends, its skeletons and witches. Sure enough, a sign suddenly appeared in the night that announced where we were: Fairies' Rock. I shivered and stepped on the accelerator.

Happily, Sophia did not insist. Because, in the end, what could I tell her that wasn't just a raw expression of my fear? Of my gnawing terror?

Louie and David, accomplices? United in a twisted and ridiculous plot? I couldn't bring myself to believe it. Their fight over the phone, at just the moment when Fred called, was enough to convince me of their discord. At the very least of a deep disagreement, most likely over me.

Or had the two associates been fighting over their loot, me? Worse: Had the disagreement over the phone been part of their farce?

"You hungry?"

My friend brought me down to more earthly concerns, pointing to a rest area with a convenience store.

"Yes. You're right."

My sandwich was rubbery and tasteless. My thoughts were hardly fresher. We ate quickly and sped back onto the highway, resolving not to stop again before we reached our destination.

We still had a good hour before we'd reach La Malouine Point, the seat of the most sumptuous villas on the coast. It faced Saint-Malo, which was wild, rough, and full of history. Dinard appeared to us like a sleeping beauty, a princess from the Belle Epoque in her dress of granite and stone pine. It felt stormy, and in the distance, we could make out heavy sea clouds rolling toward the shore.

Are our fantasies simply obsessions that we must keep ourselves from enacting? Or, instead, are they the fuel without which our libidos cannot purr?

All I know is that the few I've had the chance to test out were not pleasant in real life. Making love in water, for instance. Fred and I tried it once, while vacationing on the Balearic Islands. The salt, the sand, the water's perpetual movement, the difficulty of finding a stable position on the seafloor, the bodily fluids—nature's lubricants—washed away by the sea . . . Nothing was as nice as we'd imagined. Fred, surprised by how cold the water was, ended up losing his erection. The whole thing was unpleasant and fairly pathetic. Another bad idea. Next fantasy?

Handwritten note by me, 6/14/2009

WE SLOWED WHEN WE REACHED Avenue Poussineau to stare at the turn-of-the-century buildings, all richly ornamented with friezes, ceramic decorations, and names that made us daydream: Kerozar, Beautiful Bedrock, Flat Rock, Ker Annick . . . Brown Rocks, the house we were looking for, was at the far end of the cliff, where a coastal path traced a right angle due west. The other constructions were mostly made of granite or brownstone, but the Barlet family house was in the style of a Louis XIII hunting lodge from Versailles. Brown Rocks was larger, more imposing than its neighboring houses, and was built into the cliff, apart from all the other villas, highlighting its privileged status. We parked in front without worry. No one would question us when we went to the gate, whose sharp points dissuaded impromptu visitors.

"Now what?" Sophia inquired. "How do we get in?"

I took the giant key out of my bag.

"With *this* . . . I mean, that's what I hope."

I slipped the craggy metal object into the lock and twisted my wrist in two energetic movements. The gate did not resist. We took a few steps over the red gravel before reaching the front door, which proved easy to open, too. Security measures clearly were not up to date here, but it just went to show that the villa had been abandoned for some time. And besides, it suited us.

As soon as we set foot in the entryway, the smell of dust and mold filled our nostrils, choking us. As in ghost movies, all the furniture was covered in white sheets, which had grayed with time.

"Your man's vacation house is *so* charming!" Sophia couldn't help but comment.

It only took a few minutes to turn the electricity on, remove the sheets, and sweep up. The ground floor at least looked alive. It wasn't very late, but neither one of us had the energy just yet to go upstairs and prepare beds. And that was assuming we could find clean linens.

I rummaged through my bag for a tissue—too many mites for my allergies—and came across my phone. Five text messages and three voice mails. All from David. I didn't have a moment's hesitation before shutting it off, without consulting them.

Sophia, looking past the decrepitude, was marveling over the house's lustrous past, which shone through in many ways, especially in the sheer dimensions of the rooms:

"It's crazy to own such a beautiful place and let it go to waste . . . I'll never understand rich people. It's like they don't even care about the things they own. It must be because they have so much money . . ."

Outside of her moralizing lesson, she raised an interesting point: David wanted to have our honeymoon here, in these ruins, this dirty and dilapidated old house? I had trouble believing it.

While Sophia rummaged through the kitchen, I started exploring the upstairs. The rooms seemed frozen in a time more ancient than Aurora's tragedy. Some of them hadn't been redecorated in fifty years. There was a lot of flaking paint, and the beds looked as though they'd been molded by generations of sleepers. I did not linger on such relics. I was looking for something else. Memories, anything that could speak to the life the Barlet brothers had once had here. Something more than furniture or wall coverings. The first two rooms came up empty. The third was more promising: I yanked open the three drawers of an old dresser in dark wood. They were filled with papers, notebooks, and photo albums.

I did not ask Sophia to join me. I wanted to look through them myself, at least the first time. Most of the pictures were of vacations from a good thirty years ago. Many were beach scenes of David and Louie, smiling little boys who seemed to be quite close: on an inflatable boat, making a sand castle, geared up to go crab fishing, brandishing a crab from its pinchers, playing Jokari . . . and so on. I figured Andre Barlet must have taken the pictures. And was it just an effect of the camera, or did David always seem to be in the foreground, so self-assured, while Louie always hung in his brother's shadow, despite the fact that he was taller? The dominant and the dominated. The cadet, sure of his future victory. And his big brother, the unhappy heir, no doubt already plotting his revenge.

"Elle? Are you okay? Do you want me to come upstairs?" Sophia called up from the ground floor.

"No, no, I'm coming down. Stay there. It's even more disgusting up here."

"Do you want to go out for a drink? We aren't going to spend the evening hanging out with these nasty old things, are we?"

"Hmm . . . No thanks, I'm pooped. But you go out if you want," I encouraged her. "Just take the key. I left it on the mantel in the living room."

I heard her decisive footsteps on the floor below, and then:

"Are you sure? I think it would be good for you to go out. Clear your head."

"No, really . . . Thanks, though."

I could have used a little pick-me-up, but I had just come across some new treasures in the last bedroom. The container was not larger than a shoebox, but it was stuffed with Barlet family memories, including pictures of the parents, Andre and Hortensia, whom I had never seen before.

"Okay," she said in false resignation. "I'll stay with you, then."

"No, you should go! Have fun."

I heard a stifled laugh, the staircase creaking under her weight, her footsteps on the landing, before she appeared at the door:

"No, I'm good. Look at the treasure I found."

She was holding a rounded bottle covered in a thick layer of dust and two glasses, which she had taken the time to rinse and were still dripping with soapy water.

"What is it?" I asked, raising my head.

"Old Armagnac. Do you want some?"

"Why not . . ." I smiled.

She served us both and then kneeled down next to me and started digging through the pile.

"What are we looking for, exactly?"

"Anything that dates back to David's first marriage."

But most of the photographs, we both discovered, were of a much earlier time. When the Barlet father and mother were still a happy young couple, filled with hopes and dreams.

There were several wedding pictures. I immediately recognized the Schiaparelli dress I'd tried on the other day. It fit Hortensia perfectly, better than it ever would me. That is, if I even ended up wearing it . . .

It suddenly occurred to me that I still hadn't signed the prenup Armand had given me, and that the reasons to do so were growing fewer by the minute.

Family meals, vacations by the sea or at the mountain, Christmases in the living room at Brown Rocks . . . None of it told me anything that I didn't know already. But there was a strange absence of women in the Barlet brothers' vicinity. Even when I got to the adult photos, I didn't see any signs of fiancées or mistresses. Much less an Aurora or a Rebecca on these faded photographs and Polaroids sticking together in little piles.

Something slammed. Then a long metallic cry, strident and sinister. We jumped. The noise repeated itself a couple times. A strong wind had risen outside, enveloping the house with its panting breath. Its sea breath.

"It's nothing, it's the shutters," Sophia assured me. "The hinges must be completely rusted with this humidity."

A big gulp of Armagnac, like fire licking my esophagus, warming it like a hearth, quieting my nerves.

"I need to call Mom," I suddenly remembered before straightening.

"Okay. I'll keep looking," Sophia said absently, engrossed in the yellowed chromos.

As I made my way downstairs, I noticed through the sea-facing bay window that it was now pitch-black outside. With the exception of the Grand Jardin lighthouse and the street lamps glowing over Saint-Malo's ramparts, the horizon was blanketed in absolute darkness.

The opacity made me think of Mom.

"It's me!" I made a superhuman effort to be light.

"Hello, my girl."

The voice she had on bad days. The voice that tried so hard to hide what she was really feeling. It fooled everyone, even Laure Chappuis, but not me.

"I received a fruit basket earlier today."

"And have you tried them?"

"No . . . No, I'm not very hungry, you know. The treatments make me nauseous."

My mother indifferent to treats. Now that was a bad sign.

"Are you sure you're all right, Mom? Do you want me to come over?"

"No . . . Stay where you are, darling."

Then she cut short our conversation. Every word she spoke sounded like torture. As soon as I hung up, I dialed another number, that of Ludovic Poulain. A young man, fresh out of his residency, whom my mother had chosen to be her attending physician, out of sympathy more than anything else. Until Maude needed regular hospitalization, he was the one who took care of her; he was the one to call in case of sudden changes. Tonight, she was much worse, I could feel it.

"Dr. Poulain?"

"Yes . . . ," grumbled the young voice on the other end. "Who is calling?"

"I'm sorry to bother you so late. It's Annabelle Lorand. We've met before at my mother's house. I am Maude Lorand's daughter."

"Yes, of course." His voice softened.

"Doctor, I'm worried. I'm out of town right now. And I've just spoken with my mother over the phone . . . She seems much worse."

"Hmm . . . Shall I go and see her?"

I hadn't dared ask. But despite his young age, the doctor showed a certain degree of empathy. I prayed he would not harden, at least not so long as Mom needed him.

"If you don't mind, I would really appreciate it."

"It's no problem. I can check on her tomorrow morning, before my other appointments. My office is not far."

"Tomorrow . . . ," I breathed, incapable of hiding my disappointment.

"You want me to go now, is that it?"

"No . . ."

But I really meant *yes!*

"Don't worry . . . I understand. I'll put my shoes on and head over. I'll call later to let you know how everything goes."

As I hung up, a strong gust of wind, more violent than the others, shook the house to its foundation, sending a doleful moan through the entire structure. On this part of the coast, there was nothing between the villa and the sea, and the northerly wind lashed relentlessly at the building's antique ossature.

So long as I hadn't heard back from the doctor, I would not have the heart to continue my investigation.

"I'm going to stay down here for a bit," I cried up to Sophia. "Okay."

No television. No radio. Not a single magazine, not even old issues. I had nothing to help me wait for the news—nothing, that is, except for the book I had grabbed as I was leaving from the stack I'd purchased at La Musardine. The first on Louie's list: *Secret Women*, by Ania Oz. At that moment, I wanted to read an erotic book about as much as I wanted to go for an icy swim in the waves I could hear smashing onto the rocks outside. The waves where Aurora had drowned.

The cover was pretty: a slender-bodied woman, a heavy cameo around her neck, bathed in a purple cloud that added to her mystery. Then, as I turned the pages, I let myself get hooked on the story. It's about a writer who gets intrigued by some recent disappearances of women, and discovers an underground world where a group of Amazons have made men into sex slaves. He becomes one. At first he's an unwilling victim, but over time, he comes to like it. I couldn't help but draw a parallel: as fascinating as this story was, it was an exact inversion of my current situation. Its male-dominated twin. And I did not believe that Louie had put this book at the top of the list by accident. In addition to the obvious correspondence with my own life, I found other messages buried in its lines, which forced me to read more carefully. Is that what he expected from me: total, unconditional submission of my body? In a way, and he knew it, he had already conquered it . . . So then what did he want?

As promised, Dr. Poulain called and tried to be reassuring. He had just prescribed something that would help Mom make it through to the wedding and her trip to Los Angeles two days later. After that . . . He couldn't make any guarantees, and like me, like her, he had to put his faith in his American colleagues.

I was about to prepare some makeshift sleeping arrangements on the beds upstairs when I heard a motor roar outside. Two little honks chimed amid the racket of the storm.

I peered out the peephole on the front door. It was raining hard, and I had trouble making out the vehicle, whose headlights were pointing at the house, blinding me. They blinked twice, to the tempo of the horn. I stepped out into the torrent and headed toward the car. After advancing a few feet, I recognized Louie's limousine. But it was Richard the Chauffeur who appeared in the beaming lights, holding a large umbrella.

"Good evening," he grumbled, as affable as ever.

"Good evening. Can you explain what you're doing here?"

"I am to bring you where you are expected. That is all."

"You came all the way from Paris for that?" I inquired.

"Yes," he answered flatly, as though it were perfectly reasonable.

"And where are we going?"

"I don't know. All I have is an address."

I could have said no. I could have fled, leaving him there and shutting myself in the house. I also could have run to the base of the garden, jumped over the wall, and dived head first into the ocean, as Aurora had done before me. I could have punished the Barlets, depriving them of their latest toy.

Instead, I simply asked:

"Can you give me five minutes to change?"

"That won't be necessary. Just take the mask you received."

I proceeded unflinchingly, my blouse drenched and sticking to my chest, which was heaving wildly.

"Soph?" I yelled from the entry.

"Yes, what is it?"

"I'm going out."

"You're *what*? Are you kidding me? I just asked you ten minutes ago and you said no . . ."

I didn't know what else to say but:

"It's Louie."

No answer.

"Did you hear me?"

"Umm, yeah. But what can I do? It's your life."

I left at once, mask in hand, under the deluge.

Louie was breaking the usual codes of our meetings. He was changing the playing field. And I figured it must mean we were bringing things to another level. What else?

The car left at a slow pace, determined to deliver its package safe and sound. I was not worth more than that at the present moment, an odious thought that I found exciting.

32

In the end, what do I have to lose? What else could possibly get between my desires and me?

My thirst for truth? I've noticed that every discovery tears me further from it. My loyalty to David? What loyalty? The word seems inappropriate, considering the man betrayed me. I'm beyond that issue. From now on, and especially tonight, my body is in charge. My body is letting itself sway in the back of the limousine. My body is taking me to my latest sexual rendezvous.

The night is unfolding around us, echoing with maritime sounds and brusque gusts of wind. But I'm not paying attention to all that. It does not even surprise me when the car stops in the middle of an industrial zone, just outside of Saint-Malo. The deserted road is flanked with ominous hangars. The area does not look like a place of pleasure. I am starting to think this may be a hoax when Richard the Chauffeur parks in front of a bathroom wholesaler's spartan window. He opens the partition that separates us and gestures into the rear-view mirror. Apparently, I am expected on the opposing sidewalk.

The entrance of the Brigantine, "sauna-hammam-relaxation," looks like a beach shack grafted onto a sheet metal building. It is identical to all the neighboring rectangular structures. Holding my mask, I step inside. It reminds me of the entrance to a swimming pool. Clean, white, hygienic. A bodybuilder guy, shaved head and pectorals popping through his white T-shirt, addresses me as though we've already met:

"You're Elle. Here's a robe and your towel. The changing rooms are directly on your right."

"But don't I owe you . . . ?"

"Nothing. Everything is already paid for."

The overwhelming smell of chlorine does not lend itself to lovemaking. Two men as well built as the greeter are sitting on little benches and undressing. I am suddenly filled with uncertainty. The two men aren't paying any attention to me, even though I've started taking off my clothes as well, turning so they see my rounded rump as opposed to my breasts and bush. ~~I have always been embarrassed of the abundance of hair in that precise area.~~ They don't seem the least bit interested in my backside, and are already stroking each other's members. Their eyes are curious, hungry. And I can tell their touching will soon grow more explicit, more direct.

When I follow them into another room, my mask covering my eyes, my robe half open over my heavy breasts, my doubts are confirmed: The Brigantine is a place where men, and only men, come to meet. I am the only woman. Perhaps even the first ever to set foot here. This room is reserved for flirtation. A few dozen men with towels around their waists eye each other. Some of their hands *probe; others explore more openly. They kiss with varying degrees of ardor. One of them spots me and takes me firmly by the hand:*

"Come . . . It gets interesting over here."

Much like the colossus at the entry, this man seems to have been alerted to my presence. In fact, none of the men appear surprised to see me. They all tolerate me.

He leads me through a dimly lit corridor, lined with tiny red ceiling lamps, to a dark and cramped alcove. After my eyes adjust, there is just enough light to make out the number of people present and their respective postures. There are fifteen men.

A swell of sighs greets me as I step through a set of saloon doors. The air is permeated with noise and smells. A mix of sweat, different colognes—musky, marine, floral— and a more acrid, unmistakable aroma. Most are coupled off, missionary or doggy-style, but some are gathered in groups of three or four, and it is impossible to tell who is sucking whom, who is penetrating whom. Little by little, my embarrassment dissipates, and I decide to take advantage of what's on offer: I am the only woman, and I can watch without having to participate. I am astonished by the way a beautiful young man sucks his partner's huge member. It's more than effort or greed. In fact, he seems to be enjoying it more than the man around whom his fresh lips, now frothy with seminal liquid, are wrapped. When the other man ejaculates in his throat, he lets out a groan that almost sounds like an orgasm, and not at all like he's being suffocated, as it had appeared to me.

An active body emerges from the masses all of a sudden and faces me. Fine. Muscly. Tight. I can't take my eyes off

him. Something about his shape, the contours of his sculpted chest, is familiar. I do not dare look at his face. I'm so
scared I'll recognize him . . . But Louie's ghost disappears.
The man staring at me is darker—ethnic, I realize, when
he happens across a stronger ray of light. I don't know if
I'm relieved or disappointed.

I wonder about the meaning of this new step in our
relationship. Why this? I only see one possible answer: he
wants me to have a taste of this raw beauty. No taboos,
no barriers. These direct and sometimes rough embraces
are pure and stripped of all baggage. No one is beautiful,
no one ugly; no one rich, no one poor; no good lays, no bad
lays. ~~No small dicks, no big dicks.~~ Just desiring, hungry
cocks and asses. Erogenous zones colliding into one another,
against one another, in perfect anonymity. Nothing but
desire.

"Here, this is for you."

My guide reappears with an alarmingly big dildo. I
cannot see myself putting such a monster inside me. Much
less in front of them, no matter how occupied they may be.
So, instead, with my back against the wall, I widen my legs
a little and insert two fingers into my sopping cleft. I have
not felt this wet in a long time. My vagina sucks them up
like an avid mouth. My pelvis rocks slowly, gently, back
and forth, over my digits. My moans accentuate theirs. I am
their diva. I am their soloist. And when at last I explode, a
long and plaintive note, my eyes glued to their shining cocks,
I could swear I hear them applauding me.

I have explored the unknown.

Handwritten note by me, 6/15/2009

33

June 15, 2009

I got back to the house late—and Sophia very early, I supposed the next morning, since the house had been empty
when I returned. From what I could gather, she had ended
up abandoning the pile of old photos and going out in search
of fun. I left the gate and door open for her. I didn't hear the
sound of her parking in front of the villa or pushing open the
creaking doors. I had fallen into a weary sleep.

TWENTY-ONE MISSED CALLS, SEVEN MESSAGES.

   That is what was waiting for me on my phone when I
awoke. I was a little surprised that David had not come to
get me in person. Or at least sent one of his factotums. But
who knows: maybe Armand hadn't given me away, though
that struck me as surprising. And then, when I thought
about it, it occurred to me that it was Monday, the beginning of the workweek, when every second of his schedule
was already completely full. Tied up with his CEO duties.
That his future wife had suddenly vanished was no doubt
disagreeable, a stone in his polished shoe, but it was also

a minor event compared to the crucial deadlines awaiting him at work.

"Hey, darlin'!" I said to Sophia, who was wearing an old T-shirt and ancient panties.

Her brown curls fell over a tired face. The night had no doubt been long and well lubricated. Maybe even horizontal, too. With her, anything was possible.

"Whoa . . . softly!"

She was holding her head between her hands, covering her ears.

"Long night?"

"Hmm . . . I've had *longer*," she simpered, underscoring her salacious double meaning. "But not bad."

I waved my hand at her, playing my part as the prude. "Don't tell me. No really, don't."

"I'm not up for it anyway."

"Breakfast?"

"Definitely! Double long espresso or nothing."

The night's storm had given way to bright sunshine. The sky was clear as we drove into town, where we sat down at a table outside by the beach. There weren't many other customers. The waiter, a plump and affable young man, seemed delighted to serve two young "beautiful and sophisticated ladies." He gave us lots of presents: an additional ration of coffee, extra jam and butter, freshly pressed orange juice instead of the bottled kind we had ordered.

Is it possible to be sexually attracted to a man whose every atom disgusts you?

That is the big question this season in magazines. A writer and journalist, known for her commitment to fem-

inism, recently published a novel in which she reveals her steamy relationship with a politician who was ruined by a sexual scandal two years ago. In the book, she describes her fascination for this man she calls a "pig," who is twenty years her senior, a notorious orgy-goer, and whose addiction to sex led to his professional and very public fall. Her tell-all about how she fell for him has been a major source of fascination and scandal.

As I read various opinion pieces about her book, I can't help but wonder if I, too, have felt that kind of attraction. Not really for ugly or untouchable men. But I should probably consider why older men seem to have so much power over my young self.

An obvious answer would be that I'm subconsciously trying to find someone to replace my absent father. But there's something else. Something rawer, more animalistic in this preference. The hairier, more rugged body; the way the member is darkened by time; the heavier weight of the scrotum in my hand; the musky smell—I love the physical attributes of these old apes. I could never prefer the rosy freshness of young macaques. To please me, a man's body has to be more than a delicate caress. It has to be like an exfoliating glove, capable of scratching my skin. I've also noticed: though it's less abundant, older men's semen is stickier, thicker. I like it better.

Handwritten note by me, 6/15/2009

AFTER EATING, WE SPENT A long time looking at the sea. A statue of Alfred Hitchcock, a crow on each shoulder, stared at us. It reminded me of the villa on the cliff, a fairly convincing and disturbing allusion to the Bates residence in *Psycho*.

"It's for the festival," the waiter explained. He was a little too talkative for our taste.

"Festival?" Sophia raised an irritated eye in his direction.

"Yeah, the festival of English cinema. Oh, you have to come. There will be a lot of people, stars and everything!"

Our silence eventually won out over his parasitic babel, and we carried on with our mute staring. The day promised to be gentler, the squawk of gulls and scent of seaweed hanging on a gentle breeze.

Sophia broke our silence:

"So did you find some interesting stuff?"

"What . . . ?"

"In the house. You searched through all the drawers, right?"

"Oh, right . . . Yeah, I mean, almost. Nothing very conclusive."

"What were you hoping to find?"

The question was not really "what" but "whom."

Considering the Barlet brothers' secrecy surrounding Aurora Delbard and the role she played in their life, it was more disappointing than surprising that she was absent from the family archives. I hesitated a moment before sharing this information with my friend, then told her everything I knew about the subject.

"If I'm following you, they completely erased that girl from their past?"

"So it would appear . . ."

"That's fishy, I agree . . . ," she said. "But at the same time, if a girl died because of some rivalry that you had fostered between your sons, would you really want photos of her around your house. Really?"

She was right. Sometimes editing the past is not motivated by dark intentions. Often, when it comes to private dramas, people try to hide things out of pain and a sense of decency. The surest way of forgetting is to eliminate all traces of the tragedy.

"You're not wrong," I admitted.

"But if you want, I can help you search. I'm sure there are still things you haven't seen hidden in the back of some cupboard."

I accepted her offer of help, and we headed back to Brown Rocks. This time, we took the coastal path, which is only accessible during low tide. The narrow granite road is only partially paved and hugs the foot of the rocky Malouine Point. From there, we had a perfect view of Saint-Malo and the rest of the bay, the islands Grand and Petit Bé, Cézembre and Conchée. Midway, a red-and-white sign posted a warning: SWIMMERS, BEWARE VIOLENT CURRENT. DANGER.

After the ridge, I thought I recognized the area such as Louie had described it in the back of his limousine: the wall at the base of the villa with a little white door and a few steps leading to the path. Beneath that, large rocks peeked through the water, jagged granite as sharp as blades, between which a foot or leg could easily get caught.

"She died here."

I pointed the spot out to my friend, my voice wan.

"Here?" she asked. "But that's still the shore . . . You can't drown here! That's ridiculous!"

It was true that at low tide the danger seemed pretty slim. But with a little more water, the ocean's swells could easily trap and submerge anyone. The tide was strong and fast in the area.

As though to confirm, someone walking along the shore

pointed to a man in a wet suit who had clearly been carried off by a wave and thrown onto a sandbank some hundred fifty feet from shore. From where we were, it didn't seem far, and yet he looked really disoriented. After hesitating a few minutes, precious time in such circumstances, he ended up throwing himself in the water and fighting against the current to make it back to land.

We didn't say another word until we got back to the house. We opened all the shutters to let some fresh air through the tall windows. Then we started emptying all accessible drawers onto the dusty parquet flooring. Two of them proved impossible to open, however. And our efforts to unlock them with hangers and an old screwdriver were in vain.

Amid the ancient fumes of furniture polish and developing chemicals, we spent the following hours crouched on the ground examining each photograph, and even going over the ones I had surveyed the night before again. The findings were not miraculous—still no picture of Aurora—but there were some pretty shots. Among them were some of Andre and Hortensia, both before and after the death of the young woman. Before, their expressions were, of course, much happier than after. And there was one of Louie, young, smiling wide and carefree, his face rounder than today, in a tender embrace with a beautiful blonde. The woman had a wild look, and I barely recognized her as Rebecca. But it was her. And she was already just as affected, wearing a striped sweater reminiscent of Jean Paul Gaultier or Étienne Daho, the height of cool at the time.

"Well," Sophia lamented, "they did a good job of cleaning up."

"Yes . . . It's strange . . ."

"Strange?"

"I mean . . . Aurora left so little behind . . . It's almost like she wanted to disappear."

She clearly found my remark disconcerting but did not give it more thought and instead dived back into the piles of yellowed paper.

No use telling her where I was going with this theory. Like the women in *Secret Women*, Aurora could have decided to get rid of all traces of herself, as a kind of supreme plot to punish the Barlets for mistreating her. But the similarities stopped there: Ania Oz's Amazons hid from the world so as to reemerge in the end triumphant, and Aurora, well, she was dead. Her punishment had been considerably worse than the one reserved for those who had pushed her to such tragic extremes.

We spent our last hour at Brown Rocks searching every nook and cranny. This time, we weren't just looking for photos but for anything that could lead to Aurora or, more precisely, to any vestiges of her past.

All we found were scratched trinkets, old catalogues, and expired jars. We were about to throw in the towel, when Sophia cried:

"Look!"

Tucked between two pages of a pamphlet she had come across was a dirty and beat-up business card, which, by the looks of it, was pretty old.

> Jean-François Delbard
> Notary
> 8 Placître
> 35400 Saint-Malo

Telephone : 99 32 69 45
Fax : 99 32 69 47

"Delbard, isn't that the drowned woman's name?"

"Yes," I said succinctly.

I had never heard of Jean-François Delbard. Neither Louie nor Rebecca had ever mentioned him.

"Did you see the number?" Sophia insisted. "And the fax? This is old."

It was. And it proved that a member of Aurora's family had lived and worked in the region, most likely before she had died, judging from the numbers—only eight instead of ten. A brother? An uncle? Maybe even her father?

"What's the area code for Saint-Malo again?" I asked.

She grabbed the first advertisement handy and said, "Zero, two."

I punched the number into my phone's touch-screen keyboard and waited for it to ring. But instead, a recording informed me that it had been disconnected. For how long? A mystery. I dialed information, and the operator told me that no one by the name of Jean-François Delbard figured in her directory, nor in Dinard, nor in greater Saint-Malo. I even asked her to try again, with alternative spellings, but to no avail.

"Either he moved, or he also died," Sophia concluded after I hung up.

Dead man. Dead woman.

Her passing observation actually made me think of something.

"You're amazing!" I exclaimed, hugging her.

"What did I say?"

"Come on, let's go. I'll explain once we're on the road."

It only took us fifteen minutes to clean and lock up at Brown Rocks, leaving the house to its guarded secrets.

Happily, the records department at town hall in Dinard was still open. Unfortunately, there was no record of an Aurora Delbard, or even Barlet—neither a birth nor a death certificate.

Without skipping a beat, we went to see the people at Saint-Malo's town hall.

"Yes, I have an Aurora Delbard. Born April 12, 1970. Died December 25, 1989."

"Fuck . . . ," Sophia breathed, expressing what we were both thinking out loud. "She killed herself on Christmas day!"

Christmas night, in fact, and not in the summer, as Louie had claimed.

"Where is she buried?" I inquired.

"Are you family, Mademoiselle?"

"No . . . she was my fiancé's first wife."

She must have felt sorry for me because she offered the following:

"We don't have that kind of information here. But considering the address you gave me . . . there's a chance she's at Rocabey Cemetery. If the family has a plot there, of course."

She drew us a rough map on a brochure for tourists, and we hopped in the Beetle and rushed to the cemetery. Rocabey is a sad neighborhood in Saint-Malo, located between the train station and the merchants' port. Still, a sign at the entry indicated the celebrities buried there: Robert Surcouf, the most famous mariner of Saint-Malo, and the actor Daniel Gélin.

We wandered for several minutes before running into a grave digger with sideburns and a wheelbarrow. He scratched his head, and then remembered aloud:

"Oh, yes. Delbard . . . like the notary!"

Bingo.

"That's right." I nodded. "Like the notary. By the way, Aurora and her . . ." I paused, hoping he would complete my sentence.

"His daughter, yes. Or maybe his niece. I might be confusing them with the Dolé family. Or maybe the Bazins."

Sophia raised her eyebrows, as if to say we weren't going to get anything more out of him.

The Delbard family tomb was a slab of pink marble. It was fairly simple, with no portraits. It looked abandoned: no flowers or decorations, no sign of interest in their sepulcher. The surrounding vegetation was starting to invade. Clearly, no one was there to tend to it. There were four names listed: Amédée (1910–1985), Suzanne (1912–1999), Jean-François (1938–2005), and Aurora (1970–1989).

"She died before her father," Sophia noted.

"And even her grandmother."

Not one member of the family seemed to be with the living. There was no one to question. Unless . . .

"Her mother . . . She's not with them," Sophia observed.

"Maybe she's still alive," I speculated.

"Yeah . . . We didn't ask for her parents' names at the records department. It's closed by now."

The setting sun meant evening was upon us, and public offices abandoned for the night.

Using my smartphone's 3G connection—in passing, I noticed that David had stopped calling, and that he hadn't made any effort to reach me since late morning—I searched for the following information: *"Rebecca Sibony"* + *"Belles de Nuit."* Though the connection was weak, it gave me the following result since Belles de Nuit had been registered to Rebecca at her home: *Belles de Nuit SARL, 118 Avenue Georges Mandel, 75116 Paris CEDEX.*

"Do you want to go surprise that bitch?" Sophia's natural disposition had resurfaced.

"Yes."

"Do you really think she'll help us?"

"I don't know. It's possible."

I hoped she would.

After all, if you took David and Louie out of the equation, Rebecca was the only living witness. Not the most impartial person, sure, but still. Our trip to the sea, like the sheets at Brown Rocks, had only unveiled a tiny portion of the Barlet brothers' secret. I was counting on her to shed some light on those old memories. She had to know more than she had told me the last time I'd seen her, on Rue du Roi-de-Sicile.

Her puckish eyes looked at me from the photo, from her past self, inviting me to join her. She could prepare her answers, clean them of their lies, and fill in the gaps: I was coming.

34

June 16, 2009

Pee break. Dinner break. Gas stop. We made our way back to Paris in increments, delaying the inevitable. We were in no hurry to get answers to the questions we had been considering since Brown Rocks. If Aurora was from Saint-Malo, how had she and David met? What had really happened the night of December 25, 1989, that made the young woman throw herself into the stormy sea? Why had David taken off on Christmas day—"on business," Louie had said—leaving his brother, his parents, and, above all, his depressive young wife behind? What was their relationship to Belles de Nuit? Could it be that Aurora . . . had also been a Hotelle?

We ended up stopping at a hotel on the side of the road, somewhere between Angers and Le Mans. Neither of us had the energy to keep driving. We hadn't slept much the night before, Sophia even less than I. We'd need rest if we didn't want to get in an accident.

I am writing in almost complete darkness. I think Sophia
is already asleep, in the bed next to mine. Her breathing

is loud and regular. As for me, I can't sleep. Because of our recent discoveries? Because of everything that awaits us in Paris?

No, it's because every time I hear my friend's breath, I imagine that she's masturbating, ~~her index finger pressing into her button, a middle finger plunged into her sex.~~ This thought is not new: ever since the age of sixteen, whenever I sleep over at a girlfriend's house, I ask myself the same question: Is she touching herself? Or rather: Could she be touching herself without my noticing? The thought harasses me, and finally I slide a hand into my panties and press my clitoris, in as controlled a manner as possible, until I can't take it anymore. Did Sophia hear me tonight? Did she also wonder about my nocturnal activities? Sleeping in the same room with another person, be they of the same or opposite sex, tends to provoke this kind of question: Is the person horny? For me? For him- or herself?

Handwritten note by me, 6/16/2009

WE LEFT BEFORE DAWN THE next morning. The tunnels leading into Paris at the Porte d'Orléans, whose orange neon lights I've always liked so much, swallowed us before the day had even broken.

We took the road due west and exited at Porte de la Muette after having driven a good fifteen minutes around the city, following directions provided by Cox navigation systems.

It was still very early. That Tuesday morning in Paris, traffic was fluid and there were few cars on the road. Just bread makers, a few café workers, and garbage collectors. Five fifty, said the digital clock on the dashboard in large green numbers.

"We're not going to stop by at this hour, are we?" Sophia inquired.

"No, you're right. Coffee?"

"Coffee," she confirmed.

118 AVENUE GEORGES MANDEL WAS a large building from the seventies or eighties. It was an immaculate white, with rounded cement cavities jutting out of the facade at every window or bay window.

The entrance was just as kitsch, and finding Rebecca's name among those of all the residents took a few minutes—I noted the presence of a Barlet on the nineteenth floor. A sleepy voice answered the intercom, after what seemed to me like a long time. We were clearly waking her up.

"Yes?"

"Rebecca. It's Annabelle."

"And Sophia!" my friend hollered over my shoulder.

"I'm buzzing you in," she said. "Eleventh floor, first door on your right."

She was barefoot when she greeted us, in a silk fuchsia robe thrown over a nightie in a softer pink. Without makeup, her hair a mess, she definitely looked her fifty-odd years. I noticed wrinkles I had never seen before since they were usually so well hidden under layers of powder and foundation. But her eyes, despite their sagging lids, were exactly the same as in the stolen photograph. I wondered who could have taken it.

"Would you like something? Tea? Coffee? Water?"

She ushered us into a little sitting room with a view of the street. It was modern, clean, and stylish, and yet also filled with souvenirs and trinkets, for the most part portraits of Rebecca with an impressive number of celebrities, arm in arm, of course. Sophia's eyes widened at the sight of such and such television personality, and this or that pop star.

"No, thanks. We just had coffee," I answered for both of us.

"Okay . . . I'm going to make myself some tea, if you don't mind."

While she prepared her beverage, I had time to inspect her flat's interior. Large gray metal blocks disappeared in part under her desk, which was scattered with papers in unstable piles. I figured they must be the Belles de Nuit archives, undoubtedly carted over from the now empty offices over at Rue du Roi-de-Sicile . . .

Then, on the opposite wall, I noticed something else: underneath the pale-yellow wallpaper, I made out a door frame, a fairly noticeable thin black line just beneath the surface. *The door to Louie's apartment!* I thought, my heart thumping. I tried to calm down before the mistress of the house came back with her mug. A blanket of Shalimar followed her in and soon mixed with the scent of her steaming jasmine tea.

As I watched her mechanically stir a spoon into her sugarless tea, I thought of our last meeting and, more generally, her life. She, too, had lived a life without real flavor since she had been denied the sweetness of Louie's affections. She had been rejected by her one true love, and from what I could tell, she had never gotten over it. Nothing in love or business had been able to fill the hole in her heart.

I quickly repressed a passing thought: one room, three women . . . all possessed (or almost) by the same lover. Was it deplorable? Laughable? Revolting? . . . Or, on the contrary, exciting? Which one of us, in the end, could give

*him the most pleasure? The prettiest, the one who loved
him most . . . or, against all odds, the most recalcitrant?*

Handwritten note by me, 6/16/2009

THOUGH IT SEEMED SHE HAD been expecting the worst
from me, she clearly had not anticipated my question:

"Rebecca, when did you found Belles de Nuit?"

I already knew the answer. It was on the same document
where I had seen her address. I just wanted to hear it from her.

"In February 1992."

Exactly. Or two years after Aurora's death. Logically, then,
she could not have been one of us.

"And before Belles de Nuit?"

Sophia introduced herself into the conversation, for once
in a relevant way.

"Have you managed other agencies of the same kind?"

"No, it was the first. Before that, I was in public relations."

"For which company?"

"For different venues and also for a film distributor. But
that was a long time ago."

The celebrity friendships she showed off on her walls were
probably from that time, I speculated. Those same people had
no doubt become clients, once she'd launched the agency.

"But you didn't come here to talk about my career, did
you?" She laughed, her tone soft and nostalgic. "If you could
even call it that . . ."

Now that she had given Louie to me, now that she saw
me as the official depositary of a man she did not know
how to please, all she had left were her memories. And this
apartment—though he would soon be moving out. For good.

She who had once seemed so self-assured now looked like the remnant of an old ship battered by storms, the kind you find tucked away someplace where no one goes to see it anymore. Flaking. Crushed in parts. The rigging frayed.

"Last time we met . . . ," I continued my interrogation. "Why didn't you tell me that David owned Belles de Nuit?"

Obviously, his name did not appear on the company's registration documents. He was smarter than that. It was probably hiding behind an obscure title, one of the business's many shareholders. I hadn't had time to uncover it.

The way she batted her eyes told me that this question also came as a surprise. Then, she took a long sip of hot tea and looked at the ceiling:

"I won't even bother asking who told you that . . ."

"In any case, I wouldn't tell you," I replied with composure. "You know the rules: a journalist never reveals her sources."

I had no reason to cover for François Marchadeau. And David would undoubtedly figure out that he had been the leak. But that was between his old friend, him, and me.

"David simply loaned me some money to start the company," she said, a halfhearted exoneration. "That was more than fifteen years ago . . . That's it."

"Are you saying he doesn't have a stake in it anymore?" Sophia intervened; I could feel her growing impatient.

"He does. But he hasn't been a majority shareholder in a long time."

That would be easy to verify with a little impromptu research. But I was interested in more than administrative explanations.

"You didn't answer me: Why did you hide David's role in Belles de Nuit from me? Why not tell me that he's known all along about my activities?"

"Is it really important?" she asked, blinking.

"Yes," I answered firmly.

All I had were a handful of dates, spotty information, and a sprinkling of intuition. Nothing proved that her agency was directly linked to Aurora Delbard's tragic fate. Nothing explained the sensitive role I played between the Barlet brothers, much less the relationship between the two mysteries.

Rebecca shivered and hugged her bathrobe more tightly. She was protecting herself, drawing her frail body into a soft armor of satin.

"Lord knows David was not the best husband to Aurora . . . but he had a terrible time getting over her death."

The armband. The scars on his left forearm. I had already seen all that. No use bringing it up again. A brief smile, my way of encouraging her to go on.

"Since it had been years and he still had not come to terms with it . . . he had this idea. Unless it was Louie who had it first. I never really knew."

"What kind of idea?"

Problem: Why do we ask questions when we already know the answer?

"Belles de Nuit, of course!"

Solution: Because it hurts more when it comes from someone else's mouth. The words of others are razors; our naive quest for truth, the vein we hold out to them. It's up to them to act, to do irreparable damage.

"I don't get it," my friend cut in. "What's the connection with his ex?"

"Let's just say that David couldn't handle living alone. But he couldn't imagine entering into a relationship that might be as destructive as what he'd had with Aurora. He was afraid of the madness, the hysteria . . ."

"The agency would be a giant casting call," I breathed.

Sophia couldn't believe it either. While I sunk into the sofa, crushed, she straightened, perching her backside on the cushions' edge, on the verge of jumping.

"He never considered that maybe he had played a role in her tragedy?"

"David is not really the kind of person to doubt himself."

I had to give her that. Everything from the past couple of weeks was taking on new meaning. Since he had found me, since he had thought me worthy of succeeding Aurora, there was no reason to keep up the agency. After all, it had only been a front for his desperate quest.

I took a few deep breaths, settling myself.

"And why did he trust *you* with this mission?"

"At the time, I was out of a job. And I think Louie felt badly for leaving me again . . ."

She was speaking as though she had failed him.

"That doesn't exactly make you a competent candidate." Sophia didn't mince words.

"That's true . . . but I learned quickly. Besides, my previous work experience gave me something really important: a client list."

She confirmed my earlier hypothesis with a sweeping look over her collection of celebrity photographs.

"I thought it was a cover! Why care about your earnings?"

"David always cares." Rebecca sighed.

In other words, fake or not, the agency was not exempt from what was expected of every other Barlet Group subsidiary: it had to earn its keep.

But there was something that didn't cohere in this neat little story.

"Don't tell me it took you seventeen years to find a girl like me?"

As ordinary as me, I implied with consternation. Didn't Annabelle Lorands show up at station casting calls all year, fresh and ripe for the plucking?

"Yes," she affirmed, this time without raising her brow. "But I've told you already: David is really very demanding. About everything. And especially when it comes to the kind of women he frequents. So you can imagine for his *wife*!"

"If he wanted the perfect girl," Sophia came to my aid, "there are plenty of dating sites where you can enter your exact criteria. And believe me, candidates for marriage are a dime a dozen."

"You're right. David attracts more beautiful young women than he can possibly take to bed with him. But the sites you mention didn't exist at the time."

I ignored her barb. She was only saying the obvious, something I had no doubt been too quick to forget: the man I was supposed to marry was one of France's—if not Europe's—most eligible bachelors. Though I had trouble assessing his notoriety outside our borders.

She set her mug on the coffee table and fixed a gray strand of hair that had fallen in front of her face, a kind of call to order.

"In any case, that's not the issue . . ."

"No, but it's so ridiculous!" I finally exploded. "What do I have that's so exceptional?"

I recognized her tender and compassionate look from our last meeting.

"Well . . . It's a number of things," she equivocated. "It's hard to sum it up in three words."

"Start with three hundred," Sophia countered. "We have time."

Rebecca shot me a look suggesting it wasn't for her to say. She reiterated her point out loud, directing her words at me, as though Sophia weren't even in the room:

"I think it's up to *them* to tell you . . ."

The ambivalence of her reply was not lost on me: she wasn't saying she didn't know the answer, but that she thought it better if others told me. Them. She could have said: "It's up to David to tell you." But she had chosen to include both brothers. They were always connected.

My phone vibrated from within my bag. It wouldn't stop and interrupted my interrogation at a critical moment . . .

"Yes? Hello?" I answered coldly.

The number was blocked. But I had trouble believing that such an early-morning and persistent call could be a wrong number or a telemarketer.

"Annabelle?"

That voice. I recognized that voice. Especially the timbre. And despite its detachment from a physical person, I recognized the dramatic tone. It was grave, a voice of finality.

"Yes . . . It's me."

"It's Ludovic Poulain. I'm sorry to call you so early. I'm not disturbing you, am I?"

Tell me you dialed the wrong number, Dr. Poulain. Fill me in on the side effects of Mom's new prescriptions. Tell me whatever, anything but the real reason for your call—which, though it remained unsaid, was already like poison in my ear.

Unfeeling, I heard his words. My hand shook as I searched for something in my bag, I didn't know what. A photograph fell from my purse to the floor, the image turned facedown against the parquet.

Rebecca leaned over to pick it up. Without thinking, she turned it over. She saw herself, young, on the beach in Dinard, in Louie's arms. He was no longer in her life, and yet he was still present in every gesture, every word, every choice. She couldn't get rid of him. He was her cancer.

35

"Mom? Mom, can you hear me?"

No answer, of course. Not even a bat of the eye to show she understood. Just an inert mass in a white bed. Hospitals have a way of making our loved ones unrecognizable. We think we know their appearance by heart. Huge mistake. They're no longer your child, your friend, your dad, your mom, but a heap of flesh, sheets, and blinking machines. Don't call them Maude, Lola, or Henry. Call *that thing* a patient now. Indistinct. Almost anonymous.

Under the tubes and breathing mask, my mom looked tiny. Like a baby, one of those preemies whose lives hang on a thread, on pulsing and pumping machines. The organism sustained through artifice, life or something like it.

LAURE CHAPPUIS WAS THE ONE who had sounded the alarm. The insufferable Madame Chappuis had a useful role after all, despite her endless complaints and churlish character: she was a guardian angel. A crabby angel, but one capable of watching over my mother in case of emergency. She had just proven it. In the middle of the night, she had noticed thick smoke coming from her neighbor's air duct. Apparently, she had nothing better to do at that hour than keep an eye on the surrounding houses. She must have run out of trashy magazines and telenovelas. Or perhaps she had seen the "good doctor" come by the house earlier that night. Perhaps she had been really worried about her friend.

After Dr. Poulain's visit, Maude had felt hungry and decided to reheat the gratin dauphinois she had made the evening before. Anyone else would have popped a portion in the microwave, but she had put the whole thing in the oven, at maximum heat.

But the sedative the doctor had administered was starting to take effect. Mom fell asleep, leaving the gratin in the oven. Two hours later, the house was filled with gray smoke that threatened to asphyxiate Maude. Firefighters arrived just in time to give her some oxygen and rush her off to Max Fourestier, Nanterre's public hospital, where she went for chemotherapy treatments every three weeks.

When I finally managed to tell them what had happened, Sophia did not hesitate:

"Okay, let's go. I'm taking you," she declared, already at the door.

"No, don't worry about it, I can work it out. And besides, you have to get the car back to Peggy . . ."

"Don't be ridiculous. I told her I'd return it today—I didn't say when. Let's go!"

Rebecca remained seated in her chair, holding the photograph, incapable of movement. She offered a burdened smile as a good-bye. Nothing went her way, not even the big revelation scene. *Her* scene.

TRAFFIC WAS HEAVIER THAN WHEN we'd first gotten into Paris, and it took us almost an hour to reach Avenue de la

République, a long, charmless artery lined with low-rise buildings and decrepit houses. The high wall flanking the street is more reminiscent of a prison than a place of health. However, once you get past the front desk, Nanterre's hospital has a kind of majesty.

We walked through a courtyard and under an arch, behind which was posted an impressive list of services. At the very bottom, highlighted by little red squares, two items made me freeze: EMERGENCY ROOM – MORTUARY. I scanned through the list again, until I found ONCOLOGY, not more uplifting, really.

The smiling and attentive personnel led us to her room. Apparently, she had first been taken to the emergency room, but they had transferred her in the early morning, after the doctor had decided she no longer needed urgent care.

Sophia left me at my mother's bedside, where I ended up dozing off in my plastic chair, lulled by the regular beep of the monitors, knocked out by the ambient heat.

"Elle . . . Elle, are you okay?"

Before I could identify his voice, I recognized him from the feel of his warm hand firmly pressed into my shoulder. I didn't jump. He'd torn me from a dream, and as soon as I opened my eyes, I knew he wasn't part of it. He belonged to the ignoble reality of the hospital: dilapidated, sinister, morbid.

I wasn't really thinking about the words as they came out of my mouth, sending David away with a brutality that surprised even me, a kind of sedated fury, injected with my own pain:

"Get out." I pushed him with both hands as hard as I could. He barely moved.

"Darling . . ."

"I said get out. You don't belong here."

"At least tell me what's happening!"

"What's happening is you're leaving. You hear me?"

"For God's sake, Elle! You disappeared for two days! And now I find you here . . ."

"Scram, I said!"

"Okay, okay . . ."

He gave in and backed into the hallway, his face awash in disbelief and worry.

"I'll be in the hall," he said.

Who had told him? Rebecca, it had to be her, since I had asked Sophia for absolute discretion.

During the following hour and a half, I moved heaven and earth to meet the doctor overseeing my mom. He was a fop with salt-and-pepper hair and a precocious tan, considering how early it was in the season. By some miracle, he finally appeared around eleven.

"You wanted to see me, Mademoiselle?"

"Annabelle Lorand." I extended an anxious hand. "I'm her daughter."

I pointed to my mother, not daring to look at her directly.

"I'm Professor Laurent Banday. I'm in charge of this unit."

I heard "Band-aid" and wondered if he was telling a bad joke. But the face in front of me was calm, almost cold, and betrayed no trace of break room banter. I realized my subconscious needed to lighten the situation and could really use some med-student humor. Meanwhile, the lucid and reasonable part of me just wanted the facts.

"The incident last night . . . Did it worsen her condition?"

"No. But it did underscore your mother's extremely weak state."

"Weak . . . how weak?"

"She can't stay home by herself," he said frankly. "She needs constant care."

"You know she's supposed to leave for treatment in the United States in four days?"

If he hadn't known, he didn't show it. And Lord knows how much doctors pride themselves on masking ignorance.

"Yes, I'm aware. But I'm sorry to say that will no longer be possible. For now, we're waiting for the results of some tests I ordered last night when she was first admitted."

The hospital's George Clooney was a real professional, then, more of a Dr. Ross than a kid playing Operation. How long had he been working here, I wondered.

"But that trip is her last hope!" I cried. "You can't take it away from her just . . ."

To preserve your reputation? To justify your salary? I didn't know what vitriol I wanted to throw in his face.

He must have been accustomed to the loved ones of patients, drunk with uncertainty and despair, attacking him. He didn't seem to hold it against me, seeing more than blind suffering in my expression. I wouldn't ignore his advice. His voice grew calmer, smoother:

"Mademoiselle Lorand . . . your mother does not have long."

"I know that! That's exactly why—"

"You don't understand," he explained, squeezing my shoulder. "I'm not talking weeks but days."

How was that possible? Not long before, the same team of doctors had given her months!

"It seems we were overly optimistic in our last predictions," he admitted in a sincere tone. I was speechless. "The tests we ran last night should confirm our fears: the cancer has metas-

tasized into her vital organs. Even if we were capable of replacing her heart, lungs, and liver, it wouldn't help. All that
can be done now is to keep her comfortable, to the best of our
abilities."

Clinical. Succinct. Emotionless. Such was his delivery.
I, who had wanted him to give it to me straight, had been
granted my wish.

"You know," he went on, justifying himself, "I was the first
one here to advocate for the alternative therapy my American
colleagues are doing. If you treat the patient early on, the rates
of remission are fairly spectacular. But . . ."

"But we should have done it sooner? Is that what you're
telling me?"

"To be honest, in your mother's case, I don't think that
would have changed much. By the time we detected her
cancer, it was already too late. The chances the procedure
would be a success were already slim. The cancer was already
widespread."

Mom, who was vigilant about everything but herself. Mom
and her "Oh, it's nothing" when I told her she ought to get her
pain checked out. Mom, who, when I was still a kid, fell down
the stairs and broke her arm and didn't see the doctor for more
than a week, her arm bruised and puffy in a makeshift sling.

Mom, who always had something more important to do
than take care of herself.

"At most, we would have gained a few weeks, maybe
months . . ."

He may have found the thought reassuring, but I was
plagued with doubt, which would probably never go away,
even when Maude Lorand was buried under her pink marble
slab in some cemetery.

I ignored his hypotheticals and focused my energy on the trip's potential to save her:

"For now, I'd prefer we stick to the plan. If she can be transported, that is."

"She can . . . ," he admitted. "Well, if she comes out of the coma in time."

"Of course," I agreed, my voice calm and full of hope.

"Still, for now, it would be best if you could be here as much as possible."

I raised a round, childish, empty face and stared as though some part of me hoped a smile from him could put an end to this nightmare.

"I'm getting married the day after tomorrow," I said at last.

He was speechless for a moment, having run out of ready-made phrases, and then:

"Get married. It's probably the best thing you can do right now. For you and for her."

If he had been a few years older, he would have been an ideal father, the kind I'd always dreamed could give me away. I brushed the ridiculous thought aside.

"Do you think she'll wake up? I mean, before . . ."

I couldn't bring myself to say the word, or even any of its synonyms, no matter how euphemistic. Instead I opted for the following, more optimistic way of putting things:

" . . . before our departure?"

"Yes, of course. She still has a lot of lucid moments before her."

I appreciated his phrasing but couldn't help wondering: Lucid moments, but in the midst of what? Comas? Delirium? Was happiness any more than this: lucid moments of laughter, pleasure, and joy amid darkness?

"Don't worry," he tried to comfort me. "She'll see you again. You'll be able to speak with her."

I could have lain down like a rag doll next to Mom and waited with her until one of us left. Or turned to liquid straightaway and puddled onto the gray linoleum, which was scuffed by time and nurses' shoes.

The doctor seized my arm—this time, I realized, to keep me upright.

"Are you going to be okay?" he asked, trying to show some humanity.

"Yes . . . yes, thanks. I think I just need some air."

And as I left the room, he said:

"Don't forget to leave your cell number with the nurses on duty. They'll try to reach you if something happens, no matter the hour."

I did not, however, follow his advice and instead headed straight outside. Feeling the sun on my skin, I remembered that it would be summer in five days. I wouldn't be taking advantage of the good weather this year. There would be no golden suntan for me, certainly not like the one Professor Banday was sporting.

I had only taken a few steps around the courtyard when David suddenly appeared. It was like a bad joke. The fact that he had been waiting for me all this time was perhaps the most incongruous aspect of his presence here.

"Don't you have a meeting or something?" I barked.

He widened his eyes, disarmed. "No . . ."

"Oh, right, I'm an idiot: all your ratings are rigged anyway!"

I don't know why I said that. It was useless provocation. *Culture Mix*, my stillborn ghost show was the least of my worries. The rage I had felt after Fred's phone call seemed trivial now. Ridiculous, even.

I trotted around and around the disjointed cobblestones, twisting my ankles more than once, when suddenly his hand gripped my wrist, stopping me short.

"Will you let me explain?"

I considered him for a moment but did not recognize the man I'd found so enchanting in this suited puppet bursting with ambition, power, and pride. Even his voice seemed to have changed, suddenly stripped of its evocative qualities: more gruff now than smooth.

"Go ahead . . . ," I challenged, though I didn't expect anything from him.

He, the almighty, the superb, surprised me by his ability to play humble. His eyes, which usually looked straight into mine, wandered aimlessly over the uneven ground. He wasn't letting me go so easily.

"When I saw you in that dress on my monitor . . . your hair done up . . ."

"What? So, now you're an expert in costumes? I thought you were more interested in what was underneath."

My remark was like a slap in the face, but he didn't seem to have unpacked the allusion.

"When Dad was still managing the company, I asked him to do some screen tests with Aurora."

"In that dress, is that it?"

"No, but one like it, yes."

If he was telling the truth, I could only imagine how much of a shock it had been to see me on his screen.

I let him continue.

"I think I just . . . I couldn't stand seeing you done up like her."

I could tell by his sunken eyes that the pain was real.

"Is that why you told Guillaume not to run the show?"

"It's stupid, I know. I'm sorry."

Okay.

But what was I supposed to say? As sincere as his confession seemed, it didn't erase everything else. In no way did it make up for the things I'd heard from François and Rebecca.

I could have contented myself with his touching confession. I could have sated my thirst for information with the tears he was clearly fighting to hold back. I could have decided to forget everything and take him at his word when he promised a better life. But I already knew too much . . .

"Belles de Nuit was always only ever about one thing, wasn't it? Finding you another wife? Another Aurora?"

His face tightened into an incredulous smile. Clearly, he hadn't been expecting me to know so much. Nor that I would have the nerve to be so frank with him.

"It's not so simple . . . ," he said, casting around for an excuse.

"Yes or no: you used Rebecca's business as a private marriage agency? Yes . . . or no?" I enunciated these last words.

His embarrassment did not completely hide the irritation welling up within him. He was hopping uncomfortably, kicking the ground with the toe of his shoe, filled with nervous energy he couldn't contain.

"Yes . . . But it was Louie's idea to begin with."

"Unless it was Louie who had it first. I never really knew," Rebecca had admitted.

"But what does that really change, in the end?"

"What changes is that I didn't want it. Belles de Nuit wasn't supposed to be a trap. At least . . . not for me. Just a way for us to meet."

"And Louie?" I pressed him.

My question seemed to come as a surprise.

"Louie is an eternal bachelor. He likes the chase, you see . . . Always on the hunt for fresh meat."

The reproach struck me as though it had been meant for me. Not that I included myself among the herd from which Louie, being the good wolf that he was, chose his victims. It was more like I suddenly felt as though I were the predator David was describing, and I did not like hearing my true nature being portrayed like that. Like a vulgar form of consumption. A basic, morbid penchant.

After several sessions at the Hôtel des Charmes, I knew it was much more than that.

"For him, Belles de Nuit was a kind of godsend. All he had to do was pick up the phone and Rebecca would provide. A strange relationship, by the way, when the dealer is jealous of the stuff she's peddling to her junkie . . ."

It was one of the first times I'd heard him speak so openly about his brother. He clearly didn't have any qualms about throwing him under the bus. He didn't even try to justify his behavior or understand the reason behind his addiction to sex. He completely wrote him off, without mincing words.

"Anyway, I don't even want to know all the details, but I think sometimes it got fairly dark."

Dark?

The skulduggery Marchadeau had told me about came to mind. Louie's erotic fantasies were much less offensive by comparison.

"Dark?" I jumped. "Dark, like a porno made with sex slaves from the East?"

My remark lashed him like a whip, leaving him speechless for a moment.

"Huh?" I insisted. "Dark, like letting me sleep with your best friend the night we first met?"

Instantly, he released my hand. Judging by his expression, I could tell I had gone too far. His head sunk into his shoulders like he was defending himself against a beating. Then he composed himself, puffing up his chest in preparation for his point-by-point defense:

"The investments to which you refer were made without my knowledge."

"Really?" I was dripping with sarcasm.

"Really. The person who made them in the company's name was fired years ago. But in the wonderful world of finance, that kind of story sticks for a long time . . . Even when you're proven innocent."

I was stunned. The beast of the media had reared his head. Practiced in the art of the tricky interview, he wasn't going to give in without a fight.

"Check into it if you want. Stephen Delacroix—that's the name of the analyst I hired. And who screwed me."

"And why did he do that?"

"What do you think? He was working for the competition. To connect me to a heinous moral scandal. To get me thrown out of my job as CEO and to buy Barlet Group at a cut rate. That kind of thing happens all the time, but the media almost never talks about it."

The strategy did in fact recall what François Marchadeau had described to me over the telephone, and then on the terrace at Café Marly. Economic warfare. Anything was permitted.

Since I didn't say anything, he grimaced and provoked me:

"Ask Marchadeau if you don't believe me! Apparently the two of you are closer than I thought . . ."

Had the end of my night with Marchadeau been outside the bounds of their agreement? I quickly replayed the sequence of events in my head, so far as I now knew them: François placed an order for me with Rebecca, at David's request. David pretended to discover me during the evening, thereby avoiding the less-than-glamorous scenario of ordering me himself—would I have agreed to see him again, would I have found him all that attractive, if I had known *what* and *who* had made our magical encounter possible? Marchadeau was then supposed to get out of the way, his mission complete. But at the last minute, he changed his mind and invited me to the Hôtel des Charmes, knowing that I would never admit it to my future husband.

It all made sense. After all, David had been looking for a new wife, not the first harlot who came along . . .

It was my turn to grasp his hand. Then to draw myself to him, spontaneously, moved by a swell of emotion. He was as firm and warm as I remembered him. I did not recognize his cologne, a light citrus, just the right amount of acidity.

Why go back to him when I longed for other arms? Guilt? Remorse for having erroneously seen him as a monster?

It was easy to absolve him since, according to his account, there was nothing that needed pardoning. In the end, what could I fault him? Putting together an elaborate scheme to meet me? Using his fortune to make a better, more harmonious, and less dramatic life for himself?

In a way, what with my incessant questions, my obsession with the truth, my reporter's curiosity, which had been piqued by Rebecca and Louie's revelations, I had not been better behaved.

David was perhaps an unstable and wrathful autocrat, a demanding and fickle man who would stop at nothing to get the toys he wanted. But didn't he deserve a woman who really loved him, as opposed to someone obsessed with transparency?

He had shadowy things in his past. I did, too.

I think it was at that exact moment that Professor Band-aid's message finally sunk in: Mom was going to die, regardless of what happened with the American treatment.

Maybe in a month. Maybe a year. Or even, there, then, now. Under these paint-chipped ceilings. And I could not deal with that alone. I needed someone I could count on. I needed a David to cuddle up to for support.

I needed a solid pillar for the fragile structure that I had become.

36

June 17, 2009

When an armistice is fragile, when it is susceptible to new crises, some signs do not lie. I remember studying that in a history course on the Treaty of Versailles, which everyone now agrees contained the seeds of the Second World War.

However, nothing, no bad augur, disturbed the hours that followed. I should have been wary. The peaceful environment that greeted us at Duchesnois House was too perfect to be real.

ARTICLE ONE: PUT DOWN YOUR arms.

Against all expectations, David did not go back to the office. He made a quick call to Chloe, telling her he wouldn't be back to Barlet Tower for the rest of the day. After all, I heard him remind his assistant, it was the eve of his wedding day. Our wedding day.

In a rather comical reversal of roles, he put himself at Armand's service to help him with some last-minute details. The majordomo, red with stress, looked like he was going to drown. My future husband set himself to the task of directing workmen who were erecting the main platform, the temporary stage, and several little tents. I noticed the grass had already begun to yellow with the summer heat.

Article Two: Retreat into your camp.

I took refuge in the bedroom. Felicity had fallen asleep on the marriage contract, which had not left our conjugal bed. Excavating the document from her fur, I began initialing each page. There were three copies and the task proved tedious. Then, I hesitated for a long moment, my pen hovering over the line where I was to sign. If any gesture can be said to be automatic, it's signing one's name. However, ceding to a strange reflex of protection or reserve, I decided not to scribble my usual scrawl. I quickly traced my pen into an "Annabelle Lorand," and though it was indeed my name, signed by my very hand, it wasn't any less a lie. It was still a forgery.

Armand didn't seem to notice when at last I handed him the thick stack of papers and he checked the important pages.

"Now all we have to do is pray that Master Olivo stamps this before tomorrow afternoon," he griped.

"I trust you."

"Oh . . . your dress is back from the tailor. If you try it on now, it might save us a headache tomorrow morning."

ARTICLE THREE: TAKE OFF YOUR uniform and put on your peacetime clothing.

I immediately complied, standing alone in the bedroom in front of the mirror, glowing in the afternoon sun, which bathed the garden-facing side of the house. Through the half-open bay window, I heard workers barking at each other in various languages as well as sharp clanks of metallic pipes being assembled.

After its trip to the seamstress, the Schiaparelli dress was now even more perfectly fitted to my full curves. A second skin, a glove . . . I didn't know how to define the surprising sensation of such a seamless transition between fabric and flesh. And yet, I didn't feel anything as I gazed at myself in this perfect wrapping. I felt alien to the sublime piece. Literally, I felt like I was in somebody else's skin. Playing a role that had not been written for me. My question still remained unanswered, and was haunting me: "*What do I have that's so exceptional?*"

Was the simple girl that I was really worth seventeen years of patience and tenacious searching? What man would be crazy enough to sacrifice so much of his time for such a prosaic prize? All that for this, me, us?

ARTICLE FOUR: HONOR YOUR HEROES.

Lying against Felicity, my nose buried in her warm, fragrant fur, I let my mind wander. My thoughts were, in all appearances, idle, though something deep inside me tightened. And though I was holding *Secret Women*, I hadn't read a page. For the first time in days and days, I had not even written one single word in my Ten-Times-a-Day.

Eros and Thanatos are inextricable. Yes, but sometimes you enter so entirely into the kingdom of one that it becomes impossible to imagine the other. Then, you are one with either sex *or* death, and the other withdraws, agreeing to leave the field open for a time to its eternal partner. A brief interruption in their maddening tango.

That morning, death seemed to win out. My mother's deathbed . . . The dead woman's dress I was now wearing . . . And another deceased woman, whom I would soon be replacing at her husband's side. For his part, he was quite alive.

"YOU WON'T BE ANGRY IF I go out tonight?" I asked David, who was hunched over the guest list with Armand.

"No . . . Of course not. Where are you going?"

"Sophia has put together a last-minute bachelorette party."

"Oh . . . I see. Well, have fun." His forced smile contradicted his words.

"Honestly, I would rather stay here and help . . ."

"Why?"

"It's not really my thing. And I'm not in the mood."

"But you should go out! I'm sure it will be fun. Your Sophia seems like a hoot."

He who had planned our romance down to the last detail, who had locked up every aspect of our union, was now acting so liberal. Now he believed in spontaneity.

As for me, I was trying to convince myself that this lie would be my last. That I would be the best wife possible, regardless of how long our marriage lasted. An hour or a lifetime.

ARTICLE FIVE: REVIEW YOUR PLAN of deterrence.

I had not been surprised to find a new silver package on the table a few minutes earlier. And I had decided against a fleeting idea, which I took as a sign of my good intentions: open it in front of David. Reveal to him how his brother had infiltrated his own plan, and had been trying to steal me from him. Tell him about the Hôtel des Charmes, its rooms without numbers, the rendezvous . . .

But nothing good could come out of driving the wedge between the Barlet brothers any deeper than it already was. The score would be settled soon enough.

In addition to a magnetic key from the Hôtel des Charmes, the box contained a card and an object: a man's black boxer shorts, like the ones I had seen stretched over the buttocks of the men at the Brigantine. Which courtesan did these underthings represent? As I inspected the drawers, one detail caught my eye. In addition to the usual stitching in the front, I noticed seams in the back, over the posterior. My fingers gently explored the fabric, and came across a number of strategically placed buttons. Nothing about them was decorative. They snapped together to create a tiny trap door, not much longer or wider than a stick of gum. I had already seen this kind of thing in women's underwear, though it had always been front-side, for easy access to the vagina. That it was present on the backside was a source of wonder. Though I was instantly brought down to earth by the latest commandment:

8—Thou shalt brave the forbidden.

That is what Louie had in store for me on the eve of my wedding. The back door. The forbidden point of access. The ultimate form of capitulation, for both men and women . . . Opening a new eyelet of pleasure, a new flower of sensation. The idea was at once pleasant and fearsome.

ARTICLE SIX: CONSOLIDATE YOUR ALLIANCES.

I locked myself in the closet, away from prying ears, and called Sophia. No way I was going to that meeting alone.

"How long will it take you to get to the Hôtel des Charmes?" I whispered.

"I'm at work . . ."

"Where? Pigalle?"

"Yeah, I still have four more rotations."

I remembered the last time I saw her there, the red lighting, her finger plunged into her open sex . . .

"Please come. I'll give you the money you'd make."

"Yeah, but if I leave now, I can say good-bye to my job!"

"Fuck, Soph, you call that a job? If you want, David can make two phone calls and find you a position in a real company. No more stripteases for nasty fatsos."

It had just come out of my mouth. I was finally voicing what I really thought of her disgusting work.

"Glad to hear you could help me before I got to this point," she groused.

"I can't go alone," I insisted. "I really need you."

Nothing was more true. I needed a safety. Obviously, Sophia was probably the worst chaperone in a situation where I was trying not to be tempted by my physical desires. But then again I couldn't think of anyone else who could drop everything and come to my rescue.

SO IT WAS THAT THIRTY minutes later, I found a disheveled but punctual Sophia waiting for me in the square by the Hôtel des Charmes, right in front of the blue telephone booth where Louie had already once tortured me.

When we stepped into the lobby, Monsieur Jacques screwed up his forehead in surprise. He had not been expecting a delegation. Sometimes Hotelles came in on the arm of a man, and they always left alone. Never did they arrive here in twos, much less wearing such racy clothing. I set the tone, which was as strained as in our previous exchange:

"Which room?" I asked, cutting to the chase.

"I see you've lost your good manners, Elle . . . It's really a shame."

"Save your airs for paying guests. As you know, all I do is lie down here."

My not-so-hidden allusion to the real goings-on of his hotel made him grimace in irritation. That was Monsieur Jacques, a Tartuffe in a brothel. You could treat yourself to the most shocking perversions in his hotel so long as you never mentioned it in front of him.

He straightened, tugging at his livery, stiffening his neck, readying himself to provide the requested information . . .

"Very good. You are expected in—"

. . . when I interrupted him:

"Wait! Don't tell me. Write it here instead."

I handed him the card with the eighth commandment, blank side up. The suddenness of my decision took him aback.

"Why?"

"Just to see. Please."

He stared at us both; then my friend offered some encouragement of her own:

"Go ahead, since the young lady asked so politely."

He grasped the pen that was always sitting on his counter, the black lacquered one he tended to fiddle with, and wrote out the following in a round and ample script. I recognized it at once:

The Chevalier d'Eon
Fourth floor

My intuition had been spot-on: he was the author of the invitations, and the hotel bellboys—led up by Ysiam—were most likely his errand runners. The Hôtel des Charmes was at the center of Louie's web. It was where he would continue to coax me, so long as this chapter of our relationship was not closed.

"Thank you." I smiled graciously. "That's all I wanted to know for the moment."

We hurried toward the elevators, but suddenly I remembered something and turned around:

"Oh, right . . . I forgot something. Sophia is going to stay outside the door. And you or one of your employees had better not throw her out while I am inside."

"As you wish," he agreed without looking at me.

That night, the redheaded elevator operator was on duty. He was as silent as ever, and simply guided us to the fourth floor, the one with night-blue doors, and to the room at the end of the hall. After he unlocked the door, Sophia bade him leave with a fiery gaze, and he disappeared without further ado, leaving us on the threshold:

"Are you going to be all right, hon?"

"Yeah, don't worry . . ."

"Don't hesitate to yell if there's a problem, okay?"

"Okay. And you, where are you going to be?"

"I saw a service staircase next to the elevator. I'm going to wait behind the door."

"Super."

"Do you want me to call you when I see him?"

I was sure Louie would not miss this rendezvous. Yes, he would be coming in person this time. He wouldn't be sending an audience of sexually excited creatures or one of his male or female doubles.

"No. It wouldn't make a difference. I know what I have to do."

As I said this, I flattened my hand on the collar of my trench. The coat was too warm for the season, despite the fact that it was unlined canvas.

She winked at me one last time for encouragement and disappeared down the dimly lit hallway.

ARTICLE SEVEN: OCCUPY THE ENEMY'S deserted territory.

The Chevalier d'Eon room was brimming with rococo furnishings, which added to the oppressive atmosphere. There was one window, and as in most of the other hotel rooms, it did not open.

A thick Oriental rug, toile de Jouy wall coverings, and heavy carved-wood furniture. The most striking pieces were a dressing table with a tilting mirror and a massive damask headboard. The gilded wood of the bed's structure was topped with a silk canopy in blue, the same shade as the hallway outside.

I was burning up in my rough coat. Sweating, I felt like I was trapped in a straitjacket, and from what I could see of my face in the various reflective surfaces, my discomfort showed on my flushed cheeks. My hand was still cool, and I ran it over my exposed neck, just under my messy bun, hoping for a little relief from the sensation of being cooked alive.

But I resisted the temptation to undress. I didn't want to give away the surprise. That was paramount. It was my turn to be a few steps ahead of him. Just a few. I wanted to prove to him that I wasn't his pawn.

The door opened brusquely; perhaps my hour of liberation had finally come, and I wasn't just thinking of the suffocating coat. For the very first time, he appeared before me without hiding in the shadows. No masks, hoods, or latex suits. The scene hadn't been set to shroud him or confuse me. He was wearing one of his elegant fitted suits, which opened onto a bronze vest. He closed the door behind him with the knob of his cane, bolting it shut. Now we were each other's hostage.

"Good evening, Elle."

Before I had come up with my plan, I had considered a thousand different ways to tackle this situation. Tell him off. Send him to a purgatory of his delusional libido and twisted fantasies. Neither would really do. I suddenly found myself ill-equipped and incapable of uttering a sound. Luckily, I had thought of a plan B.

He took a step in my direction, looked me up and down, from head to toe. He seemed more troubled than happy to see me here, dutifully present. He angled the end of his walking stick toward me in an effort to lift the hem of my coat, from my knees to the midpoint of my thighs. Slowly. Excruciatingly. Sliding his knob under the rough canvas, watching the fabric rise. I waited until the cold metal was high enough between my legs; then I seized it and pulled it hard.

Reflexively, he tightened his grip on the other end of the stick, causing him to lose his balance and fall forward toward the bed.

I know: it's not nice to take advantage of your adversary's handicap.

He crashed into the gilded wood frame, his knees digging into the ground, the wind knocked out of him. Then at last he turned his head toward me.

Only then did I untie my belt and open my trench: naked breasts and torso—all I was wearing were the black cotton boxers he had sent.

ARTICLE EIGHT: ESTABLISH THE RULES for the division of power.

He picked himself up and sat on the edge of the bed. He was not wearing the arrogant smile from our first encounter at the gallery. Nor was he the suffering being, the man crushed by his past, who had taken me to the Tuileries Garden and Malmaison. He was more awestruck than annoyed, and more delighted than surprised. He looked happy, relieved even, that I was at last taking some initiative, and that he no longer needed to set the rules of our games.

I took advantage of all the confusion to slip out of my trench, letting the rigid canvas fall from my body to the ground. Then, gingerly, I stepped out of my heels.

I kneeled between his knees, pulled down his pants, and thrust my hand into his boxers for his penis. It came to attention. A growing plant whose length made up for its small girth. His foreskin retracted without my having to touch it. And the pointed shape of his tip extended from his shaft in perfect harmony. Semen had already begun to pearl on the tip's opening, and was on the verge of dripping over his gland and moistening the whole purpled rod.

I pressed my hands firmly into his thighs to prevent him from moving. Then, under his flabbergasted and powerless gaze, I dived in head first, my tongue shooting toward the base of his head. Lapping like a kitten, I licked up the drop of thick fluid and began sucking the circumference of his tip, which glistened with saliva and shone with desire. Then, without warning, I swallowed him whole.

"No . . . Not like that . . . ," he moaned. But his words directly contradicted his member, which was now comfortably lodged in my throat.

As my mouth encircled him, his hips thrust forward, begging for more, harder, faster. But with each pitch of his pelvis,

I withdrew, abandoning his sex for a second. I wanted to draw out his suffering and heighten his desire. I let the interludes grow longer and longer until I could fit in a few words:

"What do you consider forbidden?"

Thrusting him all the way into my mouth. Surprised how pleasurable it was for me.

"Possessing your brother's wife?"

Rolling my tongue over his swollen gland. It was on the verge of exploding, on the verge of unleashing its white tide, of invading me. The odor of my sex emerging now.

"Lying to her? . . . Making her come? Is that part of your plan for vengeance?"

Inserting the tip of my tongue in his meatus, feeling him withdraw in surprise by my intrusion into such a sensitive area. Resisting the urge to insert a finger inside myself. Feeling the sensitivity of my uterus, which I could tell was growing increasingly impatient.

"Isn't that enough?"

Accelerating the back-and-forth movement. Making smacking sounds—I had a lover once who swore they added to his excitement and pleasure.

"I've already told David everything."

Pushing his torso against the bed. Denying my victim any possibility of escape.

"What?" he growled.

Devoting myself once more to his ravished penis, which was now victim of my caprice. Losing him between my gleaming lips, my mouth wide open for a moment, before my cheeks contracted around him again.

I thrust him in me to the point of suffocation. He, too, became breathless. Speechless.

"But *he* loves me, you see."

He tried to break free. But his flesh quivered in my mouth, and I pressed my forehead into his lower abdomen to prevent mutiny. I was in charge now, and I intended to remain so.

"He forgave me for everything."

A last thrust, followed by a spasm: we were nearing the end.

"Stop!" he yelled. "I said, stop!"

He slapped me without warning. Not very hard, but with enough force to extract his penis from my lips. We both straightened, surprised by his brutal action. It was a daring move: out of reflex, I easily could have clamped my jaw like a guillotine and torn into his member with my teeth, cutting him in half.

"You don't understand," he said, his hard member still sticking out of his zipper.

"What don't I understand? That you're trying to make him pay for Aurora's death? That you've been using my activity at Belles de Nuit, an agency David created to find me, to blackmail me?"

He suddenly looked as I'd seen him at Malmaison: sunken-cheeked, heavyhearted.

"That's not it . . . ," he muttered. He was more vulnerable than I had ever seen him.

"What, then?" I practically screamed. "What are we doing here . . . but betraying David?"

His tell. The fleshy dimple that appears when he isn't lying.

"We're executing his plan."

"Excuse me?"

"His plan . . . ," he repeated, blank-faced.

"He isn't doing all this to hurt David," Rebecca had said.

"He's doing it for you."

For me or for his brother?

Suddenly the fog lifted over the devastated landscape. A field of ruins. All this time, I had thought they were rivals when really they were accomplices.

"You want me to believe that David asked you to bring me here, to these rooms?"

He nodded.

"Everything, the packages, the commandments . . . It was his idea?"

"Yes," he said sadly. "The idea, I mean. He let me improvise when it came to the details."

My head was spinning. I reached for the nearest piece of furniture for support, a writing table with a million little drawers.

It was worse than I ever could have imagined. I had not abandoned myself to this debauchery for as noble a cause as resentment or rancor. I was just the erotic accessory of two madmen. Two brothers who were crazy enough to share their fantasies, as well as their toys.

"But it's not what you think," he quickly added.

"Really? Because there can be a good reason behind this . . ."

I swept my arm over the room, indicating the hotel and all of our rendezvous. As I searched for the right word, I replayed every scene, one by one. They had gotten spicier, rawer, more ferocious and anonymous, giving way to the birth of my avid sex.

" . . . behind this shit!"

"Yes . . . ," he said, lowering his eyes.

"Go ahead! Tell me!"

His eyes showed a tenderness I had never seen in him. He took a deep breath before starting in on what seemed like a confession.

"He didn't want you to be like her."

Aurora. The alpha and omega of femininity according to the Barlet brothers. The standard against which they measured me, despite almost two decades of searching and incommensurable efforts to find me.

Oh, I understood what he meant. I saw what they had considered to be her sin, and what they had hoped to correct in me this time around: her sexuality. I, her replacement, would not be a doll that suffered and could not feel pleasure. To meet David's desire for perfection, they would refashion me, awaken my senses, titillate my desires, stimulate every part of my body and mind. The Elle doll would be a pleasure machine.

"He wanted you to be . . ."

He was looking for the right term, a word that, like everything that came out of his mouth, could be composed from the letters written into his own flesh. His words, body, and desire were one.

"He wanted me to be what? Your thing? Is that it? A woman you can humiliate in hotels and backrooms?"

"No. He wanted you to be complete."

I could almost see the quotation marks flying around me. Me, the incomplete woman.

I was as devastated as a defeated boxer. But I didn't wait around for the bell or the next round. I drew my hand to my hair and tugged out my comb. Before he knew what was happening, I was standing in front of him, pressing the silver object into his throat, threatening to draw blood. He tried to grab my wrist, but I held firm, gathering strength from some hitherto untapped source.

"You and David are right about one thing . . ."

"Put that thing down," he begged.

"I'll never be an Aurora. I'll never let either one of you crush me."

I pressed the metallic point harder into his skin. I could have stabbed him with it right then, leaving him for dead amid that overdone decor. A victim of his own plot, killed by his main character. I could have given in to my base instinct, the imperious need to finish him, which was more powerful than any of my most visceral desires.

"Elle, drop the comb . . . Now."

I softened my tone, but the threat was still there, the silver tooth still flush against his neck.

"I'll drop it. But first, I want you to hear one thing, Louie: this game you've been playing with me, it's over."

"Yes, I know . . . ," he moaned, a far cry from his usual arrogant tone.

"Now, I give myself whenever and to whomever I please. I *give*, do you understand? I'm not for sale. I'm not hawking myself. And no one is in charge of my body but me."

"Elle . . . Listen to me."

"No!" I gnashed. I didn't want to let him talk for one second. "You listen to me. Tomorrow I'm marrying David, whether you like it or not. If he's been manipulating me like you say . . . or if this is just another one of your ruses. I don't care. And I'm not going to bed with anyone but him. All I want is my husband."

"Please, Elle . . . there's something else."

I was deaf. Hard. Strong. There was nothing he could say that would make me change my mind.

"Go ahead, fuck every girl in Belles de Nuit's catalogue. I don't care."

Three knocks on the door drew me out of my trance.

"Elle? Elle, hon, are you okay in there?"

Sophia was getting worried. She must have heard the commotion and dampened sounds of our fight.

I dropped the comb on the parquet, where it bounced and clattered. Before he could get up, his pants crumpled around his ankles, I grabbed my coat from the floor and headed for the door. Still naked. At last I had shed the role those two had been making me play.

At the exact same moment, echoing the tintinnabulation of my hair accessory, the giant hourglass in Duchesnois House broke. I discovered it when I got home an hour later.

Thousands of shattered pieces scattered over the entry floor. Thousands of shards.

The timekeeper had been a few hours early, and had already finished its countdown. The fate it had been anticipating was now frozen in the little pile of sand in the middle of the debris: I would marry David Barlet. I would not escape my destiny, even if it was written by another. I would be his wife, his mistress, and more than that if he asked me; I would be attentive to his needs, though without ignoring my own, without losing myself in his past pain. Under no circumstance would I be an Aurora.

No. I would be me.

37

June 18, 2009

Nine o'clock and it was sparkling. The sun, eager to begin its day, was already bathing our bedroom in generous rays. David's contact at the Weather Channel had kept his promise: it was a gorgeous day, not a cloud in the sky. That was my first thought, the morning of our wedding day.

I awoke much too late for such an event. Sleeping Beauty lost in eternal slumber (it had taken me a long while to find sleep after I had gotten home from the Hôtel des Charmes), I was waiting for the kiss of redemption from my sweet prince.

"Good morning, Mrs. my wife!" David beamed when at last I opened my eyes.

Seated at the edge of the bed, he was wearing khakis and a light-yellow polo. I could already hear the busy chatter of people bustling around the house, courtyard and garden included.

"In three hours, dear sir," I echoed his playful tone, pointing to the shorter of the two steel clock hands. "Not before. For the moment, I am Miss your fiancée."

"Whatever the missus wishes. Still, the mister would like to remind Miss his fiancée that she has just barely enough time to get ready."

As he spoke, I noticed that the silk armband had changed color. It was usually pearly white, but now it was a light gray. The change was so subtle that, depending on the light and angle, it could easily be confused with the other version. I presumed, however, that this one matched David's gray suit of the day better.

"You're not dressed?" I asked.

"No. There are still a ton of things to do, and since it's supposed to be hot, I don't want to get armpit stains on my suit."

There we were. Smiling, beautiful, happy. I spoke without artifice, trying to be as carefree and casual as possible. And yet I also had to remain extremely concentrated so as not to betray the fact that I had recently learned a lot of things about him. David the manipulator. The pervert. A man who was crazy or sad enough—the same thing, really—to devote seventeen years of his life to bag an ordinary girl like me. And then twist her mind and body to make her conform to his painful memories. One woman for another, but this time she fit his expectations so well that no sickness or accident could tarnish his prefabricated happiness.

"Okay. You'd better get going! I'm sure Armand has lots for you to do." I tried not to force my smile.

"Oh, yeah. It isn't work that's lacking!" he cried as he left.

BEFORE DONNING MY CEREMONIAL GARB, and after being primped by the hairdresser and makeup girl, I threw on some gray sweats and went downstairs. The beehive of activity was impressive, exhilarating, even: each person seemed to be following an invisible thread tied tautly between the starting point and finish line. All the relevant trades were hard at work: hostesses, cloakroom attendants, laborers, gardeners, cooks, sommeliers, waiters and busboys, florists, laundrywomen, pyrotechnists, roadies and sound techs, and all manner of extras for particular guests and other functions; I had trouble identifying everyone.

"Hello, Armand," I called to the majordomo.

"Hello, Elle. Best wishes for this magnificent day!"

"Thanks."

His awkward formality made me uneasy, so much so that I hastened to change the subject.

"What are those people doing in the garden?"

I nodded discreetly in the direction of two elderly women, both wearing white cotton outfits, their hair wrapped in bright scarves. They were crisscrossing the space where the tables were set up. One held a clock, while the other raised a finger in the air.

"Oh, those are the feng shui ladies."

"Feng shui?" I asked, surprised.

"Yes. I wasn't supposed to say anything, but it's a present from Louie: he hired some specialists to survey the reception space to ensure that your wedding unfolds under the best possible conditions."

Question: Is there such thing as erotic feng shui? Can we influence the nature and quality of our encounters by arranging the space in which they take place? Would my clitoris be more sensitive depending on furniture placement and wall color? My anus more susceptible to dilate for those interested in exploring? Would my lover's erection be harder?

My advice: Choose orange for multiple orgasms!

Handwritten note by me, 6/18/2009

FROM ANYONE ELSE, THE GIFT would have been surprising, but I recognized my future brother-in-law—a man devoted to places and their memories—in it. I wondered if he would take the same precautions with his new residence, Mademoiselle Mars's old house. Probably . . . That reminded me of another question: When would he be moving in? When would the man who had subjected me to so much humiliation and distress over the past few weeks, the man who had also exposed me to such exciting intensity—when would he be our neighbor?

I left the old servant to his emergencies and continued my rounds. There was not a nook or cranny that had not been touched by the industrious army. Avoiding coatracks and platters, chairs and desks, zigzagging between tables and decorated trolleys, was a sport unto itself. I refrained from tallying the unbelievable quantity of provisions, all wrapped with incredible care. Some food items disappeared under silver domes or aluminum foil; others I barely had time to see. Amid this mountain of delicacies, I was reminded of the queen of foodies who could no longer enjoy sugared treasures, not even a crumb.

I had not been away from my phone since I'd been awake but had been delaying a call to the nurse on duty. She concisely informed me that my mother had regained consciousness but that she was still very weak. My mother's words, like her days, were numbered. From now on, she would speak parsimoniously, stripping every sentence down to the bare essentials. Listening to others also seemed to exhaust her. "I think she's kind of saving herself for you," the nurse said, making me feel guilty. At least she spared me the fateful question, the one I dreaded most: *When are you coming to see her?*

When it would be too late? When it would no longer be a question of days or hours but minutes? When she wouldn't be able to recognize me anymore?

My wandering had at least one virtue: to clear my head. I floated through the different rooms and people, careful not to get in the way. When I got to the main tent, which the workers had finished setting up the night before, I approached a young man wearing a white shirt and black vest. He was laying out name cards on immaculate porcelain plates. He seemed very young, his guest list and seating chart in one hand, his eyebrows furrowing. His level of concentration made me smile.

"Hello. How is everything going?"

"Hello . . . ," he replied, barely raising his eyes.

"I am . . . I'm the bride," I said, feeling like I should introduce myself.

My clothing contradicted this assertion, so I pointed to my well-coiffed hair, twirling a finger around the high bun.

He interrupted what he was doing and straightened at once to face me, as though I had caught him doing something he shouldn't:

"Oh, sorry! Hello, Madame! I mean, Mademoiselle. Congratulations."

I almost burst out laughing, but instead offered a playful and what I hoped was a reassuring smile.

"Thanks. But I don't want to keep you from your work."

Then I noticed the tented rectangular card he had just set on the immaculate tablecloth, from which wafted the heady scent of freshly cut flowers. LUC DORÉ, it said. To the surprise of the young man, I quickly reached for it. But it wasn't the name of the guest that made my chest tighten.

Luc Doré

No, it was the peculiar script. The very same handwriting as in my Ten-Times-a-Day.

"Excuse me," I disturbed the young man again. "Do you know who wrote the names on these cards?"

"Yes, Mademoiselle. It was Monsieur Armand."

"Are you sure?"

He puffed himself up a little, delighted to be asked about something more noble than where to place name tags, though he remained polite.

"Absolutely. I saw him do it earlier. The ink isn't even dry on all of them."

I shivered at this thought: Armand, ever Louie's accomplice, taking dictation, writing out all the scandalous things I had read over the past weeks. What had Louie offered him in exchange that would have gotten him to accept such a disgusting and thankless task? A few extra bottles? A blind eye to his pilfering from the family wine cellar?

Or was Armand as perverse as the man who had been commissioning his services? Never trust seemingly innocent old men. You never know what kind of desires are crawling in their corduroy pants, or what kind of life lies anything but dormant under their cable-stitched vests.

I wonder if Louie also kept a journal of our encounters.
Did he keep a record somewhere of what he'd felt at each
of our meetings? ~~Does he also have a Ten-Times-a-Day~~

that's even more hard-core?

He who holds his writing so dear, who wishes he could live off his pen. What words might he have found to express my turmoil, my body that hungered for him, my sex being penetrated by all those objects he had given me as a substitute for himself?

Handwritten note by me, 6/18/2009

OF COURSE, THE GUILTY MAN was nowhere to be found. Wherever I asked, I was sent to another part of the building. Ultimately, I didn't care. I knew enough already.

The door rang incessantly, its perky chime announcing a parade of suppliers and deliveries: food, flowers, bottles, various dishes and fabrics, sound or pyrotechnic equipment, etc.

I was greeted by a different kind of package when I walked through the entry on my way to the bedroom:

"It's me!"

Sophia, draped in the most scandalous dress I had ever seen, was standing there, her arms raised in a triumphant V, her hips swayed to one side in an alluring fashion.

"That's right, hon. Jaw-dropping."

She kept her pose, no doubt waiting for me to circle her a couple of times in rapture! The scrap of fabric was not only extremely close-fitting but also transparent in parts. It was shorter than any other miniskirt you could find in normal stores. Surprisingly, maybe because of its color—off-white—it wasn't vulgar.

"Holy cow! Are you looking for a man?"

"A man, I don't know . . . But I think I've found *it*!"

She didn't need to specify. I knew her well enough—her

and her obsessions—to know what she meant: her ideal outfit, the one that would make her irresistible to men. The perfect mantrap.

I nodded and made an exaggerated face in approval.

"It looks like it. Short of melting fabric to your skin, I don't see how it could get any tighter. Where did you find this marvel?"

"While Peggy and I were sorting through her old clothes. Can you believe it? She was going to throw it away!"

"But isn't Peggy two sizes smaller than you?"

"Exactly! You think you're going to turn heads by wearing clothing your size?" she argued cheekily.

"Well, when you put it like that . . ."

She smiled brightly, erasing the memory of the troubling events from the night before.

"Well, anyway. Don't you have another dress to show me?"

On the way to my bedroom, she stopped in front of every half-open door to marvel at the sumptuous decor.

"When you told me about this place, I never imagined it was so luxurious!"

I shrugged, as if to apologize and signal that, like her, I was just a guest. In no way was I responsible for this abundance of refinement. Sophia looked like she was really going to faint when at last I took out the Schiaparelli from its impressive garment bag and carefully laid it on the bed.

When she got over the shock, Sophia said in a humorous tone, her love for me far greater than any sense of bitterness or jealousy:

"Remind me to marry a billionaire in my next life. Okay?"

"No problem." I laughed. "I'll remind you."

"Will you put it on now?" she asked eagerly.

I stared at her for a second, as an idea, one worthy of our college days, dawned on me and a smile spread across my face.

"Just a second . . . I have an idea."

Then I headed into the closet, where I found bobbins of thread, a pouch filled with needles, and several scraps of colored felt.

"Wait . . . You're kidding, right?" Sophia said as I came back out.

She saw where I was going with this. She knew how much I loved to sew.

"Does it look like it?" I challenged as I threaded a needle.

"Crap, Elle, you can't customize your wedding dress! Seriously!"

"Hmm . . . You're right. It's a little too *serious* for my taste."

She was practically choking with indignation, her hand reaching toward mine to stop me from committing such blasphemy.

"No, seriously, do you know how much a dress like that costs?"

To be honest, I don't know what had gotten into me. The simplest answer that came to mind was: I wanted to be myself.

"Yes, exactly . . . ," I agreed. "That is exactly the problem: I know the price."

And I wasn't one hundred percent sure that I wanted to pay it, either today or any day. So then, why not make this silken burden more agreeable? Why not add a little color, *my* colors? Hopefully, then I could forget the woman for whom this dress had been a shroud.

Intuition: Our fantasies are like the scraps of fabric I use
to spice up my dresses. You add them here or there, livening

your real-life with color, breaking out of the monotony. You
can use them to customize your sexuality.

Some examples: A mouth welded to my sex; a torso
glued to my ass; a tongue licking my vagina from top to
bottom, as though washing it . . .

Handwritten note by me, 6/18/2009

WITH A FEW SNIPS OF my scissors and some simple stitching, I made a field of wildflowers, purposely rough and haphazardly placed. I attached them to the dress with a topstitching that I tried to make as visible as possible.

Sophia didn't know what to say or do to stop me from committing such carnage.

"Aren't you scared of how David will react?"

"Scared? No . . . I'm not scared anymore," I replied without one second's hesitation.

As I thrust my needle into the fabric with rage, I told her about Armand's complicity—this time there was proof—in the Barlet brothers' detective-novel plots. Knowing that, I felt at liberty to plant a few seeds of fantasy and rebellion in their perfect little story line. They were so relentless I very well could follow in Aurora's footsteps.

"Now I understand how Louie knew so much about me before we even met. Easy: he had two spies!"

"Know what, exactly?" Sophia asked.

"You wouldn't believe it. Things that only come up in pillow talk."

Sophia has a high tolerance for twisted plans. But even she has her limits, her morals. And respect for privacy is one of them.

"Do you mean David told him about how you fucked?"

"Based on some of the messages . . ."

I paused a second to take inventory of all the little secrets I had told David—if he wasn't the source, then I didn't even want to know where Louie was getting his information—which had later appeared in the notebook: the first time I had touched myself; how I liked doing it doggy-style; my abnormal sensitivity to intimate smells; my orgasms, how I screamed *no* instead of *yes* . . .

" . . . There's no other possible explanation."

"Gross!" Sophia sneered like a teenager.

We giggled, covering our mouths with massive tufts of silk.

My alterations were soon finished. Sophia didn't say much, since she knew I really didn't give a damn if she cried murder. Then, like that time when David took me on the dining room table, the one time when he actually made me come, I stepped into that amazing dress.

"Wow! Just: wow!" she exclaimed, wide-eyed. "I don't know if mine says 'fuck me' . . . but yours definitely screams 'marry me.'"

I was laughing my head off when my phone started vibrating. I had set it on the bed while sewing. I didn't recognize the number.

Under Sophia's concerned gaze, I entered into a conversation with an impressive number of monosyllabic affirmations.

"Was that the hospital?"

"Yes . . . ," I whispered.

"It's . . ."

The end. The limit. The conclusion. The very last breath. Everyone's terminus, and for one woman in particular. Sophia had all manner of euphemisms to choose from, but in the end, she was speechless.

I put my phone on the bed, as though the thick comforter might swallow it up, together with all the bad news.

"No, it's not over yet . . . but she's asking for me. Apparently, she's really insisting. I have to go."

"Do you want me to come?"

"No . . . No, stay here with Armand. He's going to need you if we have to delay things."

"Okay. What time do the guests arrive?"

"Noon, for cocktails."

I threw on the first pair of ballet flats I could find and headed for the stairs without saying another word. Sophia called behind me:

"Hey! Aren't you going to tell David?"

"You do it," I yelled over my shoulder.

"But he doesn't even know me!"

Her powerless cry did not slow me down. I was already outside, running west down Rue de la Tour-des-Dames, my feet hitting the hot asphalt like a tam-tam drum. With every step, a muffled but skull-splitting vibration throbbed through my temples.

I made my way to the nearest taxi station, in front of the Église de la Trinité. A white Peugeot was waiting when I arrived, the black chauffeur spilling out the window, along with the sputtering sounds of the Formula One. He sped as fast as one of those race cars, making it to Max Fourestier Hospital in no time.

ONE COULD SEE DEATH'S DIFFERENT faces in the oncology wing: bald and emaciated, the pajamaed infirm dragging their drips like they were a thousand years old, exhausted nurses who didn't look much better than their patients . . . Everyone was so out of it that no one noticed my eccentric outfit, nor even my entry into Mom's room outside of visiting hours.

As for me, I only saw her. She was buried under even more tubes than on my last visit. Though it was weak, the blinking of her eyes told me she was still there, alert. I drew my chair up to her bed and leaned over her dying body.

"Mom . . . Mom, it's me, it's Elle."

She blinked to show she understood. I didn't need a doctor to give me the prognosis: she was out of her coma, but this was her last encore before the end. This time it was definitive.

We would never see America together. We would never have the chance to try for a miracle across the ocean. The adventure stopped here.

"I can see that you hear me, but are you able to speak?"

Her yes was so weak that it almost could have been confused with a timid gurgle from her drip.

"Come closer," she mouthed, too breathless to say the words out loud. "It's Louie . . ."

She was about to die, and her last words were of the man who had been torturing and exciting me. A man whose name she had never before spoken in my presence, and with whom she had been exchanging secrets.

"What is it? What did he do to you, Mom?"

" . . . He gave me all this."

All I noticed were two giant flower bouquets and a box of chocolate as large as her bedside table. But I knew she was referring to more than these trifles, and that she also saw him as an anonymous benefactor who had showered her with presents.

"I know . . . But how did you . . ."

She placed a trembling, bony finger on my lips, silencing me. As if to say that my questions were superfluous, that she had more answers for me than I questions.

"He came to deliver them . . ."

"Today, you mean?"

"No. Every time."

"Louie? He came to see you in Nanterre?"

I never would have guessed that. Already the fact that they spoke over the phone was a surprise. But Louie visiting Maude at her little house on Rue Rigault . . . it was beyond comprehension.

She nodded.

"Did he come often?"

Then something strange happened. A smile slowly spread across her face, transforming its fading features into a beaming icon.

Nevertheless, the effort to speak still seemed colossal.

"Almost every day. And when he couldn't come, he called."

The famous phone calls Fred had discovered. Their memory seemed to tear her from the relentless pain that held her in its jaws like a bad dog.

There was no denying that, no matter Louie Barlet's motivations, he had brought my mother comfort—joy, even—that I had been incapable of offering. It was absurd, unjust. I had to bite the inside of my cheeks to keep myself from exploding.

"Mom . . . I have something important to ask you: When did Louie start visiting you? Do you remember?"

"Yes, yes . . . I'm dying, not crazy!" she protested in a barely audible voice, a final surge before death. "It must be three months. Maybe more."

In other words, probably before I first met David, during the period I now thought of as the "approach." Once they had gotten a sense of the specimen that I was, the two Barlet brothers had patiently started acquainting themselves with the people—Maude, Sophia, Fred, etc.—who made up my circle of intimates. That way none of the people I loved would be against my entry into their family, and the infernal duo would only have to call on them to get to me.

But that didn't exactly explain why Louie had gone to see my mother so often. The fact that she had been flattered to receive such attention was understandable. But what pleasure did that dandy take in seeing her? My mother was old, poor, unsophisticated—everything that ought to have sent that erotomaniacal aesthete running. Why play his role any more than was necessary?

"Why didn't you ever tell me?"

"He didn't want me to. It was our little secret. Like the *Stets*."

"You mean the States?" I corrected without thinking.

"Yes. He was supposed to come with me," she said as proudly as her thready voice would allow.

I thought she was delirious, and that it was the morphine talking. The translucent liquid dripped through tubes into her veins in what were no doubt considerable doses.

"Are you sure?"

"Look in my bag . . ."

Her exhausted, clouded, and bloodshot eyes pointed to the coffee table on the other side of the bed.

Her tired leather bag did not contain much, and I had no trouble digging out a red, white, and blue envelope on which was embossed a lined planisphere. Inside, I found not one but two round-trip tickets for Los Angeles, dated June 20, in business class.

Her reluctance for me to join her now took on new meaning. It hadn't been about selflessness, or the sacrifice of a mother for her child. My torturer and my mother were apparently so close that she had fallen into his traps all by herself. Thanks to him, she had been able to revisit what it was like to be twenty-one and taste the lightness and folly of youth. And for that I thanked him.

She breathed deeply, in a way I found concerning. Exhausted from our exchange, however brief, she added:

"I think he loves you a lot, too . . ."

I didn't know what to say to that, so I asked:

"Did he say that?"

She was out of breath and couldn't utter another word. Instead, she nodded almost imperceptibly.

"When?"

Again, she used her eyes to point: the fresh flowers, the box of untouched chocolates . . . both things that had not been there the night before. The message was clear: today. This morning. Maybe even just before I got there.

Then her tired gaze noticed my dress, and she gathered what little energy she had left to take it all in and say:

"You are so beautiful. Louie must be so proud."

I did not correct her on my fiancé's first name. But maybe it hadn't been an error. Perhaps it was her way of sanctifying a choice she'd noticed slowly growing in me. Of giving me her blessing.

I held her head in my hands and buried my nose in her neck, which was now a bony hollow, a swath of desiccated gray flesh. Despite the overwhelming scent of detergent and medicine, I still caught a whiff of her rose perfume. Or maybe I imagined it, I couldn't say. I stayed like that for a while, taking solace in her touch. I couldn't get enough of her—I, her daughter, who had already received so much and given so little. Even these past few weeks, busy as I had been with my false illusions.

During that time, Louie had been by her side. He had given her comfort and attenuated the painful side effects of her sickness. Her mouth must have felt less dry to her, her dizziness less affecting, her moments of weakness more surmountable.

He would forever be the angel of her final days.

Mom blinked several times, trying to catch my attention. Or was it simply a reflex, a muscular tremor announcing the end?

Her catheter clicked, releasing what seemed to me like a rather large dose of analgesic. The screen monitoring her heart remained unchanged. Still, I felt her go into a state of consciousness that I could not access. It was impossible to say whether or not she would be back again, maybe once more or even several times, before it was all over. My face was practically touching hers, but her irises avoided me. Her eyelids shuttered, and she kept looking left. What had she wanted to tell me?

I looked around the room as though I were seeing it for the first time. Everything was empty and jaundiced. Outside of Louie's gifts, the only noticeable object was a little pink sweater that the good Dr. Poulain must have grabbed for Mom on their way out of the house to the ambulance.

The one and only closet was divided into hanging and shelf space and was half open. I almost fell from my chair when I noticed the package occupying one of its shelves.

A silver package. It appeared that Louie had left it there himself, for me.

My head was spinning, but I still managed to stand and collect the package from the dusty particle board. Impatiently, I tore the paper. At the bottom, I found just one card on which was written, as usual, a commandment:

9—*Thou shalt marry his fantasies.*

What fantasies? And more importantly, whose?

I placed the card on the yellow sheet, a pure little rectangle that contrasted sharply with its environs. I removed the tissue paper from the box. I was so surprised by what I found underneath that I did not move for several seconds. Then, with bated breath, I grabbed the little stack of photos and started looking at them, one by one. I struggled not to rush through them. I didn't want to miss any details.

Meanwhile, starting with the very first snapshot—a picture taken on the steps of some town hall (in Dinard?) on David and Aurora's wedding day—I had the feeling I was at last coming out of months of blindness. I was seeing things clearly for the first time. The evidence was before me, on that yellowed paper. It bored into my eyes. Would I have preferred not to have seen? Not to have known?

Picture after picture. I would have thought the effect would dissipate, become less striking, less flagrant. But the opposite occurred. The more I saw Aurora such as she had been, such as she had lived—here arm in arm with Hortensia by the sea, there lying on the beach in a polka-dot bikini—the more I could not deny the horrible truth, the implacable fact that was as cutting as the rocks that had killed her: I was her doppelganger. And she was mine. Twin sisters born two decades apart, both fallen victim to a common fate.

It wasn't just a vague resemblance. We had the same curves, the same long brown hair, green eyes, and freckles over our noses and cheeks. In every way, down to the specific shape of our face, the fold of our eyelids, and the fleshy indecency of our lips, everything was the same.

"I'll never be an Aurora," I remembered promising myself the night before at the Hôtel des Charmes, with Louie at my mercy. And yet that is what I had been, ever since the second when David—or was it Louie or Rebecca?—had seen me in the Belles de Nuit catalogue . . . and in each moment after that: the miraculous night when David and I first met, his proposal on the boat . . . even during those times when I felt like a lowly ball in a game of racquets between the two brothers.

In the last three pictures, Aurora was wearing a little corolla dress that fell just above her knees. Its giant flowers and cut were strikingly similar to the one the girl in wardrobe at BTV had chosen for me to wear on my first show. Had David given her the idea? Or had it been a coincidence, as he had claimed, that explained his impulsive decision not to air my show?

Seventeen years to find her clone. No doubt David had rejected dozens of potential candidates. Until me. Until I appeared, the ghost of another woman, the palimpsest of a history that was not my own and that they wanted to thrust upon me.

But I wasn't more perfect than Aurora, Aurora the madwoman, Aurora the untouchable, the frigid—no more than she had been before me. That's where Louie and his mission came in: erase the pure memory of the saint and make me into a full and sensual woman with desires and orgasms, where the original had gotten lost in a world stripped of all pleasure, a place of suffering. That had been the reason behind every rendezvous: my sexual education. "All I do is reveal," he had said in a moment of sincerity. Reveal to me the infinitely colorful palette of pleasurable options, while preserving me intact for his brother. That is why he had never penetrated me. That is why he had upheld the distance between student and teacher.

The last picture also came as a shock. It had been taken at the Sauvage Gallery the night Louie and I had first met. I hadn't realized someone had taken our picture. We were facing each other. Looking at each other intensely. Both lost in that strange tension between us. It wasn't the best memory I had of him. And yet it acted like liquid magic, exciting the silver salts of my memory: Louie who had watched over my mother; Louie who had given Sophia what she'd needed to survive in a time of desperation; Louie who had found a job for Fred; Louie who had written my name into the city . . . Louie who, despite his brother's mission for him, had been like a guardian angel in these troubled times.

Louie who, to use Rebecca's words, had done it all for me. Only for me. And in spite of his brother.

"Is everything okay, Mademoiselle?"

I was panting and lost like a little girl in my rumpled wedding dress, holding my stack of photographs. The nurse who ran into me in the hall caught me at my lowest. My sobs were long and uninterrupted, at once heavy and comforting. Before leaving my mother's side, I had said my tender good-byes, kissing her forehead, then her cheeks. There was nothing more I could do. I could not bear to see what would come next. I had closed her eyelids, still warm and trembling, over her pupils, where the light was slowly dying, two little flames that death would soon extinguish forever.

The nurse asked again:

"Are you okay? Do you want to sit down? Or have a glass of water?"

What could I say? That I had lost a mother and gained a lover in the same moment? That I was leaving my mom's deathbed to run into the arms of the one I loved? That at last my physical desires and my heart were in alignment? That I could finally give free rein to what I had felt during our promenades and also, though more fleetingly, when we'd met at the Hôtel des Charmes? And that the more the real Louie—who was so different from all the masks he wore and so close to the picture Rebecca had painted—showed himself, the more my doubts disappeared?

I could have said nothing. Or opted for something prosaic.

But I chose otherwise. Another angle.

I let a gentle smile spread over my tear-soaked lips.

"Thanks. I'm *going* to be fine . . . I'm going to be much better, now."

38

Nothing was less sure. I was just a disheveled bride with tears running down my face. I tiptoed down the hall, which smelled of bleach and ether. I pitched from wall to wall, a tiny metallic pinball shooting into my new life. I was ready . . .

. . . and yet still so uncertain. Just a hair away from collapsing onto the green linoleum. Incapable of seeing beyond my present pain.

Annabelle = Aurora. A simple equation, but one I simply could not wrap my head around, much less accept.

And what if that declaration in pictures was Louie's final ruse? What if I was entering into the last phase of David's plan, a plan his brother had carried out—for reasons that still escaped me (guilt?)—to the letter?

However, I had seen him be sincere, thanks to his tell, his dimple. "There's something else," he had murmured the night before as I was leaving the room. Something else to tell me, to show me . . . or to inflict upon me?

THE PEOPLE WAITING FOR BUS 378 took no notice of my outfit or distress. They were too busy toting heavy bags and ruminating over their own problems. I couldn't be the first disheveled bride they'd seen riding the bus. That was one of the benefits of poor neighborhoods: everyone had too many of their own issues to care about those of others. A form of indifferent respect protected everyone's individual misery.

At last the bus came, and the compact little group pressed up against the automatic door, which opened with a *shhk*.

I had left Duchesnois House in such haste that I had nothing on me except a little pouch with my keys and a pack of tissues that I had been using to sponge up tears and makeup. The taxi I'd taken to get there had been paid for by BTV. But I was completely without resources when the driver, a man with a shaved head and a hoop in his right ear, said:

"Your ticket, Mademoiselle . . ."

"Oh, right . . . ," I stuttered.

I rummaged through my bag, dropped it in an embarrassing clatter, stooped to pick up my keys from amid impatient shoes, which were on the verge of crushing me and clamoring into the vehicle, when a firm hand helped me up.

"It's okay, she's with me."

The face was not totally alien.

"Super. My congratulations to the young bride," the driver said sarcastically. "But she still has to pay."

The mystery man—brown hair, medium build, in rather elegant weekend wear—quickly dug into the pocket of his jeans and withdrew a two-euro coin, which he slapped onto the counter. The driver's tone seemed to have annoyed him.

"There you go. Happy?"

"Your change," the other replied dryly. "And your ticket."

My savior took the magnetized card, validated it, and guided me to a seat, where I collapsed without saying a word. My gaze was sucked into the uninterrupted row of miserable homes and concrete high-rises. Though the sun was shining, this part of the periphery, an industrial no-man's-land with housing projects and unending strips of highway, had a sinister poetry about it.

"You don't recognize me?" the providential man with the timid smile inquired.

I looked at him, then admitted:

"No . . . I mean, not really."

"Bertrand Passadier. We spoke the other day on the RER train."

One day months ago vaguely floated back to me, like thick fog. What was he doing here, on a Thursday at noon? Was he on vacation already? Had he taken the day off to visit someone? Regardless, I didn't care.

"Maybe," I conceded.

"No, we did. I remember it well. You must have moved to Paris."

I didn't respond. What could I say? How to describe the monumental fiasco that these past few weeks had been? How to share the ruins that my life had become? But a tiny germ of hope had just emerged, at my dying mother's bedside.

"I have. But I'm moving back to Nanterre."

"Really? But what about your dress . . ." He looked at my outfit with surprise and curiosity.

"It's just a costume."

"Oh. That surprised me, too . . ."

This poor guy was always a few steps behind my reality and my lies.

I searched nervously through my pouch, only to discover that I had left my phone in the conjugal bedroom, where I would never sleep again.

"Do you have a phone?" I asked, eyeing him bleakly.

"Yes, of course."

"Could you make a call for me?"

"You mean for me to make it?"

"Yes."

He withdrew the latest smartphone from his jacket and held it toward me.

"You don't want to borrow it?"

"No . . . No, I want you to make the call."

I had no desire to hear Armand lecture me, catch the sound of the brouhaha of guests growing impatient behind him, or listen to David screaming for him to hand over the phone.

I dictated the number for Duchesnois House to a disconcerted Bertrand Passadier, whose index finger hovered over the green button.

"Who is supposed to answer?" he asked.

"It doesn't matter . . . the people I was staying with in Paris."

"What do you want me to tell them exactly?"

"Just say you're calling on behalf of Aurora . . ."

The message seemed fairly obvious to me. That way David would know that I knew. And all the masks would fall, and the way David saw my face would become apparent to all: the image of someone who was not me. That of his dead wife, the one and only Madame David Barlet. His spouse for life. Or, rather, death.

" . . . Aurora, that's your name?" He smiled, hitting on me like an idiot.

"Yes," I lied. "Tell them that Aurora wants her things sent to Nanterre . . . And tell them that she's never coming back."

"Are you sure?"

He had thought our meeting was just a happy coincidence, but now a shadow crossed his face as he realized how dramatic this situation really was.

"Yes."

"And what if the person asks to speak with you?"

"Tell them . . . that I'm not with you. You're just a messenger."

He nodded and did as he was told, repeating what I had said word for word. When I heard confused voices raised over the speaker, I made a sign for him to hang up and cut off the hysteria and efforts to talk to me. The driver, uninhibited by obstacles or traffic lights, had stepped on the accelerator, and the bus 378 was taking me far, far away.

"The place I just called," he pried, though with empathy. "That's your wedding, isn't it?"

"It *was*, yes. But not anymore."

"Are you sure?"

Again I didn't know what to say. I was not sure of anything. Except perhaps my survival instincts, which were telling me to get as far away as possible from Rue de la Tour-des-Dames.

It wasn't hard to imagine what chaos I had left behind me. David drunk with anger. A disappointed Armand. Sophia burdened with justifying my desertion. The other guests, speechless. No one daring believe this Hollywood drama. Everyone unsure whether to politely leave or to stay and comfort the groom I had left in the lurch.

The caterers were no doubt already packing up the foodstuffs, alcohol, sweets. The flowers were already drooping in their vases—an act of indignation—the water stagnating. Everyone was already starting to offer their embarrassed lines, giving false promises to help out in any way, and hurrying to escape this disaster zone, for fear that they, too, would be infected. Some misfortunes are considered contagious.

WHEN WE GOT OFF THE bus at the end of the line with all the other passengers, my Good Samaritan of public transportation handed me his business card, of simple and cheap stock, the kind you can order online:

"Here . . . In case you ever need to talk. About anything."

I took it, but as soon as he disappeared around the corner pharmacy that faced the station, I threw it in the trash. I didn't need a Bertrand Passadier in my life any more than a Fred or a David.

Has Bertrand Passadier been masturbating to me these past couple of weeks? No, the real question is, how many times has he thought about me while masturbating? Had I made him come more than his other mental pictures, or than those bitches he no doubt ogles on the Internet?

We should all have some kind of radar, an erotic crystal ball, to tell us right away if we're going to sleep with someone who attracts us or not. How much disappointment would that nip in the bud? How much tension, conflict, how many wars, even, could be avoided with such a gadget? How much time and energy would be saved for more noble causes? Instead, we spend our lives running after the beautiful and sexy . . .

Handwritten note by me, 6/19/2009

IT FELT STRANGE GETTING BACK to Mom's silent and deserted house. I knew that from now on, I would be the only person there. And though I may have grown up there, I had the impression I was intruding on my mother's stuff, a collection of dusty old things. The whole house still smelled like something was burning. No one had thought to air it out after she'd been rushed to the hospital.

In the living room, next to all the pictures of me, I found what was left of the presents Louie had brought her. Every box and scrap of wrapping paper had been carefully saved. Macaroons, calissons from Aix, fruit candies . . . I inspected them, and idly tasted a few of the remaining treats. I did not want to imagine all the sorting that would have to be done, the trash bags that would have to be filled by the dozen, packing up everything from her life in plastic and taking it to the curb come garbage day.

In my room—I could not even remember the last time I had been there—I was struck by a shiny piece of silver paper crumpled up in the wastepaper basket. It gleamed in the midday light like a fallen disco ball, as comical as it was out of place. At one time, Mom would have emptied it right away, during one of her multiple-times-a-week cleaning sessions. But recently, she hadn't had the strength to make it upstairs, and had made do with minimal tidying.

The home phone rang from the entry, tearing me from my heavy thoughts. I hesitated for a second before running to answer it. After just two rings, it stopped, then started up again after three seconds exactly, then two more rings, then it stopped, and so on: Sophia's and my code, to be used in cases of emergency.

"Soph?"

"It's me. I don't have much time."

"Are you still there?"

"Yes. I mean, I just stepped outside, but David won't leave me alone."

"I'm so sorry . . ."

"Don't be, I swear. The man is insane. Ever since Armand got that phone call from your friend, he's been terrorizing everyone. Screaming at the personnel. He threw some people out who tried to keep him from going berserk . . ."

I had trouble imagining him acting so violent. And yet . . .

"At the same time, he has good reason," I admitted.

"That's why I'm calling: he knows you're at your mom's house. He's coming to get you."

I could always barricade myself in, like Mom and I had done once when Fred came over drunk and angry. I trusted David to come up with better ways to persuade me than banging angrily on a glass door. Didn't he know important people on the police force?

"Thank you, my Soph."

"No problem. But get out of there."

She was right: I needed to leave, and fast. No sense waiting for a confrontation that would only turn against me, and from which I didn't expect to gain anything. The truth was written on my face, on each aspect of me that reminded him of his past. Of *their* past.

"Actually, is Louie there?"

"No, I haven't seen him."

Louie's absence was no accident. He knew I would find his last present right before I was to be married. He knew it would come as a shock. Even the commandment echoed the snapshots and David's plot: *Thou shalt marry his fantasies*.

After hanging up, I climbed the stairs four by four. The silver paper kept eyeing me from its receptacle. Despite its bling and the illusions of its reflective surface, it had been more authentic than any of the presents David had ever given me. Despite all the mystery, it had shown me something about myself that had been buried deep inside. It had given me permission to discover new sensations and desires.

Louie had told me a million times: the games he had made up for me had no other goal but to reveal me to myself. And they had nothing to do with his brother's twisted mind. They came from him, him alone, and his love for me.

What was I waiting for? What more did I need to spur me to action?

I seized the crumpled paper, and discovered a second ball made from the same material hiding underneath the first. The wrapping from his first package. That was just what I needed. That was how I would put an end to the cycle that had begun a dozen days earlier. At the very bottom of the wastepaper basket, I at last found the original box.

I knew what I had to do before running. I didn't have any doubts about the contents or the recipient. As luck had it, there were still condoms in the medicine cabinet, from back when I was with Fred. I took one and placed it in the box. Since I didn't have a blank card, I penned the following order on a Post-it:

10—I shall submit myself to my master.

Aren't the most binding commandments the ones the faithful write for themselves? The ones they choose and write, even in an act of submission . . . I liked the idea of playing with Louie's codes. Of stealing his rhetoric, at the risk of paraphrasing.

But the intention was all mine.

I want to submit myself, open myself up and get wet for you, forever. I want to invent new organs for myself, new orifices, new sexes for your pleasure. I want to change my DNA and give you a body the likes of which no other man has seen. I want to redefine the concept of submission for you. I want to be a woman to replace all others, the one who awakens both the beast and the gentle lamb in you, and at last reconciles both sides in you.

Handwritten note by me, 6/19/2009

I WRAPPED EVERYTHING UP IN haste. All I had left to do was write his name and address on a blank sheet of paper and tape it on the front of the package:

LOUIE BARLET

I wasn't sure which address to put. But since Louie had wanted to live in the shadows, this one made the most sense:

118 Avenue Georges Mandel
75016 Paris

My hand was shaking, my writing sloppy. Still, it was legible enough to make it into the right hands. Hands I imagined tearing the paper before running to me, this time free from fraternal obligations.

I deliberately did not include a time and place to meet. Shouldn't it be obvious? Ten o'clock. He knew where.

As for the room, he wouldn't need his eyes or brains to guess, just his memory. And his nose. I borrowed Mom's rose perfume, which I found in its usual spot on the dresser in her bedroom. I sprayed the package generously. Rose like Château de Malmaison. Rose like Josephine. Rose like the scent of a woman who only wants her Bonaparte.

It was getting late, danger drew nigh, and yet I had not finished with what I had to write. I jotted the following lines in haste on a loose sheet of paper without crossing anything out:

David,

We never truly examine our motivations behind sharing our lives with one man or one woman.

I'm afraid that in your case, with respect to me, you knew all too well.

I do not want to become another, even if you love me like mad, even if you manage to fashion me into the one I am to replace, but without the "faults." Contrary to what I said in my message to Armand, I am Annabelle, Elle, not Aurora. We may look the same on the outside, but our hearts could not be more different. I want to live. I want to enjoy every second.

I will leave you to chase her spirit, and I shall honor my own.

I am truly sorry if some of my future choices hurt you. Let's call it even, then.

Much love,

Elle

I slid my letter into an envelope. I reached under my dress for the pictures of Aurora, which I had tucked under the elastic of my underwear, and included it in the message. I put a stamp on the front and set it on the living room table. I was sure that somehow David would end up finding it.

Finally, I went to the antique rotary phone and dialed the general number for the Barlet Group. I didn't even remember having memorized it.

"Yes, hello, it's Annabelle Lorand, from BTV."

"Hello, could you give me your number, please?"

"Yes, zero, six, eighteen."

I had chosen it, of course. My birthday. Today. June eighteenth. The day that turned my world upside down.

"Perfect. What can I do for you, Mademoiselle?"

"I need you to pick up a letter from 29 Rue Rigault in Nanterre."

"Destination, please?"

"118 Avenue Georges Mandel, in the 16th Arrondissement in Paris."

"Very good. Is it an urgent package?"

"Yes. *Very* urgent," I impressed.

"Got it. Have a nice day . . ."

"Wait! Could you pick it up at 27 Rue Rigault instead?"

"Yes, of course. What's the resident's name?"

"Madame Chappuis. Laure Chappuis."

"Okay. 27 Rue Rigault, then."

"That's right. Thank you."

MADAME CHAPPUIS WAS NOT THE least bit astonished to see me in her home wearing a wedding dress, my makeup smeared in black streaks over my cheeks, nor that I was there just after one o'clock, when the ceremony was supposed to be taking place; even the unusual favor I was asking of her came as no surprise. The only thing she cared about was my mom and her condition. For her, that explained everything. Laure Chappuis loved her neighbor. Like a friend, maybe even like a sister. It could be seen in the two fat tears running down her withered cheeks, taking a little powder with them on the way. After decades of blunt friendship and snide comments, on this day she finally allowed herself to express her true feelings and lose the sourpuss mask.

SHE PROMISED TO TAKE GOOD care of my package and closed the door without another word. Though it had not been my intention, I had just pushed her a little closer to her grave as well.

In my own way, I was escaping the one in which David had wanted to imprison me.

39

My name is Annabelle Caroline Lorand.

But everyone calls me Elle. All my friends, anyway. I was born on June 18, 1986, at exactly ten p.m.

AND AT EXACTLY TEN P.M. on June 18, 2009, on the very day, minute, second of my twenty-third birthday, I stepped into the Josephine de Beauharnais room of the Hôtel des Charmes. My teenage years had dragged on for too long. And as I entered the room, I knew it was time to leave them behind. Enter and shed this skin that no longer suited me. My budding love had slowly been stripping me of it. Enter and banish the indecisive shape of a young, chubby girl in order to become the accomplished woman that Louie had always seen in me. Polished. Refined by his discerning eye and able hands. Leave my old self behind and bloom.

Born from my own sex.

AFTER LEAVING NANTERRE, I SPENT the day wandering Paris in my patchwork wedding dress, holding my ballet flats in one hand, my bare feet on the hot asphalt. The sun was shining; it was already summer. Summer and its crowded terraces; summer and its skimpy outfits that show off thighs, middles, shoulders; summer and its pickup artists, who emerge from hibernation with the sun's first rays. As I meandered, I let myself be flattered. It was like a sweet echo of the happiness growing inside me. A fire waiting to be unleashed. Tonight.

"Hey, girl! Marry me!"

"Sorry, not today." I laughed.

"Come on, don't be like that, marry me! You got the dress, the class, everything! I'll be your man! We can make a ton of babies."

And the guy did a suggestive hip movement as he bit his incisors into his lower lip.

At least people noticed my outfit here. But males in heat weren't the only ones to do a double take when they saw me. For little girls, I was a fairy-tale princess. For teenagers, a punk-rock bride. For adults, a kind of madwoman, a crazy person, maybe even someone dangerous like a junkie, better to avoid me; some even changed sidewalks when they saw me coming.

I didn't care. I ignored the attention. I was exhausted, but I felt great. The concrete had worn my feet, which seemed to float above the hot ground, as though carried by a cushion of air. I wasn't afraid of anything anymore because I now knew where I was going. Toward unbound happiness. I thought of Mom and knew without having to hear it that she would have encouraged me to seize this moment and live my life.

BACK IN THE KITCHEN IN Nanterre, I had taken a few ten-euro bills from the old coffee grinder. "Emergency treasure," Mom had called it. I used it to buy a few Monacos and a little snack in a bistro.

The place was pretty rustic, and still had a phone behind the counter. The proprietor, a redheaded woman in her fifties, shot me a complicit smile as she handed it to me.

"Here, sweetheart! You have five minutes to tell him no."

"I'm saying yes right now!" a drunk from the other side of the gleaming bar cried. "Did you see this girl, Simone? She reminds me of my Vero . . ."

"Ha! Exactly, your Vero said no. So just leave the girl alone, okay?"

I called Max Fourestier Hospital. Mom's condition was critical but stable. Every passing minute could be the one, but it was impossible to tell when it would happen. I gave the nurse Sophia's number, telling her to call in case of emergency. At least until the following day. After that . . . I had no idea where I would be or if I would even be reachable.

After this crucial check-in, I went back to my walk, crossing the center of Paris, feeling carefree. I was as light as my heart was full of emotion.

I stopped in front of the Louvre des Antiquaires and ogled the antique canes. Good-bye, vintage watches. Now I only had eyes for elegant walking sticks whose fine silver, ruby, ivory knobs had fascinating stories to tell.

I DON'T REALLY KNOW HOW I made it to Rue du Chemin Vert. I instinctually recognized the row of bazaars and kebab shops. Then the sign and bordeaux-colored awning. When I rang the bell, ten pairs of male eyes turned in concert and stared at my silk-and-felt-clad silhouette. I thought I recognized one or two faces from my previous visit.

I carefully avoided the *Pink Pussy* books and went straight for a copy of *Secret Women* that was sitting on one of the tables marked LITERATURE. I still had fifty pages left and decided to purchase a second copy.

I spent my last euros on the book and headed back out past the Père Lachaise cemetery. I set up shop on the first bench I found in the sun, in the tree-lined and shady Boulevard de Ménilmontant. Amid the white noise of traffic, I had no trouble diving right into my reading.

First of all, I found the end of the book disconcerting. The main character, the author who goes looking for his wife, who has disappeared into a city's subterranean labyrinth, ends up accepting his new condition as an erotic slave for the cult of women. And now that he's Cyprie and Sophie's thing, he is committed to their idea of creating a new community of Amazons.

The parallel with my current situation was obvious. I, too, was ready to surrender myself completely and without reserve. My thirst for discovery seemed unquenchable. But much like the novel's narrator, I wasn't only interested in the wanton. I was abandoning myself to Louie, but it was not simply a reaction to his treatments, the capitulation of my overstimulated senses. Nor was I submitting myself to the unmentionable out of love. I finally understood: it was a blossoming of my whole being. Like peeling fruit, each new electric touch had removed a layer, session after session, until my quivering flesh was completely naked. And loving. Until my feelings were completely out in the open.

The light ended up convincing me. The flounce of my dress was scrunched up around my thighs. My eyes were closed. I let the heat pour into my skin, which became more and more sensitive with every passing minute. The afternoon drew on like a dream. I heard the voices of passersby, and a few snippets from my nights at the Hôtel des Charmes. I felt as though I were visiting all of its rooms, one after the other, and that each one awoke in me a new sensation, a novel desire. Behind each door, I found a letter left for me by my Alphabet Man. Could it be that the hotel had exactly twenty-six rooms? I liked the thought, and let my mind wander, giving in to reverie.

I also imagined someone delivering my silver package to Avenue Mandel. Louie opening the door and then exploring the contents of the box, his beautiful emaciated face twisted in surprise.

Melted into a grave smile.

AROUND DINNERTIME, I TOOK THE metro for our rendez-vous. I got off at the Notre-Dame-de-Lorette station and could have avoided Rue de la Rochefoucauld to get up to Pigalle. But something told me to turn left on Rue Saint-Lazare until it intersected with Rue de la Tour-des-Dames. I was only a few steps away from Duchesnois House. From where I stood, the panic that had taken hold after my earlier disappearance seemed to have subsided. The guests had probably all left long before, after they had run out of consolations and words of encouragement.

I only noticed two rental trucks, both with their back doors wide open, one filled with untouched comestibles, the other with planks and metallic tubes from one of the platforms or tents. I wondered if Madonna, whose private concert was supposed to be the shining moment of the reception, had also been inconvenienced by my defection. Or if someone had warned her.

There I was, contemplating this situation, when a thick silhouette coming out of the circular courtyard bumped into me.

"Elle!"

I started running. Armand, who was once again wearing his corduroys and a vest, chased after me.

"Elle! Come back!"

Thanks to the street's fairly pronounced downward slope, and despite the layers of silk between my legs, I had no trouble losing him. By the time I reached the intersection with the Rue d'Aumale, it was clear he wouldn't catch up with me. I glanced over my shoulder and saw him retreat, probably to tell his master about my recent appearance.

It was stupid of me to go. But I suppose it had been necessary. You can only leave your old skin behind after having duly burned it. I'd needed to measure what I had decided to lose in order to value what I was about to gain.

I wondered if I should call Sophia, then decided against it. What could she tell me that I couldn't guess? I was leaving David's wrath behind me, and there was nothing anyone could say to change my mind. Rather than dwell on a past that was impossible to rewrite, I was much happier to think of the present, which was lively and sweet, and filled with promise and new sensations.

HONESTLY, I COULD NOT SIT still. The more the hour approached, the less capable I was of staying calm, much less sitting down. I got some pho from a Vietnamese takeout place and ate it standing up, a few steps from the hotel, stuffing each forkful into my mouth as though my life depended on it.

Over the course of the final hour, the shops started closing one by one. I walked through the neighborhood, doing the same loop over and over, noticing little changes with each rotation. I felt more and more as though I belonged here. I was at last becoming an Athenian. Perhaps I wasn't as accustomed as Louie at reading every architectural detail as though it were speaking to me, but I was becoming affected by its poetry. The neighborhood was inscribing itself in me, just as my name had once been written on it.

On that note, I did not regret having left my second copy of the *Secret Women* on the bench on Boulevard de Ménilmontant. Soon some stranger would find it and get lost in the stupefying city where women were the masters. That mysterious reader would decide whether to become one of them or one of their toys. I didn't care: it was up to him or her.

TEN OH-ONE. 22 + 1 = 23. I am twenty-three years old.

I push open the gilded door of the Josephine. Monsieur Jacques gave me a keycard, no questions asked. He almost seemed relieved to see me. I am now also part of this hotel. Along with Marie, Margaretha, Caroline, Esther, Lola, and the others. I am one of them now.

The room is as it was when I visited it two weeks ago, with my athletic client. But then I only saw it in the dark, and here it is bathed in the light of the setting sun. The star only disappeared three minutes ago, if that, and the building is covered in its dying glow. The window is open. The light dives through it, licking the gilding.

LOUIE IS STANDING IN THE middle of the room.

Naked. Fragile.

He is waiting for me.

He also looks different in this light. For the first time, he is also presenting himself to me without artifice. Not even his eternal cane. Just him, at the mercy of a new history that is just beginning. Just him and his suddenly vulnerable attitude. He is open like the blank pages of a new notebook that we will write together. Despite my invitation, neither one of us shall order the other around, from here on out. We shall only be as we are now: eager to discover each other and accept the present moment, ready to let whatever must blossom between us burst forth. No expectations. No plots.

SILENTLY, HE WATCHES ME ENTER the room. He puts a finger over his lips. All words are superfluous tonight. I stop a few paces from him. I'm savoring the moment. I want to feel myself against his skin, muss myself up with his desire, roll around in our sweat, our scents, and gild myself in his love.

The light has chiseled him into a statue of white skin and long muscles, a perfection of flesh that I long to grasp and bite. I am discovering him for the first time. In his entirety. In his grace. I am reveling in his harmony. Who says that only a woman's body is fascinating?

My appetite for him is whole, intact, devouring, a warm ball that thumps in my chest, my belly, my sex. Soon, I won't be able to contain myself. Soon, it won't just be a question of bodies groping, kneading, converging. Soon, we will love each other.

But we don't need to rush things, his eyes keep telling me.

AS THE SUN SLOWLY FINISHES its descent behind the white meringue of the Sacré Coeur, Louie's body is plunged into darkness. All that remains in the light is his profile and his upper left shoulder. On this latter, I am only just noticing a new tattoo: his initials in old English script woven around a black-ink climbing rosebush. No colors, just lines and shadowy shades of gray. A thorny branch shooting out from the bush runs through the hollow of his clavicle to the base of his neck, where a timid bud blossoms. It must be a recent addition; otherwise I would have seen it before, peeking out from under his shirt collar.

And here he is before my very eyes: the Alphabet Man who will write his own language on me. He will find the right words. Not to play with me but to express, inhale, and feel.

HIS PRESENCE ALONE MAKES THE air vibrate like the quiet music playing all around us, innervating every particle of dust: *Words like violence break the silence, come crashing in, into my little world.*

The various aspects of the room's decor seem to dissolve, becoming one of the floating particles. Soon, everything else disappears; there is only him. And me. And this light.

HE SLOWLY STEPS TOWARD ME. He isn't in a hurry. Neither of us are. We have all night to study the lines between us, the rough draft of our narrative.

His eyes dive into me, piercing me sweetly. Incandescent points at once light up deep inside me. They blaze, they burn me. *Painful to me, pierce right through me. Can't you understand, oh my little girl?* Louie hammers the point home, tapping his finger on his lips in time to the electronic music, signaling his instructions. I grasp my lesson: our bodies, and only our bodies, shall be allowed to express themselves. They alone are up to the task of bandaging wounds and filling the cracks that have been keeping us apart.

His hands act first, as messengers of pleasure to come. They are closer to me than ever. So elegant and yet so firm and powerful.

Delicately, they remove my layers of silk. The dress melts softly to the Oriental carpet. All I am wearing now are an immaculate demi-cup bra and panties. His trembling hands naturally find the small of my back. My body shines at his touch. We melt into each other, our skin becoming one fabric. *All I ever wanted, all I ever needed, is here in my arms. Words are very unnecessary, they can only do harm.* At last I am his. At last he is mine. We have won. We have overcome all obstacles. We have found each other.

Yet a shiver runs through him, telling me he is still incredulous: he still can't believe it. So he tightens his embrace. He holds me. He doesn't want to let me go. He grips me close, afraid I might fly away. And yet I still sense that he wants me to be free. That his love for me will not be a suffocating jail. Not anymore.

I also begin to tremble so violently I'm afraid I might collapse. His contact holds me upright. Every new touch practically makes me faint. He is the cause and the solution. The sickness . . . and its remedy. I want to fall into his chest, feel his strength, and give myself to him entirely.

That is not what he wants. He picks me up. He wants me upright, open, proud. Divine. I won't be a rag doll in his arms. He hasn't led me through so many steps to discover my inner wealth of resources to then have me simply abandon myself to him. Has anyone ever loved me as he does? Has anyone ever desired me to the point of causing inextricable pleasure and pain in me? Tears well in my eyes.

But it is not time to relax. I must act. I must confront him, too. I must climb him like a mountain. I must plant my claws in him like an ice axe. He has already conquered me, body, heart, and soul. I want to possess him, like a man possesses a woman. It is my turn to flush new blood into his organs. It is my turn to give him life.

LAUGHTER FROM THE NIGHT OUTSIDE rings through the window. But the sound does not disturb us. We are burning for each other. We have barely touched, and yet our bodies are already feasting on each other. The surface of our skin seems to have escaped from a planet that has gotten too close to its star. More contact will only be painful.

His cologne blends with his body's smell, which I am discovering for the first time. I can also make out his sex's perfume emanating from between his thighs. His penis is eager, hungry. It points into me, erasing what is left of the distance between us. I have the feeling our intimate parts will blend with as much grace as our scents. That the bouquet of our skin and hair will be harmonious. Touchdown.

YES, THIS TIME I AM the one to initiate, to conquer. I grab his member—the softness of the skin on his shaft is a delightful surprise—and gently guide it to my wet lips. His sex brushes against my clitoris, sending out an electric charge. Something in me explodes, rending the ultimate chasm, the one that has been waiting for just this moment.

My throat suddenly tightens as a ball of lava hurtles from my chest to my vagina, sending delicious pleasure through my body. I arch my back, thrust my pelvis forward, and open my avid lips. I moan with desire, but stop when a new tremor shakes my lower body. I am burning and liquefying all at once.

Years of desire are finally being unleashed, and I find myself submerged in them like a mariner surprised by a giant swell. I stagger, then grab ahold of myself. I am still standing, my body is mine.

I have been waiting for one thing over the past several weeks: him in me. He has been hoping for the same thing for the past sev-

eral months. Waiting for a lifetime, waiting for me. He alone can satisfy me.

Still, his sex alone cannot erase all that he has put me through. That would be too easy. I am going to need to experience a lot more pleasure to make up for it. If he wants me to love him even more, I am going to need thousands of kisses, able caresses, and looks saturated with desire and love.

I will also need to tend to him, to torture his senses, be lewd, vicious, relentless, in order to forget our twisted beginnings planned by someone else.

But I have no doubt that in the end—once our bodies are united, melted into one orgasmic cry, a heavy and sticky magma—all the hurtful things we have said will be erased.

As if to confirm this thought, we are jolted by another eruption borne from the joining of our sexes. The volcanic activity that unites us is just getting started.

I AM MASTURBATING HIM GENTLY against my thigh. He has been teasing me all this time with agonizing desire. I, too, want to draw out his frustration, to the point of explosion. Until he can't take it anymore. Until he begs. Until he rubs himself against me like a dog driven mad. Until he barks his need for me. Until he bites me. It is his turn to be my toy.

So I play, with care and tenderness, as with what we hold most dear. My hand looks minuscule next to his member. I have trouble grasping it in its entirety. I like that it has grown so immense for me. I tickle it with my fingers, making his shaft tremble. He sighs in delight. At some intervals, I imprison him in my palm like a little bird, and then I set him free again. At another moment, my hand feels a pulse in his inflated, sweating member, as though his heart were limitless and beating in every one of his organs.

The more I play with him, the more he suffers, I can feel it. His panting has given way to long moans. An almost continuous howl. He is going crazy. He begs in a deep voice that resonates like a bell in my ears:

"Take me . . . Take me, now."

The fact that he pleads with me like a woman radiates through my innermost depths. He is offering himself to me, and I am deeply moved. Outside, the day has disappeared. Only a few remnants of light from the lampposts on the square outside distinguish our bodies from the shadows.

I feel the liquid of his desire stipple my thigh and melt into the river of fluid that has already slickened the area. Our fluids are now one. They coat me in one same desire. It is getting harder and harder to restrain myself. But doesn't being the mistress of our games entitle me to succumb as I see fit? To give myself as I please?

Our bodies are now grafted to each other. They swell under our heavy breathing, which presses them and molds them together. A sweet prelude to the fusion of our sexes. But again, we aren't in a hurry. One hour, one night, one life of desire is opening up before us.

HE TRIES TO INSERT A finger inside me. But I withdraw it. I want to accompany his touch as it journeys slowly over my pelvis to the edge of my swollen lips, diving into the wild bush that covers them, to the avid, emerging point. My love peak. The contact of his index finger on my fleshy mound draws a new tear from me. He is no longer a savage laying me to waste, a mercenary only doing his job. He is the man who desires all

of me. The one I greet like a hero with my miniature triumphant arch.

He knows it. He begins tracing circles around my button,
driving me wild with desire. His eyes mist over, and he closes
them to concentrate on the sensations blossoming under the
pads of his fingers. He takes pleasure in seeing me so close to
explosion. He loves loving me. My hips sway uncontrollably.
My body is no longer mine. Now it will only obey his expert
hands. We rock in unison, our movements supple and fluid.
Ours is a dance in which every step defines us, invents us.

I search his face. A silent wave washes through us both. At
this moment, we are standing at the edge of a precipice, and
it is the most delicious sensation we have ever known. And
this is just the beginning. We stay here, petrified, savoring the
moment like an endless hard candy. A tart second. I refrain
from saying sweet nothings, from uttering "I love you." It's still
too early for declarations. Nothing could be more expressive
right now than our bodies.

His attention to my lips is exquisite. I close my eyes and let
the orgasm rise over the horizon of my innermost depths. It
comes like a tsunami, crashing into my whole body, from my
belly button to my lips, threatening to wipe everything out.
Louie presses his sex into my hip, panting heavily. Is he going
to come with me? Is it possible to feel so much pleasure, so
quickly, and with just a few gentle touches?

I AM THE WOMAN IN our common fall, the angel of our voluptuous undoing. I take him by the hand like a girl on her first
time. I lead him to the bed. We have all the time in the world
to explore our pleasures, but for now I know what I want. I
remember a quote from Saint-Exupéry, author of *The Little*

Prince, that my girlfriends in high school always used to write on their notebooks: "Love does not consist in gazing at each other, but in looking outward together in the same direction."

Tonight, for the first time, we are not making love face-to-face. We are experiencing ecstasy while looking in the same direction. Our orgasms take aim at the same far-off and invisible target. The firmament.

I stretch out on my stomach, spreading my thighs just wide enough to give him room. My arched back gives way to the proud and generous curve of my buttocks. My crotch peeks out from the hollow between my legs, shining with desire. It has never blared its wish to be taken with such force. Louie lies down on top of me, though without crushing me, as though he were a comforter of skin and flesh. He is long and warm and soft, though a bit angular in parts. He is solid. His incredibly firm shoulders, chest, and stomach meld perfectly with every nook and cranny of my body's surface.

With one hand, he reaches for the small silver wrapper lying on the bedside table. Again with one hand, he manages to tear open the package and remove its contents. Still with one hand, he rolls the condom over his member, which I can feel pressing urgently against my buttocks. He doesn't need it. I could do without. But he respects my commandment.

He enters me slowly, bit by bit, emotion by emotion. A feeling of well-being and fulfillment invades my senses. My body is receiving him for the first time, and yet my vagina recognizes him. He is as I have seen him before, and felt him in my mouth. Long and slender. He touches the sensitive parts of my innermost depths with precision. Gently, when it comes to probing me where the threshold between pleasure and pain is particularly tenuous. Forcefully, when he rocks in and out of me. The walls of my sex envelop him perfectly, guiding first his tip, then his shaft through my intimate folds. I invite, aspirate, devour him. I open myself wide so he can invade my whole being. He slides in me again and again. He is tenderly excavating me. Occasionally, he withdraws so we can savor the moment. And then when he fills me again, we experience the pleasure of rediscovering each other anew.

Another tremor runs through me like a wave unfurling. One, then another crashes down into my crotch, which keeps opening wider and wider for him. Two giant flowers seem to bloom at this moment, one on top, one on bottom. They share the same root, the same lifeblood.

As the first orgasm hits me, I bury my face into a pillow. I twist left and right. My head rebels. My sex surrenders. I am shaking uncontrollably. My mouth is gaping. My cheeks are hidden by my hair. But my lips peek through the curtain. They are as fleshy as an orchid. His teeth try to sink into them. He rams harder against my soft backside. He quickens his pace. My insides are aflame. He does not let up. He will not be satisfied with one ecstatic moment. He wants to exhaust us both with pleasure. Wear us out with love. Carpet bomb us with sex. Hiroshima, my love.

HIS RIGHT HAND IS STRETCHED out over my front side, clutching my vulva. His middle finger is pressed into my clitoris again with authority. Though at first wary, my pink mound has given in, engorging and clamoring for more. An almost painful sensation shoots through it, joining the low rumble emanating around my uterus. The two vibrations meet at last. They become one, plucking my vocal cords, which ring out and excite the wild man, who growls as he ejaculates in spurts as intense as lightning.

At this point, my prior lovers would have collapsed into a heap. He, on the other hand, continues to rise and fall inside of me, hard and resolute. I realize that this is just the beginning, and my pussy spasms in radiant delight. Neither of us are close to being done.

"More . . ."

I do not wait for a reply. I know there will be more. There will be more nights, days, hotel rooms. We will make thousands of rules and transgress them all.

His tenacity is proof of how much he wants and desires me. Perhaps even loves me. No, my happiness immediately corrects: he definitely loves me. Completely, even. A strange glow seems to emanate from our bodies, a miraculous halo, the dawn of orgasms to come. The light envelops us, suspending us in midair. We are fragile and trembling like two butterflies in love.

The room around us has disappeared. And the sky above has cracked open invitingly. A ball of light carries us up with it, suspending us in space. We are in orbit, two fetuses grafted to each other. We contemplate the new earth being born below. It can only last a second; it can last billions of years. Time and space are meaningless; only the union of our bodies matters. We aren't sleeping, we aren't dreaming: we're savoring the moment, recreating the world according to our pleasure. Elle and Louie. He and I.

Without stopping his gentle movement in and out of me, he reaches for a drawer in the table on our left. He withdraws a flat object that I don't immediately recognize, but which has a strangely familiar glint.

My Ten-Times-a-Day! Louie places it on the bed near my face. I could pick out its silver cover from among a thousand notebooks. He opens it to the last page, which is not written in my hand. I don't need to know how he got ahold of it.

As I leaf through it, I see our confessions dancing over the pages in a two-step that has now become one.

I smile. I've understood. Seeing this, he covers my neck in light kisses, sending shivers through my body and awakening other appetites, in the space between my thighs.

I desire you completely, fatally. I want to spend my life exploring you, and I know I will never be able to discover all of you. The more I possess you, the more secrets you will hold. The more your sex will be a mysterious continent rich in resources. The more it will jealously guard its pleasures.

Promise me.

Handwritten note by Louie, 6/18/2009

AGAIN HE STRETCHES OUT HIS arm and withdraws a small object that can fit in his hand. He places it on the cover of our notebook. A key. Not a magnetic card, a real key. Unpolished metal, heavy. A tag is tied to its head. Despite the darkness, I manage to read the handwritten message:

Welcome to
room number one.

Room number one?
I almost break our silence to ask. But I refrain. A moment

later, it becomes clear. The rooms at the Hôtel des Charmes aren't numbered because it is up to each person to live her own experiences and attribute numbers accordingly.

The Josephine will therefore always be room number one for me. It is where I experienced my first orgasm as a woman, a woman who chose to abandon herself to a man in order to know more pleasure. It was where we spent our first night together.

THE HALO OF LIGHT HASN'T dissipated. On the contrary, it has become more intense than ever. I feel it all around us. It is surprisingly familiar. Now, it will be with us forever.

However, the musical theme has changed. The first song was imbued with so much meaning. Now, the selection is softer, more hypnotic. I wonder what it is called.

"'Home,'" Louie whispers with a smile.

Both the title of the song and the new status of this hotel. We both know it will forever be the seat of our pleasure. Our haven. Our home.

I HAVE NEVER BELONGED TO that category of women who see all hotel rooms as identical, all one and the same, each an anonymous space without any character or personality.

Now I know why.

ACKNOWLEDGMENTS

I would like to thank my agent, Anna Jarota.

Thanks also to her wonderful team: Ted, Gwladys, Marc, Anne, and anyone I may be forgetting.

Thanks to editors from all over the globe who believed in this project and put faith in me as a French writer, with all my untranslatable Gallicisms!

Thanks to my father, who nurtured my adult imagination, and for the books he had around the house when I was young.

Thanks to all the tattoo artists who participated, in their way, during the months in which this project gestated, and particularly to the amazing girls at Dragon Tattoo.

Thanks to Alphabet Man, who is less virtual than he believes.

Thanks to my friends and their unwavering support and occasional goading: Valérie, Thomas and Miguel, Sophie, Éric, Florence, Virginie, Cécile, Ovidie, etc.

Finally, thanks to Emmanuelle, who will hopefully forgive all the (numerous?) things I have borrowed. But as she once said to me about my work: "I'm a writer—everything you say or do may end up in my novel."

She had no idea . . .

THEMATIC BIBLIOGRAPHY

For those interested in music, a soundtrack of sorts (in no particular order):

Nocturne no. 20 in C-sharp minor, Frédéric Chopin
"More Than This," *Roxy Music*
"Neighborhood #1 (Tunnels)," *Arcade Fire*
"69 Année érotique," *Serge Gainsbourg*
Boléro, *Maurice Ravel*
"Karmacoma," *Massive Attack*
"Dancin'," *Chris Isaak*
"Forever Without End," *Jocelyn Pook*
"If You'll Be Mine," *Babybird*
Trio for Piano, op. 100, second movement, Franz Schubert
Burst Apart, *The Antlers*
"If You Run," *The Boxer Rebellion*
"Carolyn's Fingers," *Cocteau Twins*
"L'Amour," *Dominique A*
"Party Day," *Cosmo Vitelli*
"Shadow Magnet," *Lisa Gerrard and Pieter Bourke*
"The Last Beat of My Heart," *DeVotchKa*
"Something Good," *Paul Haig*
"By This River," *Brian Eno*

"Bela Lugosi's Dead," Camping Car
"Walker," Cascadeur
"Willow Tree," Chad VanGaalen
Für Alina, *Arvo Pärt*
"Hoppípolla," Sigur Rós
Gnossienne *no. 1, Erik Satie*
Theme to The Persuaders!, *John Barry*
"I Sold My Hands for Food So Please Feed Me," Get Well Soon
"See My Eyes," DWNTWN
"Breathe," Télépopmusic
"Surface to Air," The Chemical Brothers
"Consequence," The Notwist
"Go With the Flow," Lacquer
"A Pure Person," Lim Giong
"Lady Sleep," Maximilian Hecker
"A New Error," Moderat
"Your Silent Face," New Order
"Our Darkness," Anne Clark
"Sehnsucht," Ellen Allien
"All I Want," Kodaline
"How It Ended," The Drums
"Enjoy the Silence," Depeche Mode
"Home," Wave Machines

For those interested in compiling a library of erotic literature of their own, here is Louie Barlet's complete list of recommendations (in chronological order, from their date of publication):

Hymn to Aphrodite, *Sappho*
Satyricon, *Petronius*
The Art of Love, *Ovid*

The Decameron, *Boccaccio*

The Canterbury Tales, *Geoffrey Chaucer*

The Lives of the Gallant Ladies, *Brantôme*

Forbidden Fruit: Selected Tales in Verse, *Jean de La Fontaine*

Giorgio Baffo's erotic sonnets

The Story of My Life, *Giacomo Casanova*

The Sopha: A Moral Tale, *Claude Crébillon*

Fanny Hill; or, The Memoirs of a Woman of Pleasure,
    John Cleland

Erotica Biblion, *Honoré-Gabriel de Mirabeau*

Le Pornographe, *Nicolas-Edme Restif de la Bretonne*

Philosophy in the Bedroom, *Marquis de Sade*

My Secret Life, *Anonymous*

L'Enfant du bordel, *Pigault-Lebrun*

Gamiani, or Two Nights of Excess, *Alfred de Musset*

Venus in Furs, *Leopold von Sacher-Masoch*

Chansons pour elle (Songs for Her), *Paul Verlaine*

Journal d'une enfant vicieuse, *Hugues Rebell*

The Eleven Thousand Rods, *Guillaume Apollinaire*

The Exploits of a Young Don Juan, *Guillaume Apollinaire*

The Young Girl's Handbook of Good Manners for Use in
    Educational Establishments, *Pierre Louÿs*

Irene's Cunt, *Louis Aragon*

Story of the Eye, *Georges Bataille*

Lady Chatterley's Lover, *D.H. Lawrence*

Tropic of Cancer, *Henry Miller*

Our Lady of the Flowers, *Jean Genet*

Sexus, *Henry Miller*

Story of O, *Pauline Réage*

Lolita, *Vladimir Nabokov*

Emmanuelle, *Emmanuelle Arsan*

Septentrion, *Louis Calaferte*

The Margin, *André Pieyre de Mandiargues*

Portnoy's Complaint, *Philip Roth*

Delta of Venus, *Anaïs Nin*

Tales of Ordinary Madness, *Charles Bukowski*

The Two of Us, *Alberto Moravia*

Fear of Flying, *Erica Jong*

Les Mémoires d'une culotte, *Aymé Dubois-Jolly*

Lunes de fiel (Bitter Moon, *Roman Polanski film adaptation*),
   Pascal Bruckner

The Lover, *Marguerite Duras*

L'Orage, *Régine Deforges*

The Butcher: And Other Erotica, *Alina Reyes*

La Femme de papier, *Françoise Rey*

The Mechanics of Women, *Louie Calaferte*

Autoportrait en érection, *Guillaume Fabert*

Baise-moi, *Virginie Despentes*

Sex vox dominam, *Richard Morgiève*

Éros mécanique, *Pierre Bourgeade*

In My Room, *Guillaume Dustan*

La Foire aux cochons, *Esparbec*

The Ages of Lulu, *Almudena Grandes*

Vers chez les blancs, *Philippe Djian*

The Sexual Life of Catherine M., *Catherine Millet*

The Surrender: An Erotic Memoir, *Toni Bentley*

Femmes secrètes (Secret Women), *Ania Oz*